Gakuen ALICE

Volume 15

Created by Tachibana Higuchi

DISCARDED

TOKYOPOP

HAMBURG // LONDON // LOS ANGELES // TOKYO

Gakuen Alice

Contents

Chapter 83 7
Chapter 84 39
Chapter 85 70
Chapter 86 103
Chapter 87 133
Chapter 88 163

Story and Character Introductions

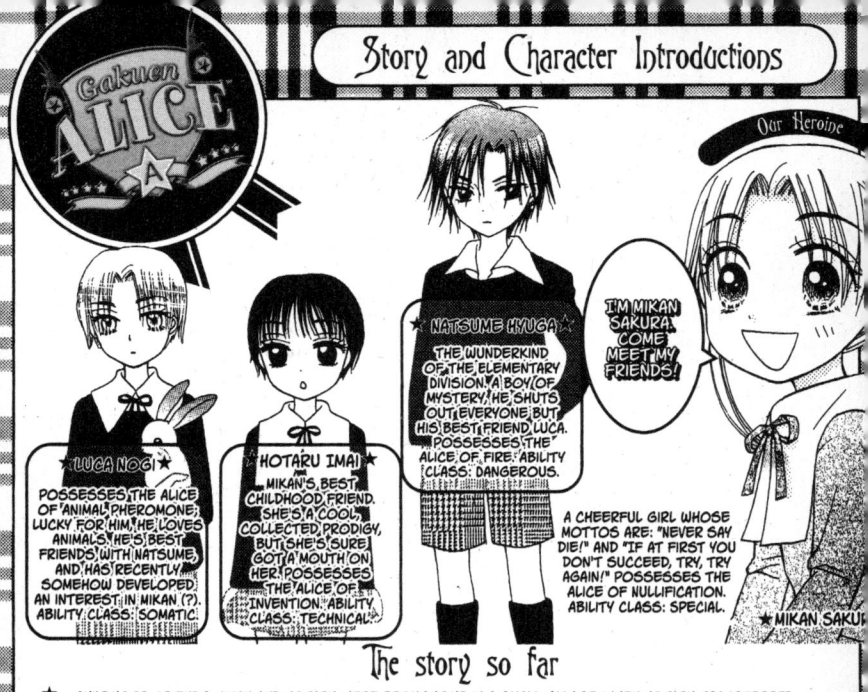

Our Heroine
I'M MIKAN SAKURA. COME MEET MY FRIENDS!
★MIKAN SAKU
A CHEERFUL GIRL WHOSE MOTTOS ARE: "NEVER SAY DIE!" AND "IF AT FIRST YOU DON'T SUCCEED, TRY, TRY AGAIN!" POSSESSES THE ALICE OF NULLIFICATION. ABILITY CLASS: SPECIAL.
★NATSUME HYUGA★
THE WUNDERKIND OF THE ELEMENTARY DIVISION. A BOY OF MYSTERY, HE SHUTS OUT EVERYONE BUT HIS BEST FRIEND LUCA. POSSESSES THE ALICE OF FIRE. ABILITY CLASS: DANGEROUS.
★HOTARU IMAI★
MIKAN'S BEST CHILDHOOD FRIEND. SHE'S A COOL, COLLECTED PRODIGY, BUT SHE'S SURE GOT A MOUTH ON HER. POSSESSES THE ALICE OF INVENTION. ABILITY CLASS: TECHNICAL.
★LUCA NOGI★
POSSESSES THE ALICE OF ANIMAL PHEROMONE; LUCKY FOR HIM, HE LOVES ANIMALS. HE'S BEST FRIENDS WITH NATSUME, AND HAS RECENTLY SOMEHOW DEVELOPED AN INTEREST IN MIKAN (?). ABILITY CLASS: SOMATIC.

The story so far

★ CHILDHOOD FRIENDS MIKAN AND HOTARU WERE BROUGHT UP IN A SMALL VILLAGE. WHEN HOTARU TRANSFERRED TO THE ALICE ACADEMY FOR PEOPLE WITH MYSTERIOUS POWERS (OR 'ALICES'), MIKAN FOLLOWED HER! HER SCHOOL LIFE'S ROCKY SOMETIMES, BUT SHE'S TRYING HARD TO LIVE BY HER MOTTO: "NEVER SAY DIE!"

★ THANKS TO HER SIGNATURE TENACITY, MIKAN WAS PROMOTED FROM A NO-STAR TO A SINGLE AND IS FLYING HIGH!

★ THROUGH FUN AND TERRIFYING ENCOUNTERS, SUCH AS THE SCHOOL FESTIVAL, CHRISTMAS PARTY, AND Z INCIDENT, MIKAN AWAKENS HER NULLIFICATION ALICE.

★ THE NEW YEAR KICKS OFF WITH AN INCIDENT AT THE JUNIOR DIVISION FLOWER GARDEN ASSOCIATION, WHICH UNEARTHS NATSUME'S LITTLE SISTER AOI, WHO HAD BEEN HELD CAPTIVE AT THE SCHOOL--MIKAN AND CO. HELP TO RETURN HER HOME SAFELY.

IF YOU WERE TO ASK ABOUT HOW EVERYONE IN CLASS POUNCED ON HER WELL!! OF COURSE THEY DID!
She's beautiful!
HEY, KOIZUMI-SAN, WHERE ARE YOU FROM?
LUNA KOIZUMI-CHAN...!!
She's so graceful...
So neat and clean!
WHAT KIND OF ALICE DO YOU HAVE?
She looks like she smells nice!
HOW OLD ARE YOU?!
WHA... WHAT'S THIS...!
WE HAD HIGH HOPES FOR THE COSPLAY OF THE BEAUTIFUL YOUNG GENIUS, HOTARU IMAI...!
Bang!

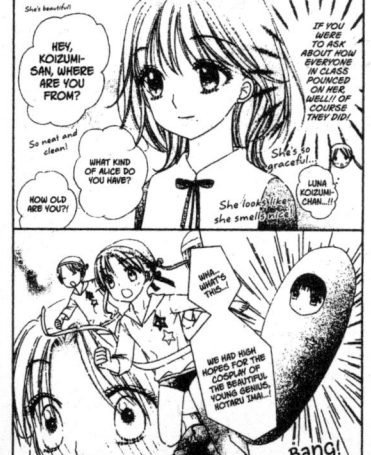

★ SPRING ARRIVES, AND MIKAN AND HER FRIENDS GRADUATE TO THE SIXTH GRADE WITHOUT A SCRATCH. A NEW STUDENT, LUNA KOIZUMI, TRANSFERS IN TO MIKAN'S CLASS B! LUNA, WHO CLAIMS TO BE A SICKLY GIRL, SEEMS TO BE PLOTTING SOMETHING?!

★ THE FIRST FUN EVENT OF THE NEW TERM, THE ATHLETIC MEET, BEGINS. DIVIDED INTO RED AND WHITE TEAMS, THE ENTIRE SCHOOL COMPETES, INCLUDING THE TEACHERS. AT THE REVOLVING COSPLAY DOOR, NO ONE KNOWS WHAT THEY WILL BE DRESSED IN, AND HOTARU FINDS HERSELF COSPLAYING COD ROE!! WHO WILL BE THE NEXT VICTIM...?!

What is Alice Academy?

THE ULTIMATE TALENT SCHOOL THAT ADMITS ONLY SPECIAL PRODIGIES WHO POSESS MYSTERIOUS POWERS CALLED "ALICES." EXTREMELY STRICT, THE ACADEMY PROHIBITS STUDENT CONTACT WITH THE OUTSIDE WORLD--INCLUDING PARENTS.

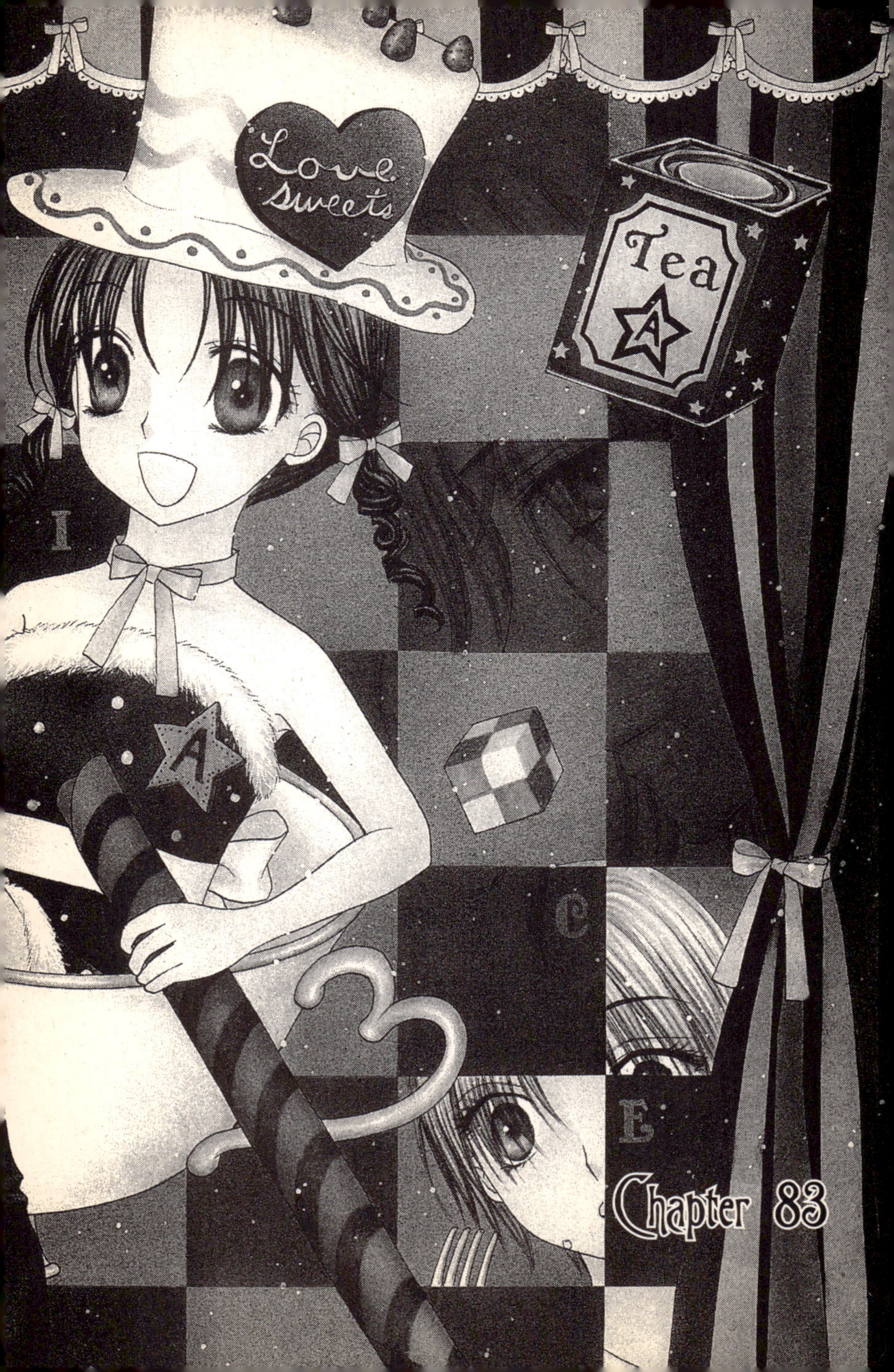
Love sweets
Tea
A
A
I
C
E
Chapter 83

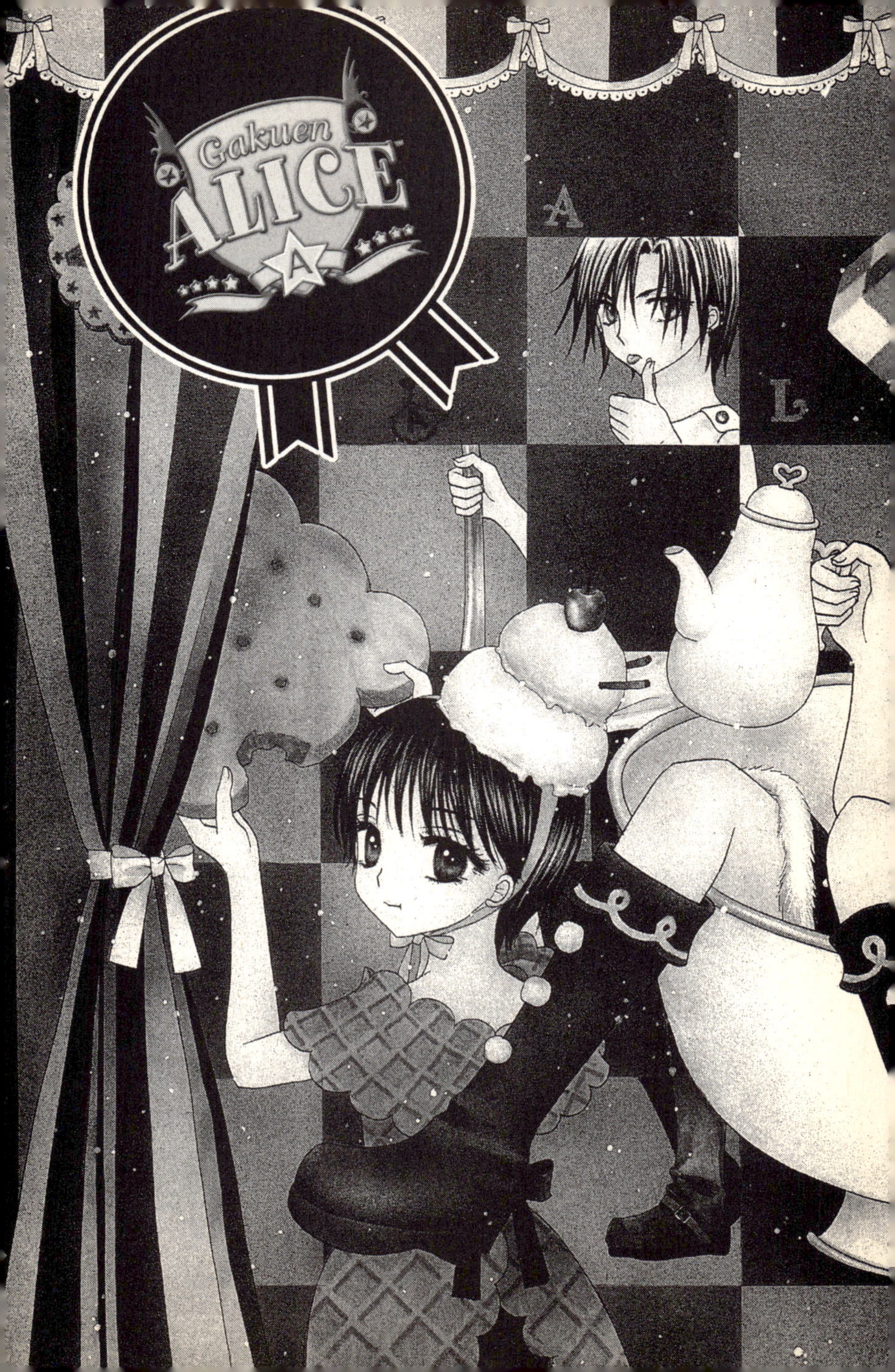
Gakuen
ALICE

Time for a Character Psychology Test (13)

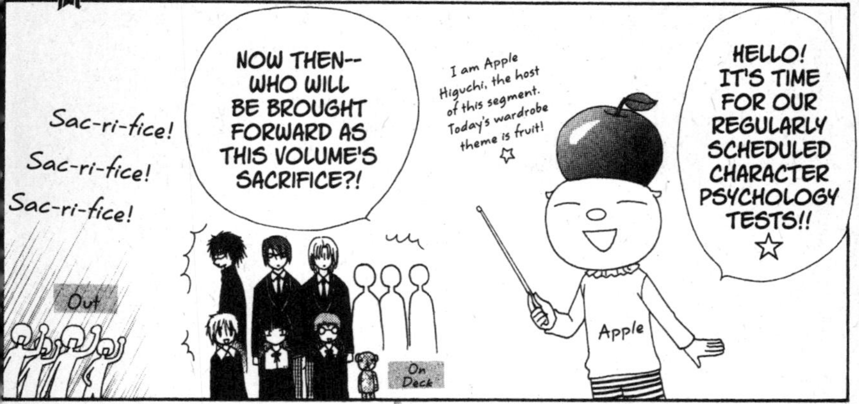
HELLO! IT'S TIME FOR OUR REGULARLY SCHEDULED CHARACTER PSYCHOLOGY TESTS!! ☆
I am Apple Higuchi, the host of this segment. Today's wardrobe theme is fruit! ☆
Apple
NOW THEN-- WHO WILL BE BROUGHT FORWARD AS THIS VOLUME'S SACRIFICE?!
Sac-ri-fice!
Sac-ri-fice!
Sac-ri-fice!
On Deck
Out

AS WITH BEFORE, HERE'S AN EXPLANATION OF THE RULES.

	You		

Write the names of whoever comes to mind in the empty spaces, wherever you like (you can write more than one).

Who you want to raise.	You	Who you want to kick around.	Who you want to be raised by.
(Who you want to serve.) Who you want to be kicked around by.	Who you want as a partner.	Who you want as a friend.	Your rival.

These are the test answers (?).

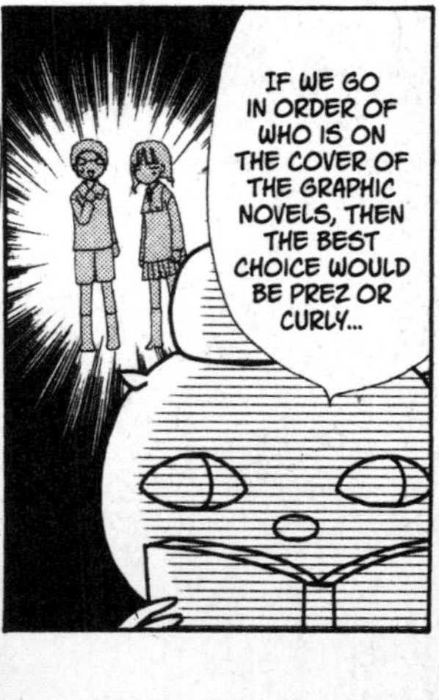
IF WE GO IN ORDER OF WHO IS ON THE COVER OF THE GRAPHIC NOVELS, THEN THE BEST CHOICE WOULD BE PREZ OR CURLY...

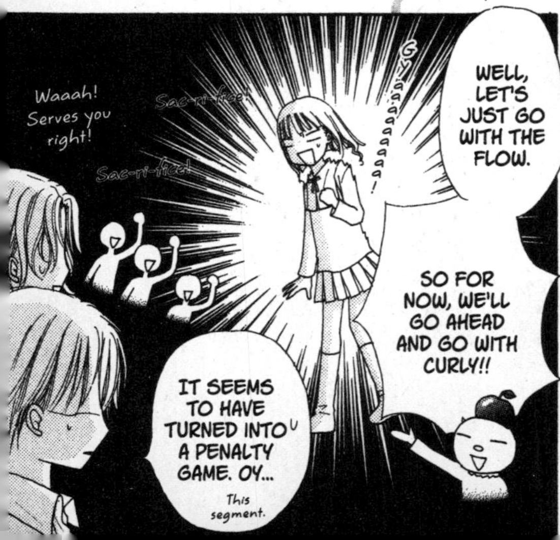
WELL, LET'S JUST GO WITH THE FLOW.
GYAaaaaaaaaa!
Sac-ri-fice!
Waaah! Serves you right!
Sac-ri-fice!
SO FOR NOW, WE'LL GO AHEAD AND GO WITH CURLY!!
IT SEEMS TO HAVE TURNED INTO A PENALTY GAME. OY...
This segment.

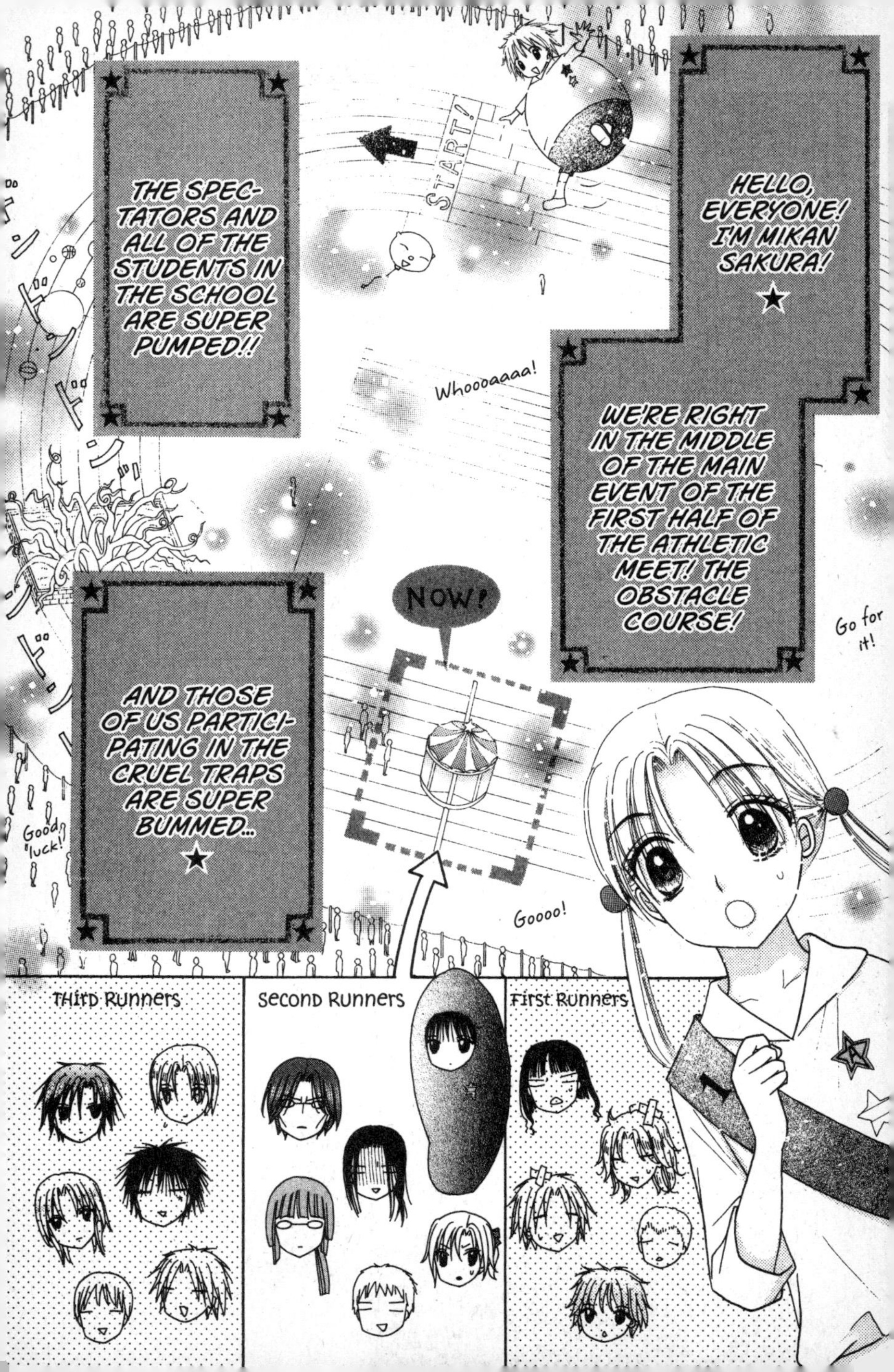

START!
HELLO, EVERYONE! I'M MIKAN SAKURA! ★
WE'RE RIGHT IN THE MIDDLE OF THE MAIN EVENT OF THE FIRST HALF OF THE ATHLETIC MEET! THE OBSTACLE COURSE!
THE SPEC-TATORS AND ALL OF THE STUDENTS IN THE SCHOOL ARE SUPER PUMPED!!
Whoooaaaa!
Go for it!
NOW!
AND THOSE OF US PARTICI-PATING IN THE CRUEL TRAPS ARE SUPER BUMMED... ★
Goooo!
Good luck!
First Runners
Second Runners
Third Runners

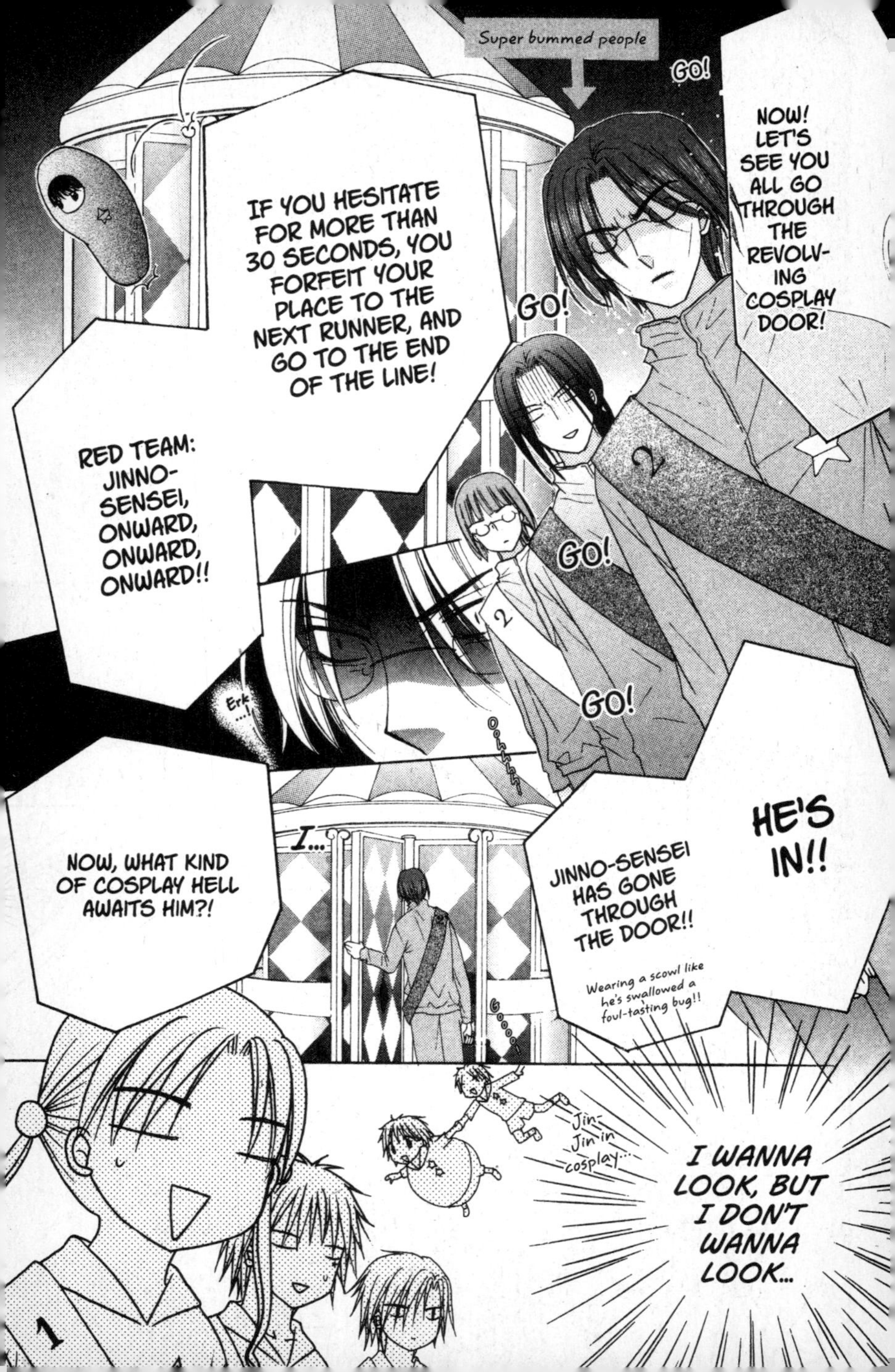

Super bummed people
GO!
NOW! LET'S SEE YOU ALL GO THROUGH THE REVOLV-ING COSPLAY DOOR!
GO!
IF YOU HESITATE FOR MORE THAN 30 SECONDS, YOU FORFEIT YOUR PLACE TO THE NEXT RUNNER, AND GO TO THE END OF THE LINE!
RED TEAM: JINNO-SENSEI, ONWARD, ONWARD, ONWARD!!
GO!
GO!
Erk ...!
HE'S IN!!
JINNO-SENSEI HAS GONE THROUGH THE DOOR!!
Wearing a scowl like he's swallowed a foul-tasting bug!!
I...
NOW, WHAT KIND OF COSPLAY HELL AWAITS HIM?!
I WANNA LOOK, BUT I DON'T WANNA LOOK...
Jin-Jin in cosplay...

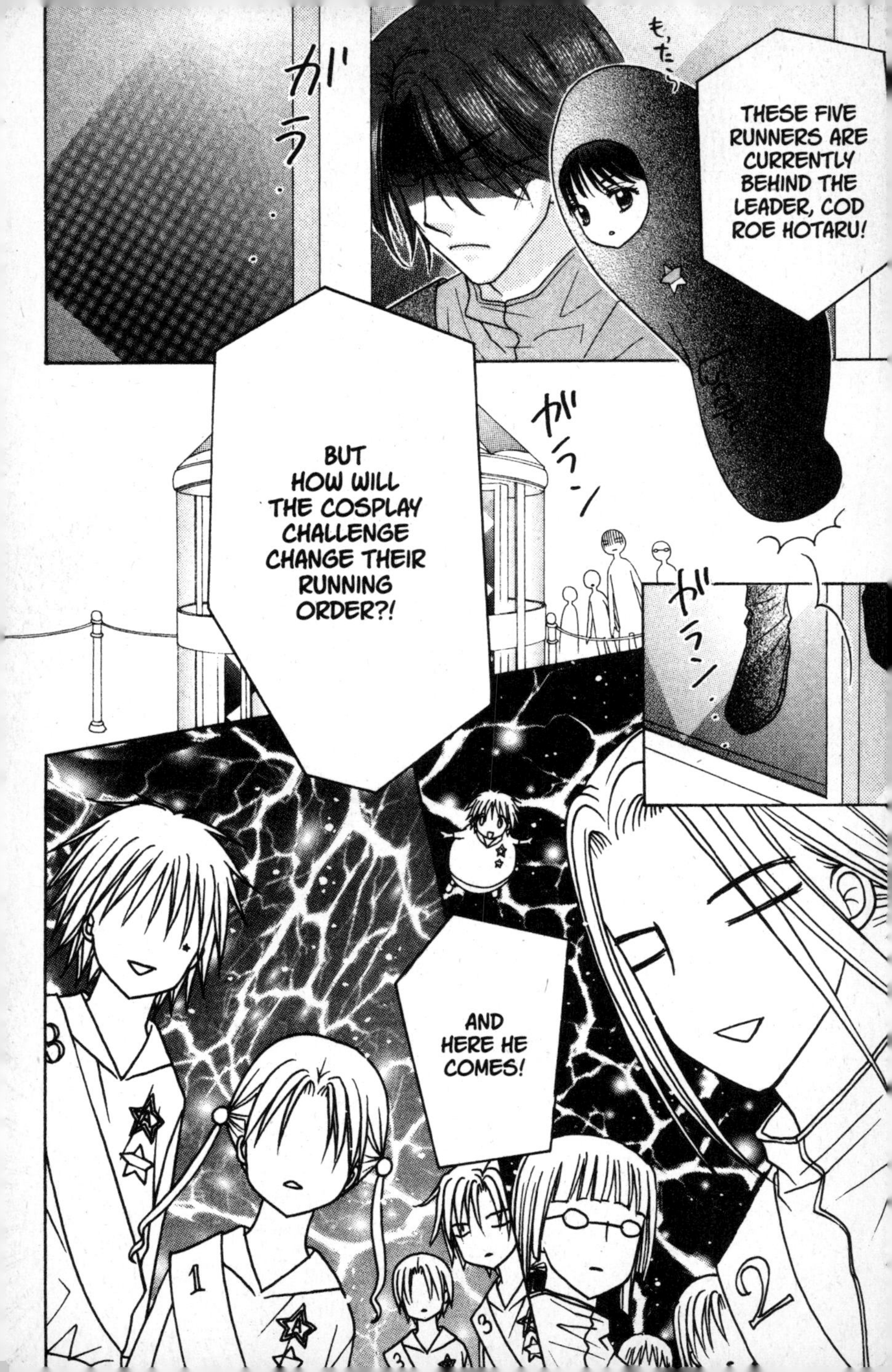

THESE FIVE RUNNERS ARE CURRENTLY BEHIND THE LEADER, COD ROE HOTARU!
ガラ
BUT HOW WILL THE COSPLAY CHALLENGE CHANGE THEIR RUNNING ORDER?!
がラン
がラン
AND HERE HE COMES!

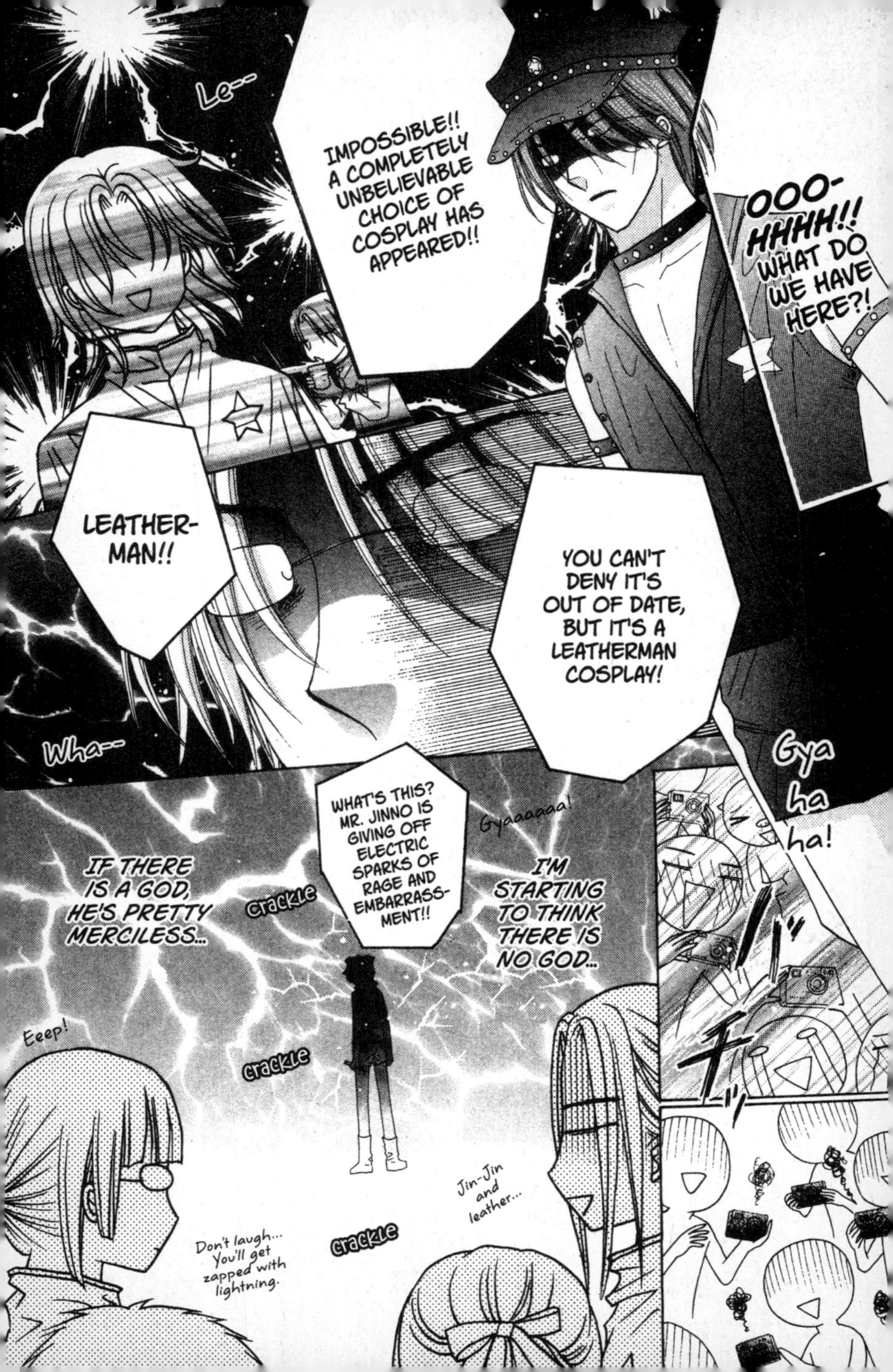
OOO-HHHH!! WHAT DO WE HAVE HERE?!
IMPOSSIBLE!! A COMPLETELY UNBELIEVABLE CHOICE OF COSPLAY HAS APPEARED!!
Le--
LEATHER-MAN!!
YOU CAN'T DENY IT'S OUT OF DATE, BUT IT'S A LEATHERMAN COSPLAY!
Wha--
Gya ha ha!
WHAT'S THIS? MR. JINNO IS GIVING OFF ELECTRIC SPARKS OF RAGE AND EMBARRASS-MENT!!
Gyaaaaaaa!
I'M STARTING TO THINK THERE IS NO GOD...
IF THERE IS A GOD, HE'S PRETTY MERCILESS...
crackle
crackle
crackle
Eeep!
Jin-Jin and leather...
Don't laugh... You'll get zapped with lightning.

Read at Your Own Discretion.

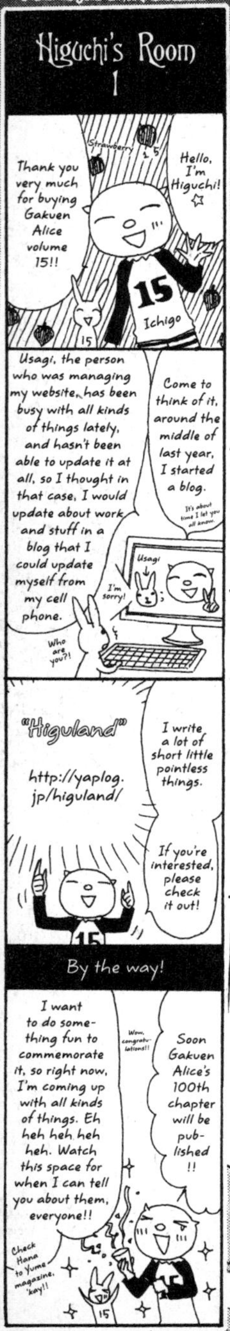

Loach on over to two.

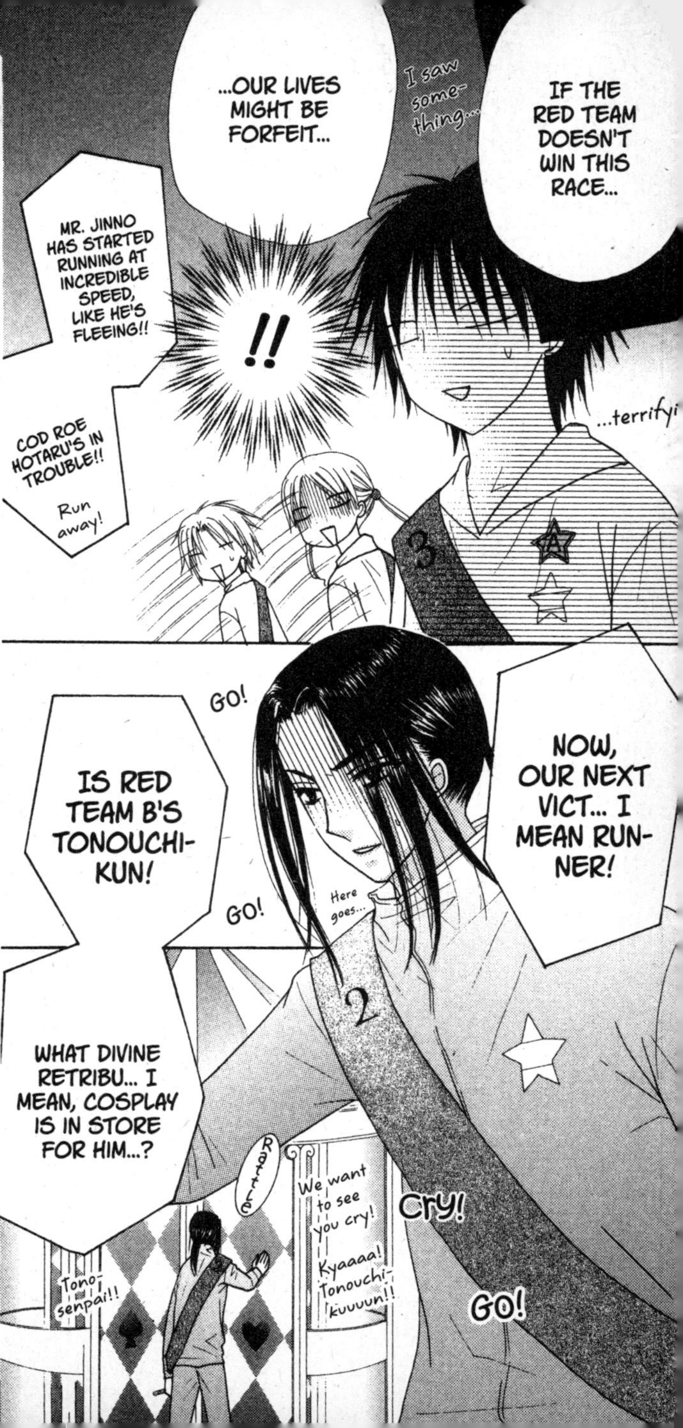

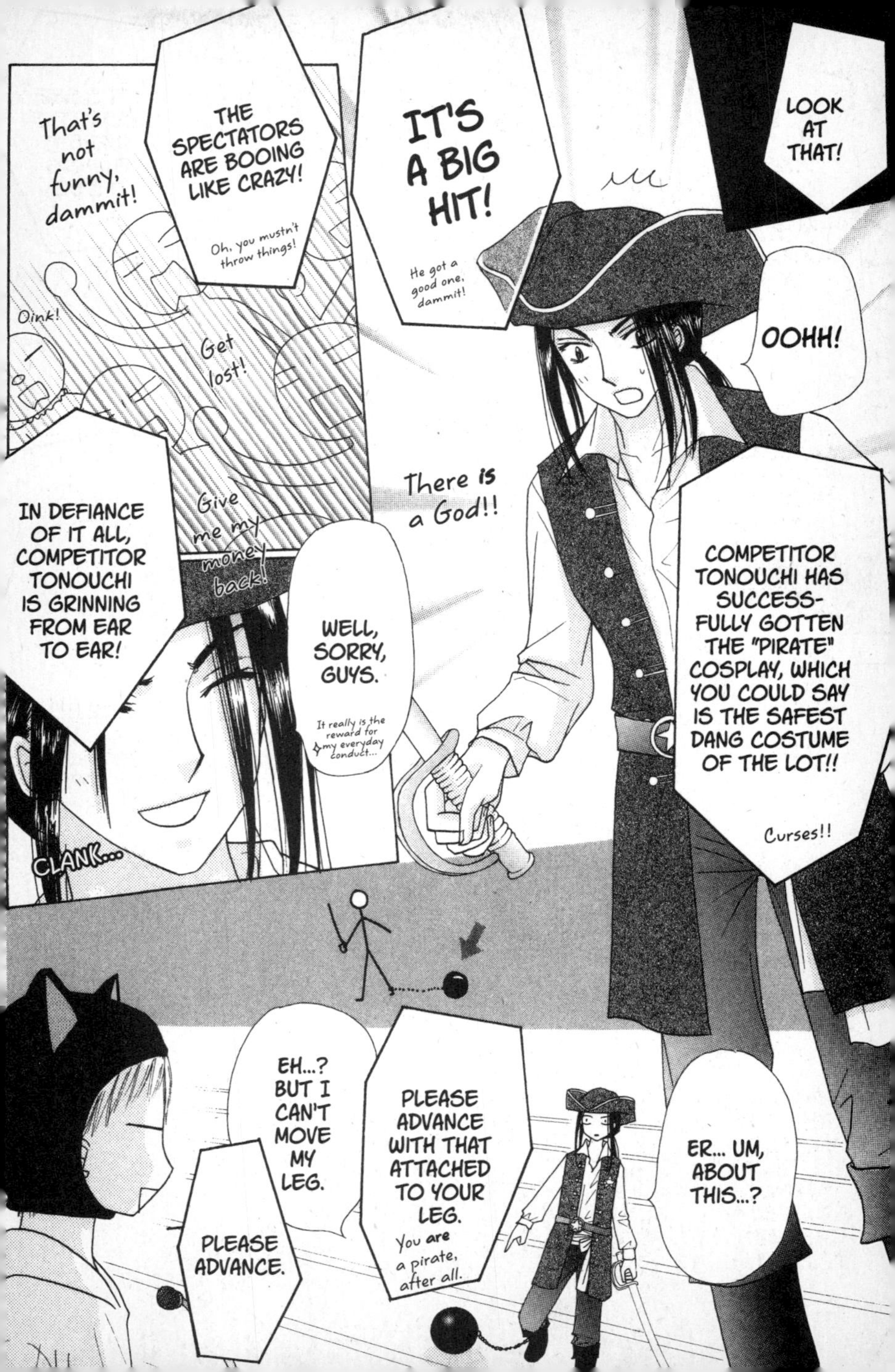
LOOK AT THAT!
OOHH!
IT'S A BIG HIT!
He got a good one, dammit!
THE SPECTATORS ARE BOOING LIKE CRAZY!
Oh, you mustn't throw things!
That's not funny, dammit!
Oink!
Get lost!
There is a God!!
COMPETITOR TONOUCHI HAS SUCCESS-FULLY GOTTEN THE "PIRATE" COSPLAY, WHICH YOU COULD SAY IS THE SAFEST DANG COSTUME OF THE LOT!!
Curses!!
WELL, SORRY, GUYS.
It really is the reward for my everyday conduct...
Give me my money back!
IN DEFIANCE OF IT ALL, COMPETITOR TONOUCHI IS GRINNING FROM EAR TO EAR!
CLANK...
ER... UM, ABOUT THIS...?
PLEASE ADVANCE WITH THAT ATTACHED TO YOUR LEG.
You are a pirate, after all.
EH...? BUT I CAN'T MOVE MY LEG.
PLEASE ADVANCE.

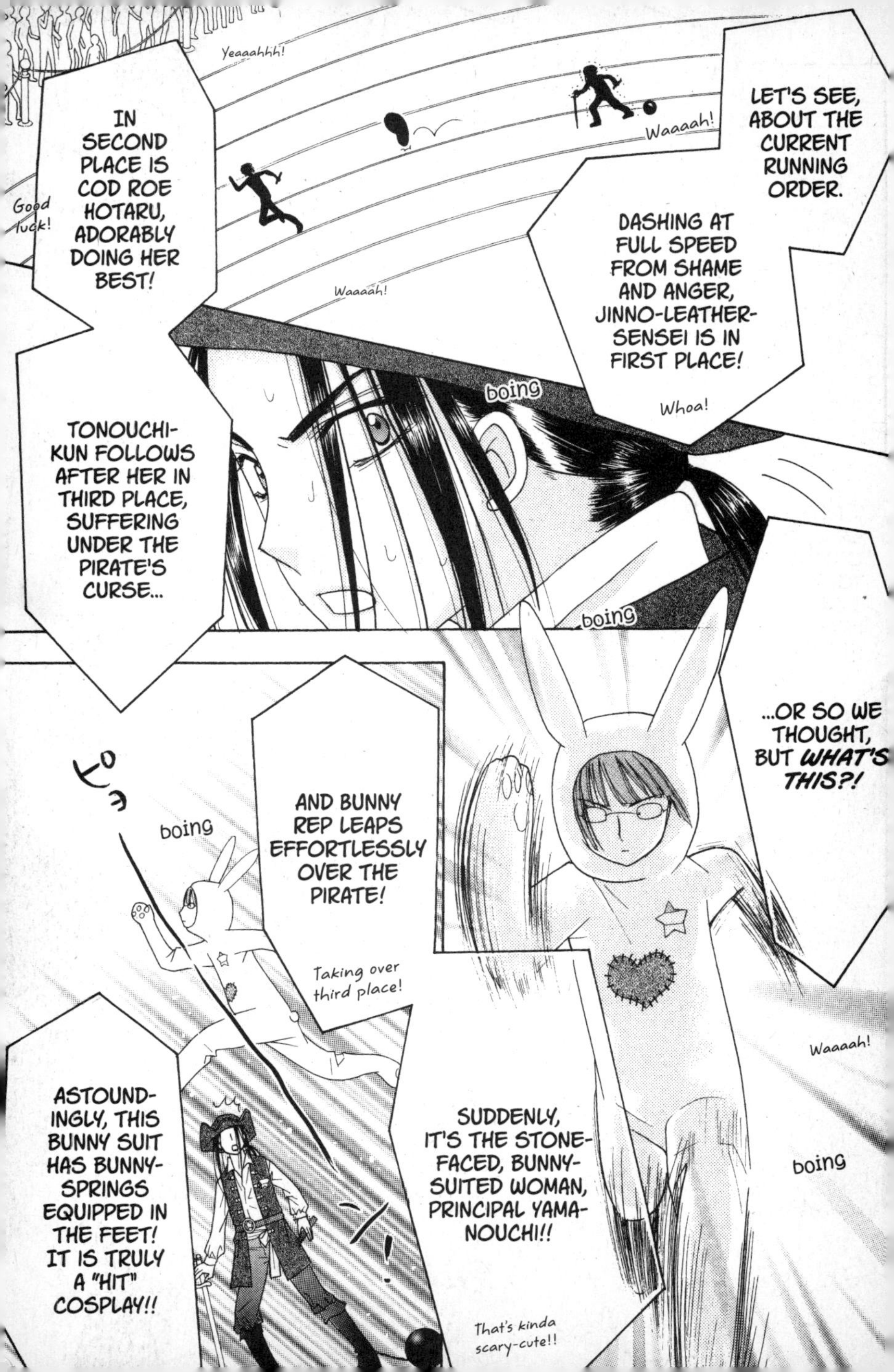
LET'S SEE, ABOUT THE CURRENT RUNNING ORDER.
DASHING AT FULL SPEED FROM SHAME AND ANGER, JINNO-LEATHER-SENSEI IS IN FIRST PLACE!
Waaaah!
Yeaaahhh!
IN SECOND PLACE IS COD ROE HOTARU, ADORABLY DOING HER BEST!
Good luck!
Waaaah!
boing
Whoa!
TONOUCHI-KUN FOLLOWS AFTER HER IN THIRD PLACE, SUFFERING UNDER THE PIRATE'S CURSE...
boing
...OR SO WE THOUGHT, BUT ***WHAT'S THIS?!***
AND BUNNY REP LEAPS EFFORTLESSLY OVER THE PIRATE!
boing
Taking over third place!
Waaaah!
SUDDENLY, IT'S THE STONE-FACED, BUNNY-SUITED WOMAN, PRINCIPAL YAMA-NOUCHI!!
boing
ASTOUND-INGLY, THIS BUNNY SUIT HAS BUNNY-SPRINGS EQUIPPED IN THE FEET! IT IS TRULY A "HIT" COSPLAY!!
That's kinda scary-cute!!

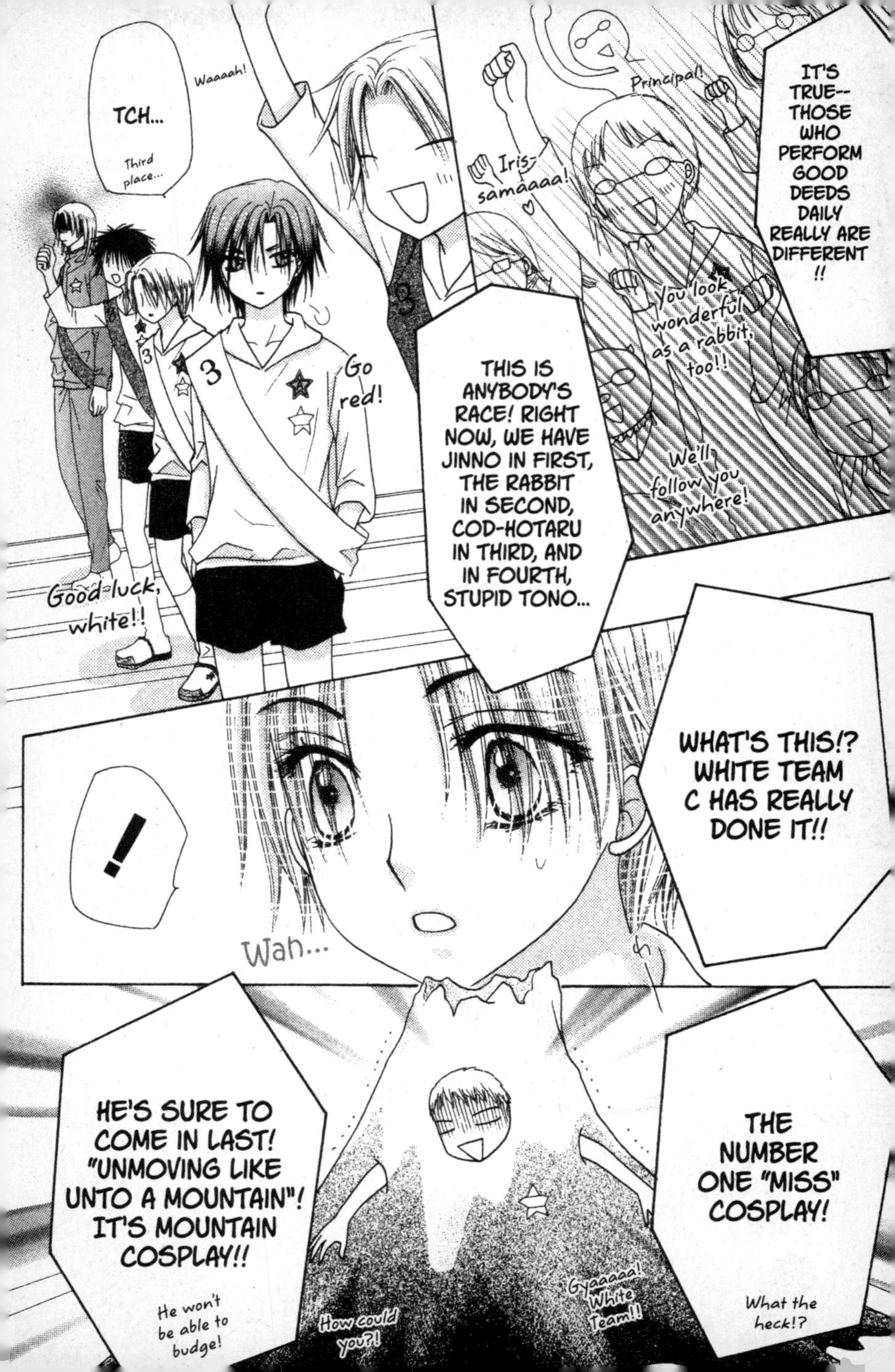
IT'S TRUE--THOSE WHO PERFORM GOOD DEEDS DAILY REALLY ARE DIFFERENT!!
Principal!
Iris-samaaaa! ♡
You look wonderful as a rabbit, too!!
We'll follow you anywhere!
THIS IS ANYBODY'S RACE! RIGHT NOW, WE HAVE JINNO IN FIRST, THE RABBIT IN SECOND, COD-HOTARU IN THIRD, AND IN FOURTH, STUPID TONO...
Waaaah!
TCH...
Third place...
Go red!
Good luck, white!!
WHAT'S THIS!? WHITE TEAM C HAS REALLY DONE IT!!
!
Wah...
THE NUMBER ONE "MISS" COSPLAY!
HE'S SURE TO COME IN LAST! "UNMOVING LIKE UNTO A MOUNTAIN"! IT'S MOUNTAIN COSPLAY!!
What the heck!?
Gyaaaaa! White Team!!
How could you?!
He won't be able to budge!

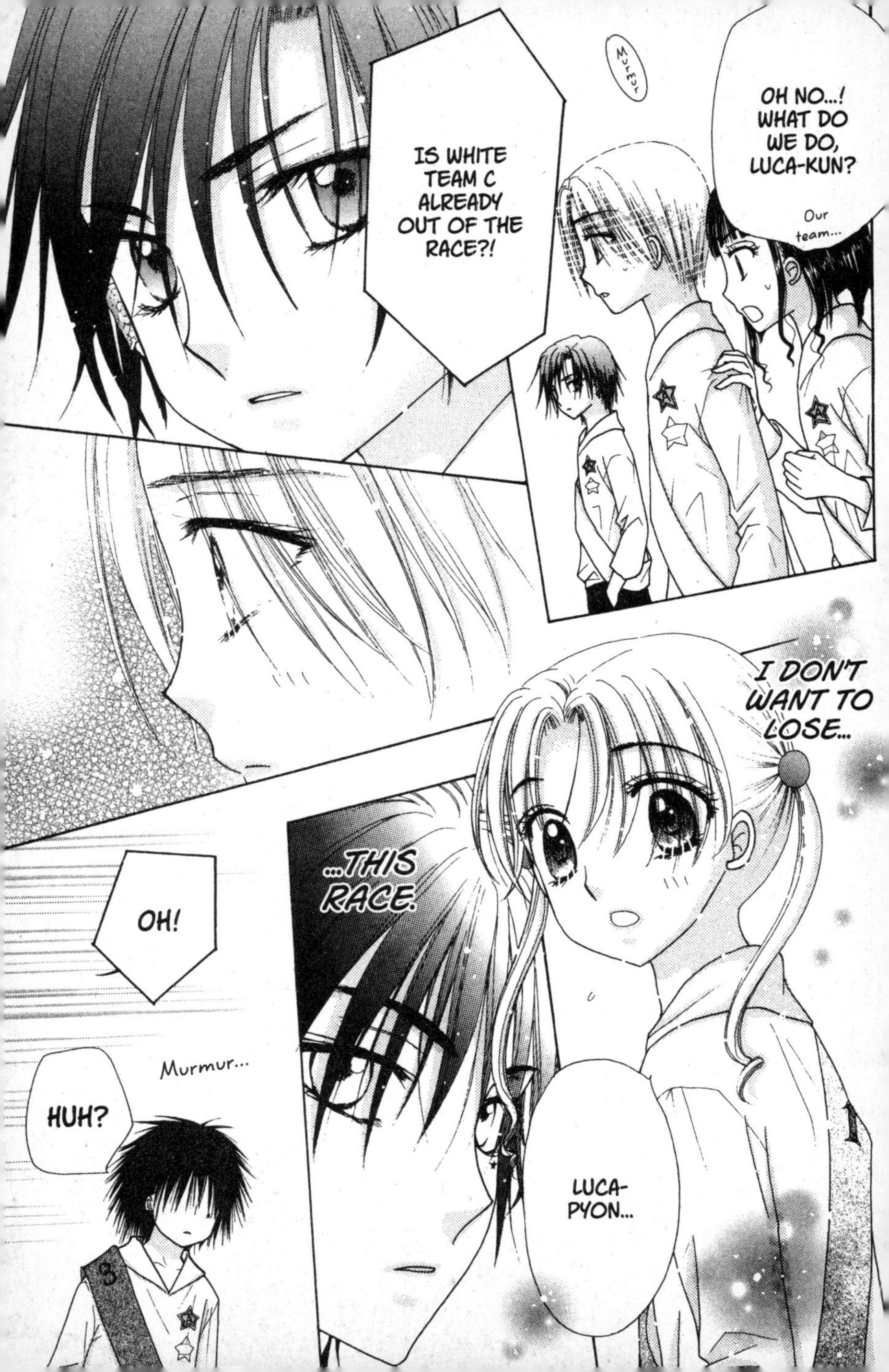
OH NO...! WHAT DO WE DO, LUCA-KUN?
Our team...
Murmur
IS WHITE TEAM C ALREADY OUT OF THE RACE?!
I DON'T WANT TO LOSE...
...THIS RACE.
OH!
LUCA-PYON...
Murmur...
HUH?

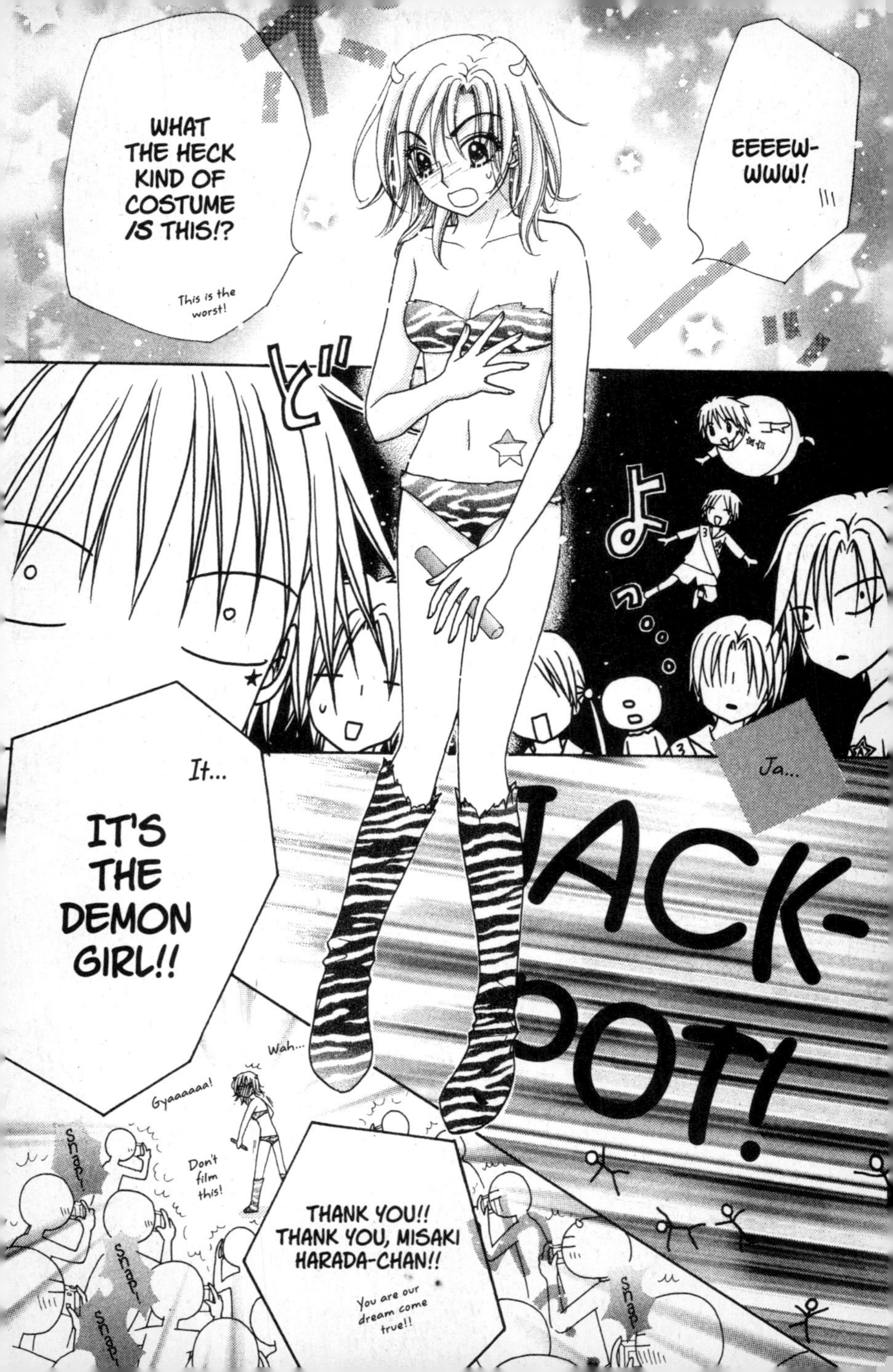
EEEEW-WWW!
WHAT THE HECK KIND OF COSTUME IS THIS!?
This is the worst!
Ja...
JACK-POT!
It...
IT'S THE DEMON GIRL!!
Wah...
Gyaaaaaa!
Don't film this!
THANK YOU!! THANK YOU, MISAKI HARADA-CHAN!!
You are our dream come true!!

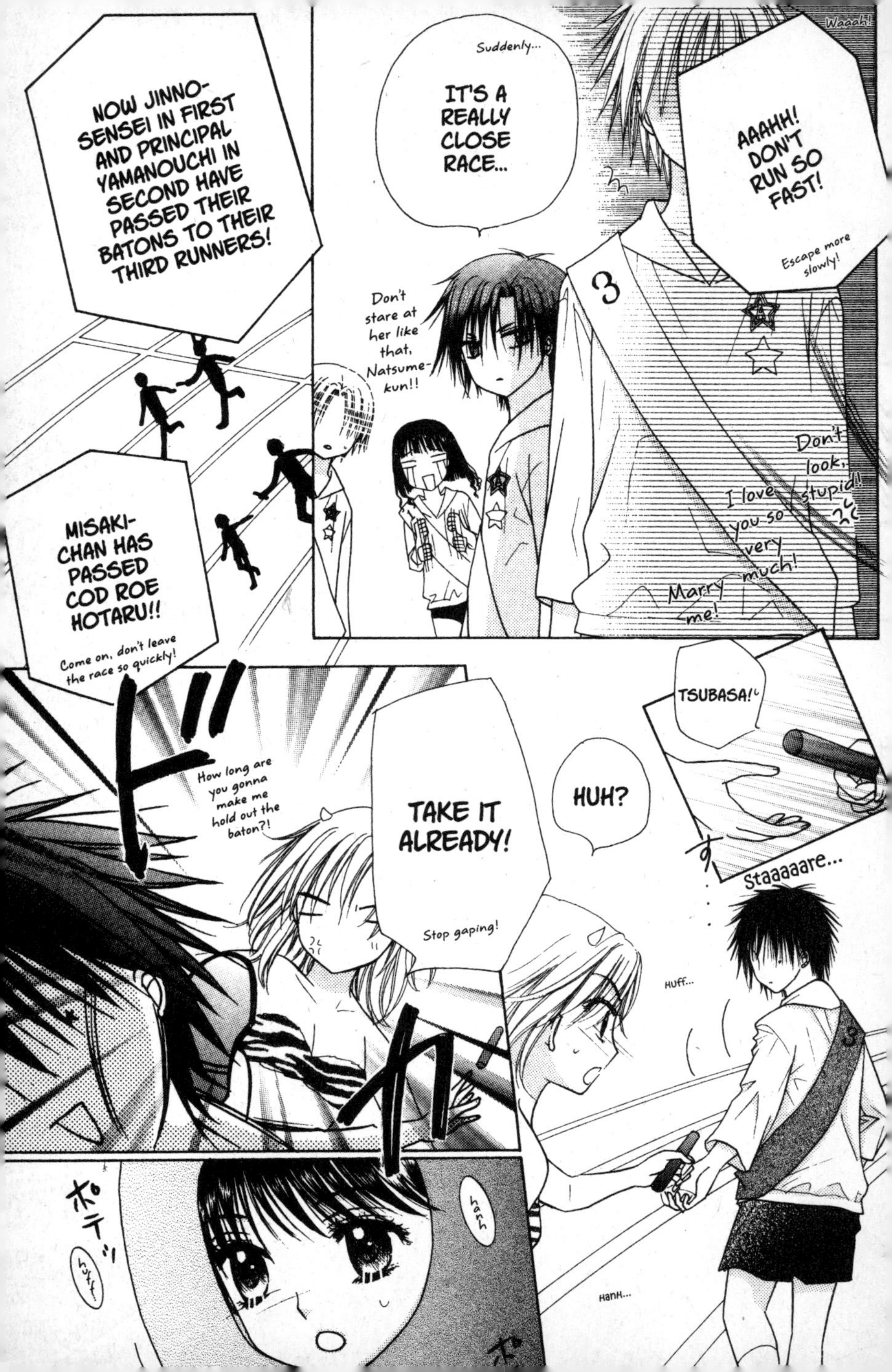

Waaah!
AAAHH! DON'T RUN SO FAST!
Escape more slowly!
Don't look, stupid!
I love you so very much!
Marry me!
Suddenly...
IT'S A REALLY CLOSE RACE...
Don't stare at her like that, Natsume-kun!!
NOW JINNO-SENSEI IN FIRST AND PRINCIPAL YAMANOUCHI IN SECOND HAVE PASSED THEIR BATONS TO THEIR THIRD RUNNERS!
MISAKI-CHAN HAS PASSED COD ROE HOTARU!!
Come on, don't leave the race so quickly!
TSUBASA!
HUH?
Staaaaare...
HUFF...
HanH...
TAKE IT ALREADY!
Stop gaping!
How long are you gonna make me hold out the baton?!
hanh
huff

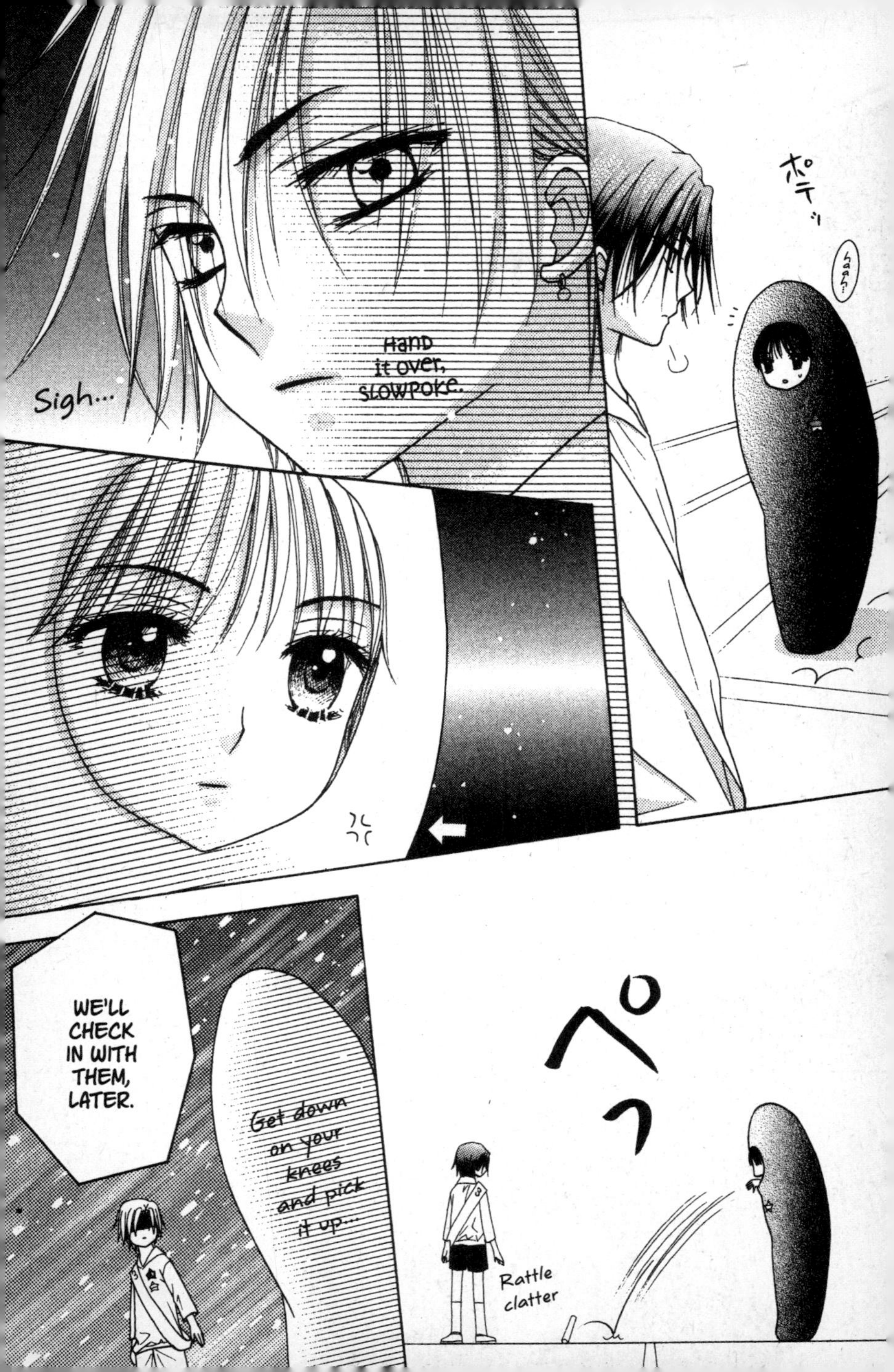
ポテッ
haah...
Hand it over, slowpoke.
Sigh...
ペっ
Rattle clatter
Get down on your knees and pick it up...
WE'LL CHECK IN WITH THEM, LATER.

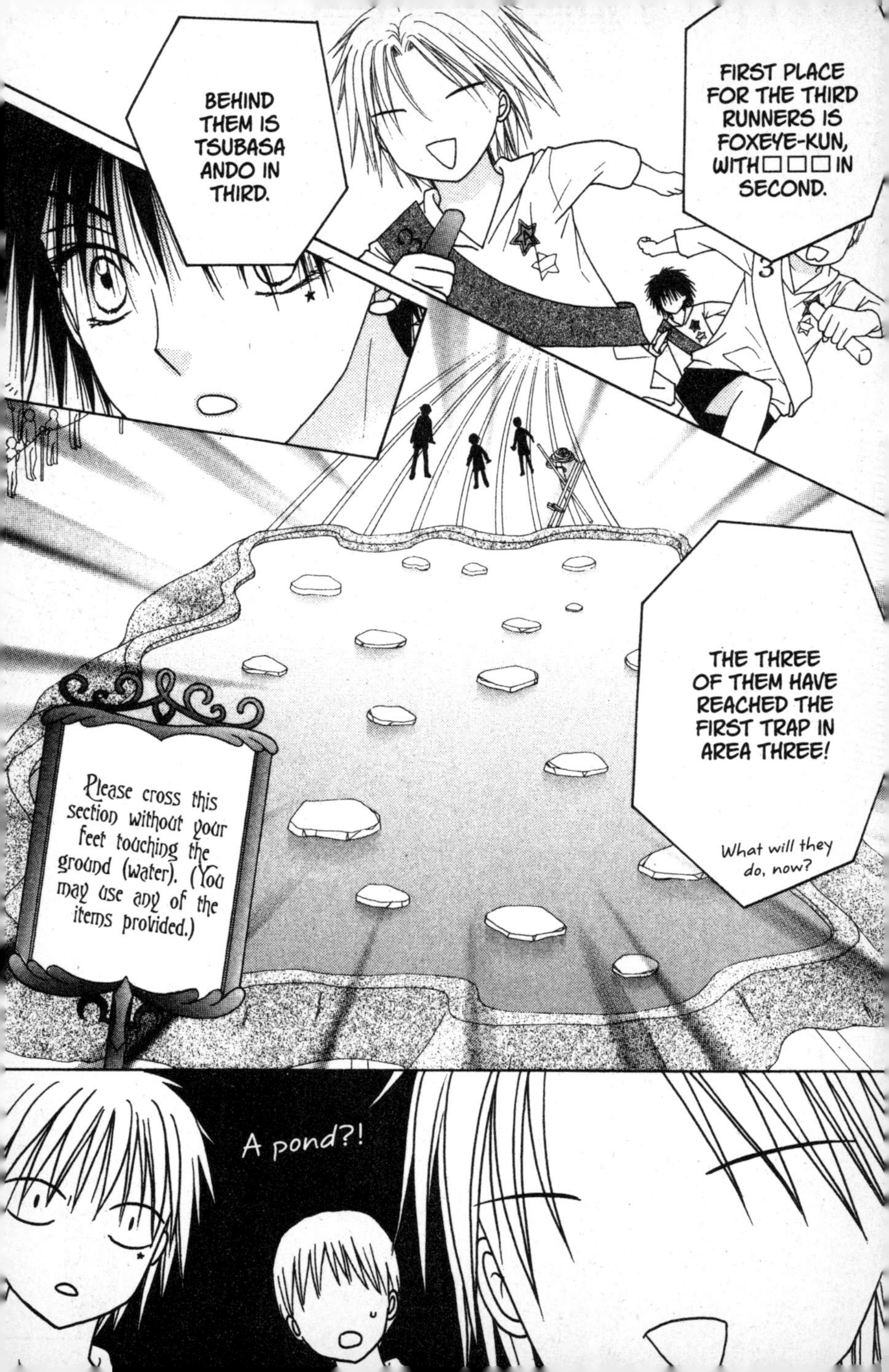
FIRST PLACE FOR THE THIRD RUNNERS IS FOXEYE-KUN, WITH□□□ IN SECOND.
BEHIND THEM IS TSUBASA ANDO IN THIRD.
THE THREE OF THEM HAVE REACHED THE FIRST TRAP IN AREA THREE!
What will they do, now?
Please cross this section without your feet touching the ground (water). (You may use any of the items provided.)
A pond?!

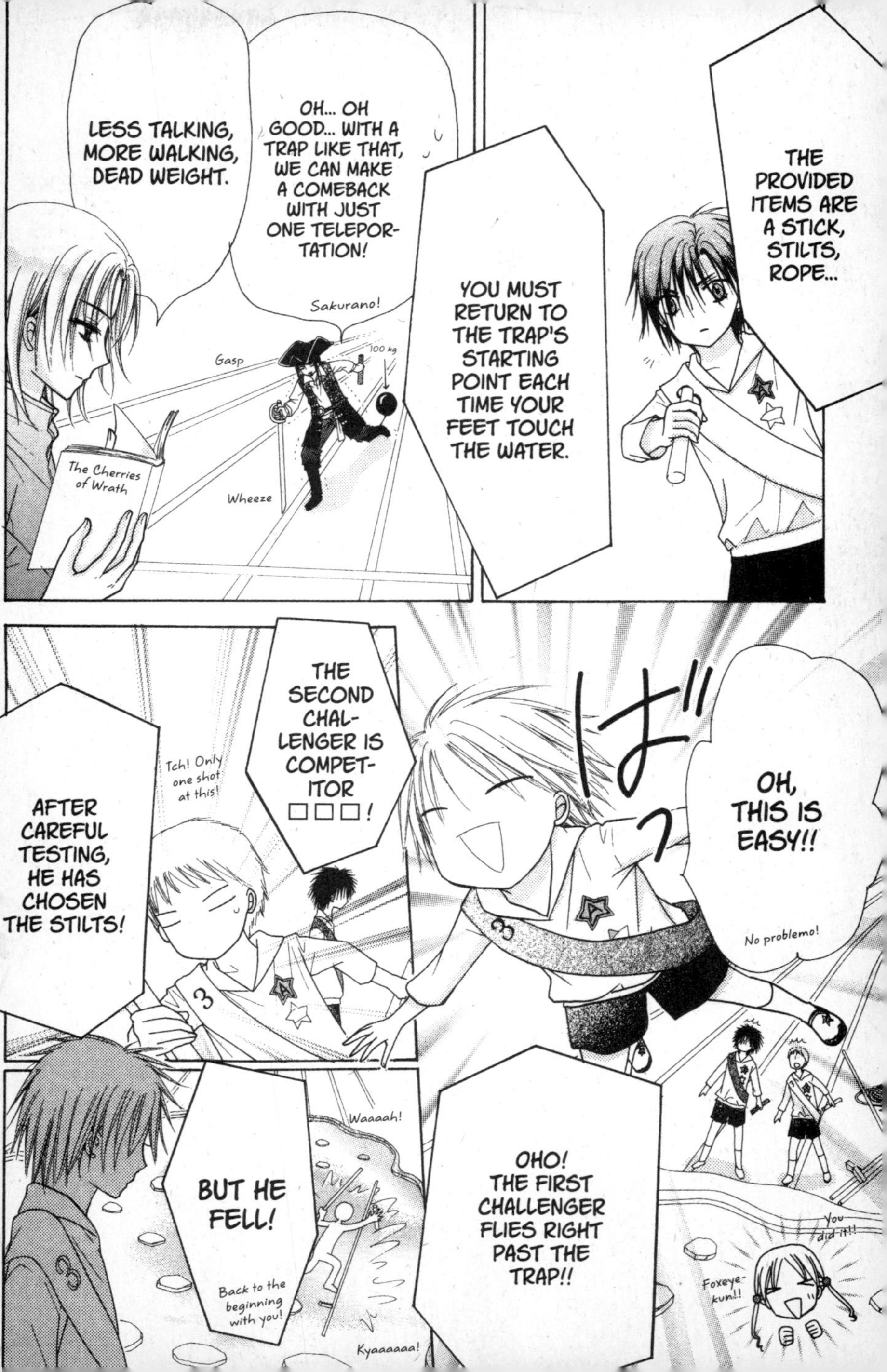

THE PROVIDED ITEMS ARE A STICK, STILTS, ROPE...
YOU MUST RETURN TO THE TRAP'S STARTING POINT EACH TIME YOUR FEET TOUCH THE WATER.
OH... OH GOOD... WITH A TRAP LIKE THAT, WE CAN MAKE A COMEBACK WITH JUST ONE TELEPOR-TATION!
Sakurano!
100 kg
Gasp
Wheeze
LESS TALKING, MORE WALKING, DEAD WEIGHT.
The Cherries of Wrath
ばっ
OH, THIS IS EASY!!
No problemo!
OHO! THE FIRST CHALLENGER FLIES RIGHT PAST THE TRAP!!
You did it!!
Foxeye-kun!!
THE SECOND CHALLENGER IS COMPET-ITOR □□□!
Tch! Only one shot at this!
AFTER CAREFUL TESTING, HE HAS CHOSEN THE STILTS!
BUT HE FELL!
Waaaah!
Back to the beginning with you!
Kyaaaaaa!

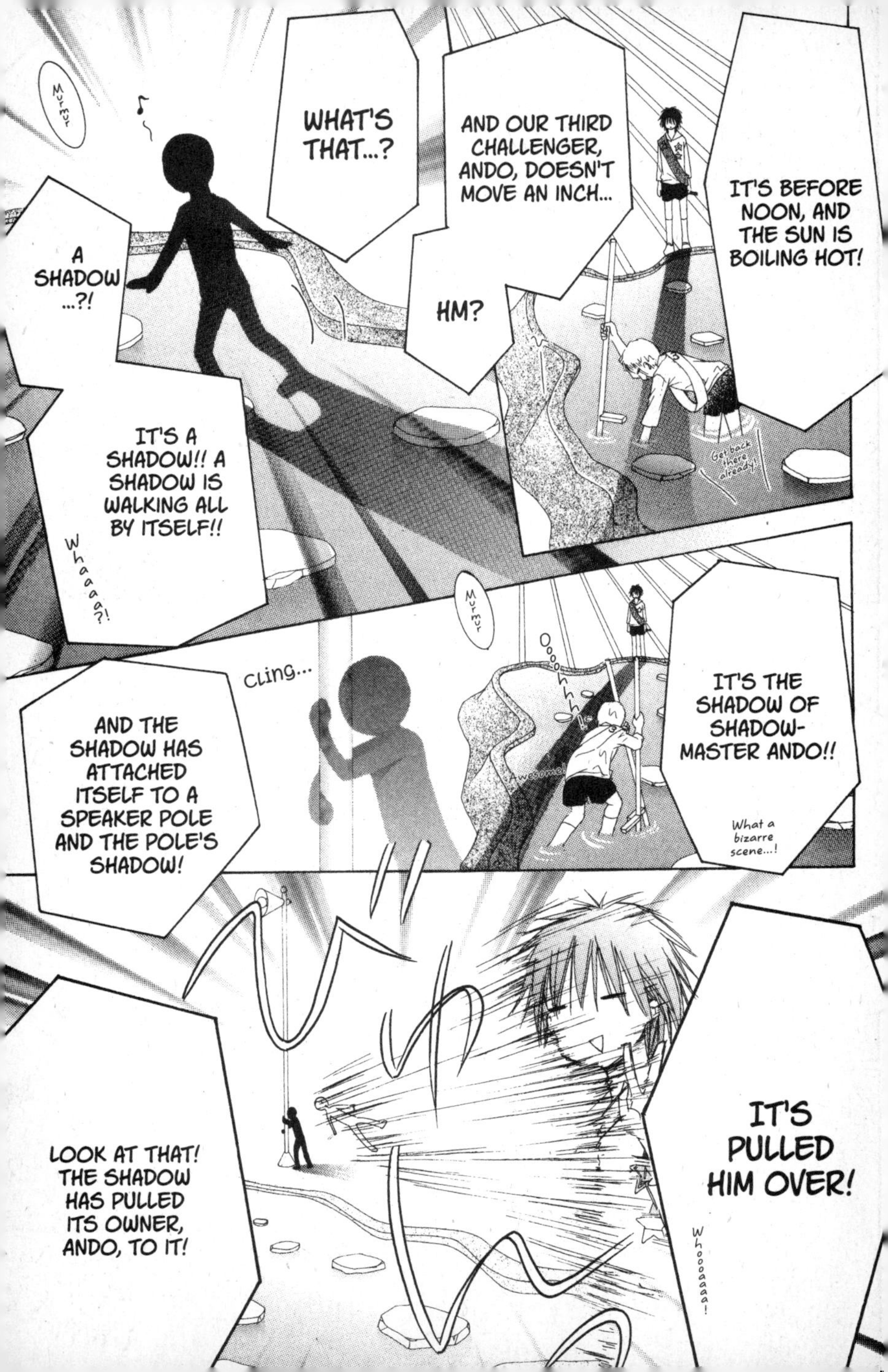
IT'S BEFORE NOON, AND THE SUN IS BOILING HOT!
AND OUR THIRD CHALLENGER, ANDO, DOESN'T MOVE AN INCH...
HM?
Get back there already!
WHAT'S THAT...?
Murmur
A SHADOW ...?!
IT'S A SHADOW!! A SHADOW IS WALKING ALL BY ITSELF!!
Whaaaaa?!
Murmur
Ooooohhh!!
Awesome!
IT'S THE SHADOW OF SHADOW-MASTER ANDO!!
What a bizarre scene...!
Cling...
AND THE SHADOW HAS ATTACHED ITSELF TO A SPEAKER POLE AND THE POLE'S SHADOW!
IT'S PULLED HIM OVER!
Whoooaaaaa!
LOOK AT THAT! THE SHADOW HAS PULLED ITS OWNER, ANDO, TO IT!

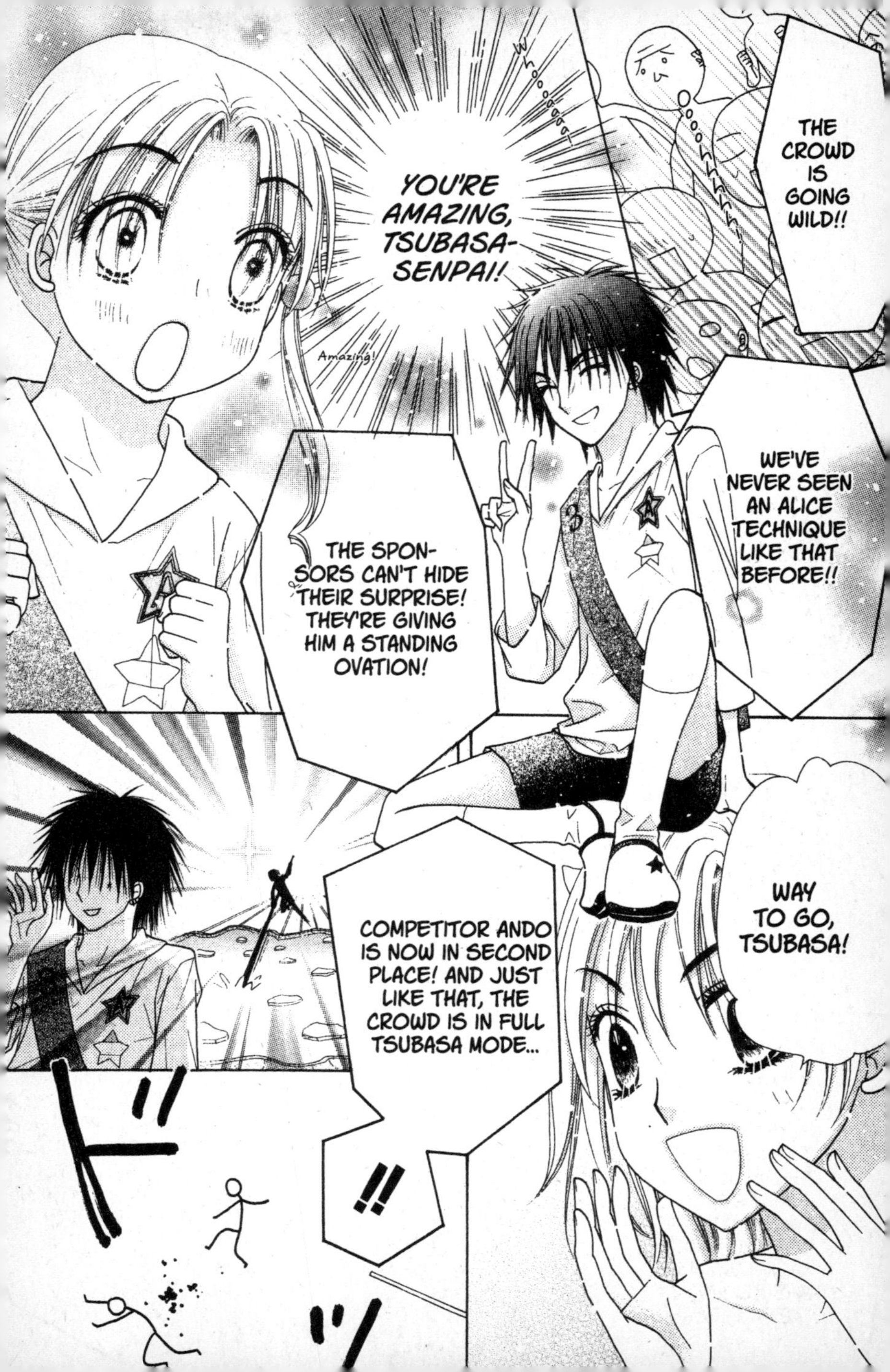
THE CROWD IS GOING WILD!!
YOU'RE AMAZING, TSUBASA-SENPAI!
Amazing!
WE'VE NEVER SEEN AN ALICE TECHNIQUE LIKE THAT BEFORE!!
THE SPON-SORS CAN'T HIDE THEIR SURPRISE! THEY'RE GIVING HIM A STANDING OVATION!
WAY TO GO, TSUBASA!
COMPETITOR ANDO IS NOW IN SECOND PLACE! AND JUST LIKE THAT, THE CROWD IS IN FULL TSUBASA MODE...
!!
ドッ

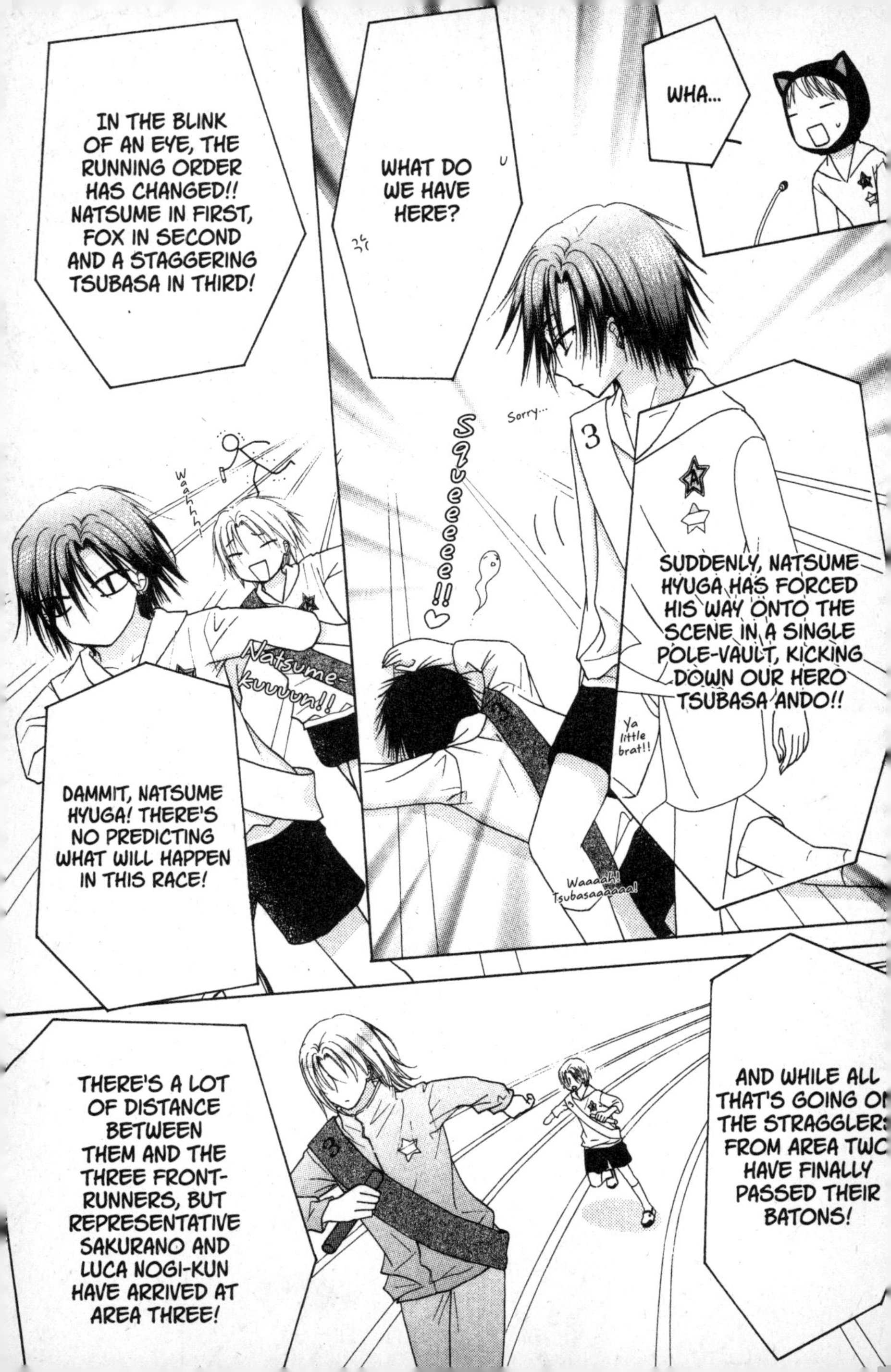
WHA...
WHAT DO WE HAVE HERE?
Sorry...
SUDDENLY, NATSUME HYUGA HAS FORCED HIS WAY ONTO THE SCENE IN A SINGLE POLE-VAULT, KICKING DOWN OUR HERO TSUBASA ANDO!!
Squeeeeeee!!
Ya little brat!!
Waaaah! Tsubasaaaaaa!
IN THE BLINK OF AN EYE, THE RUNNING ORDER HAS CHANGED!! NATSUME IN FIRST, FOX IN SECOND AND A STAGGERING TSUBASA IN THIRD!
Waahhh!
Natsume-kuuuun!!
DAMMIT, NATSUME HYUGA! THERE'S NO PREDICTING WHAT WILL HAPPEN IN THIS RACE!
AND WHILE ALL THAT'S GOING ON THE STRAGGLERS FROM AREA TWO HAVE FINALLY PASSED THEIR BATONS!
THERE'S A LOT OF DISTANCE BETWEEN THEM AND THE THREE FRONT-RUNNERS, BUT REPRESENTATIVE SAKURANO AND LUCA NOGI-KUN HAVE ARRIVED AT AREA THREE!

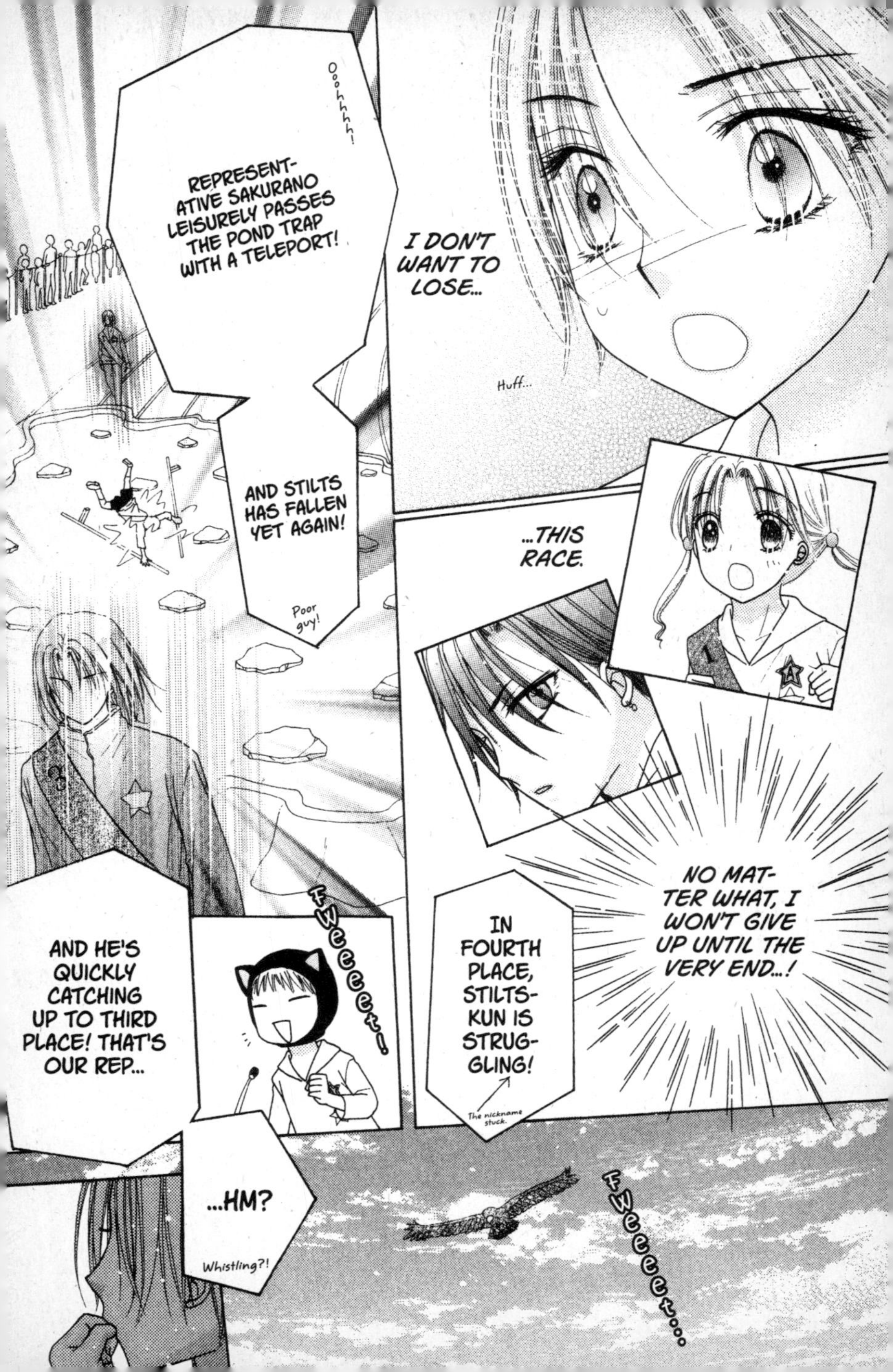
I DON'T WANT TO LOSE...
Huff...
...THIS RACE.
NO MATTER WHAT, I WON'T GIVE UP UNTIL THE VERY END...!
Ooohhhh!
REPRESENTATIVE SAKURANO LEISURELY PASSES THE POND TRAP WITH A TELEPORT!
AND STILTS HAS FALLEN YET AGAIN!
Poor guy!
IN FOURTH PLACE, STILTS-KUN IS STRUGGLING!
The nickname stuck.
Fweeeet!
AND HE'S QUICKLY CATCHING UP TO THIRD PLACE! THAT'S OUR REP...
Fweeeet...
...HM?
Whistling?!

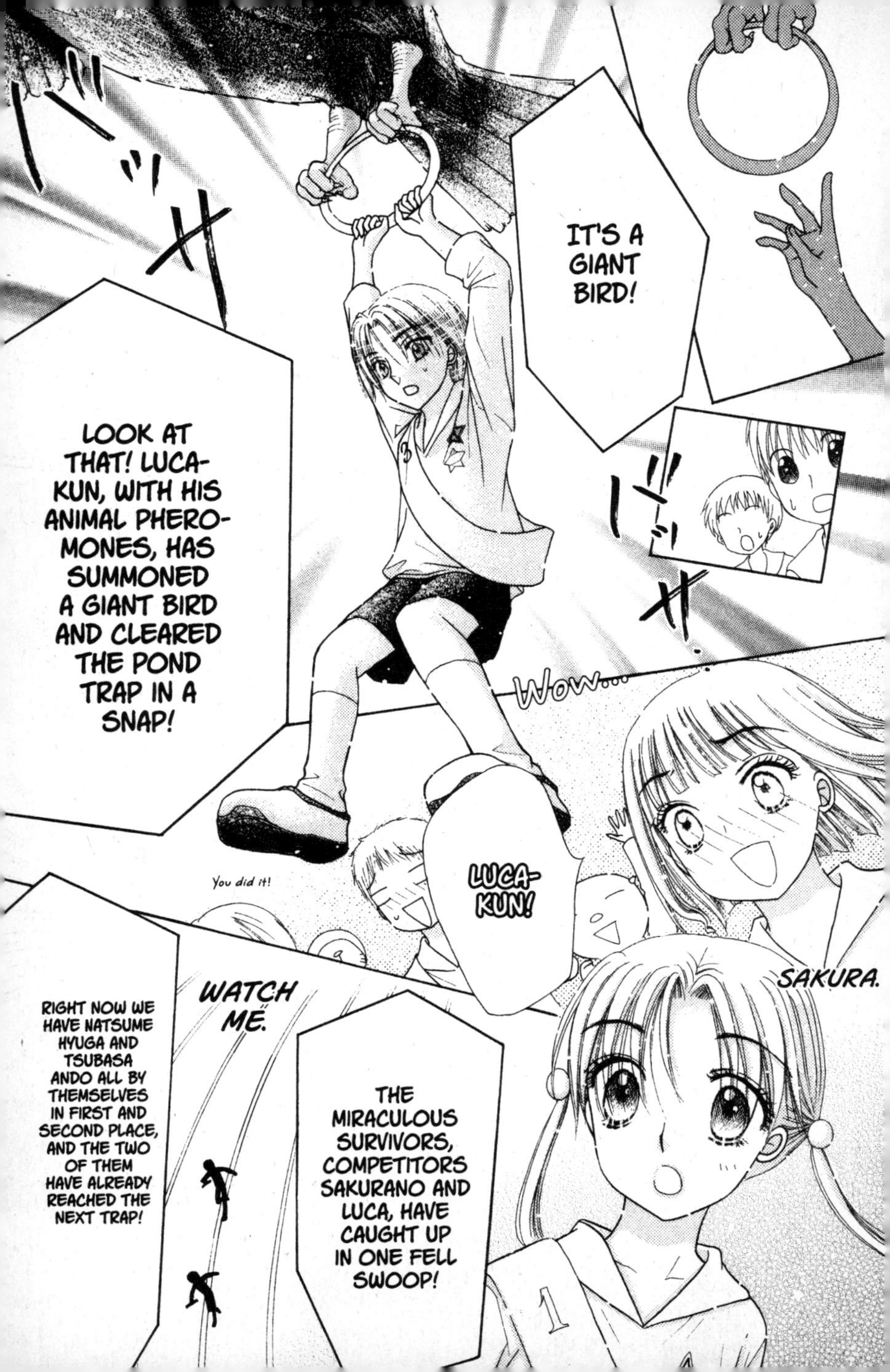
IT'S A GIANT BIRD!
LOOK AT THAT! LUCA-KUN, WITH HIS ANIMAL PHEROMONES, HAS SUMMONED A GIANT BIRD AND CLEARED THE POND TRAP IN A SNAP!
Wow...
LUCA-KUN!
You did it!
SAKURA.
THE MIRACULOUS SURVIVORS, COMPETITORS SAKURANO AND LUCA, HAVE CAUGHT UP IN ONE FELL SWOOP!
WATCH ME.
RIGHT NOW WE HAVE NATSUME HYUGA AND TSUBASA ANDO ALL BY THEMSELVES IN FIRST AND SECOND PLACE, AND THE TWO OF THEM HAVE ALREADY REACHED THE NEXT TRAP!

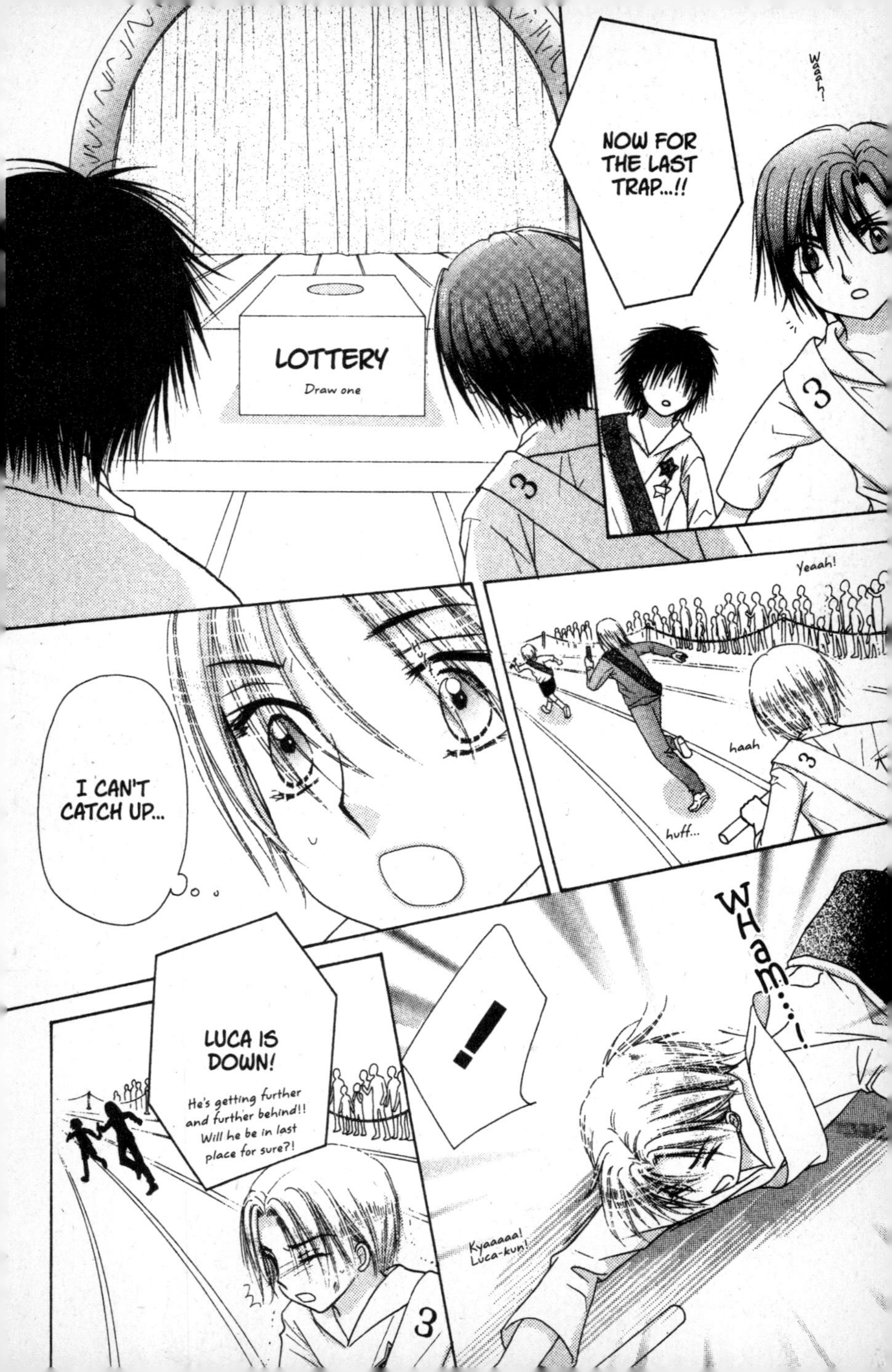

Waaah!
NOW FOR THE LAST TRAP...!!
LOTTERY
Draw one
Yeaah!
haah
huff...
I CAN'T CATCH UP...
WHAM...!
Kyaaaaa! Luca-kun!
!
LUCA IS DOWN!
He's getting further and further behind!! Will he be in last place for sure?!

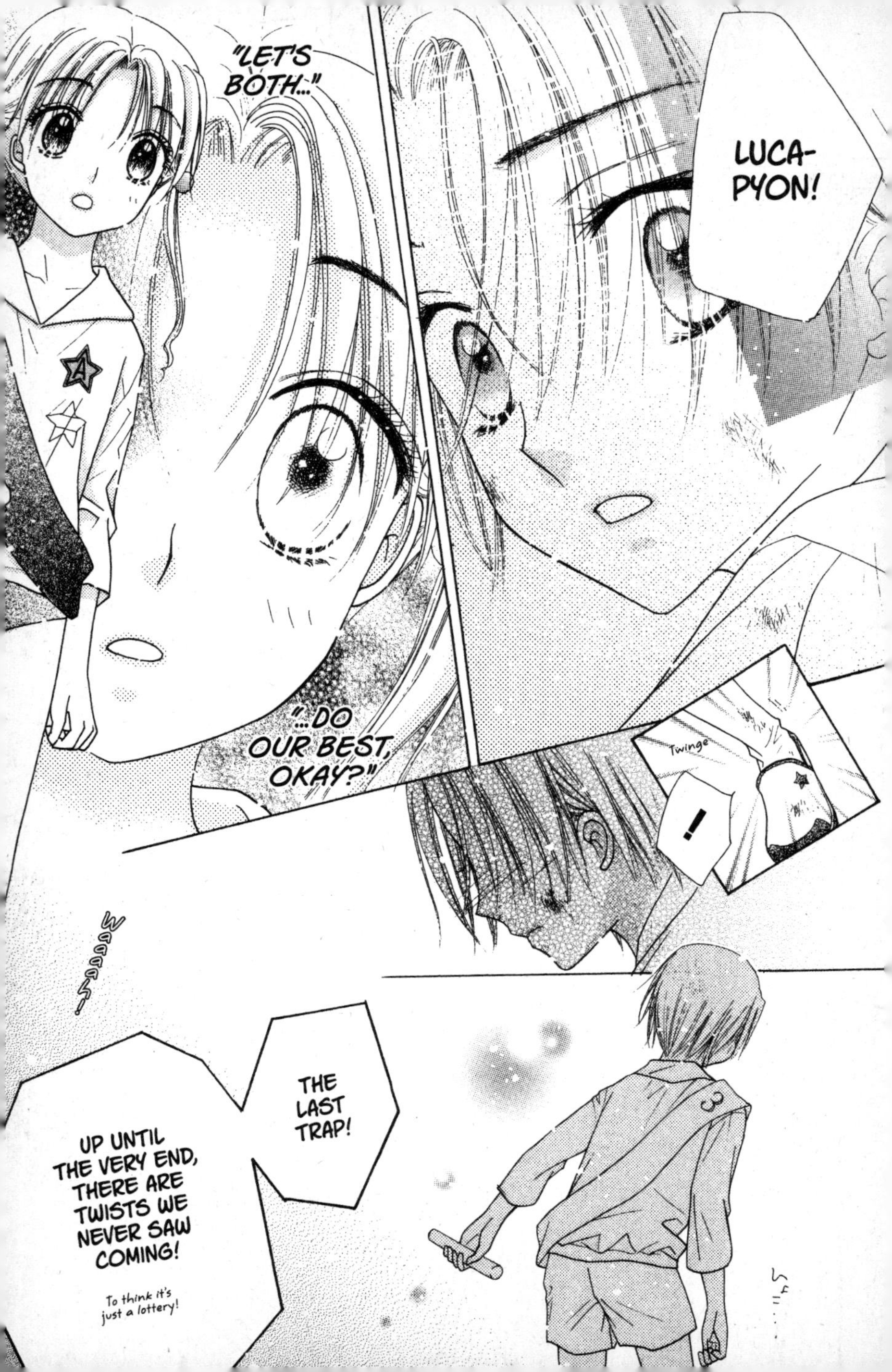
LUCA-PYON!
"LET'S BOTH..."
"...DO OUR BEST, OKAY?"
Twinge
!
THE LAST TRAP!
UP UNTIL THE VERY END, THERE ARE TWISTS WE NEVER SAW COMING!
To think it's just a lottery!
Waaaah!

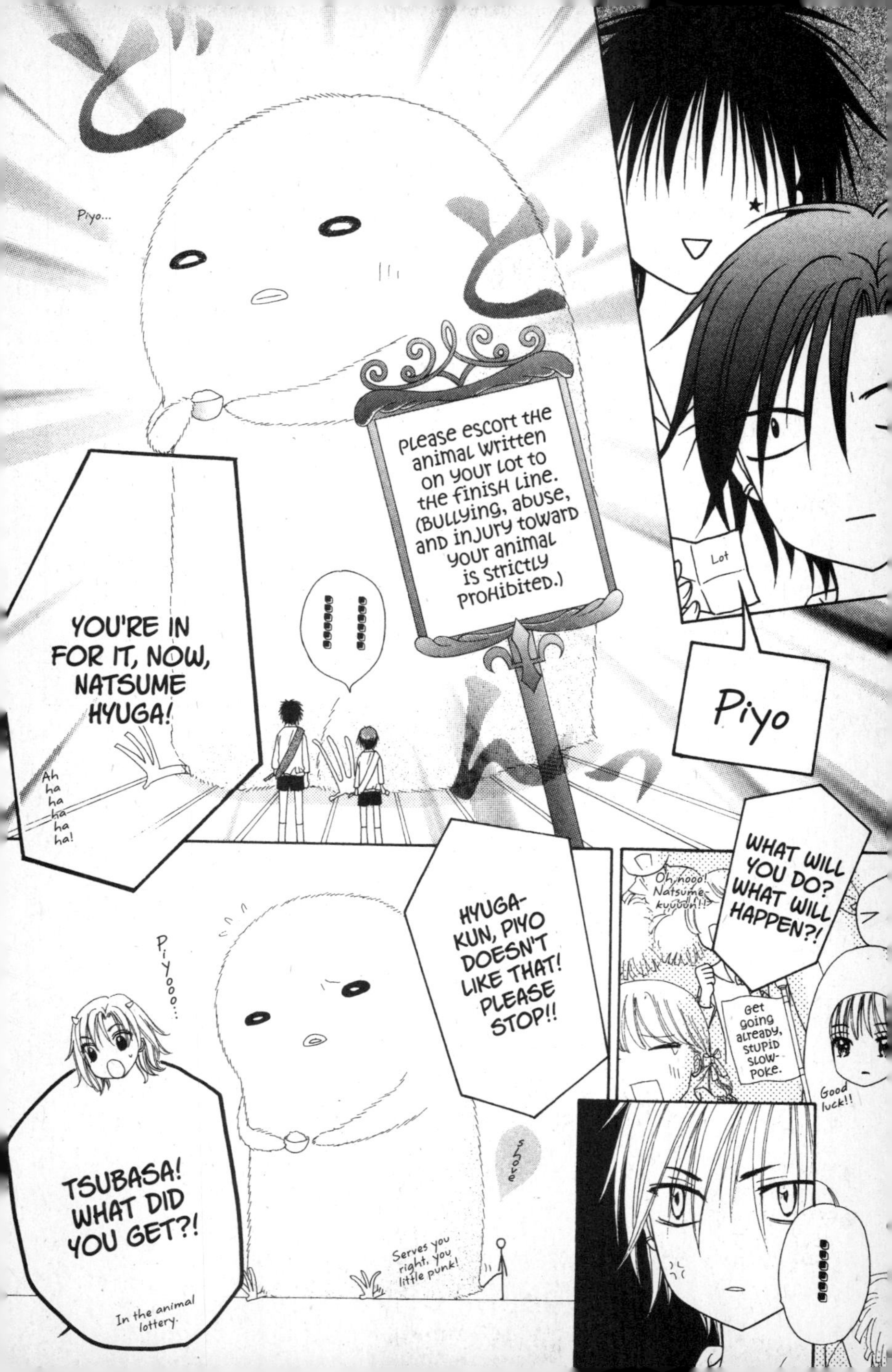
Lot
Piyo
Piyo...
Please escort the animal written on your lot to the finish line. (Bullying, abuse, and injury toward your animal is strictly prohibited.)
......!!
YOU'RE IN FOR IT, NOW, NATSUME HYUGA!
Ah ha ha ha ha ha!
WHAT WILL YOU DO? WHAT WILL HAPPEN?!
Oh, nooo! Natsume-kuuuun!!
Get going already, stupid slow-poke.
Good luck!!
......
HYUGA-KUN, PIYO DOESN'T LIKE THAT! PLEASE STOP!!
Piyooo...
shove
TSUBASA! WHAT DID YOU GET?!
Serves you right, you little punk!
In the animal lottery.

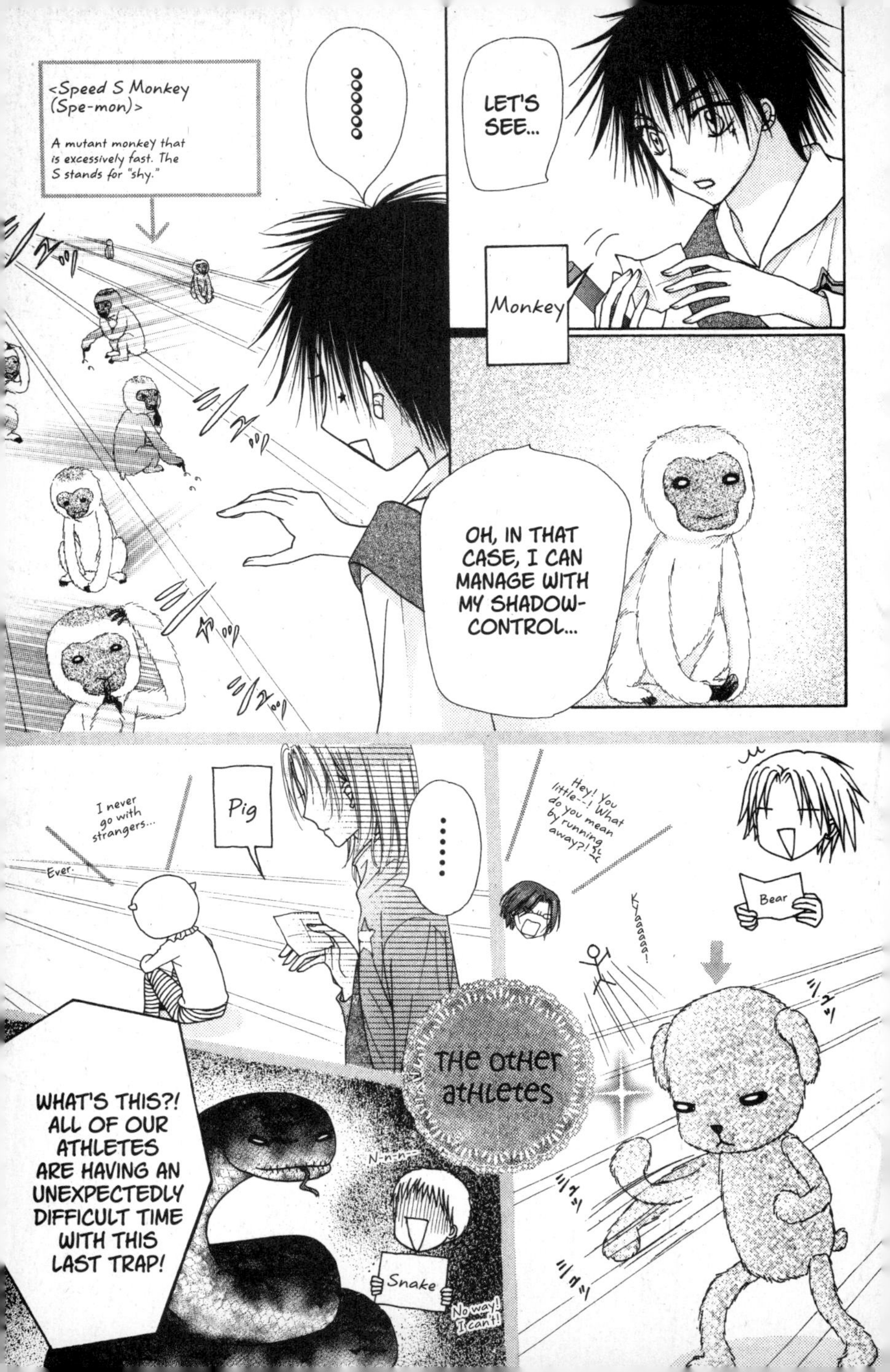

LET'S SEE...
Monkey
OH, IN THAT CASE, I CAN MANAGE WITH MY SHADOW-CONTROL...
......
<Speed S Monkey (Spe-mon)>
A mutant monkey that is excessively fast. The S stands for "shy."
Hey! You little--! What do you mean by running away?!
Kyaaaaaa!
Bear
......
Pig
I never go with strangers...
Ever.
THE OTHER ATHLETES
WHAT'S THIS?! ALL OF OUR ATHLETES ARE HAVING AN UNEXPECTEDLY DIFFICULT TIME WITH THIS LAST TRAP!
N-n-n--
Snake
No way! I can't!

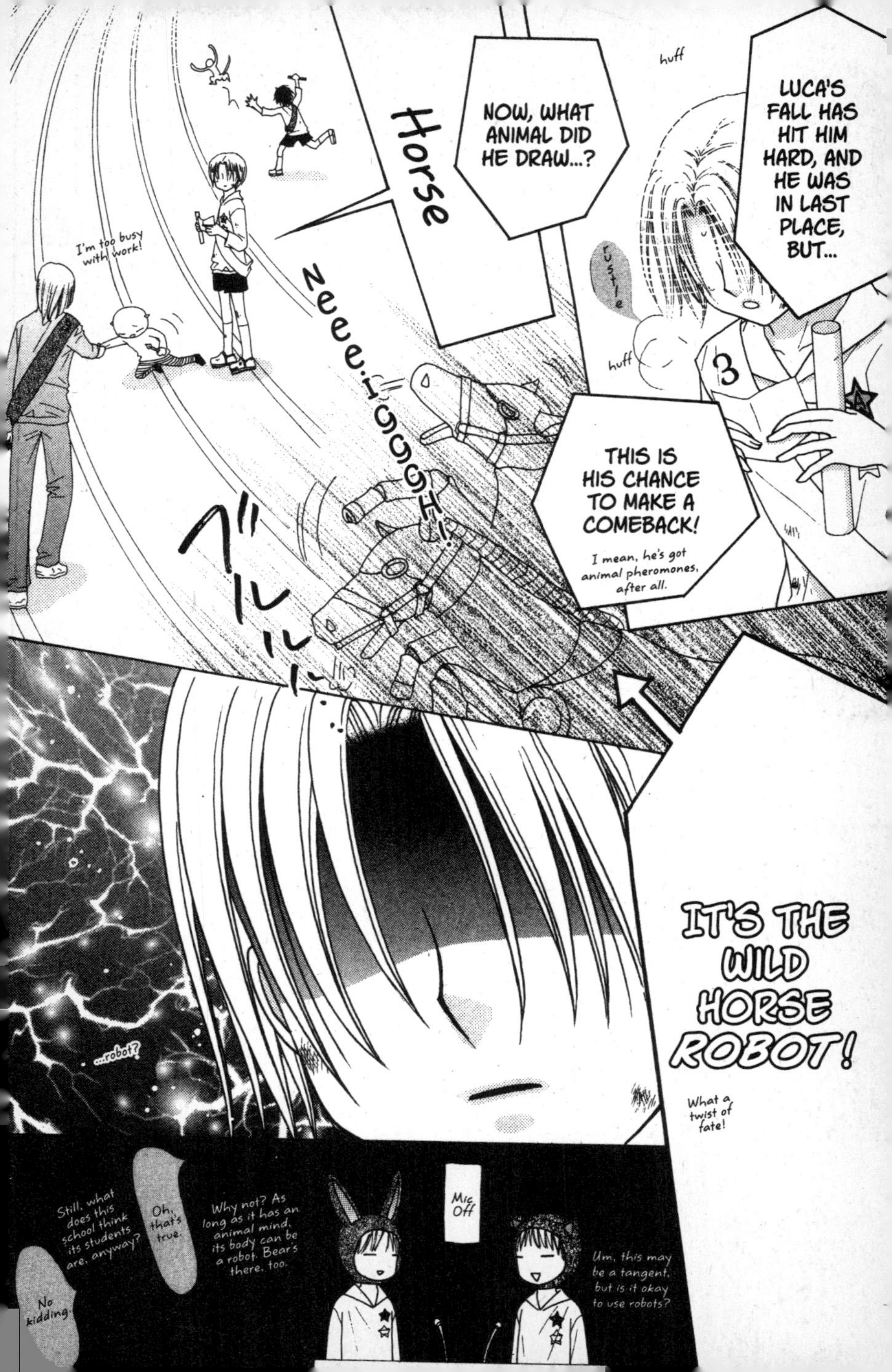
huff
LUCA'S FALL HAS HIT HIM HARD, AND HE WAS IN LAST PLACE, BUT...
rustle
huff
THIS IS HIS CHANCE TO MAKE A COMEBACK!
I mean, he's got animal pheromones, after all.
NOW, WHAT ANIMAL DID HE DRAW...?
Horse
Neeee...iggggh!
I'm too busy with work!
IT'S THE WILD HORSE ROBOT!
What a twist of fate!
...robot?
Um, this may be a tangent, but is it okay to use robots?
Mic Off
Why not? As long as it has an animal mind, its body can be a robot. Bear's there, too.
Oh, that's true.
Still, what does this school think its students are, anyway?
No kidding.

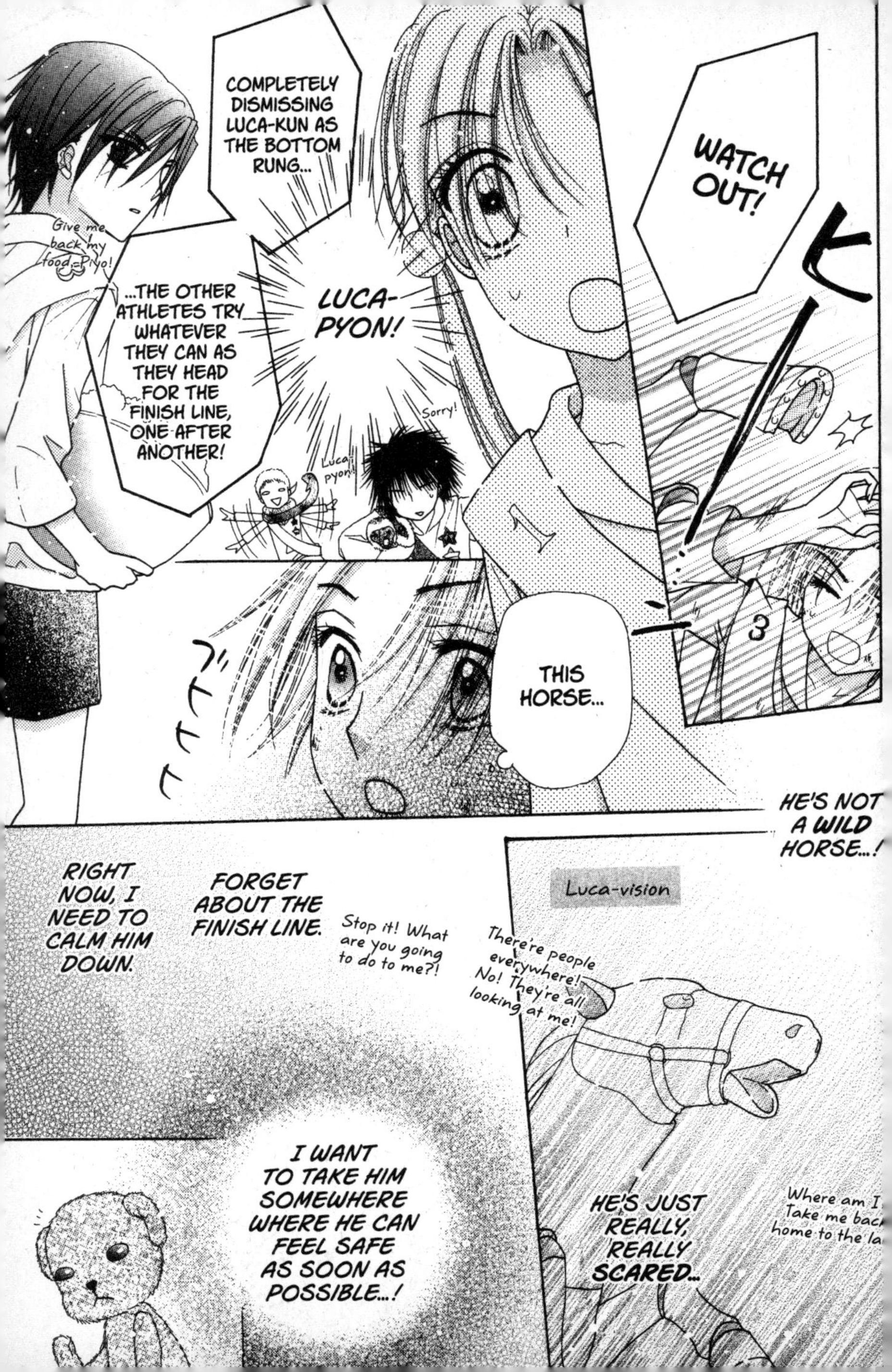

COMPLETELY DISMISSING LUCA-KUN AS THE BOTTOM RUNG...
...THE OTHER ATHLETES TRY WHATEVER THEY CAN AS THEY HEAD FOR THE FINISH LINE, ONE AFTER ANOTHER!
WATCH OUT!
LUCA-PYON!
Sorry!
Luca-pyon!
Give me back my food-Piyo!
THIS HORSE...
HE'S NOT A WILD HORSE...!
Luca-vision
There're people everywhere! No! They're all looking at me!
Where am I
Take me bac
home to the la
HE'S JUST REALLY, REALLY SCARED...
FORGET ABOUT THE FINISH LINE.
RIGHT NOW, I NEED TO CALM HIM DOWN.
Stop it! What are you going to do to me?!
I WANT TO TAKE HIM SOMEWHERE WHERE HE CAN FEEL SAFE AS SOON AS POSSIBLE...!

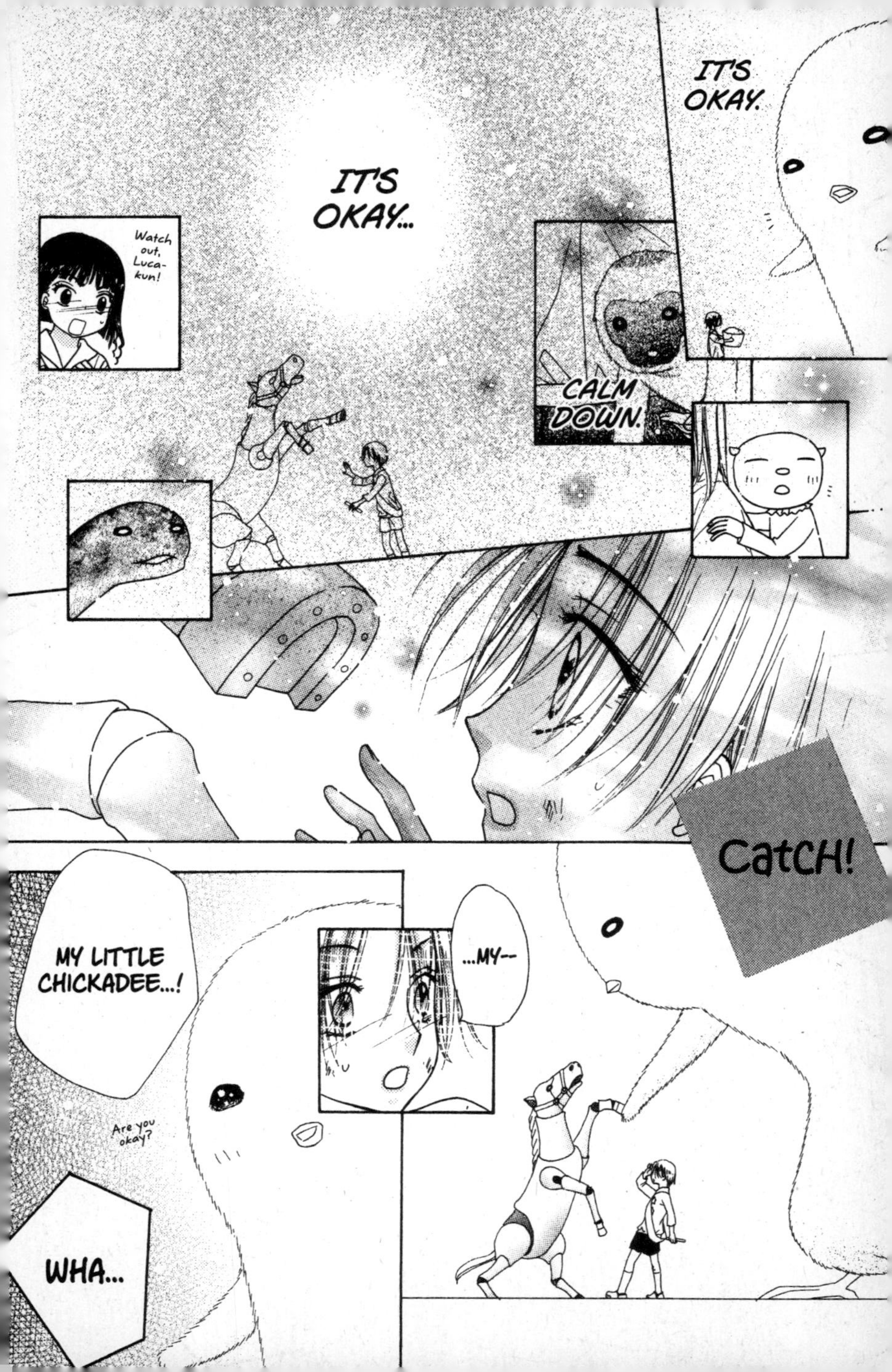
IT'S OKAY.
IT'S OKAY...
CALM DOWN.
Watch out, Luca-kun!
Catch!
...MY--
MY LITTLE CHICKADEE...!
Are you okay?
WHA...

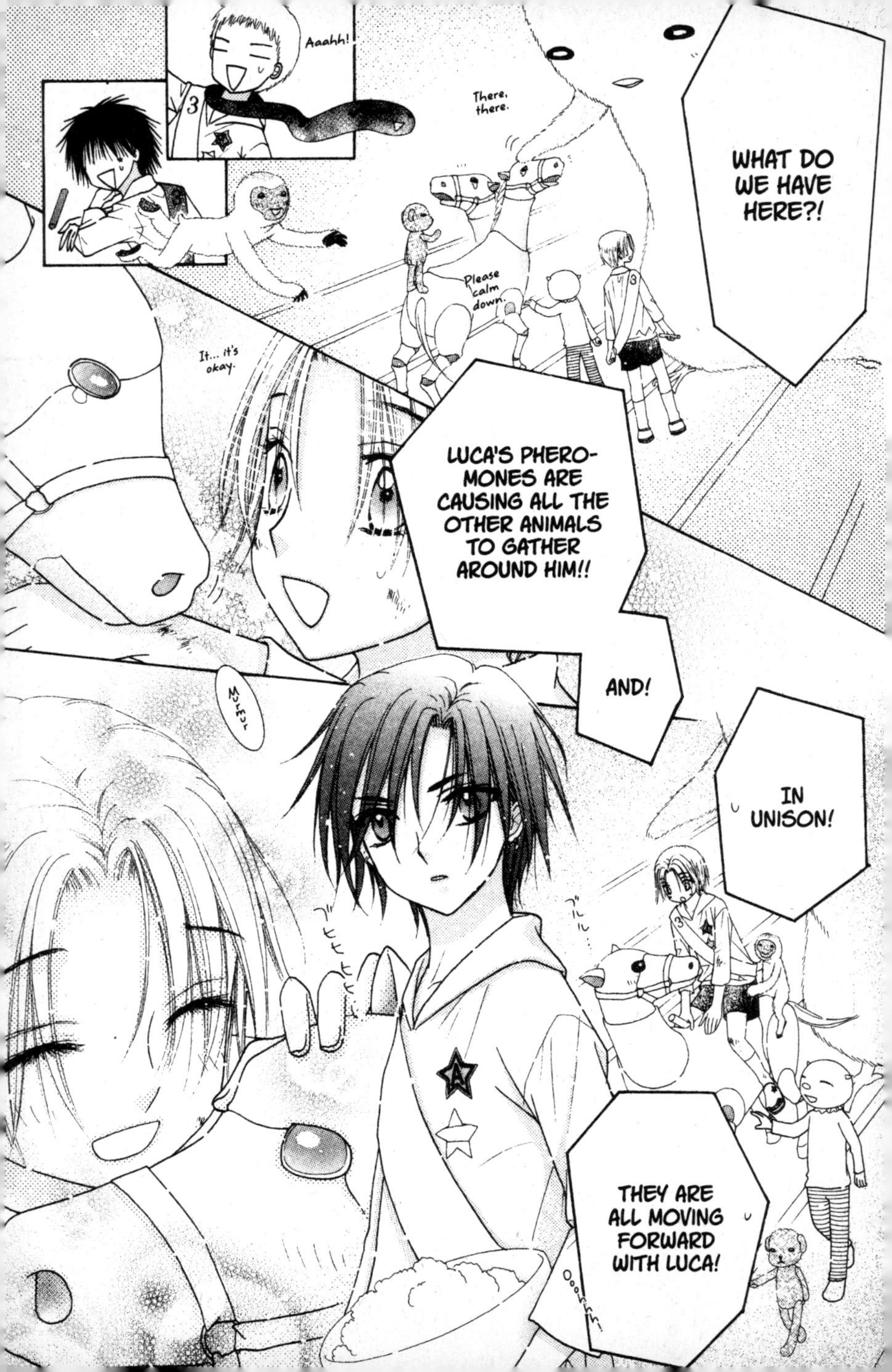

WHAT DO WE HAVE HERE?!
There, there.
Aaahh!
Please calm down.
It... it's okay.
LUCA'S PHEROMONES ARE CAUSING ALL THE OTHER ANIMALS TO GATHER AROUND HIM!!
AND!
IN UNISON!
ブルル…
ブヒヒヒ
Murmur
THEY ARE ALL MOVING FORWARD WITH LUCA!
Ooohhh!

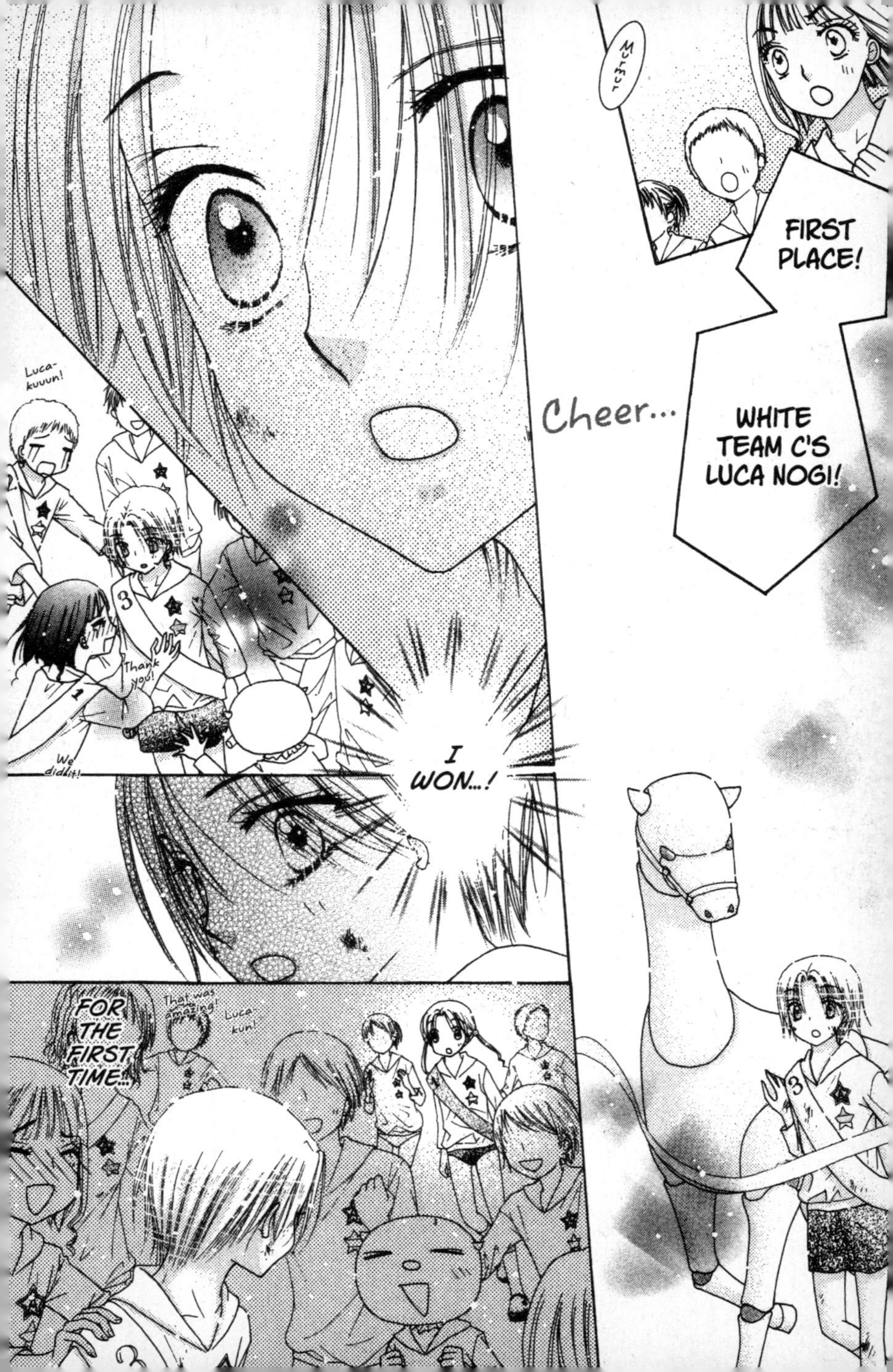

Murmur
FIRST PLACE!
WHITE TEAM C'S LUCA NOGI!
Cheer...
Luca-kuuun!
Thank you!
We did it!
I WON...!
FOR THE FIRST TIME...!
That was amazing!
Luca-kun!

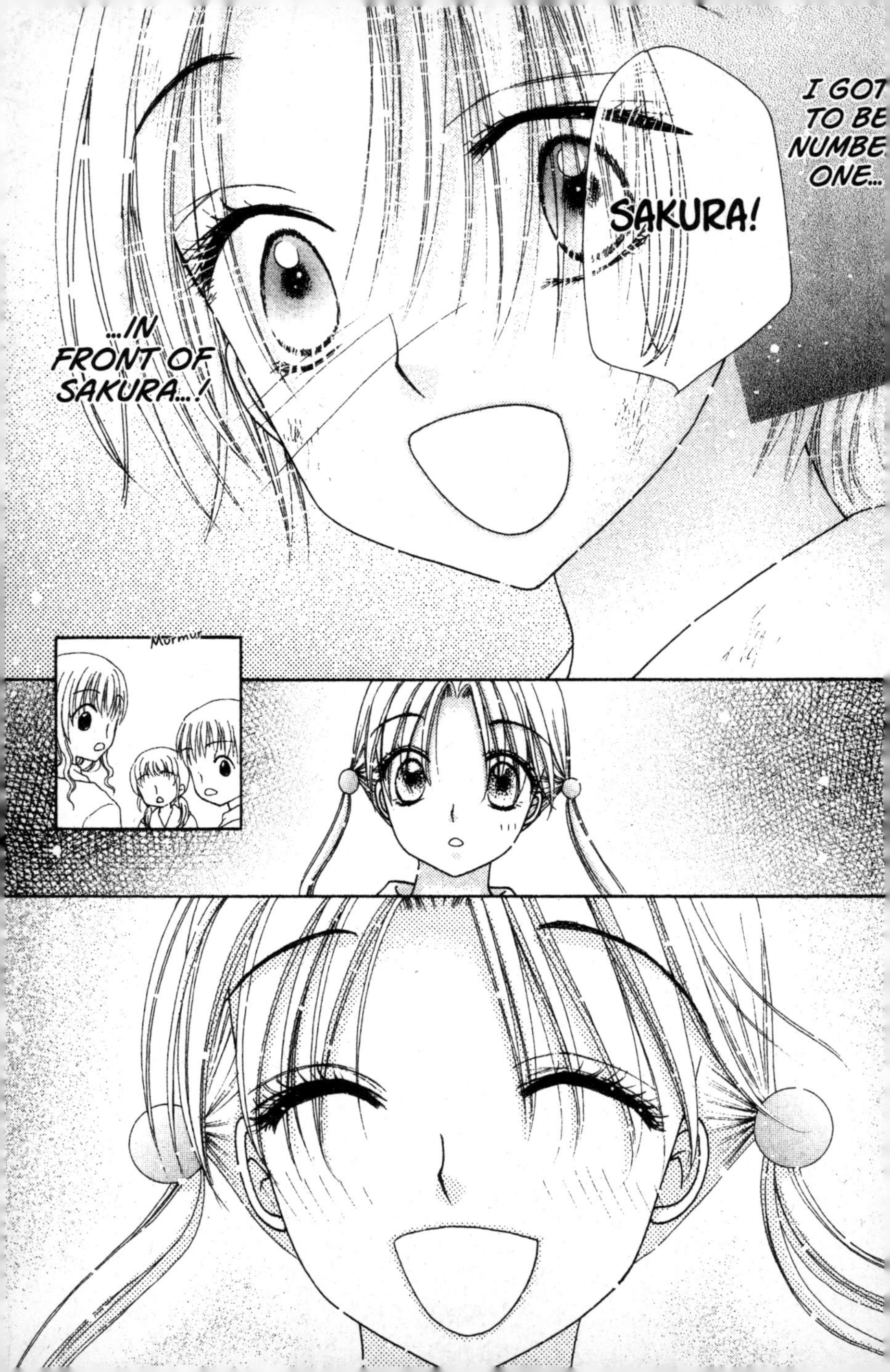
I GOT TO BE NUMBE ONE...
SAKURA!
...IN FRONT OF SAKURA...!
Murmur

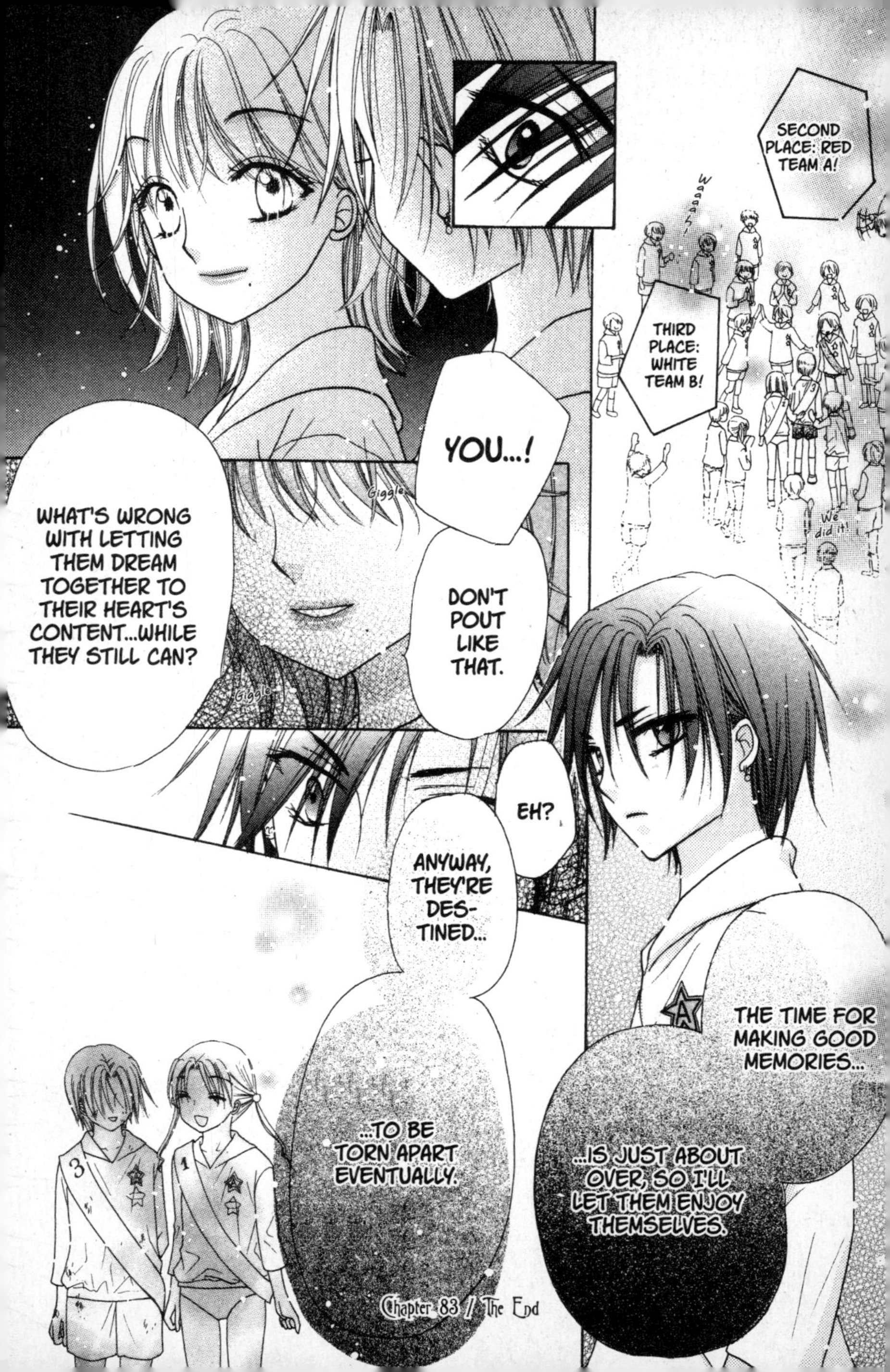
SECOND PLACE: RED TEAM A!
Waaaa!
THIRD PLACE: WHITE TEAM B!
We did it!
YOU...!
Giggle
Giggle
DON'T POUT LIKE THAT.
WHAT'S WRONG WITH LETTING THEM DREAM TOGETHER TO THEIR HEART'S CONTENT...WHILE THEY STILL CAN?
EH?
ANYWAY, THEY'RE DES-TINED...
...TO BE TORN APART EVENTUALLY.
THE TIME FOR MAKING GOOD MEMORIES...
...IS JUST ABOUT OVER, SO I'LL LET THEM ENJOY THEMSELVES.
Chapter 83 / The End

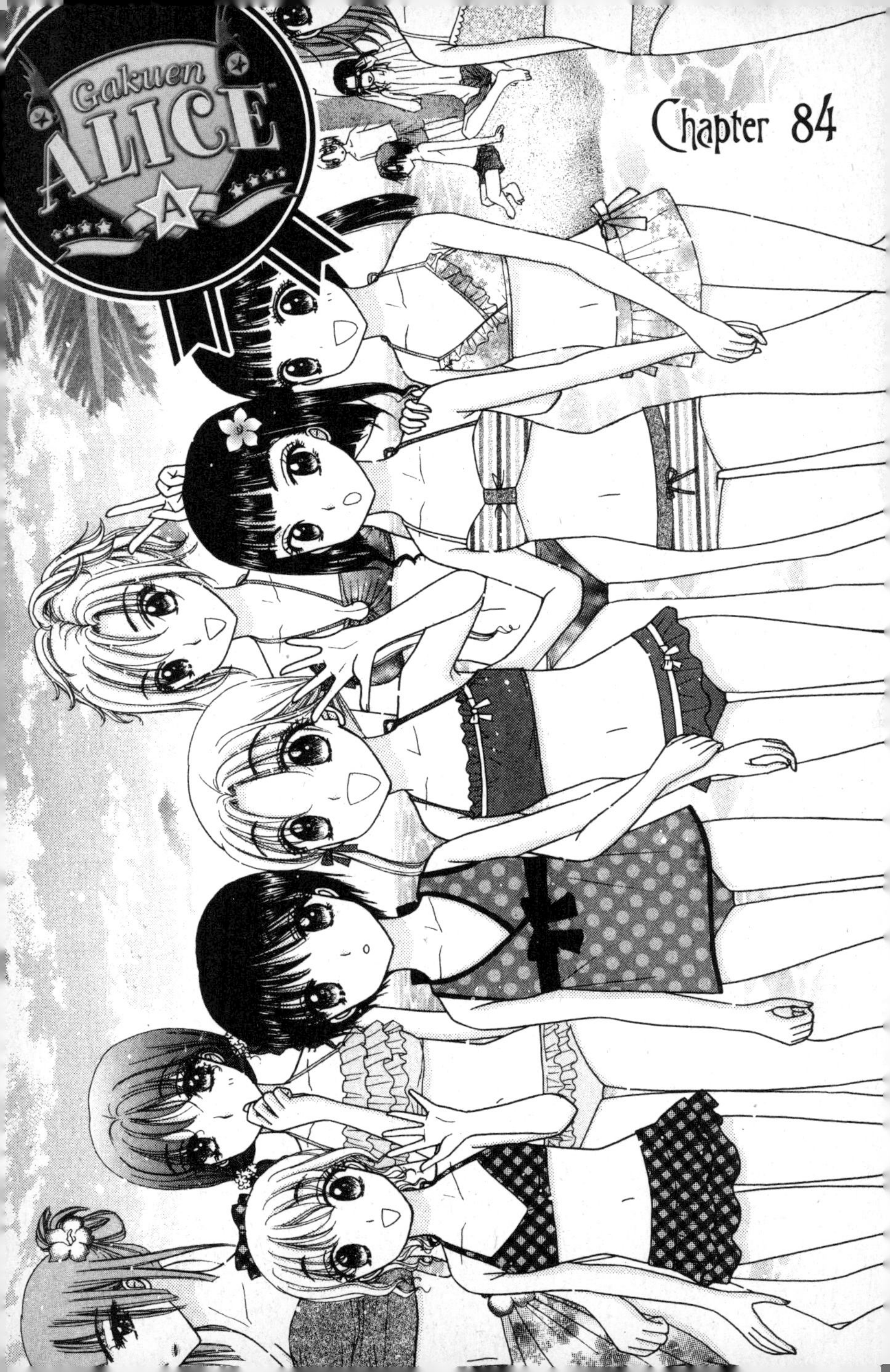
Gakuen ALICE
Chapter 84

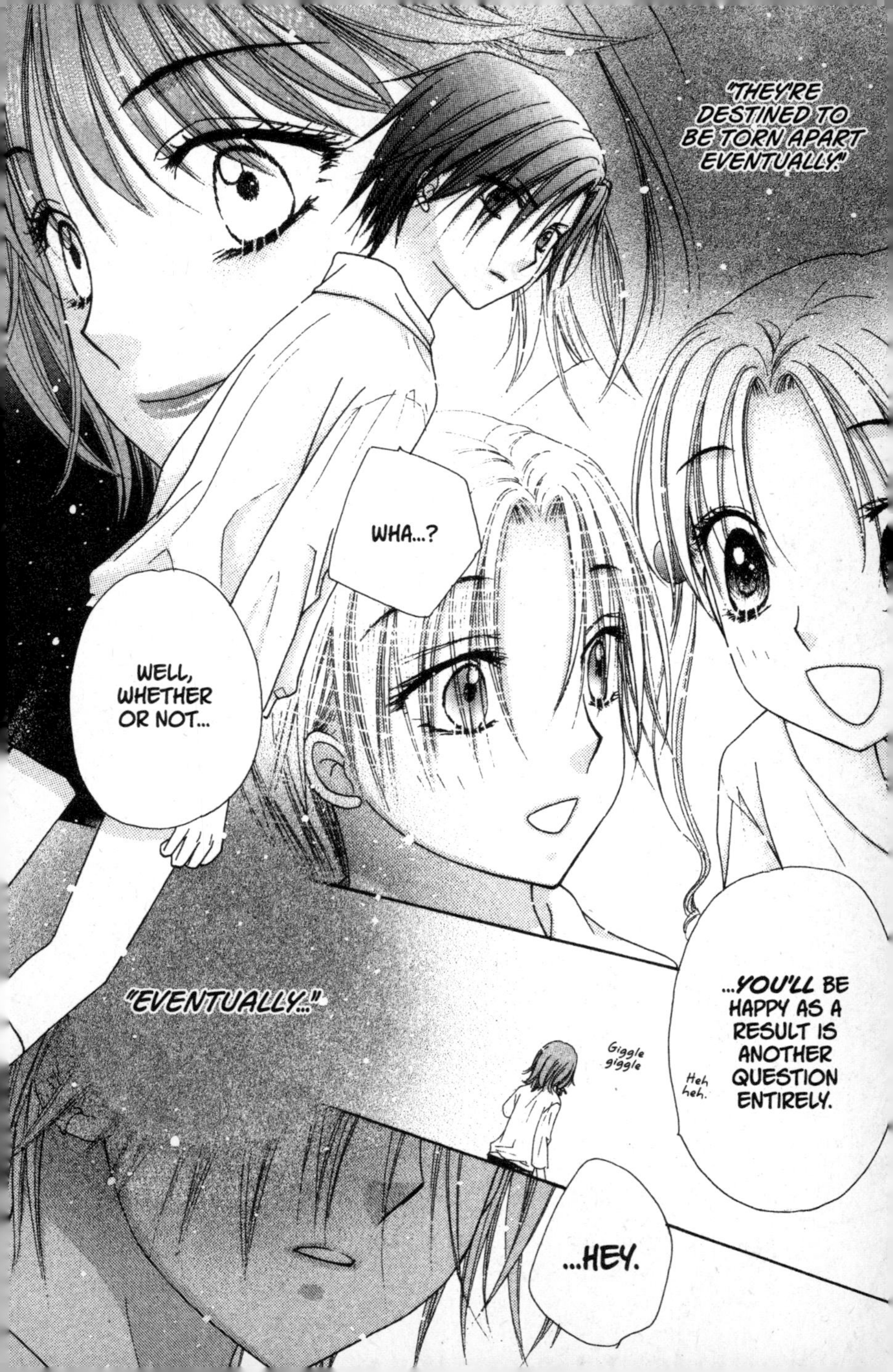
"THEY'RE DESTINED TO BE TORN APART EVENTUALLY."
WHA...?
WELL, WHETHER OR NOT...
...YOU'LL BE HAPPY AS A RESULT IS ANOTHER QUESTION ENTIRELY.
Heh heh.
Giggle giggle
"EVENTUALLY..."
...HEY.

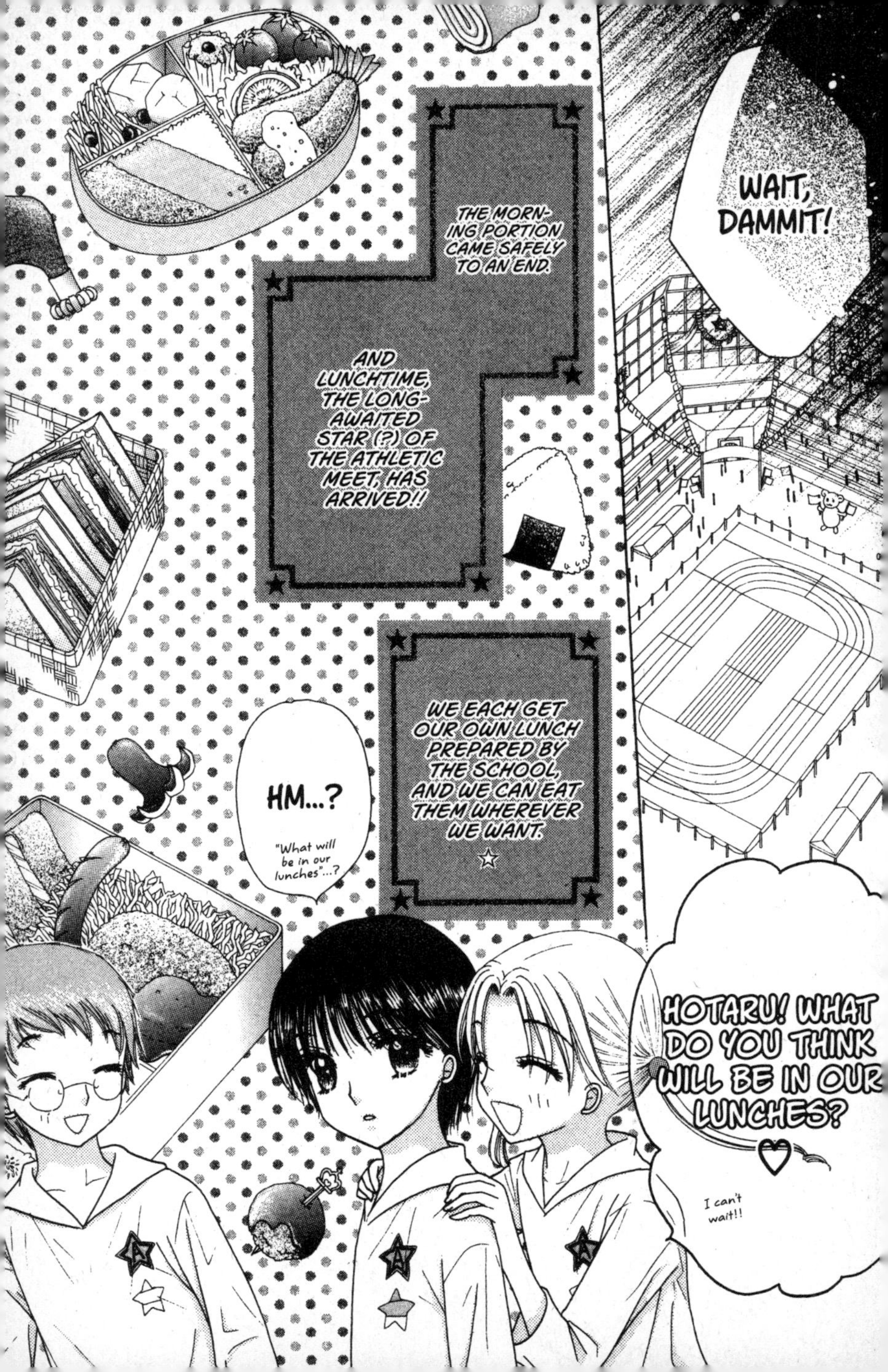
WAIT, DAMMIT!
THE MORNING PORTION CAME SAFELY TO AN END.
AND LUNCHTIME, THE LONG-AWAITED STAR (?) OF THE ATHLETIC MEET, HAS ARRIVED!!
WE EACH GET OUR OWN LUNCH PREPARED BY THE SCHOOL, AND WE CAN EAT THEM WHEREVER WE WANT. ☆
HOTARU! WHAT DO YOU THINK WILL BE IN OUR LUNCHES? ♡
I can't wait!!
HM...?
"What will be in our lunches"...?

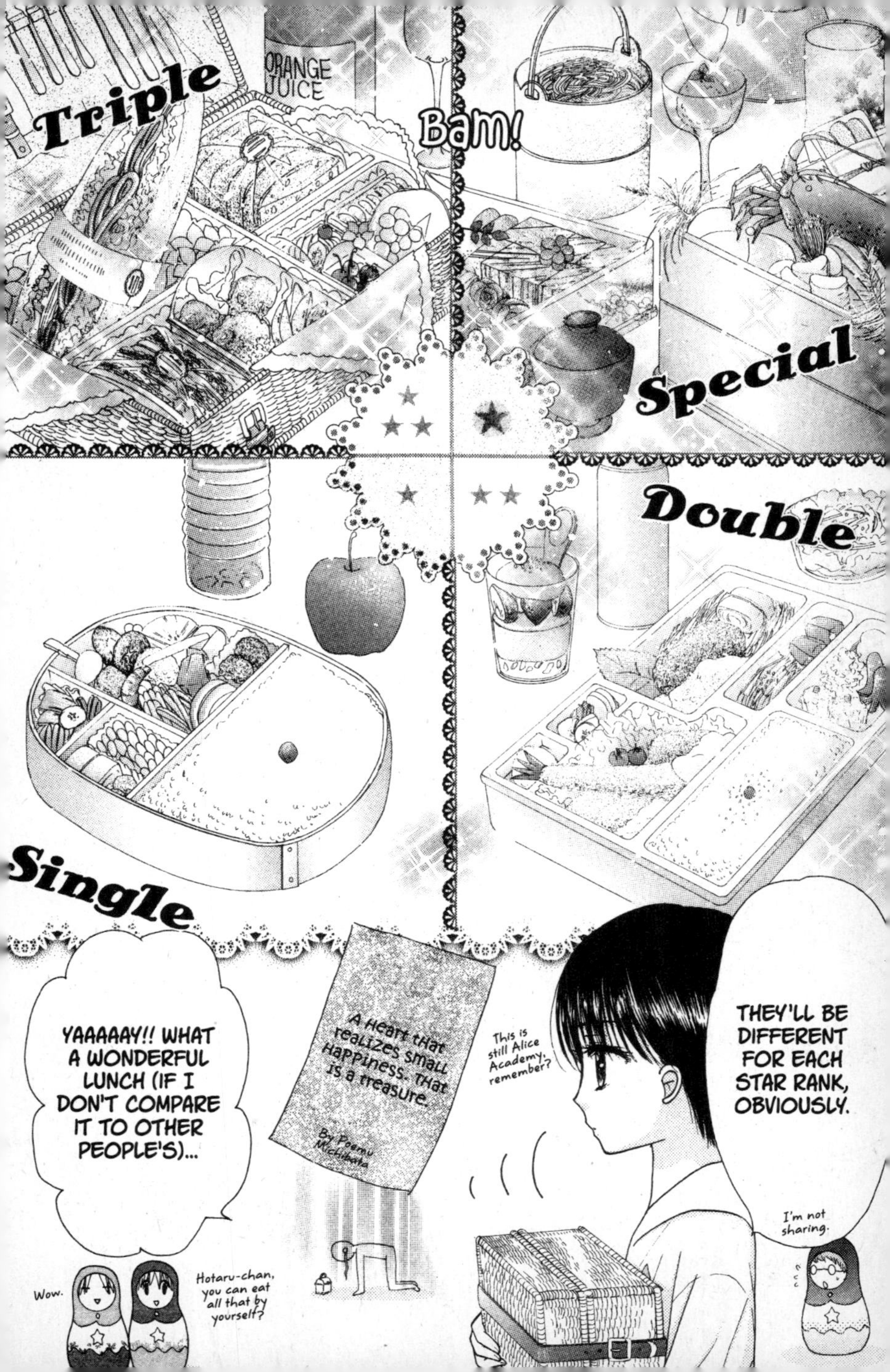
Special
Triple
ORANGE JUICE
Bam!
Double
Single
THEY'LL BE DIFFERENT FOR EACH STAR RANK, OBVIOUSLY.
I'm not sharing.
This is still Alice Academy, remember?
A heart that realizes small happiness. That is a treasure.
By Poemu Michibata
YAAAAAY!! WHAT A WONDERFUL LUNCH (IF I DON'T COMPARE IT TO OTHER PEOPLE'S)...
Hotaru-chan, you can eat all that by yourself?
Wow.

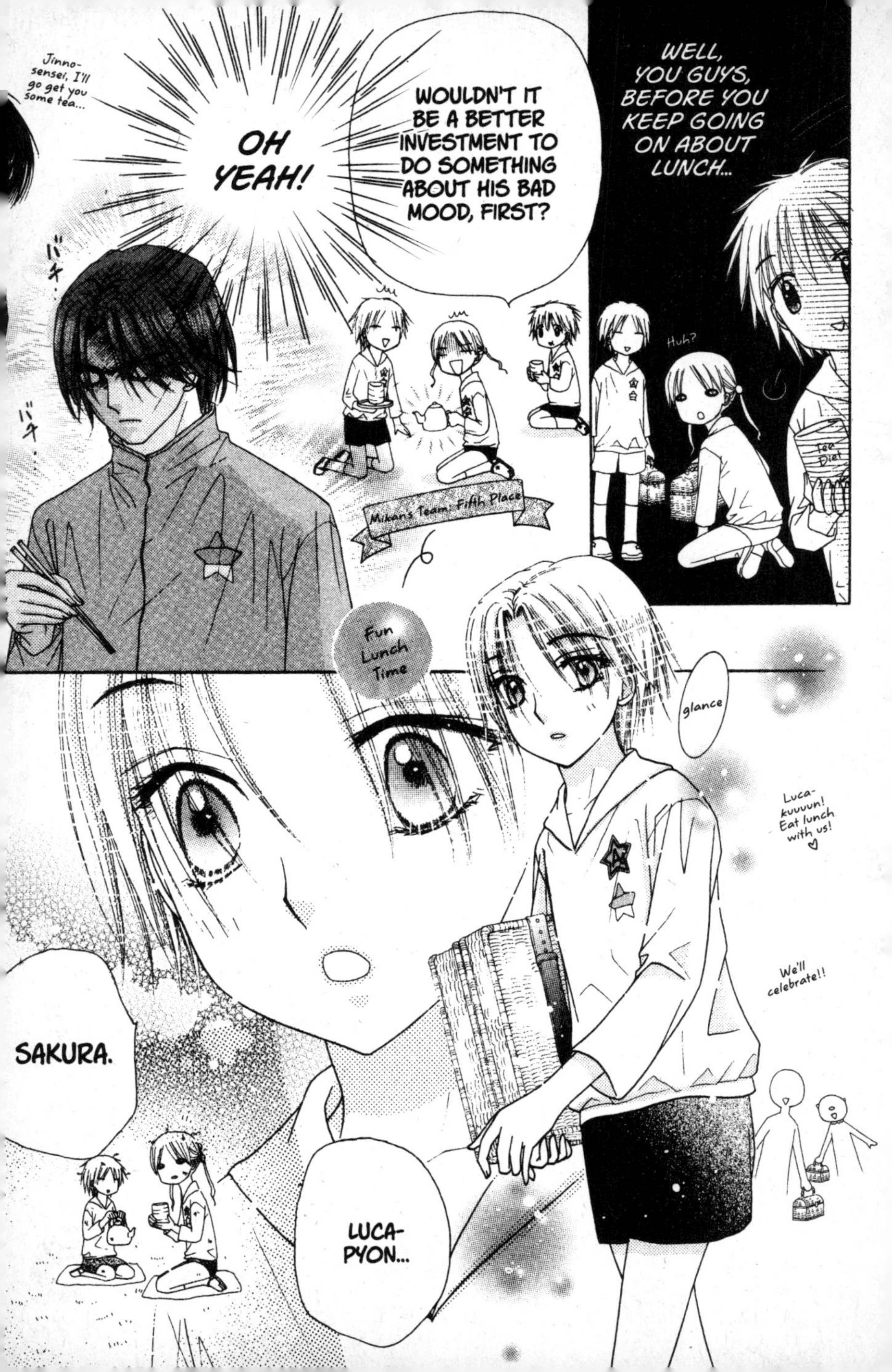
WELL, YOU GUYS, BEFORE YOU KEEP GOING ON ABOUT LUNCH...
Huh?
Tea Diet
WOULDN'T IT BE A BETTER INVESTMENT TO DO SOMETHING ABOUT HIS BAD MOOD, FIRST?
OH YEAH!
Jinno-sensei, I'll go get you some tea...
Mikan's Team: Fifth Place
Fun Lunch Time
glance
Luca-kuuuun! Eat lunch with us! ♥
We'll celebrate!!
LUCA-PYON...
SAKURA.

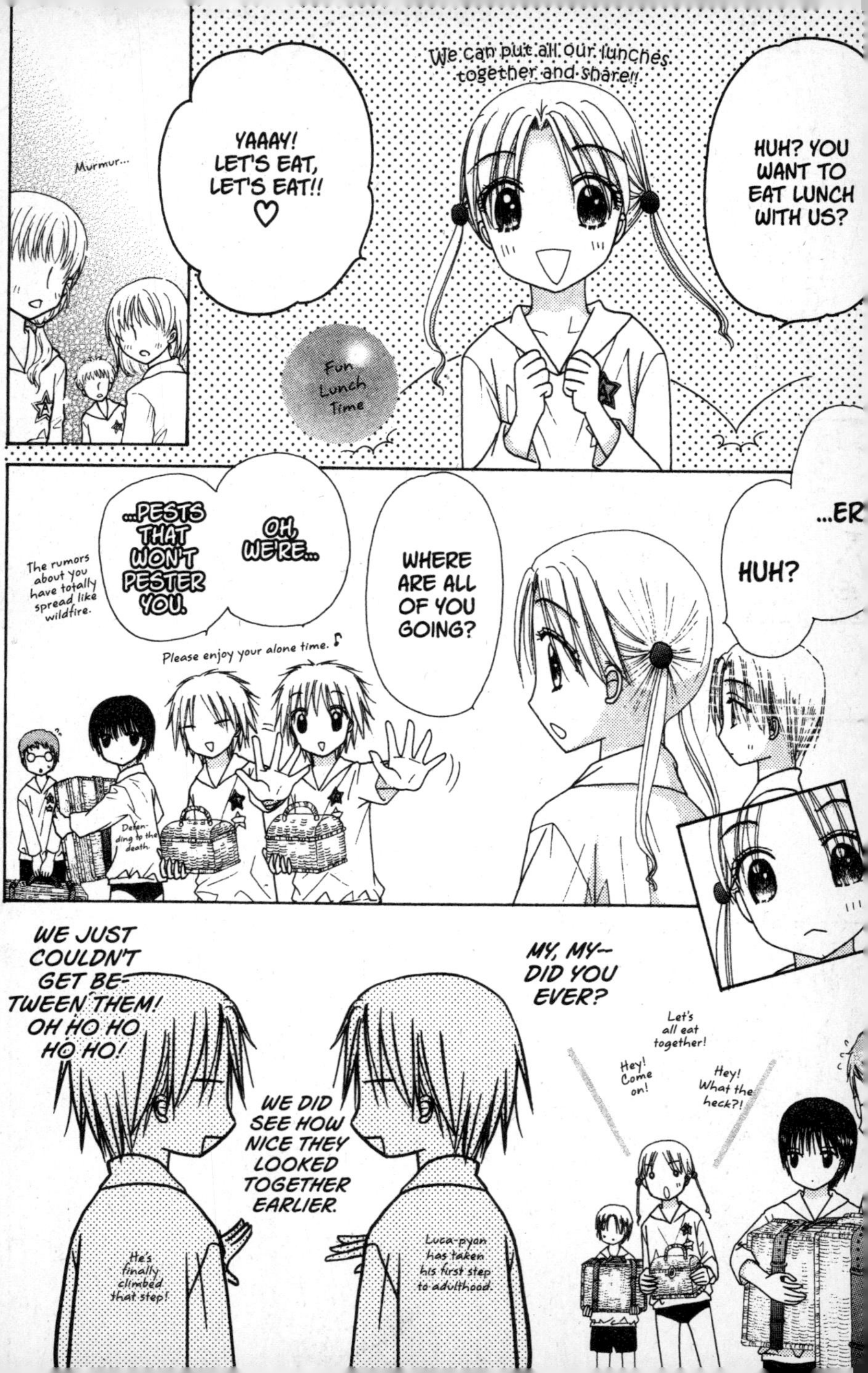
HUH? YOU WANT TO EAT LUNCH WITH US?
We can put all our lunches together and share!!
YAAAY! LET'S EAT, LET'S EAT!! ♡
Fun Lunch Time
Murmur...
...ER
HUH?
WHERE ARE ALL OF YOU GOING?
OH, WE'RE...
...PESTS THAT WON'T PESTER YOU.
The rumors about you have totally spread like wildfire.
Please enjoy your alone time. ♪
Defending to the death.
MY, MY-- DID YOU EVER?
Let's all eat together!
Hey! What the heck?!
Hey! Come on!
WE DID SEE HOW NICE THEY LOOKED TOGETHER EARLIER.
Luca-pyon has taken his first step to adulthood.
WE JUST COULDN'T GET BE-TWEEN THEM! OH HO HO HO HO!
He's finally climbed that step!

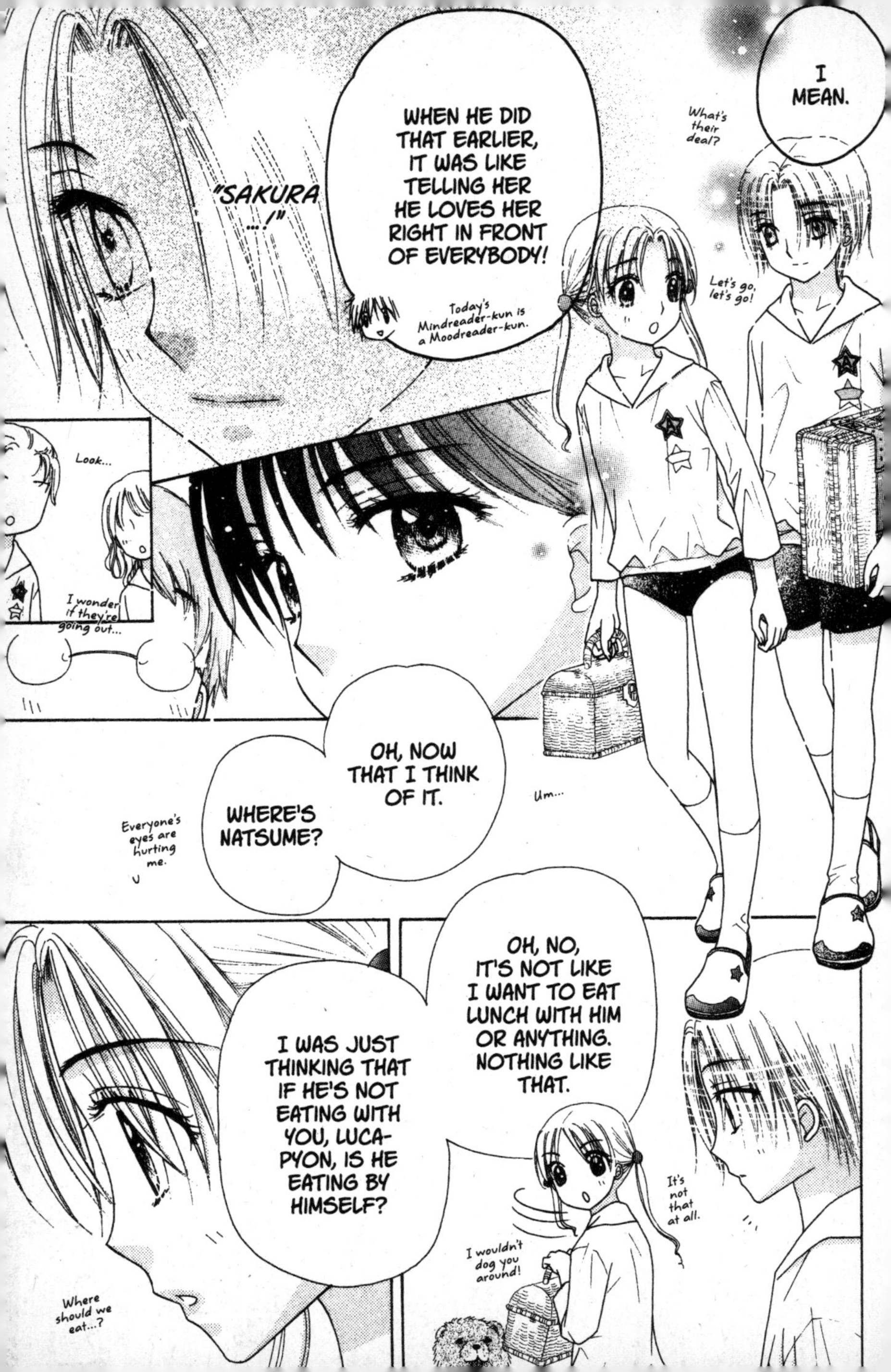
I MEAN.
What's their deal?
Let's go, let's go!
WHEN HE DID THAT EARLIER, IT WAS LIKE TELLING HER HE LOVES HER RIGHT IN FRONT OF EVERYBODY!
Today's Mindreader-kun is a Moodreader-kun.
"SAKURA ...!"
Look...
I wonder if they're going out...
Um...
OH, NOW THAT I THINK OF IT.
WHERE'S NATSUME?
Everyone's eyes are hurting me.
OH, NO, IT'S NOT LIKE I WANT TO EAT LUNCH WITH HIM OR ANYTHING. NOTHING LIKE THAT.
It's not that at all.
I wouldn't dog you around!
I WAS JUST THINKING THAT IF HE'S NOT EATING WITH YOU, LUCA-PYON, IS HE EATING BY HIMSELF?
Where should we eat...?

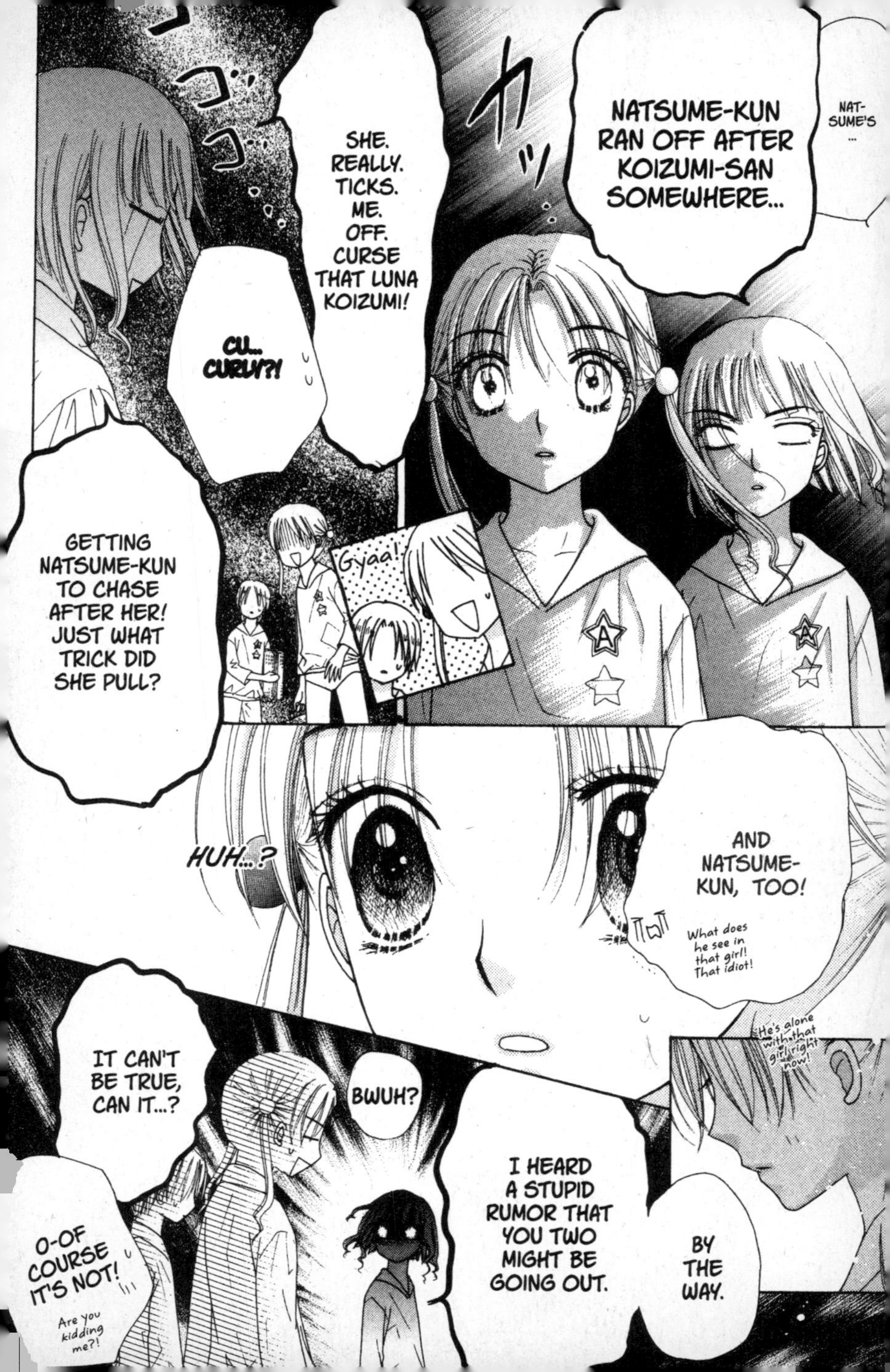

NAT-SUME'S ...
NATSUME-KUN RAN OFF AFTER KOIZUMI-SAN SOMEWHERE...
SHE. REALLY. TICKS. ME. OFF. CURSE THAT LUNA KOIZUMI!
CU... CURLY?!
GETTING NATSUME-KUN TO CHASE AFTER HER! JUST WHAT TRICK DID SHE PULL?
Gyaa!
AND NATSUME-KUN, TOO!
What does he see in that girl! That idiot!
HUH...?
He's alone with that girl right now!
BY THE WAY.
I HEARD A STUPID RUMOR THAT YOU TWO MIGHT BE GOING OUT.
BWUH?
IT CAN'T BE TRUE, CAN IT...?
O-OF COURSE IT'S NOT!
Are you kidding me?!

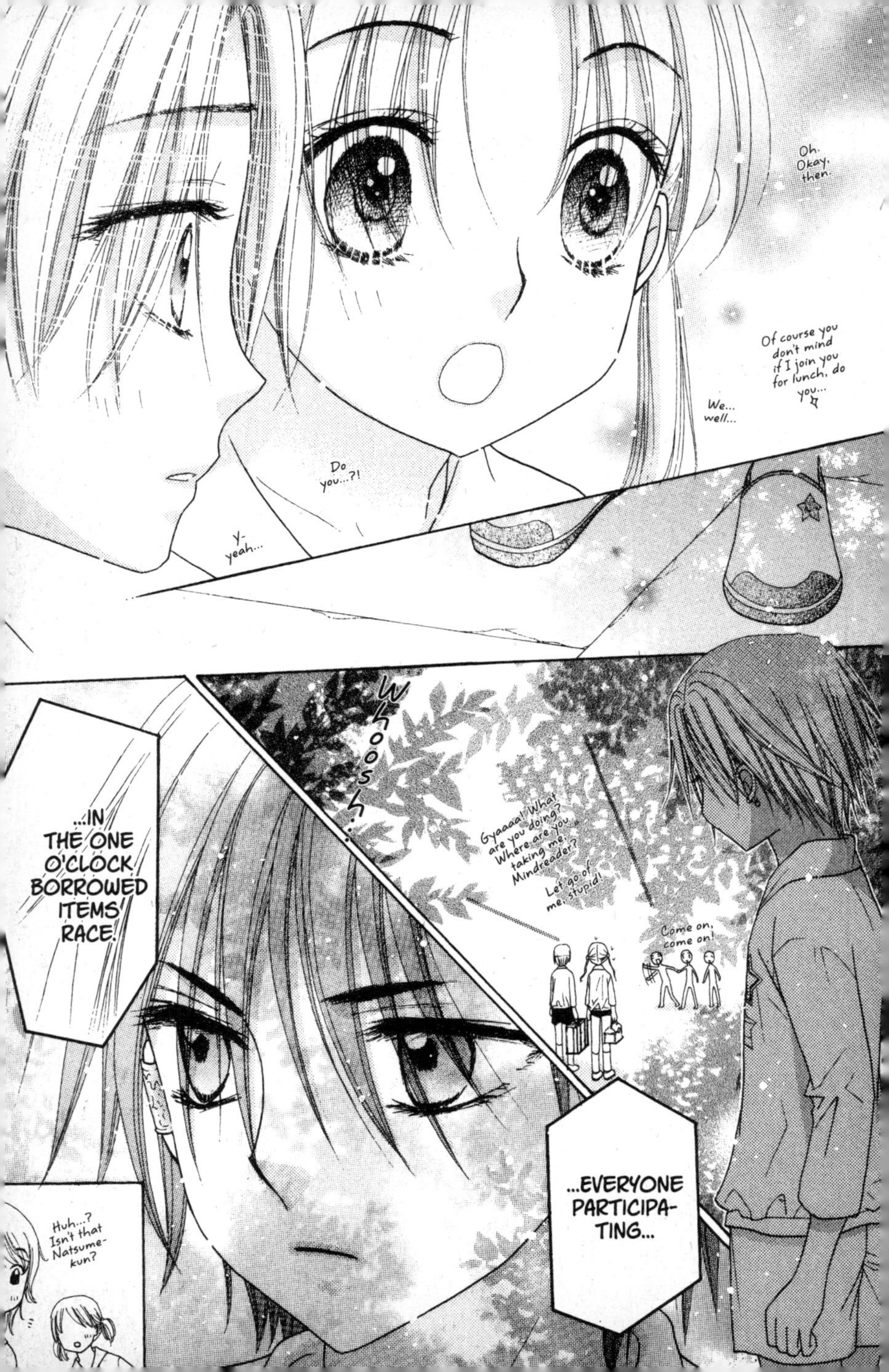
Oh. Okay, then.
Of course you don't mind if I join you for lunch, do you...
We... well...
Do you...?!
Y-yeah...
Whoosh...
Gyaaaa! What are you doing? Where are you taking me, Mindreader?
Let go of me, stupid!
Come on, come on!
...EVERYONE PARTICIPATING...
...IN THE ONE O'CLOCK BORROWED ITEMS RACE.
Huh...? Isn't that Natsume-kun?

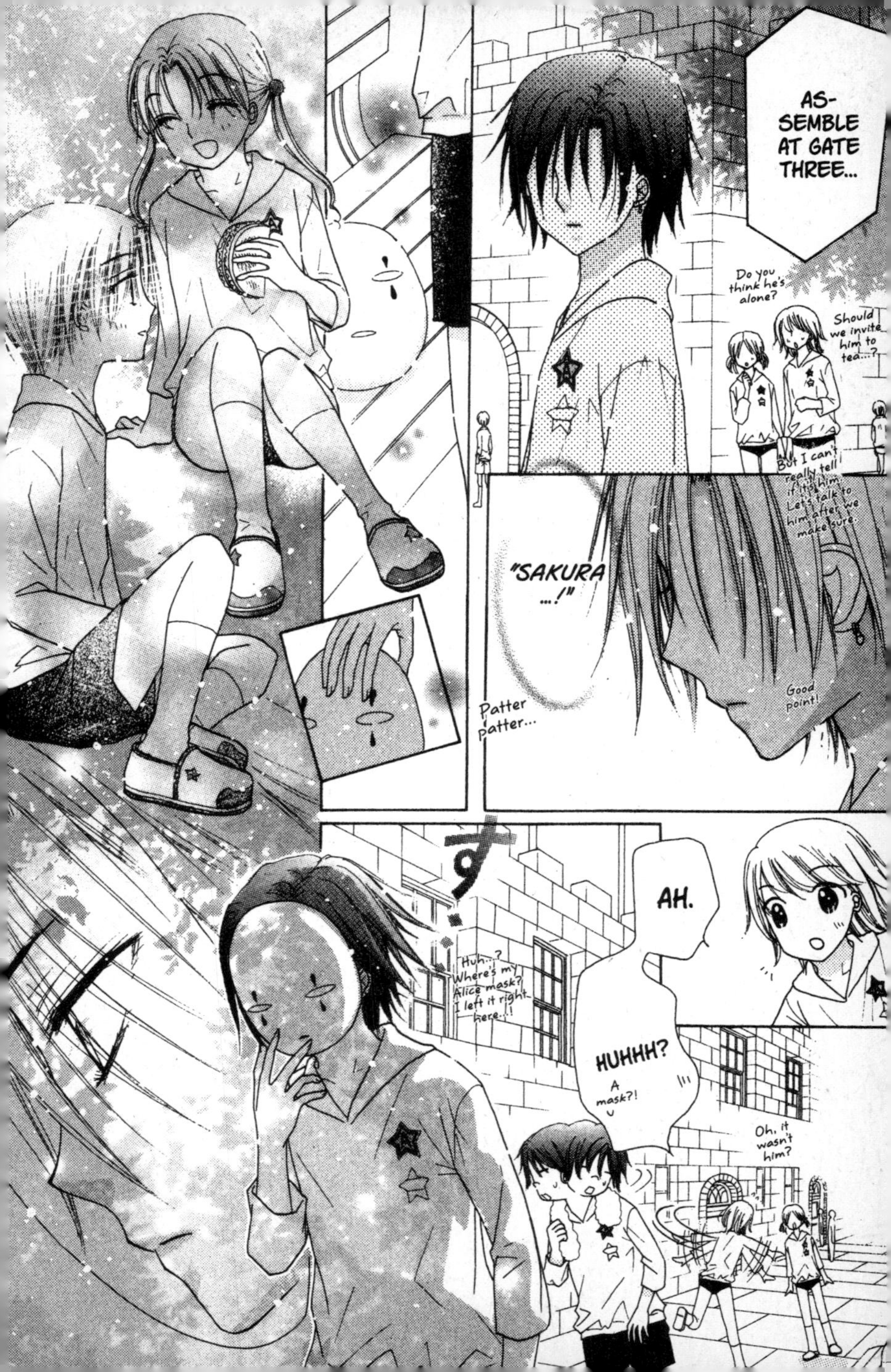
AS-SEMBLE AT GATE THREE...
Do you think he's alone?
Should we invite him to tea...?
But I can't really tell if it's him. Let's talk to him after we make sure.
Good point!
"SAKURA ...!"
Patter patter...
AH.
HUHHH?
A mask?!
Oh, it wasn't him?
す
Huh..? Where's my Alice mask? I left it right here...!

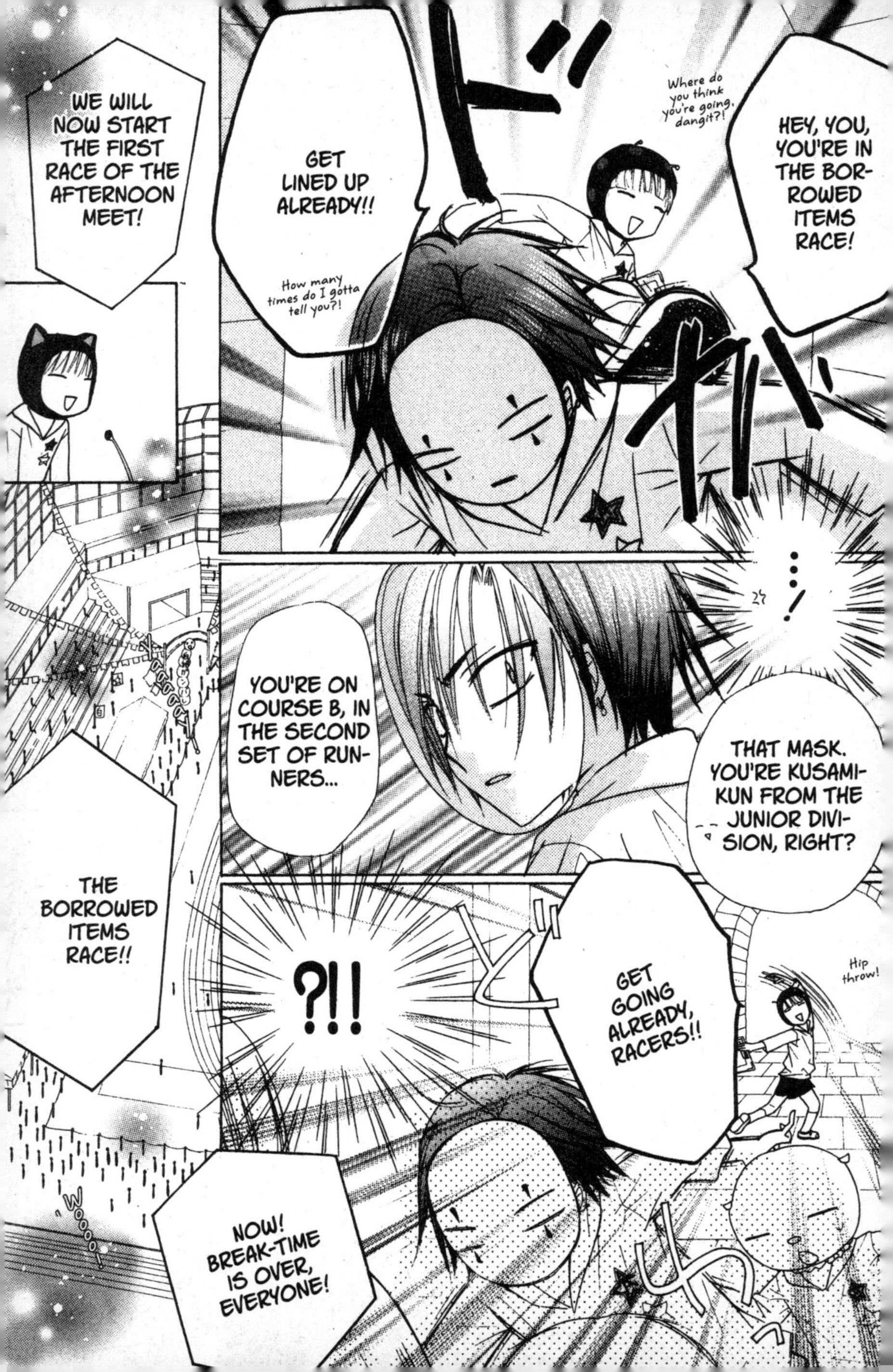
HEY, YOU, YOU'RE IN THE BORROWED ITEMS RACE!
Where do you think you're going, dangit?!
GET LINED UP ALREADY!!
How many times do I gotta tell you?!
...!
THAT MASK. YOU'RE KUSAMI-KUN FROM THE JUNIOR DIVISION, RIGHT?
YOU'RE ON COURSE B, IN THE SECOND SET OF RUNNERS...
Hip throw!
GET GOING ALREADY, RACERS!!
?!!
WE WILL NOW START THE FIRST RACE OF THE AFTERNOON MEET!
THE BORROWED ITEMS RACE!!
Wooo-!
NOW! BREAK-TIME IS OVER, EVERYONE!

Waaah!	

WHAT ARE YOU SPACING OUT FOR, KUSAMORON!

THIS IS ANOTHER POPULAR TRADITIONAL RACE THAT'S MORE COMPLICATED THAN IT SEEMS!

YO, KUSAMORON! DO YOUR BEST!

Borrowed items race?

OH! WHAT'S UP, KUSAMORON? YOU'RE SO INTENSE RIGHT NOW...

I'M GETTING A MERCILESS, DANGEROUS VIBE FROM YOU...

NOW TO EXPLAIN THE RULES!!

What happened to your usual dopey personality?

...GUH?!

Do bad things and they'll come back to get you...

"Kusa..."?

TCH...

How did this happen?

Is he owner of the mask I took?

THE RULES ARE SIMPLE! DRAW FROM THE LOTTERY AT THE MIDWAY POINT OF THE RACE, GET THE ITEM OR PERSON WRITTEN ON THE PAPER, AND TAKE IT/THEM WITH YOU TO THE FINISH LINE!

I NEED TO GET OUT OF HERE FAST...

Yeaah!

...Ugh, why am I in this race.

HOWEVER!

participants

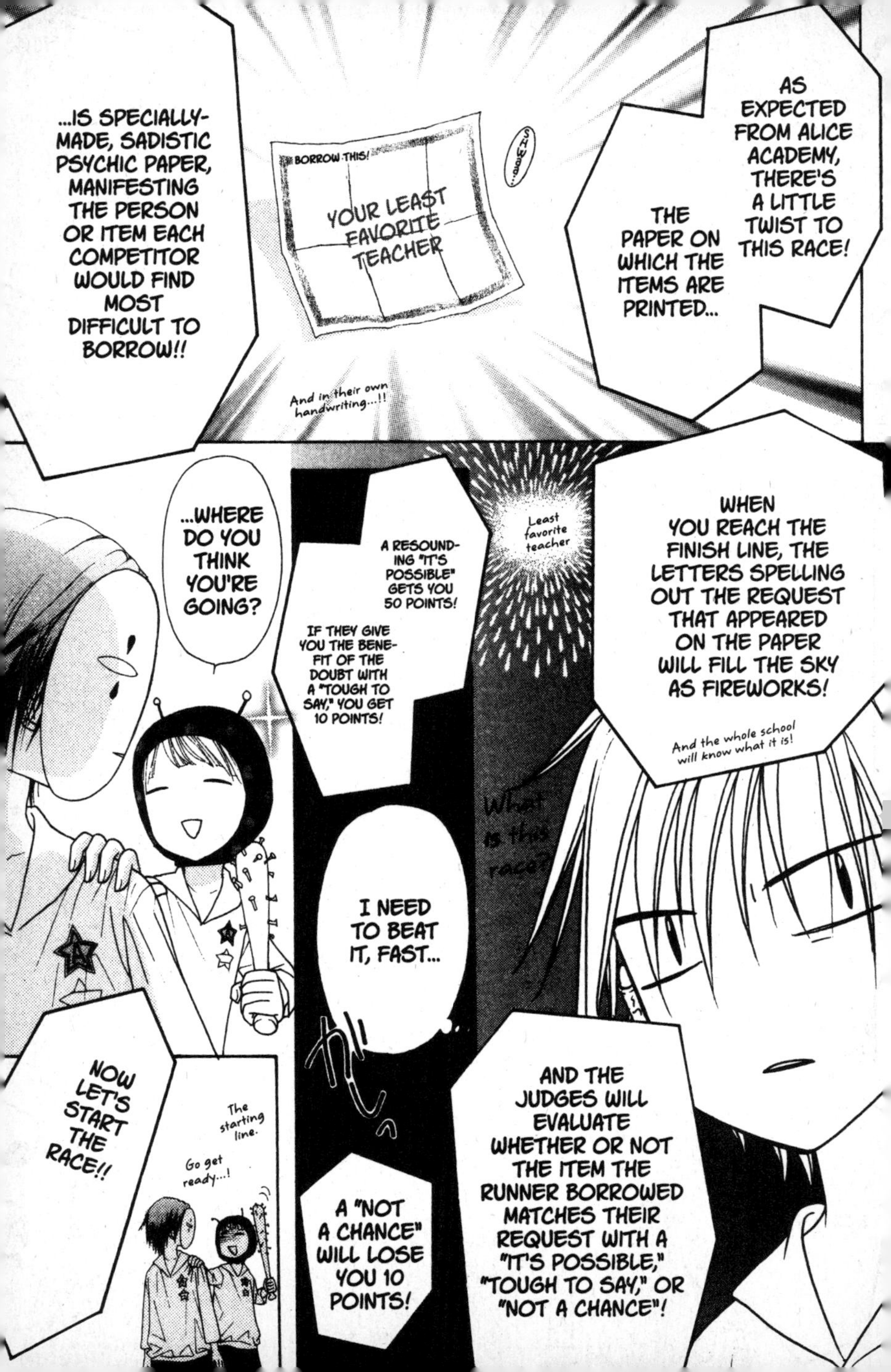
AS EXPECTED FROM ALICE ACADEMY, THERE'S A LITTLE TWIST TO THIS RACE!
THE PAPER ON WHICH THE ITEMS ARE PRINTED...
BORROW THIS!
YOUR LEAST FAVORITE TEACHER
...IS SPECIALLY-MADE, SADISTIC PSYCHIC PAPER, MANIFESTING THE PERSON OR ITEM EACH COMPETITOR WOULD FIND MOST DIFFICULT TO BORROW!!
And in their own handwriting...!!
WHEN YOU REACH THE FINISH LINE, THE LETTERS SPELLING OUT THE REQUEST THAT APPEARED ON THE PAPER WILL FILL THE SKY AS FIREWORKS!
And the whole school will know what it is!
What is this race?
Least favorite teacher
AND THE JUDGES WILL EVALUATE WHETHER OR NOT THE ITEM THE RUNNER BORROWED MATCHES THEIR REQUEST WITH A "IT'S POSSIBLE," "TOUGH TO SAY," OR "NOT A CHANCE"!
A RESOUNDING "IT'S POSSIBLE" GETS YOU 50 POINTS!
IF THEY GIVE YOU THE BENEFIT OF THE DOUBT WITH A "TOUGH TO SAY," YOU GET 10 POINTS!
I NEED TO BEAT IT, FAST...
A "NOT A CHANCE" WILL LOSE YOU 10 POINTS!
...WHERE DO YOU THINK YOU'RE GOING?
NOW LET'S START THE RACE!!
The starting line.
Go get ready...!

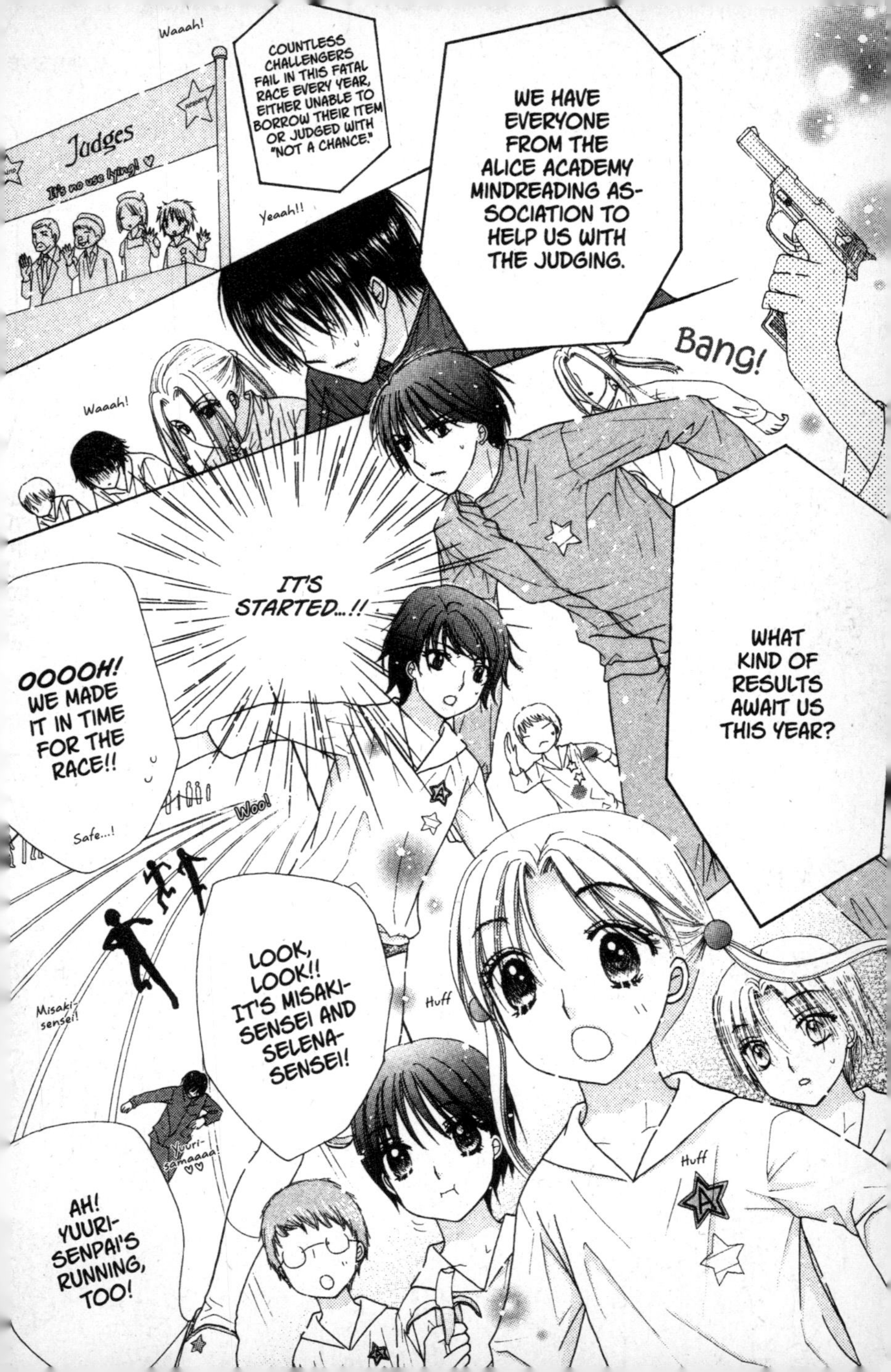

WE HAVE EVERYONE FROM THE ALICE ACADEMY MINDREADING AS-SOCIATION TO HELP US WITH THE JUDGING.
COUNTLESS CHALLENGERS FAIL IN THIS FATAL RACE EVERY YEAR, EITHER UNABLE TO BORROW THEIR ITEM OR JUDGED WITH "NOT A CHANCE."
Waaah!
Judges
It's no use lying! ♡
Yeaah!!
Bang!
Waaah!
WHAT KIND OF RESULTS AWAIT US THIS YEAR?
IT'S STARTED...!!
OOOOH! WE MADE IT IN TIME FOR THE RACE!!
Woo!
Safe...!
Huff
LOOK, LOOK!! IT'S MISAKI-SENSEI AND SELENA-SENSEI!
Misaki-sensei!
Huff
Yuuri-samaaaa! ♡♡
AH! YUURI-SENPAI'S RUNNING, TOO!

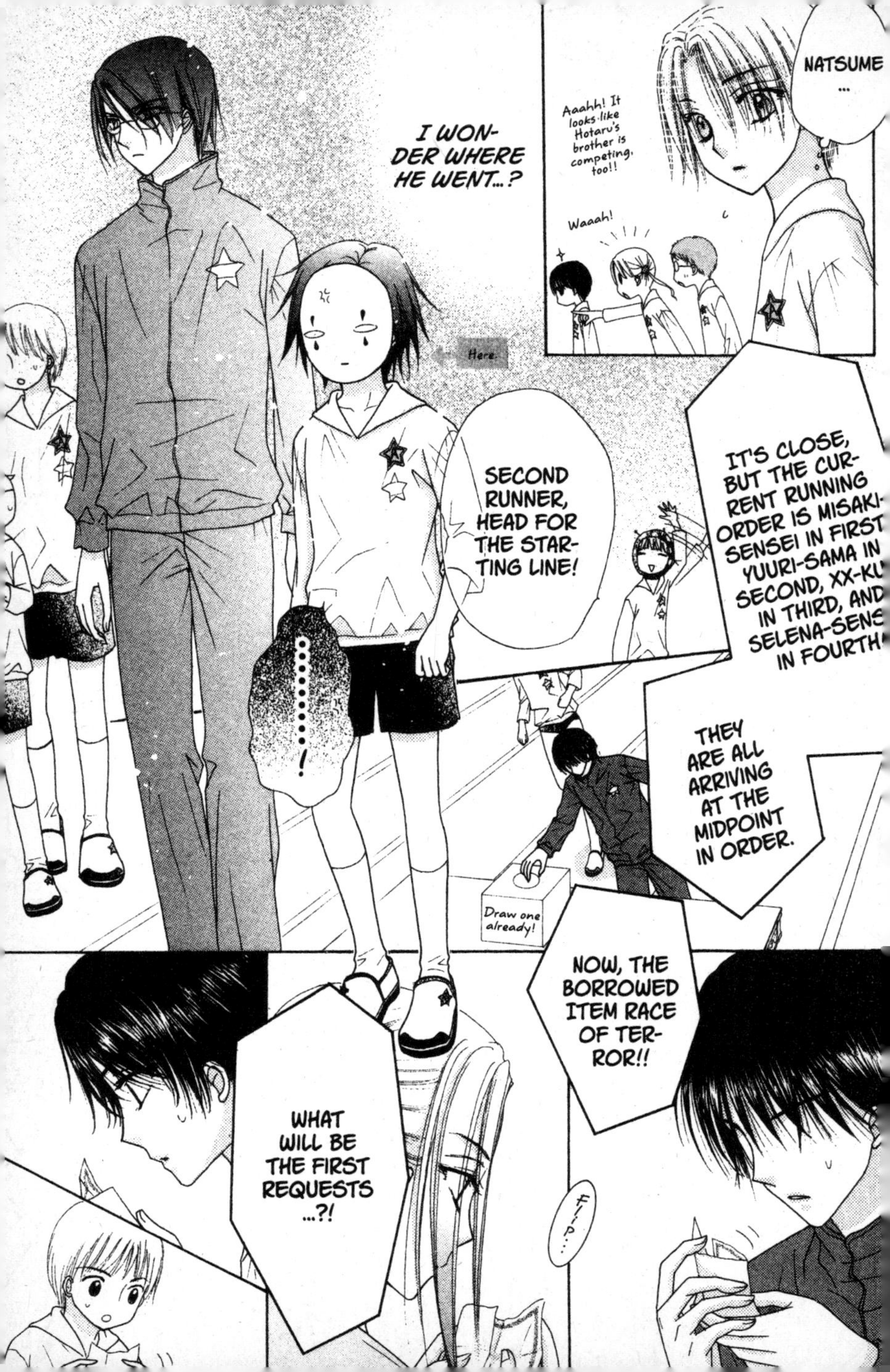
NATSUME ...
Aaahh! It looks like Hotaru's brother is competing, too!!
Waaah!
I WONDER WHERE HE WENT...?
Here.
......!
IT'S CLOSE, BUT THE CURRENT RUNNING ORDER IS MISAKI-SENSEI IN FIRST, YUURI-SAMA IN SECOND, XX-KU IN THIRD, AND SELENA-SENS IN FOURTH
SECOND RUNNER, HEAD FOR THE STARTING LINE!
THEY ARE ALL ARRIVING AT THE MIDPOINT IN ORDER.
Draw one already!
NOW, THE BORROWED ITEM RACE OF TERROR!!
Flip...
WHAT WILL BE THE FIRST REQUESTS ...?!

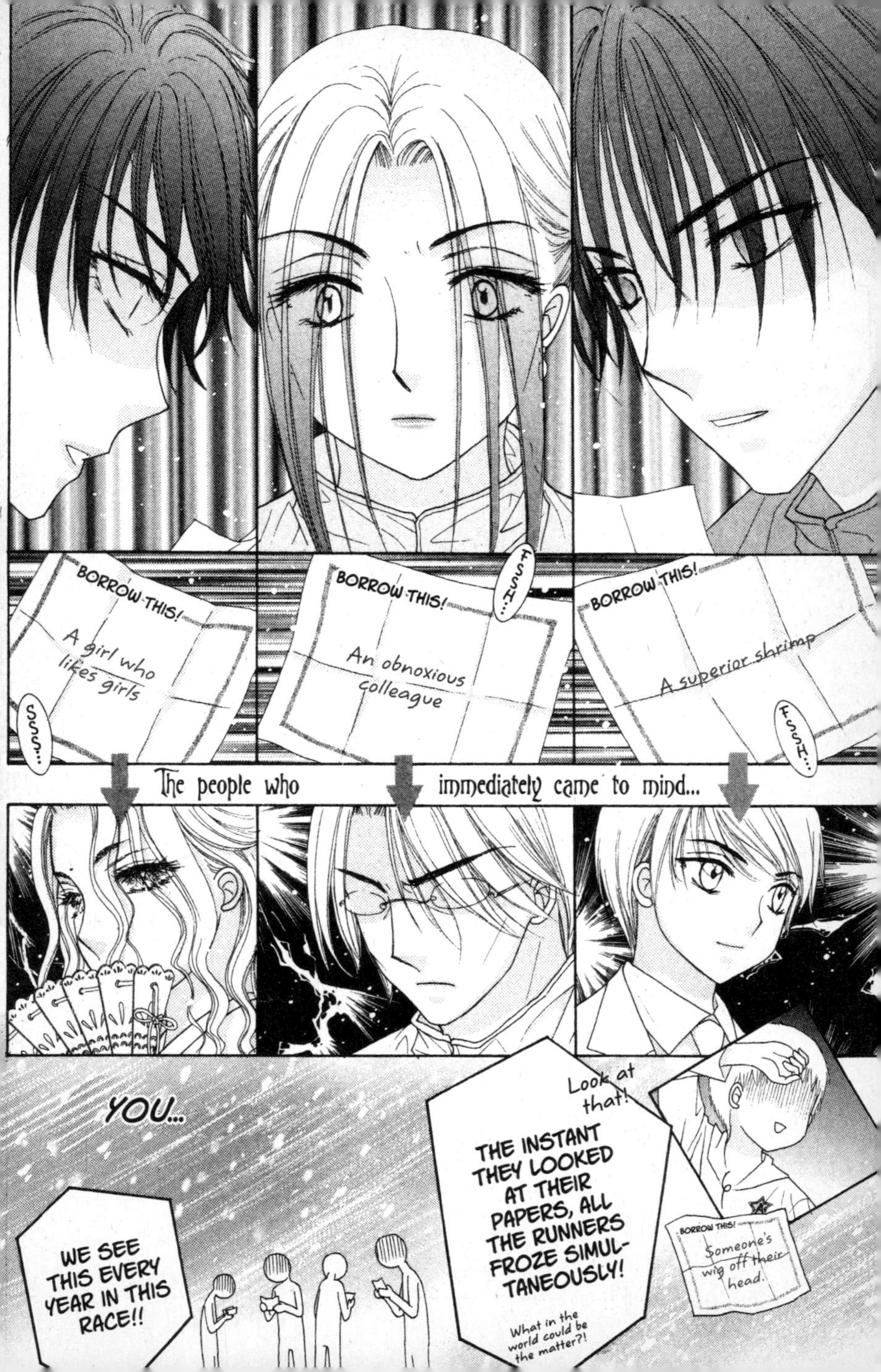

BORROW THIS!
A superior shrimp
FSSH...
FSSH...
BORROW THIS!
An obnoxious colleague
BORROW THIS!
A girl who likes girls
SSS...
The people who immediately came to mind...
BORROW THIS!
Someone's wig off their head.
Look at that!
THE INSTANT THEY LOOKED AT THEIR PAPERS, ALL THE RUNNERS FROZE SIMULTANEOUSLY!
What in the world could be the matter?!
YOU...
WE SEE THIS EVERY YEAR IN THIS RACE!!

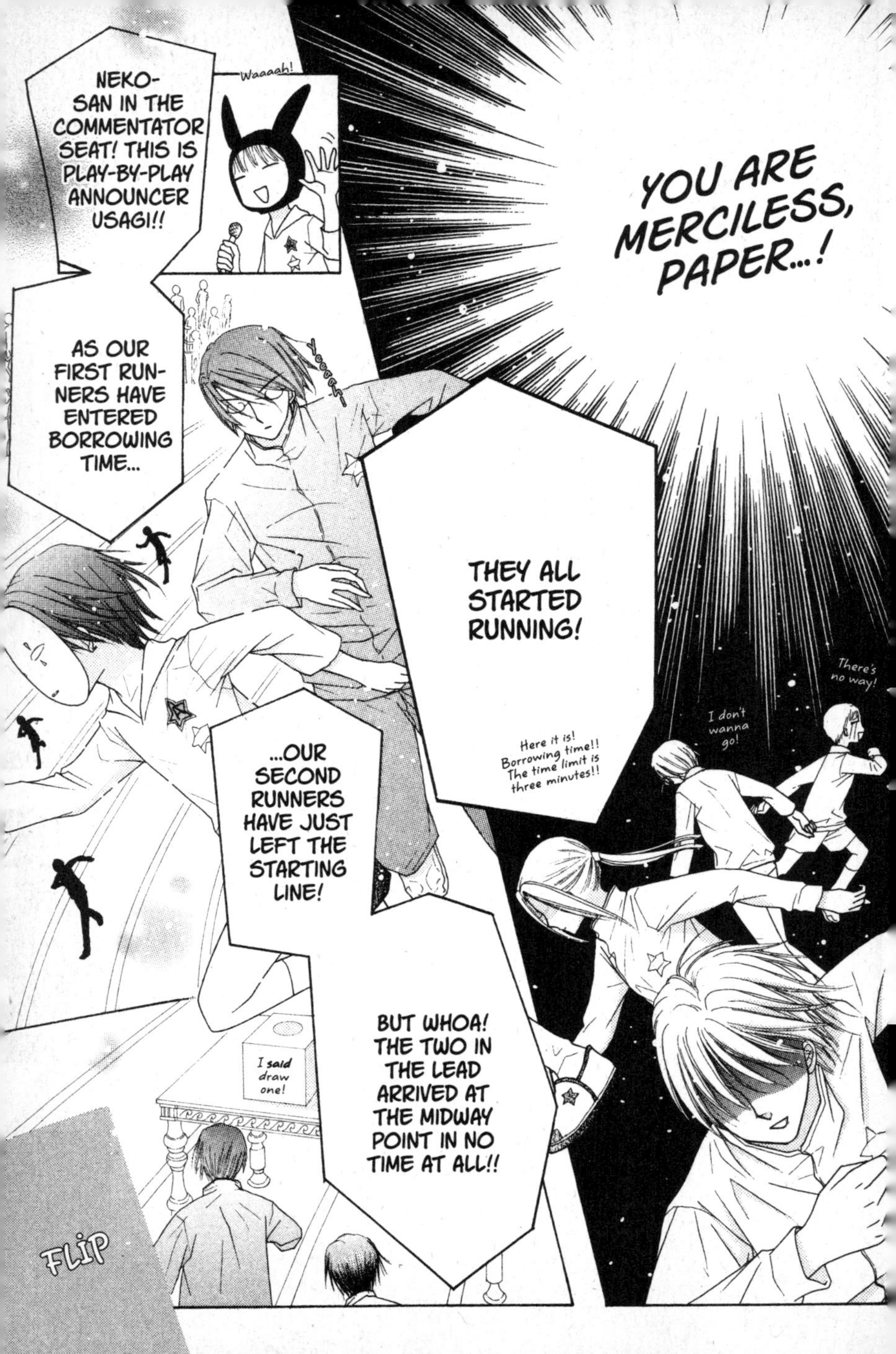
YOU ARE MERCILESS, PAPER...!
Waaaah!
NEKO-SAN IN THE COMMENTATOR SEAT! THIS IS PLAY-BY-PLAY ANNOUNCER USAGI!!
THEY ALL STARTED RUNNING!
Yeeaah!
AS OUR FIRST RUNNERS HAVE ENTERED BORROWING TIME...
...OUR SECOND RUNNERS HAVE JUST LEFT THE STARTING LINE!
There's no way!
I don't wanna go!
Here it is! Borrowing time!! The time limit is three minutes!!
BUT WHOA! THE TWO IN THE LEAD ARRIVED AT THE MIDWAY POINT IN NO TIME AT ALL!!
I said draw one!
FLIP

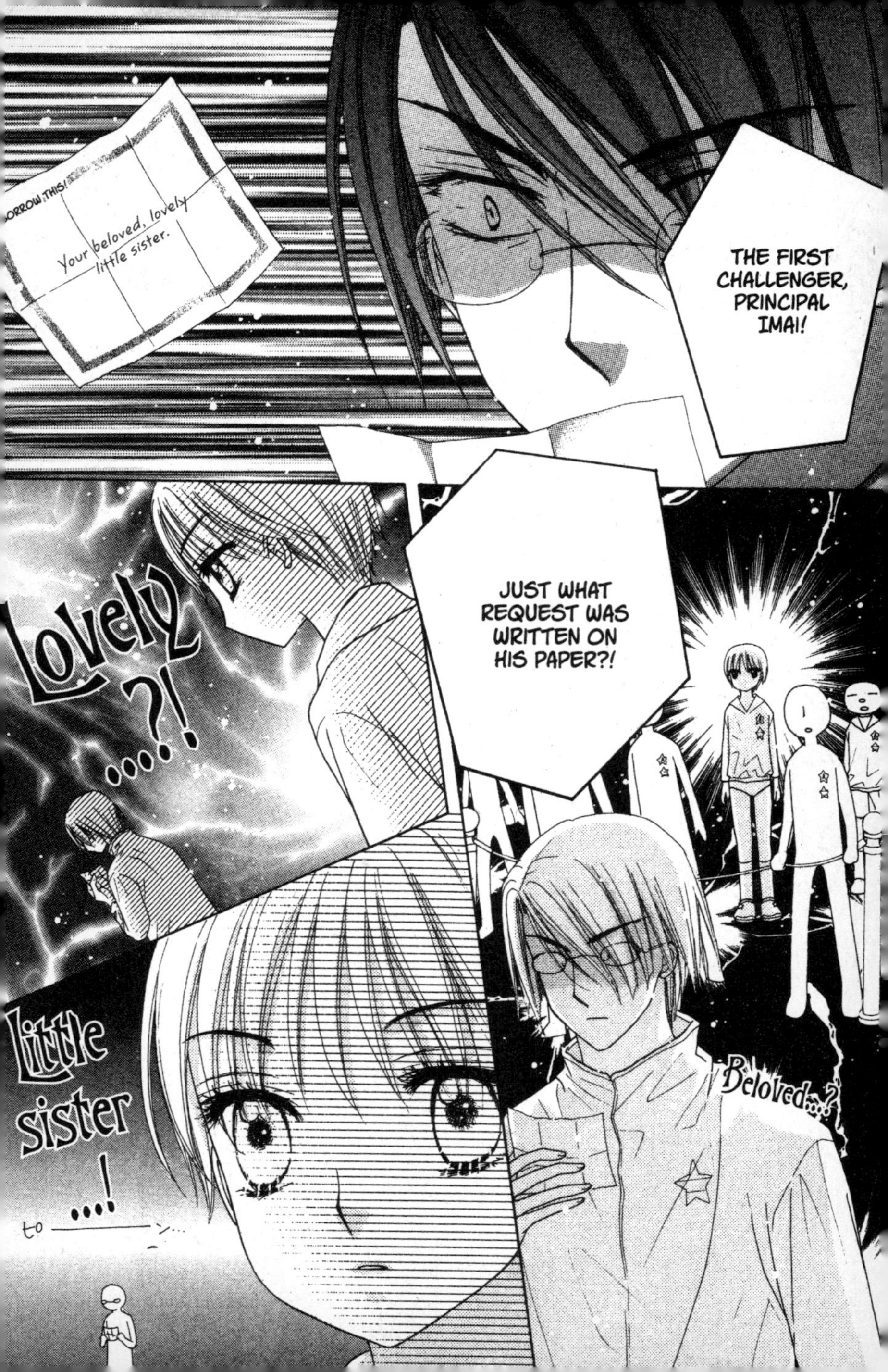
THE FIRST CHALLENGER, PRINCIPAL IMAI!
ORROW THIS!
Your beloved, lovely little sister.
JUST WHAT REQUEST WAS WRITTEN ON HIS PAPER?!
Beloved...?
Lovely ...?!
Little sister ...!

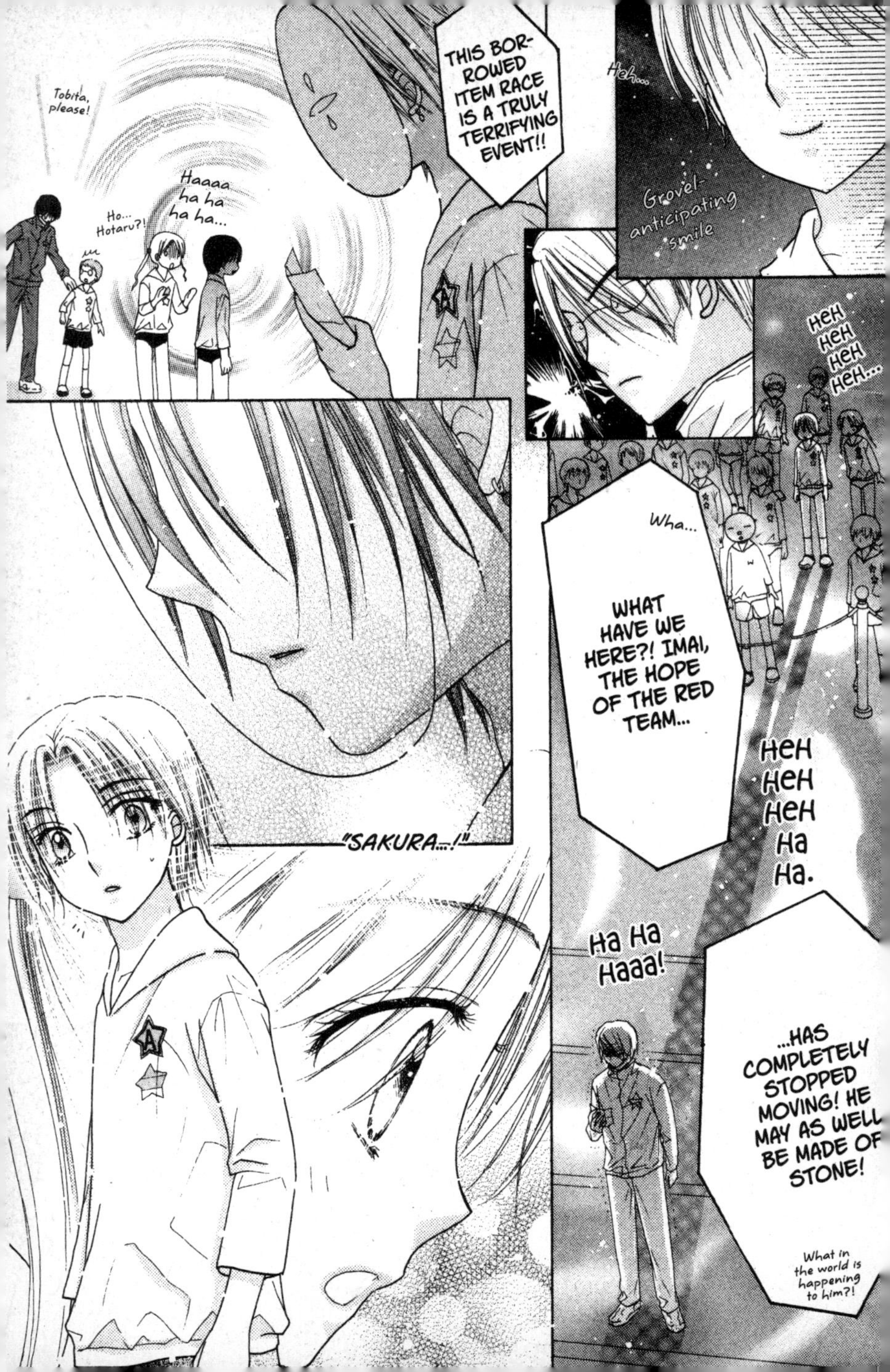
Heh...
Grovel-anticipating smile
THIS BOR-ROWED ITEM RACE IS A TRULY TERRIFYING EVENT!!
Tobita, please!
Haaaa ha ha ha ha...
Ho... Hotaru?!
HEH HEH HEH HEH...
Wha...
WHAT HAVE WE HERE?! IMAI, THE HOPE OF THE RED TEAM...
HEH HEH HEH Ha Ha.
Ha Ha Haaa!
...HAS COMPLETELY STOPPED MOVING! HE MAY AS WELL BE MADE OF STONE!
What in the world is happening to him?!
"SAKURA...!"

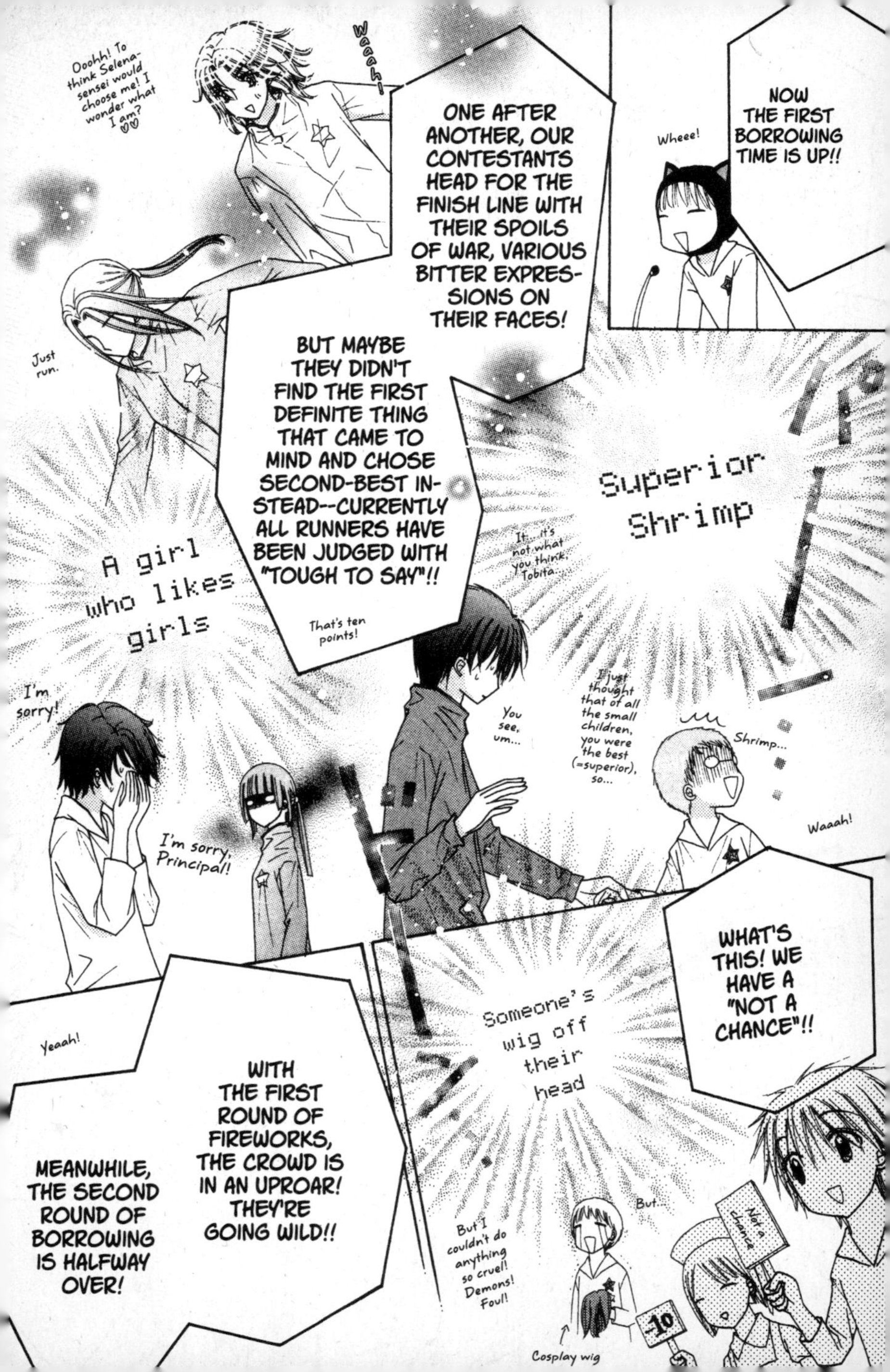

NOW THE FIRST BORROWING TIME IS UP!!
Wheee!
ONE AFTER ANOTHER, OUR CONTESTANTS HEAD FOR THE FINISH LINE WITH THEIR SPOILS OF WAR, VARIOUS BITTER EXPRESSIONS ON THEIR FACES!
Waaah!
Ooohh! To think Selena-sensei would choose me! I wonder what I am? ♡♡
Just run.
BUT MAYBE THEY DIDN'T FIND THE FIRST DEFINITE THING THAT CAME TO MIND AND CHOSE SECOND-BEST INSTEAD--CURRENTLY ALL RUNNERS HAVE BEEN JUDGED WITH "TOUGH TO SAY"!!
That's ten points!
Superior Shrimp
It... it's not what you think, Tobita...
A girl who likes girls
You see, um...
I just thought that of all the small children, you were the best (=superior), so...
Shrimp...
Waaah!
I'm sorry!
I'm sorry, Principal!
WHAT'S THIS! WE HAVE A "NOT A CHANCE"!!
Someone's wig off their head
Yeaah!
WITH THE FIRST ROUND OF FIREWORKS, THE CROWD IS IN AN UPROAR! THEY'RE GOING WILD!!
MEANWHILE, THE SECOND ROUND OF BORROWING IS HALFWAY OVER!
But...
But I couldn't do anything so cruel! Demons! Foul!
Not a chance
-10
Cosplay wig

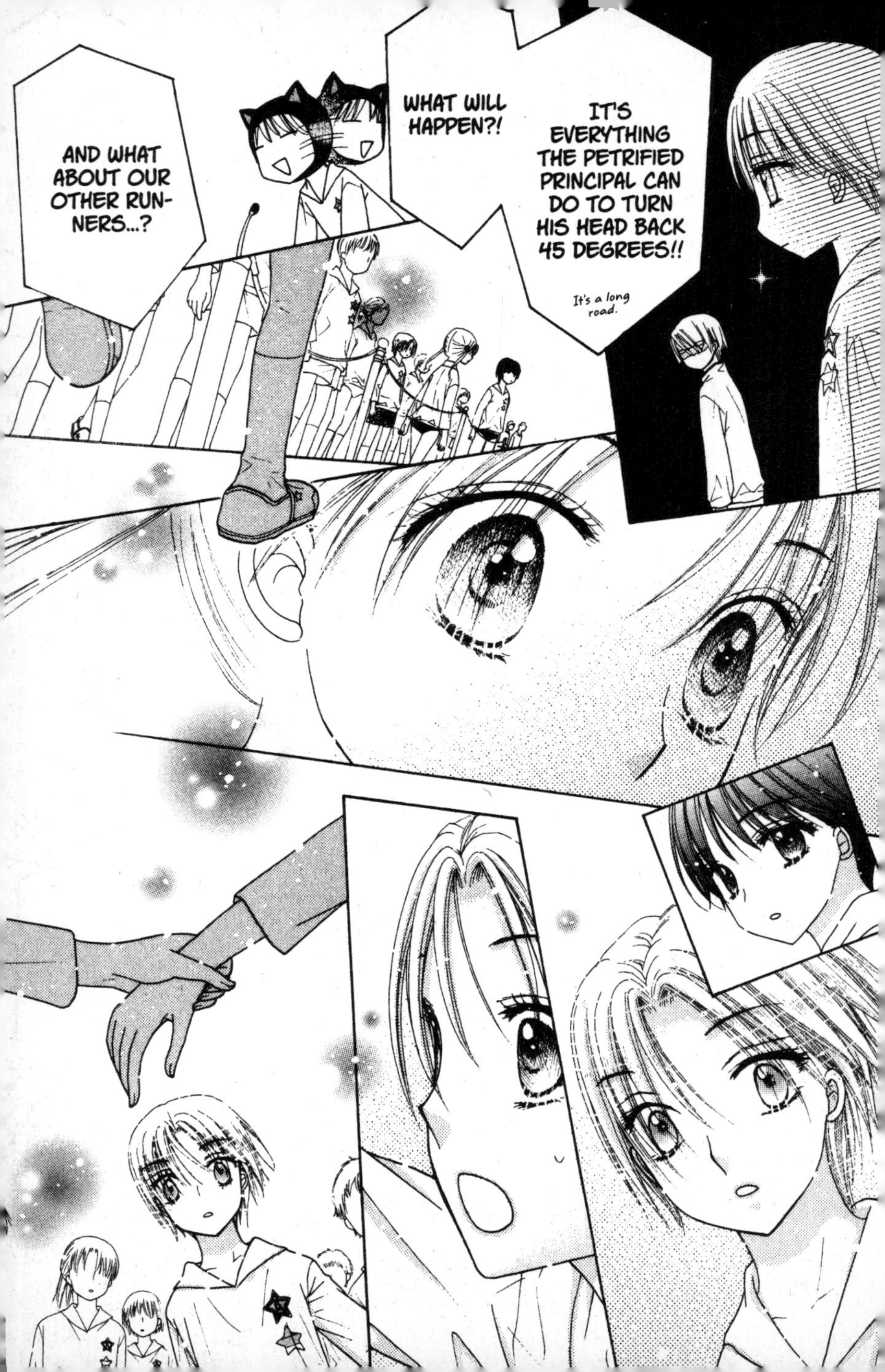
IT'S EVERYTHING THE PETRIFIED PRINCIPAL CAN DO TO TURN HIS HEAD BACK 45 DEGREES!!
It's a long road.
WHAT WILL HAPPEN?!
AND WHAT ABOUT OUR OTHER RUN-NERS...?

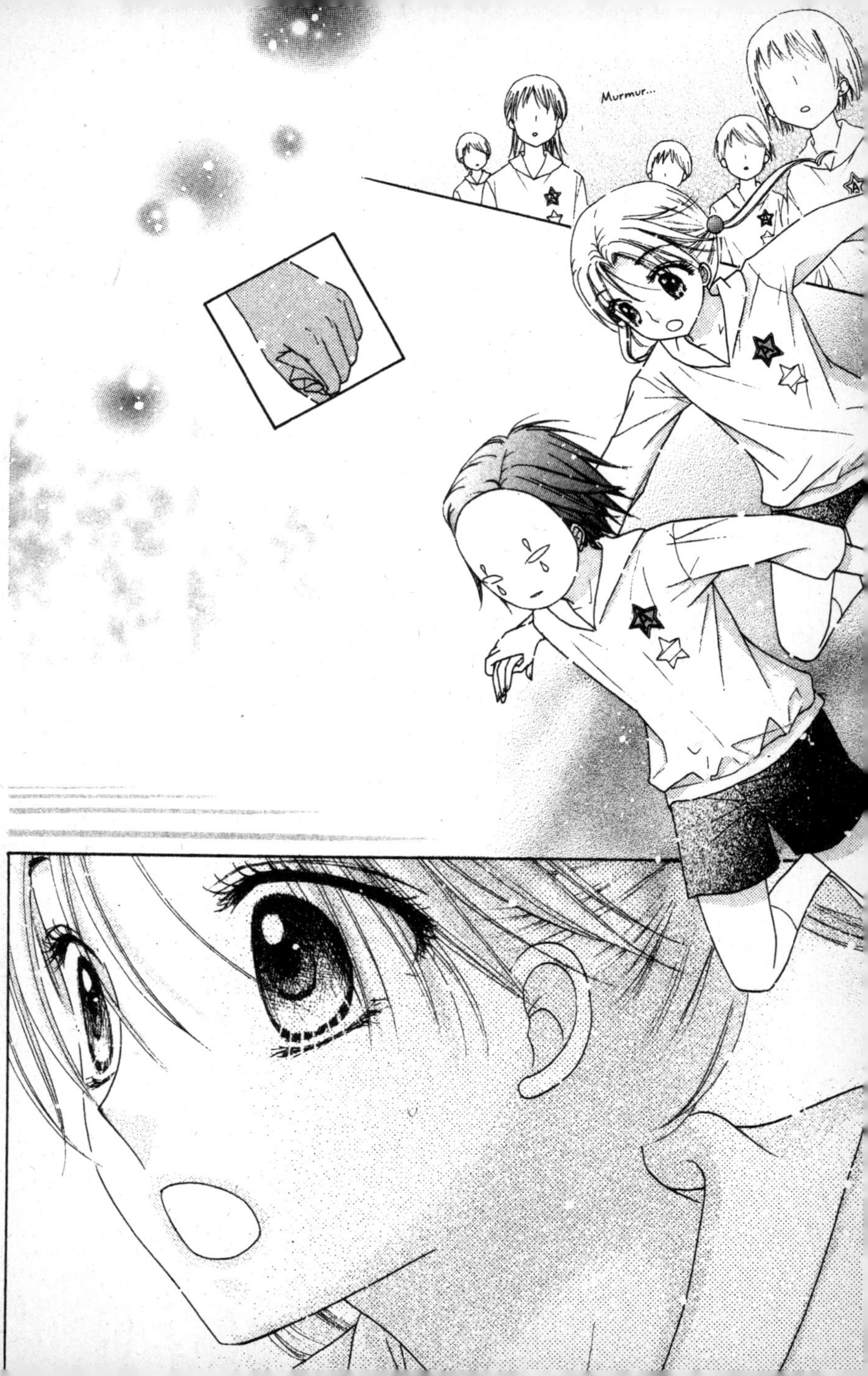
Murmur...

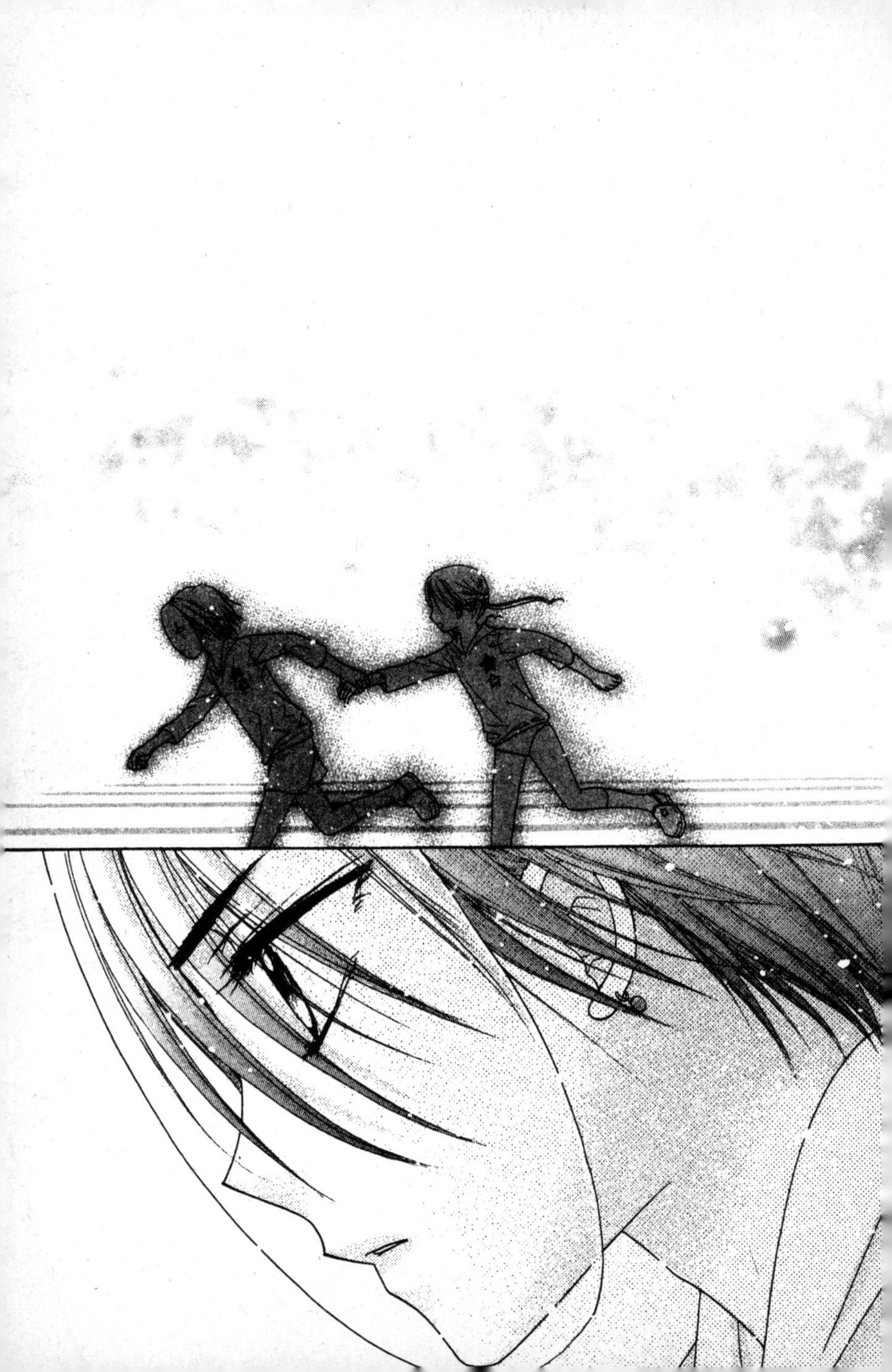

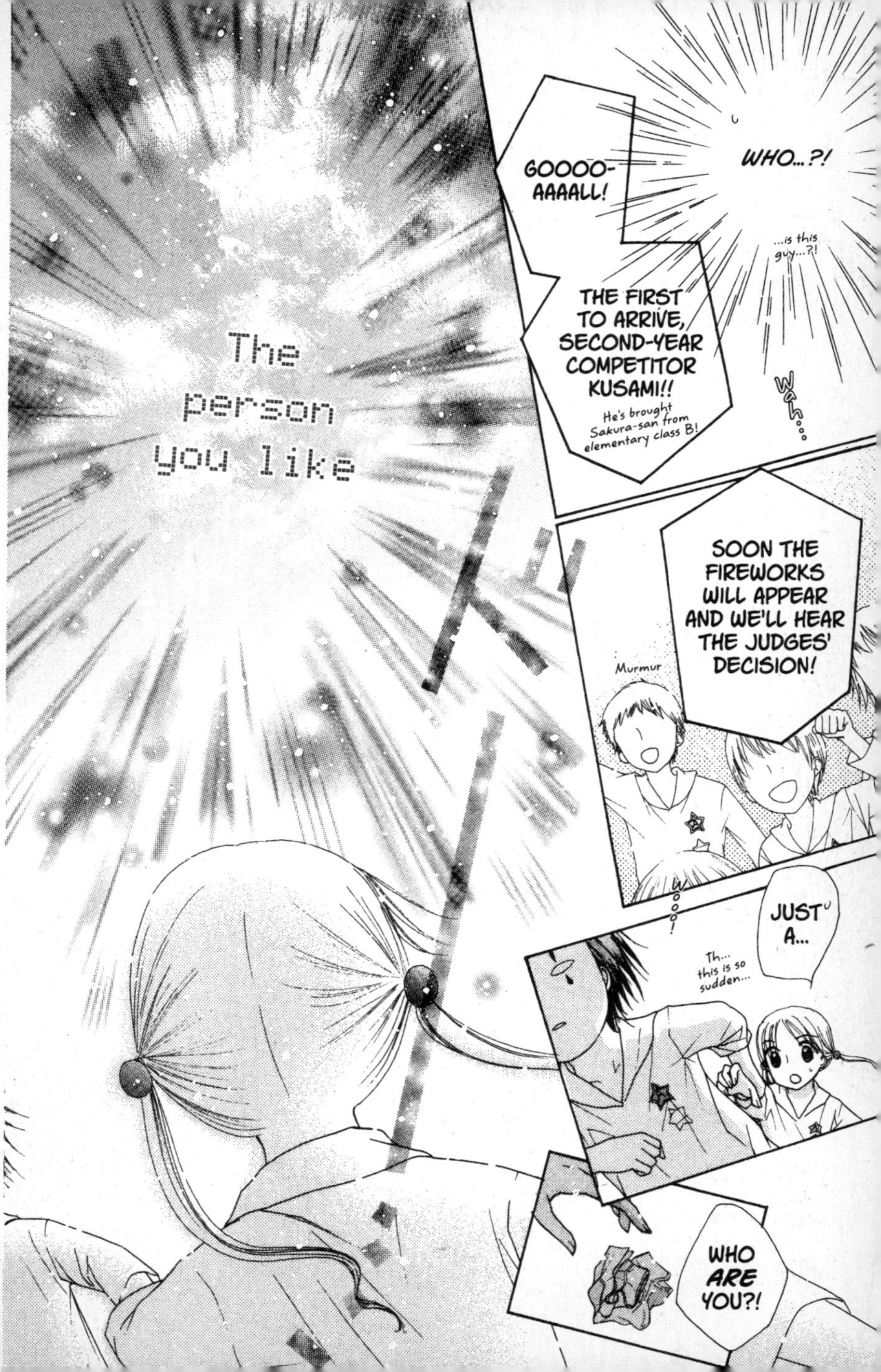
WHO...?!
...is this guy...?!
GOOOO-AAAALL!
THE FIRST TO ARRIVE, SECOND-YEAR COMPETITOR KUSAMI!!
He's brought Sakura-san from elementary class B!
Wah...
SOON THE FIREWORKS WILL APPEAR AND WE'LL HEAR THE JUDGES' DECISION!
Murmur
Wooo!
JUST A...
Th... this is so sudden...
WHO *ARE* YOU?!
The person you like

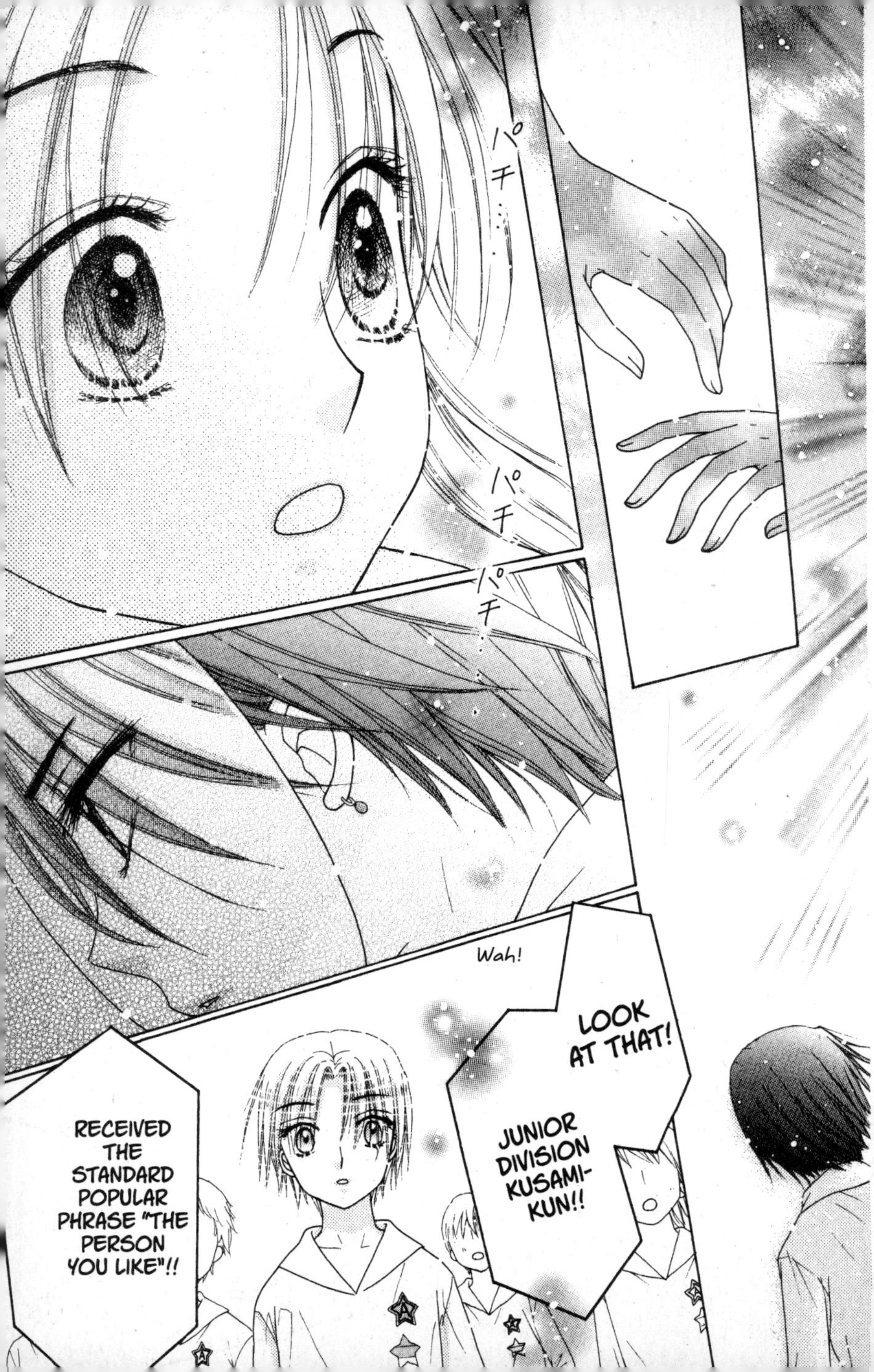
パチ…
パチ
パチ…
Wah!
LOOK AT THAT!
JUNIOR DIVISION KUSAMI-KUN!!
RECEIVED THE STANDARD POPULAR PHRASE "THE PERSON YOU LIKE"!!

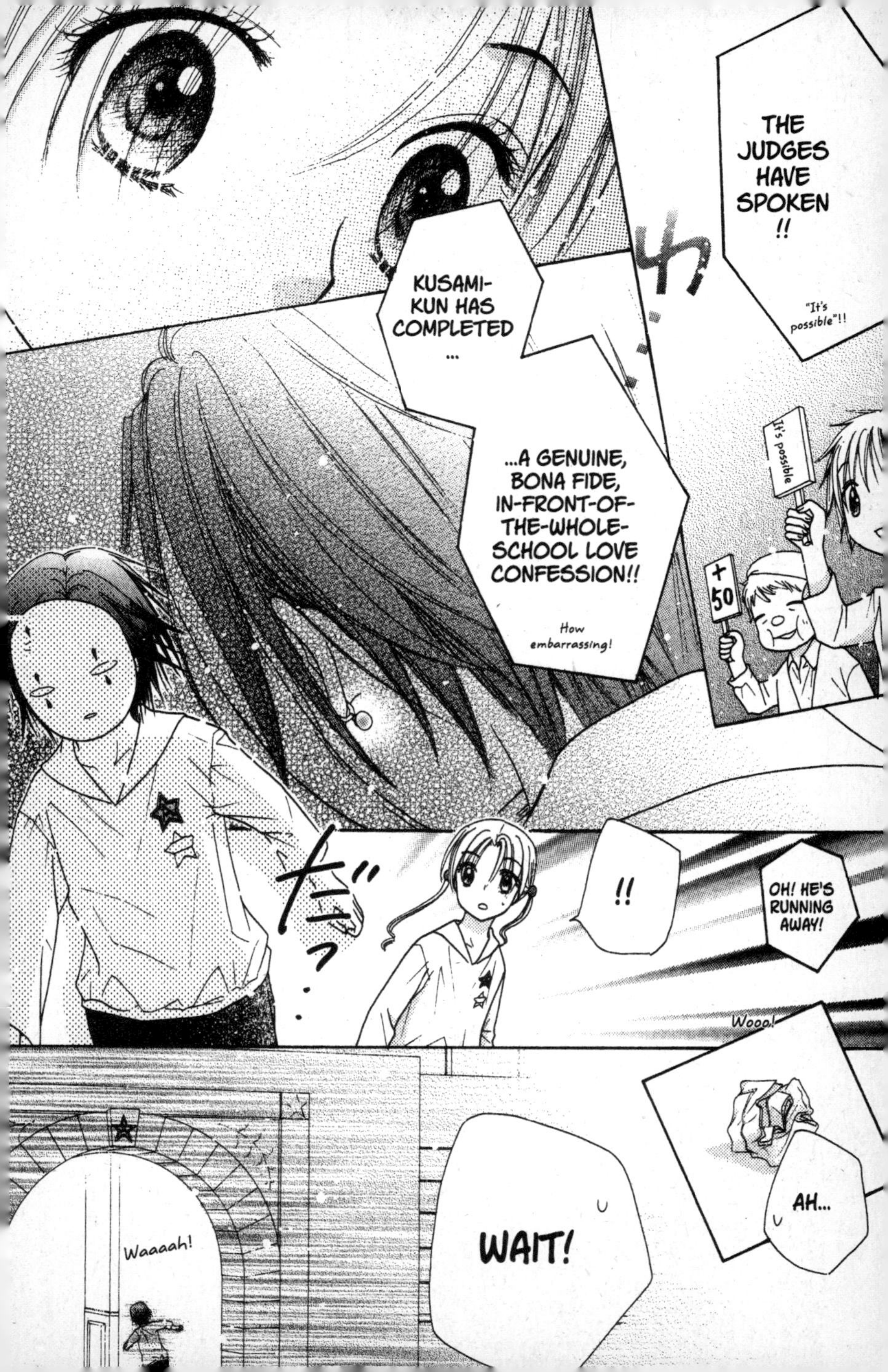
THE JUDGES HAVE SPOKEN !!
"It's possible"!!
It's possible
+50
KUSAMI-KUN HAS COMPLETED ...
...A GENUINE, BONA FIDE, IN-FRONT-OF-THE-WHOLE-SCHOOL LOVE CONFESSION!!
How embarrassing!
OH! HE'S RUNNING AWAY!
!!
Wooo!
AH...
WAIT!
Waaaah!

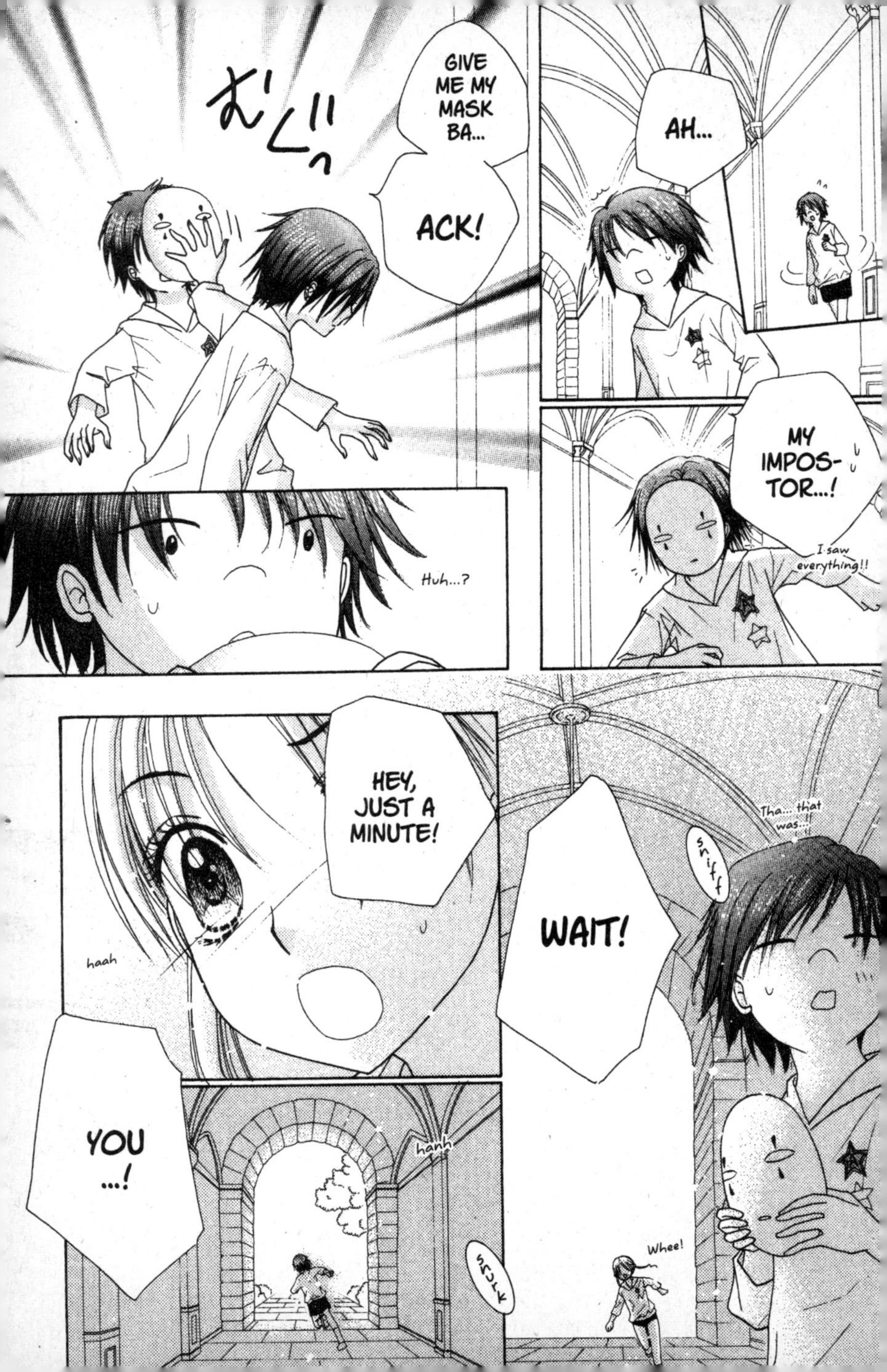
AH...
MY IMPOSTOR...!
I saw everything!!
むぐっ
GIVE ME MY MASK BA...
ACK!
Huh...?
Tha... that was...
sniff
WAIT!
Whee!
HEY, JUST A MINUTE!
haah
YOU ...!
hanh
snurk

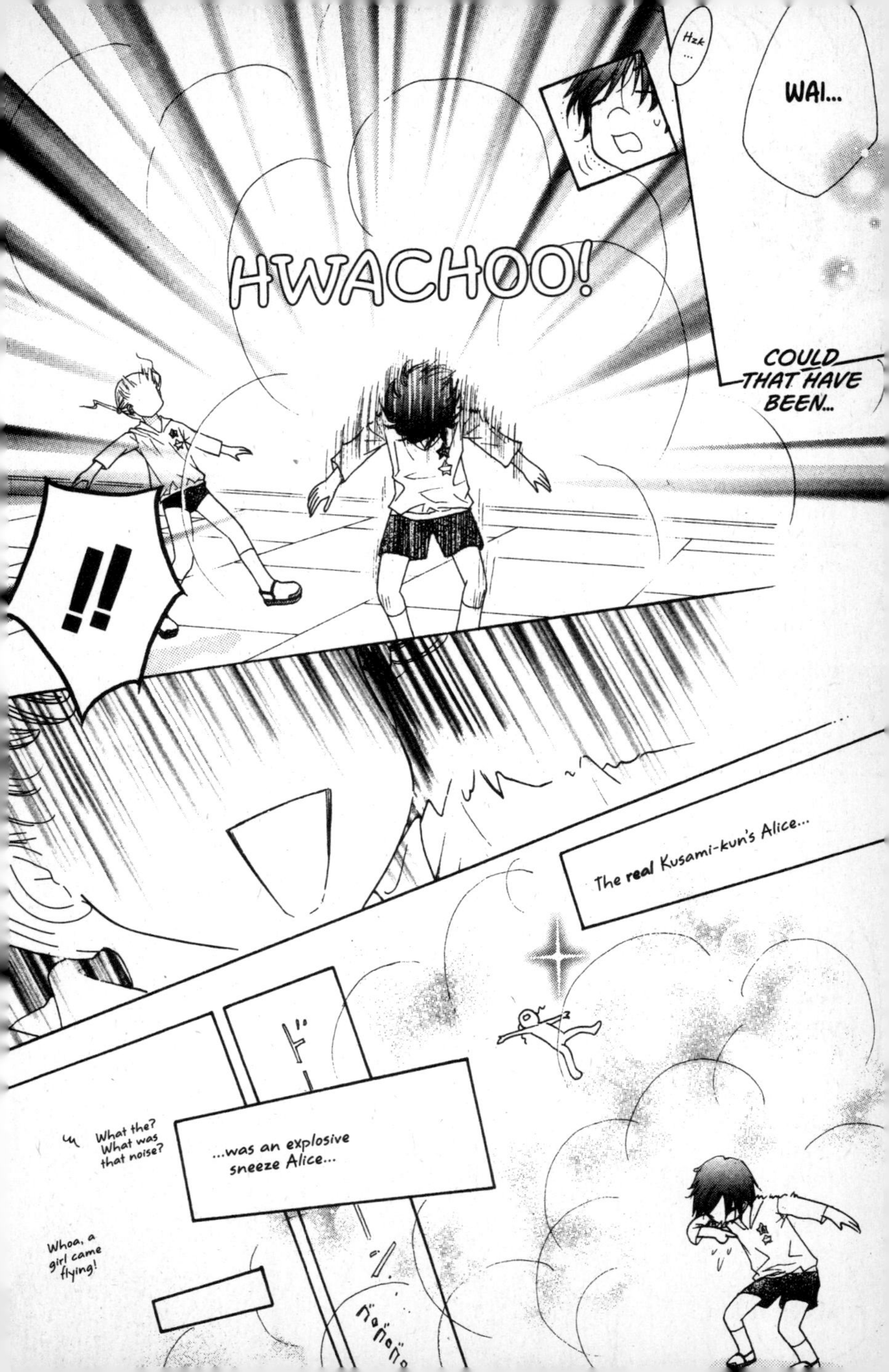
WAI...
COULD THAT HAVE BEEN...
Hzk ...
HWACHOO!
!!
The real Kusami-kun's Alice...
...was an explosive sneeze Alice...
What the? What was that noise?
Whoa, a girl came flying!

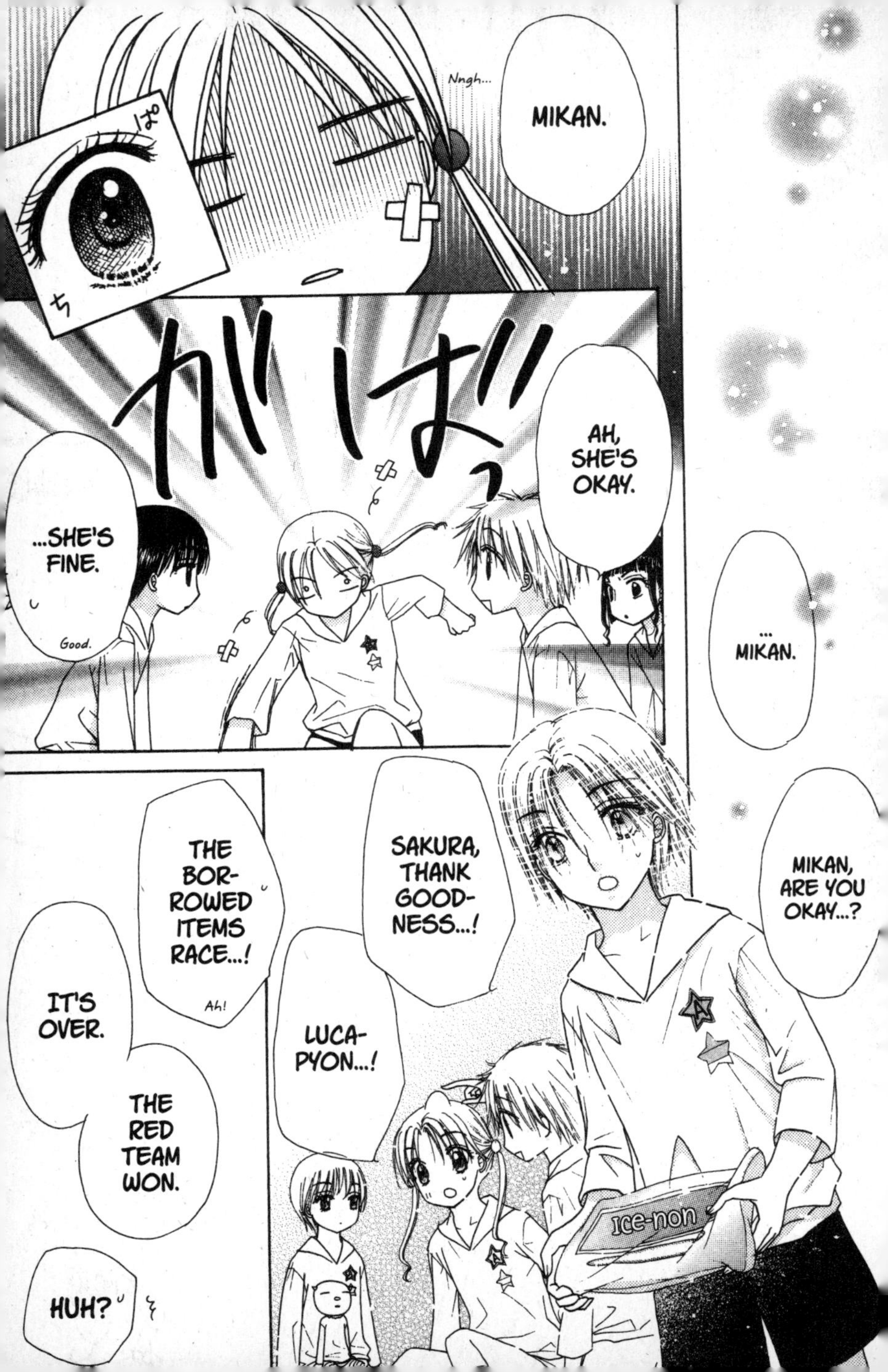
MIKAN.
Nngh...
ぱち
...
MIKAN.
がばっ
AH, SHE'S OKAY.
...SHE'S FINE.
Good.
MIKAN, ARE YOU OKAY...?
SAKURA, THANK GOODNESS...!
LUCA-PYON...!
THE BORROWED ITEMS RACE...!
Ah!
IT'S OVER.
THE RED TEAM WON.
HUH?
Ice-non

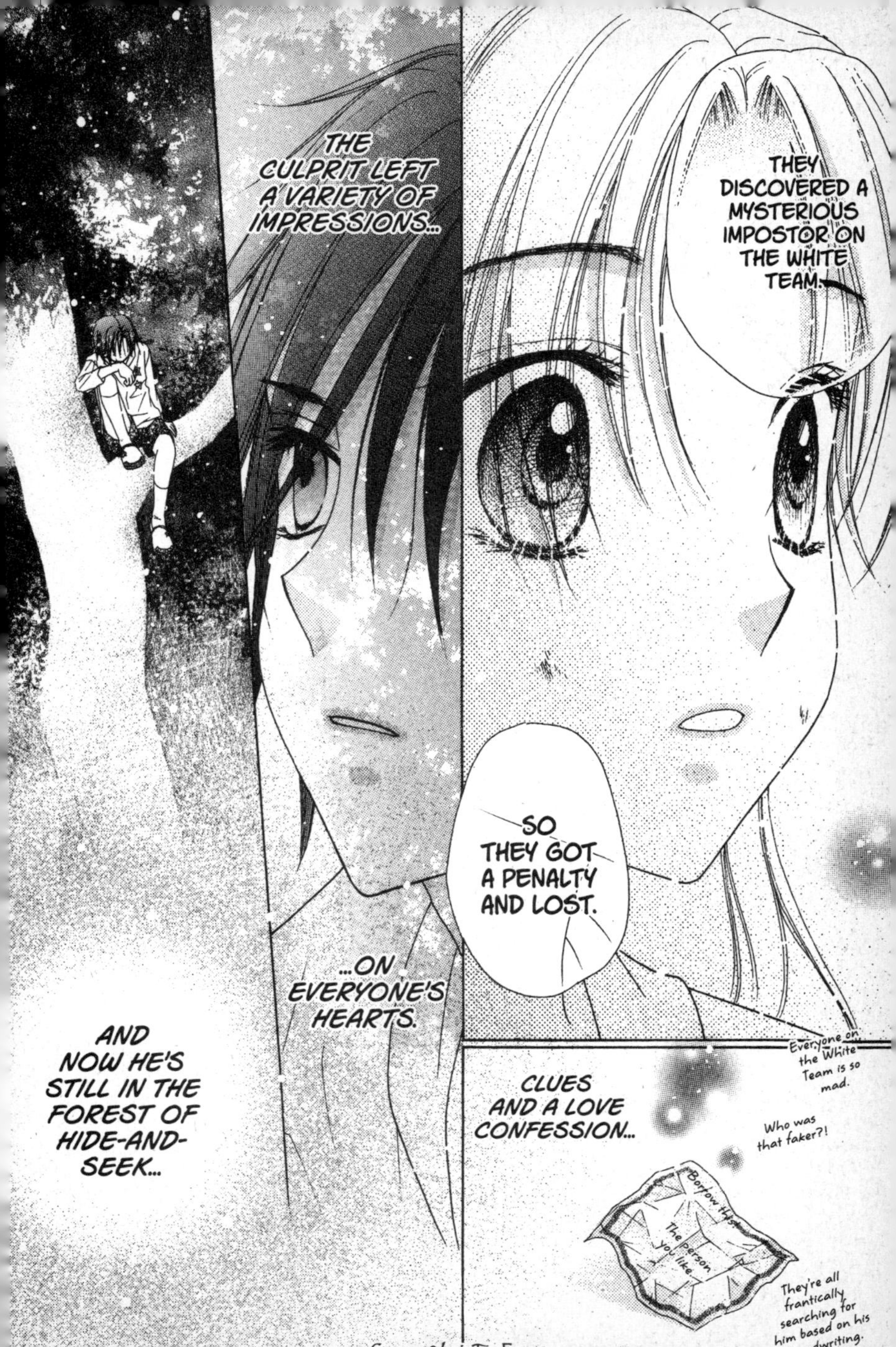
THEY DISCOVERED A MYSTERIOUS IMPOSTOR ON THE WHITE TEAM.
SO THEY GOT A PENALTY AND LOST.
Everyone on the White Team is so mad.
Who was that faker?!
CLUES AND A LOVE CONFESSION...
Borrow this: The person you like.
They're all frantically searching for him based on his handwriting.
THE CULPRIT LEFT A VARIETY OF IMPRESSIONS...
...ON EVERYONE'S HEARTS.
AND NOW HE'S STILL IN THE FOREST OF HIDE-AND-SEEK...

Chapter 84 / The End

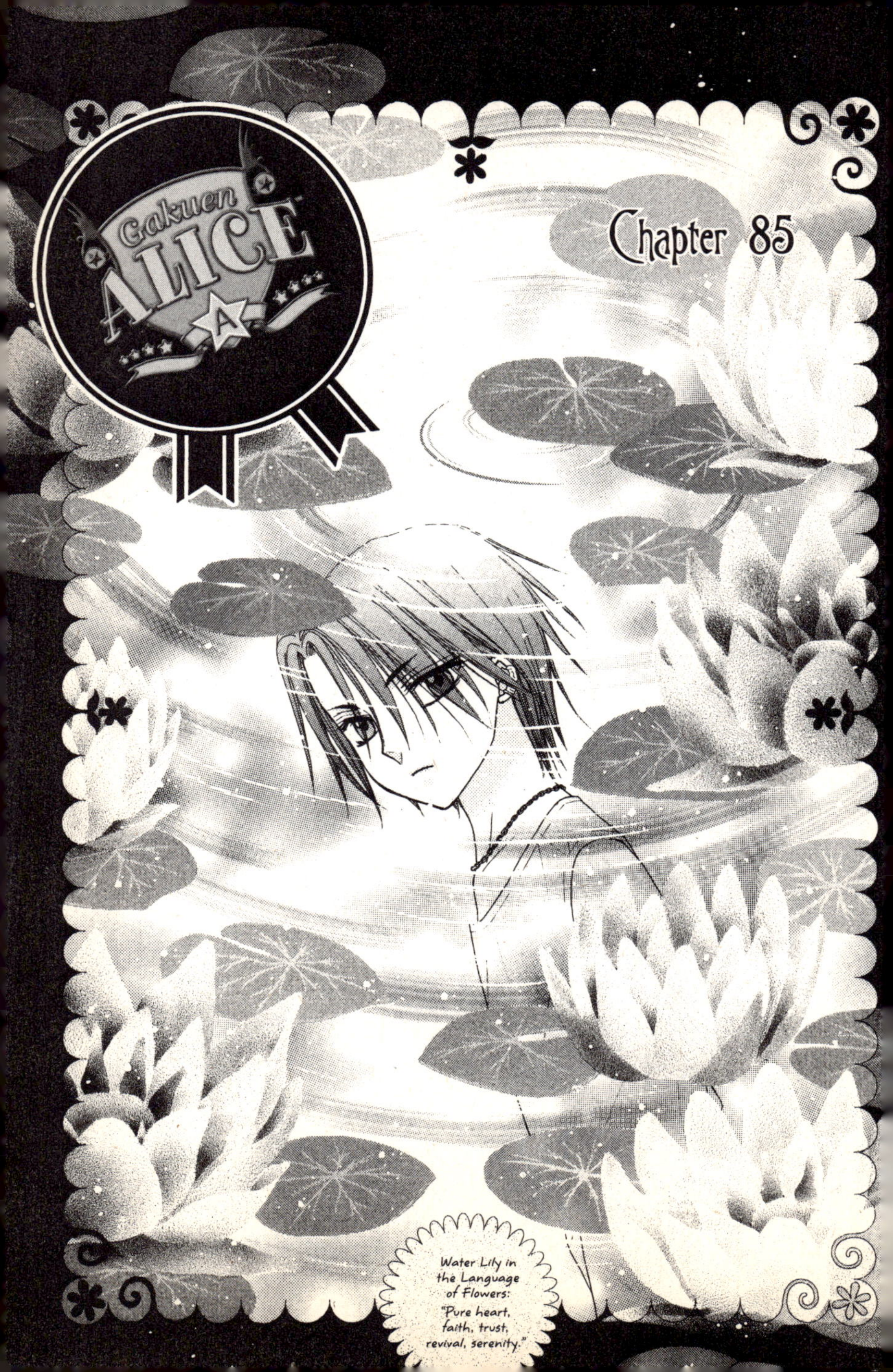
Gakuen ALICE
Chapter 85
Water Lily in the Language of Flowers: "Pure heart, faith, trust, revival, serenity."

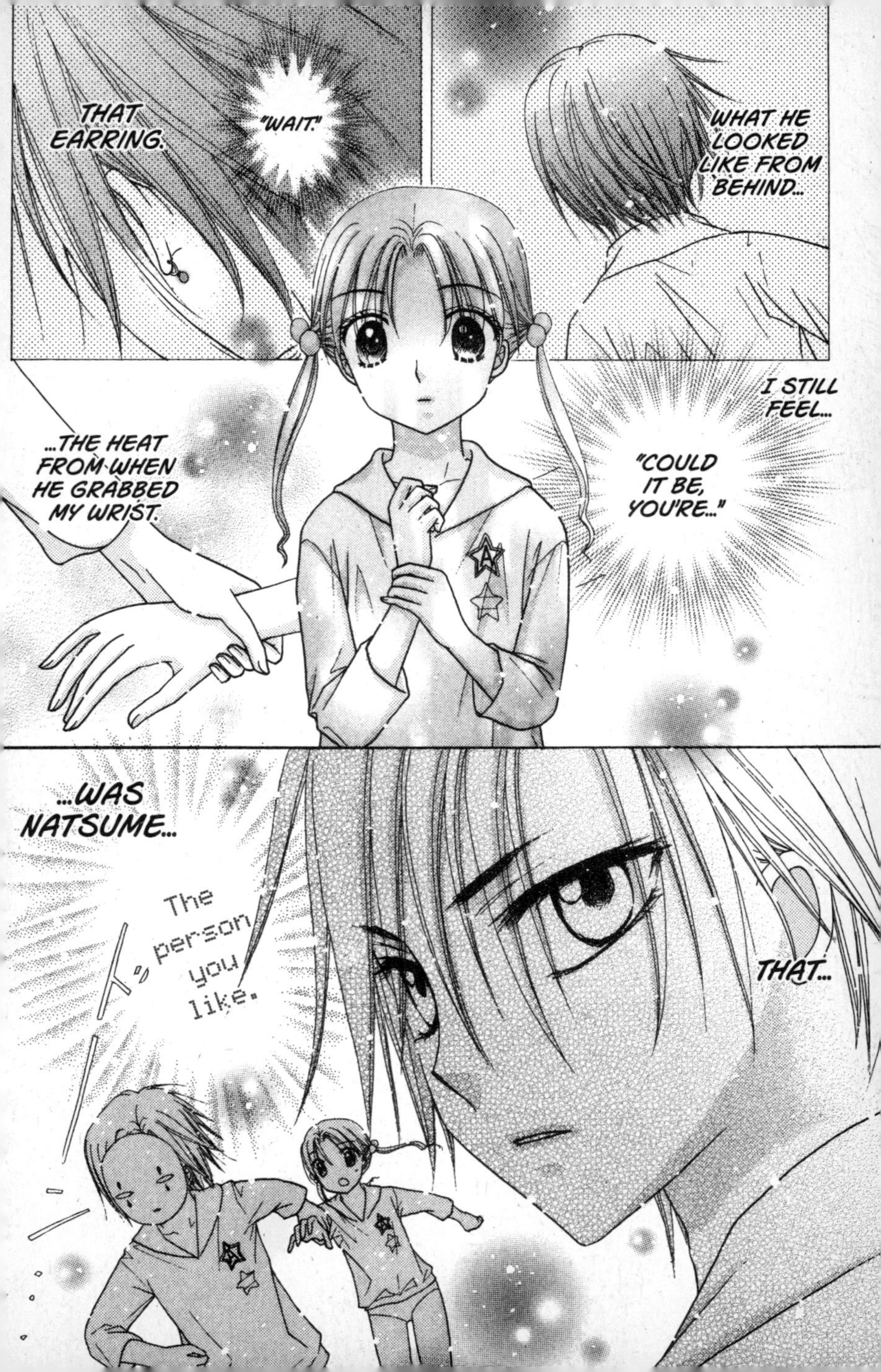
WHAT HE LOOKED LIKE FROM BEHIND...
"WAIT."
THAT EARRING.
I STILL FEEL...
"COULD IT BE, YOU'RE..."
...THE HEAT FROM WHEN HE GRABBED MY WRIST.
THAT...
...WAS NATSUME...
The person you like.

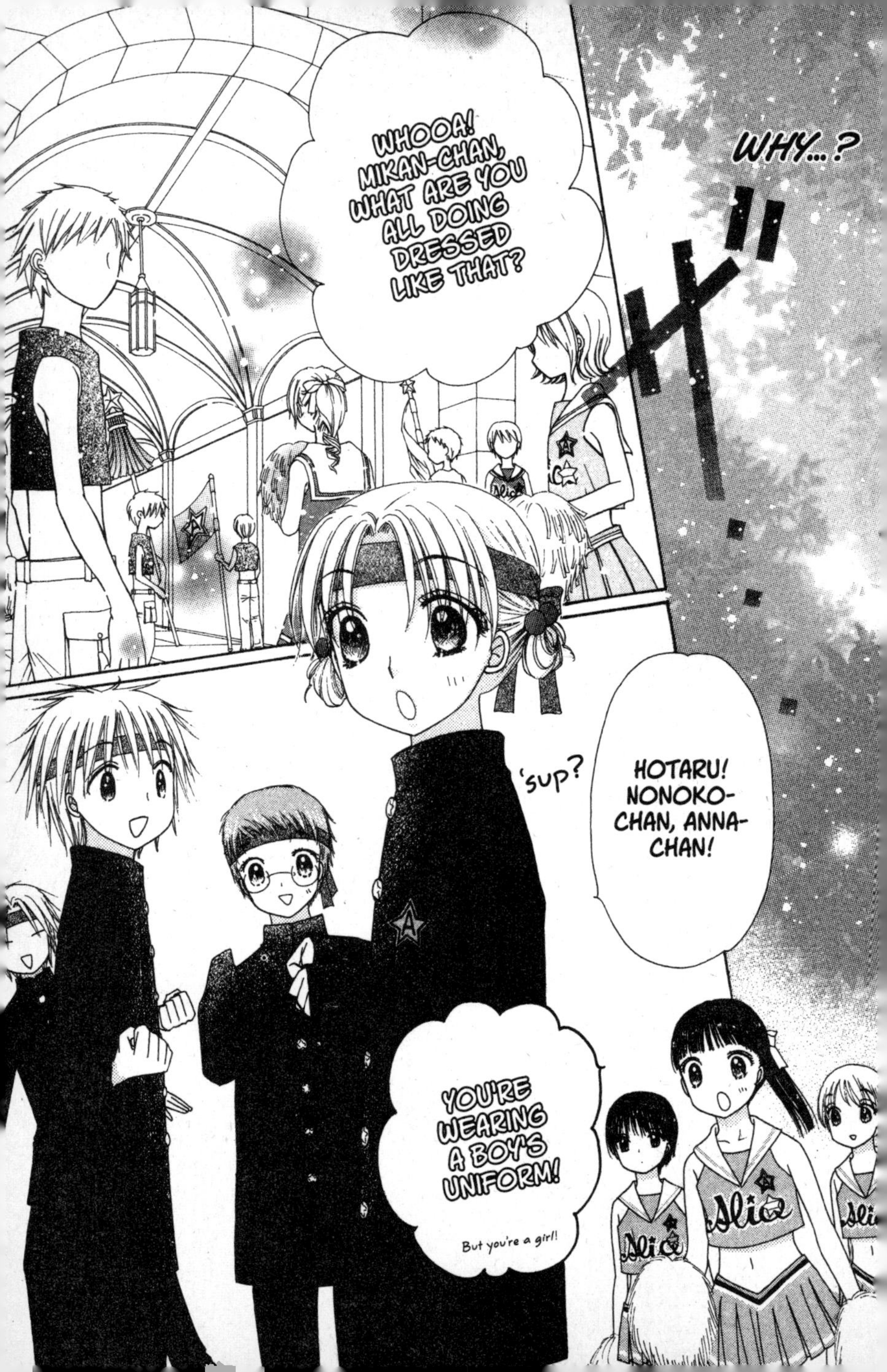
WHY...?
WHOOA! MIKAN-CHAN, WHAT ARE YOU ALL DOING DRESSED LIKE THAT?
HOTARU! NONOKO-CHAN, ANNA-CHAN!
'sup?
YOU'RE WEARING A BOY'S UNIFORM!
But you're a girl!

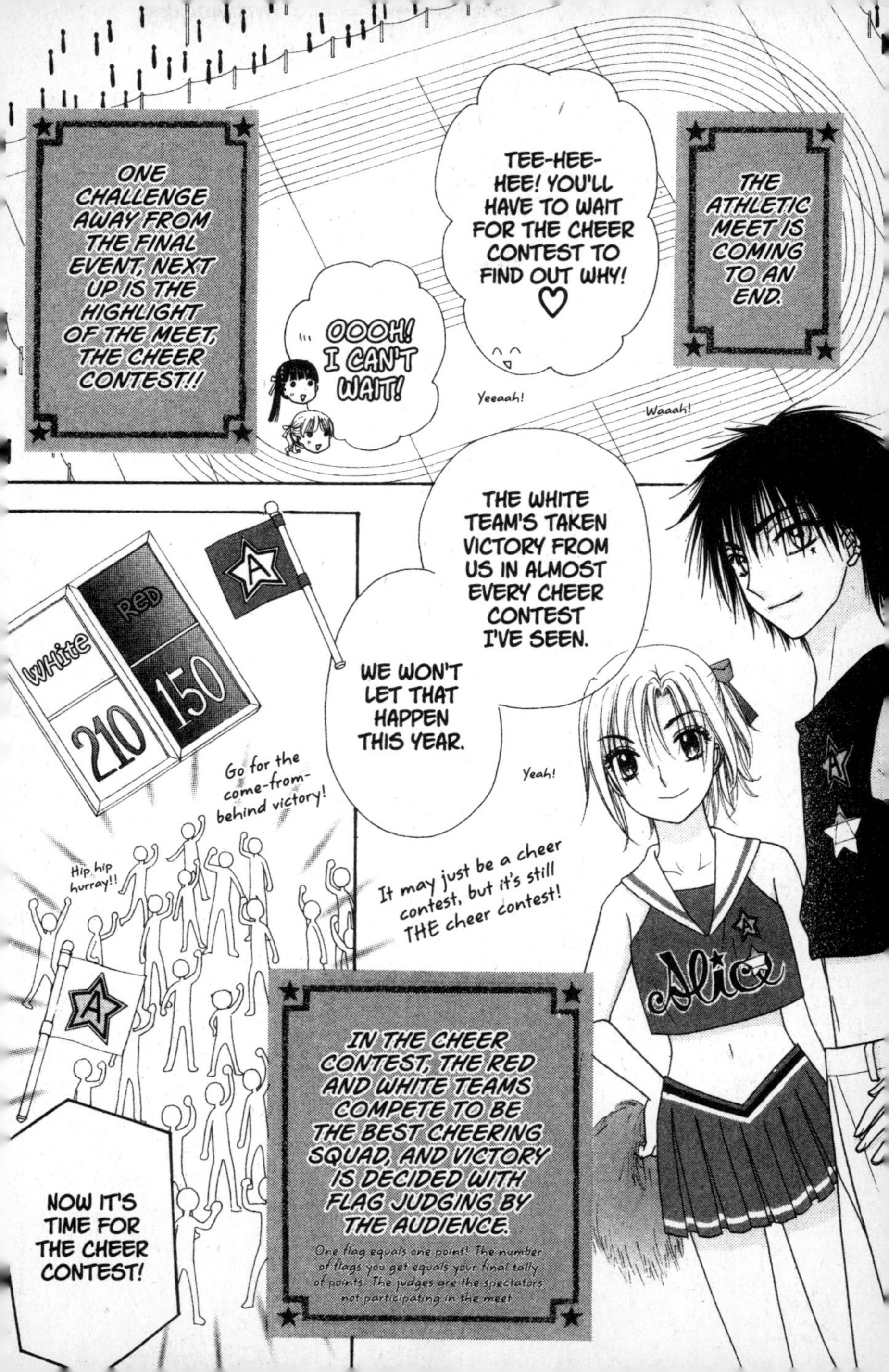
THE ATHLETIC MEET IS COMING TO AN END.
TEE-HEE-HEE! YOU'LL HAVE TO WAIT FOR THE CHEER CONTEST TO FIND OUT WHY! ♡
Waaah!
Yeeaah!
OOOH! I CAN'T WAIT!
ONE CHALLENGE AWAY FROM THE FINAL EVENT, NEXT UP IS THE HIGHLIGHT OF THE MEET, THE CHEER CONTEST!!
THE WHITE TEAM'S TAKEN VICTORY FROM US IN ALMOST EVERY CHEER CONTEST I'VE SEEN.
WE WON'T LET THAT HAPPEN THIS YEAR.
Yeah!
It may just be a cheer contest, but it's still THE cheer contest!
IN THE CHEER CONTEST, THE RED AND WHITE TEAMS COMPETE TO BE THE BEST CHEERING SQUAD, AND VICTORY IS DECIDED WITH FLAG JUDGING BY THE AUDIENCE.
One flag equals one point! The number of flags you get equals your final tally of points. The judges are the spectators not participating in the meet.
RED
WHITE
150
210
Go for the come-from-behind victory!
Hip hip hurray!!
NOW IT'S TIME FOR THE CHEER CONTEST!

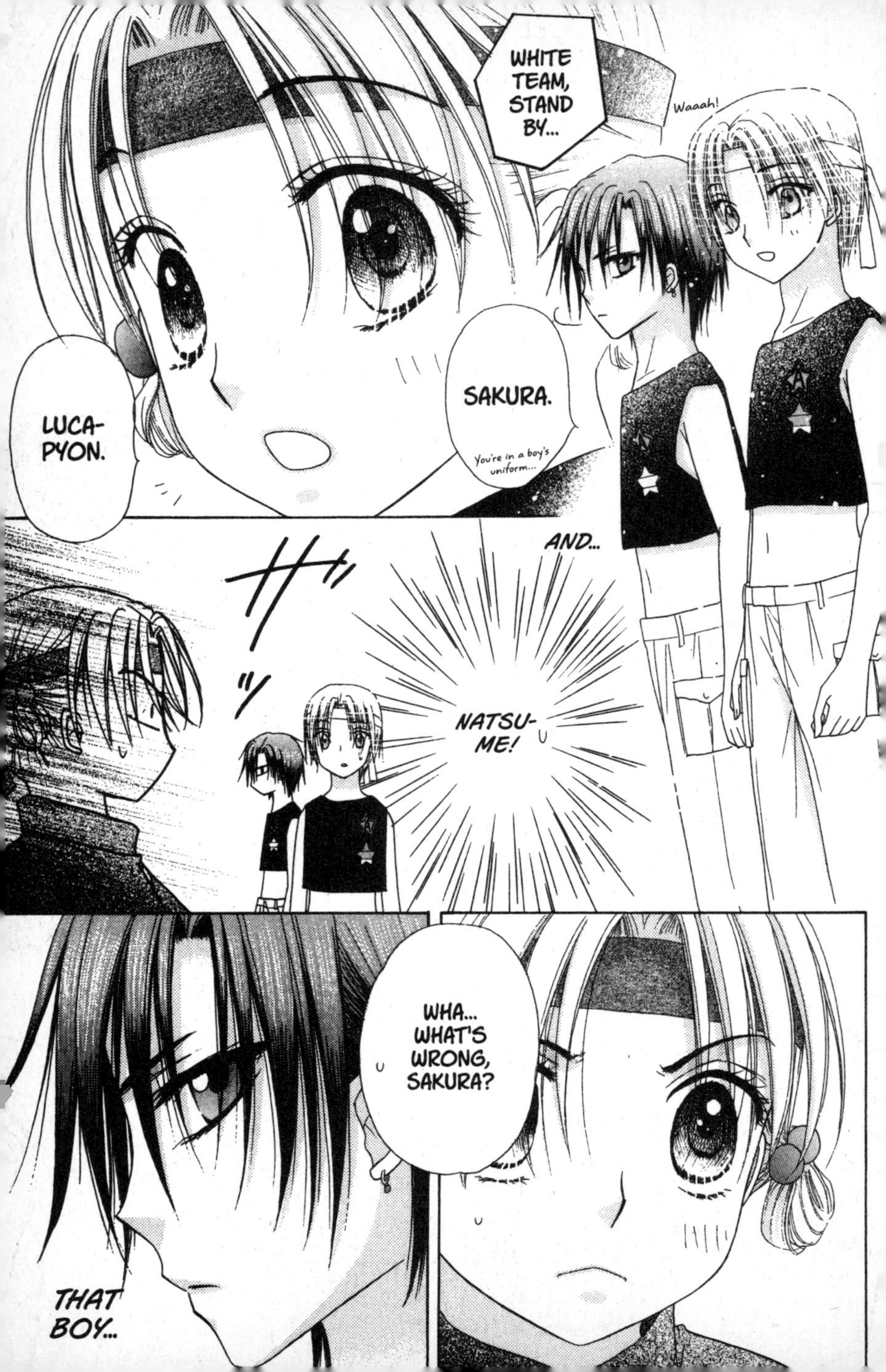

WHITE TEAM, STAND BY...
Waaah!
SAKURA.
You're in a boy's uniform...
LUCA-PYON.
AND...
NATSU-ME!
WHA... WHAT'S WRONG, SAKURA?
THAT BOY...

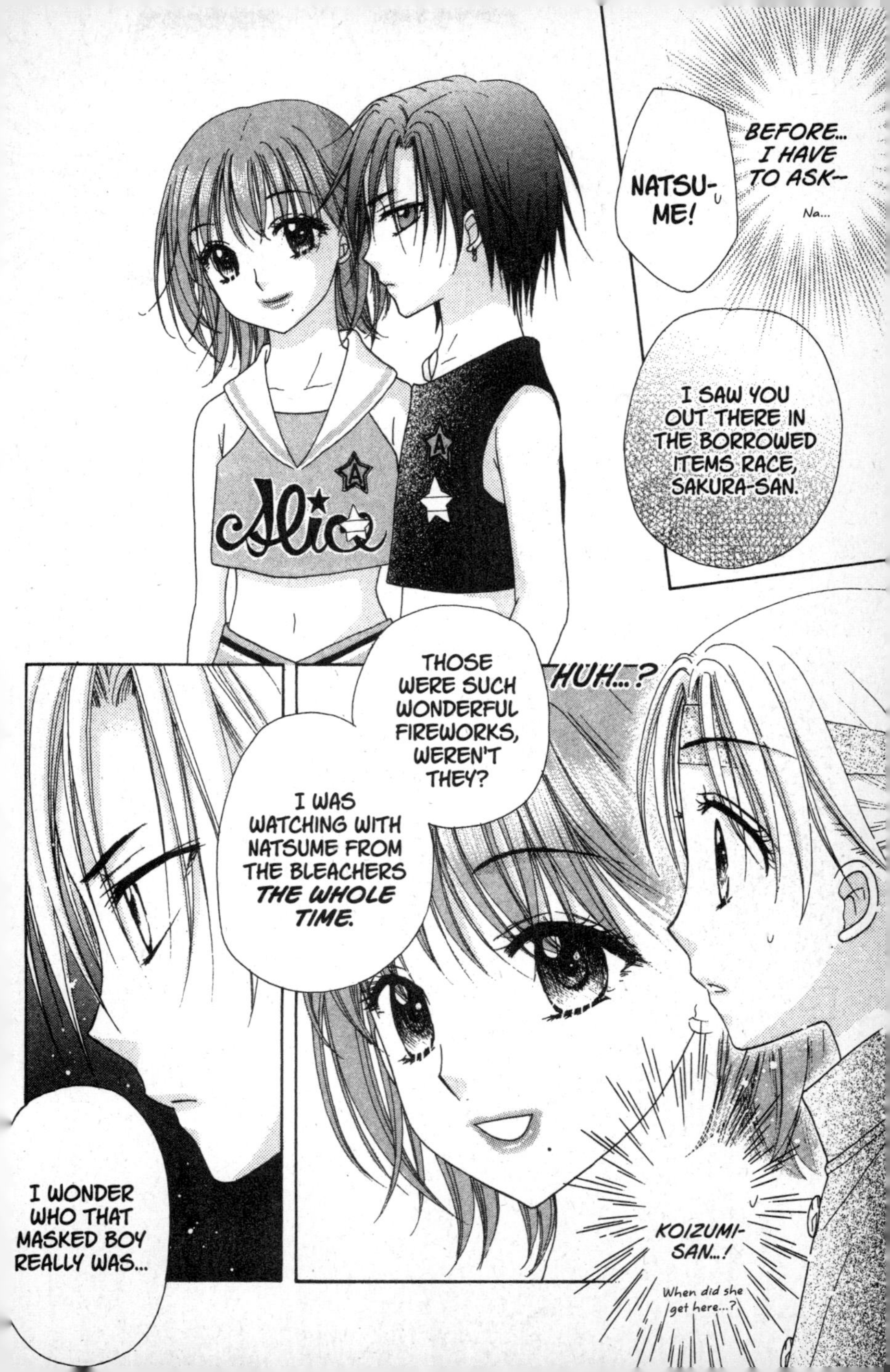
BEFORE... I HAVE TO ASK~
Na...
NATSU-ME!
I SAW YOU OUT THERE IN THE BORROWED ITEMS RACE, SAKURA-SAN.
HUH...?
THOSE WERE SUCH WONDERFUL FIREWORKS, WEREN'T THEY?
I WAS WATCHING WITH NATSUME FROM THE BLEACHERS *THE WHOLE TIME.*
KOIZUMI-SAN...!
When did she get here...?
I WONDER WHO THAT MASKED BOY REALLY WAS...

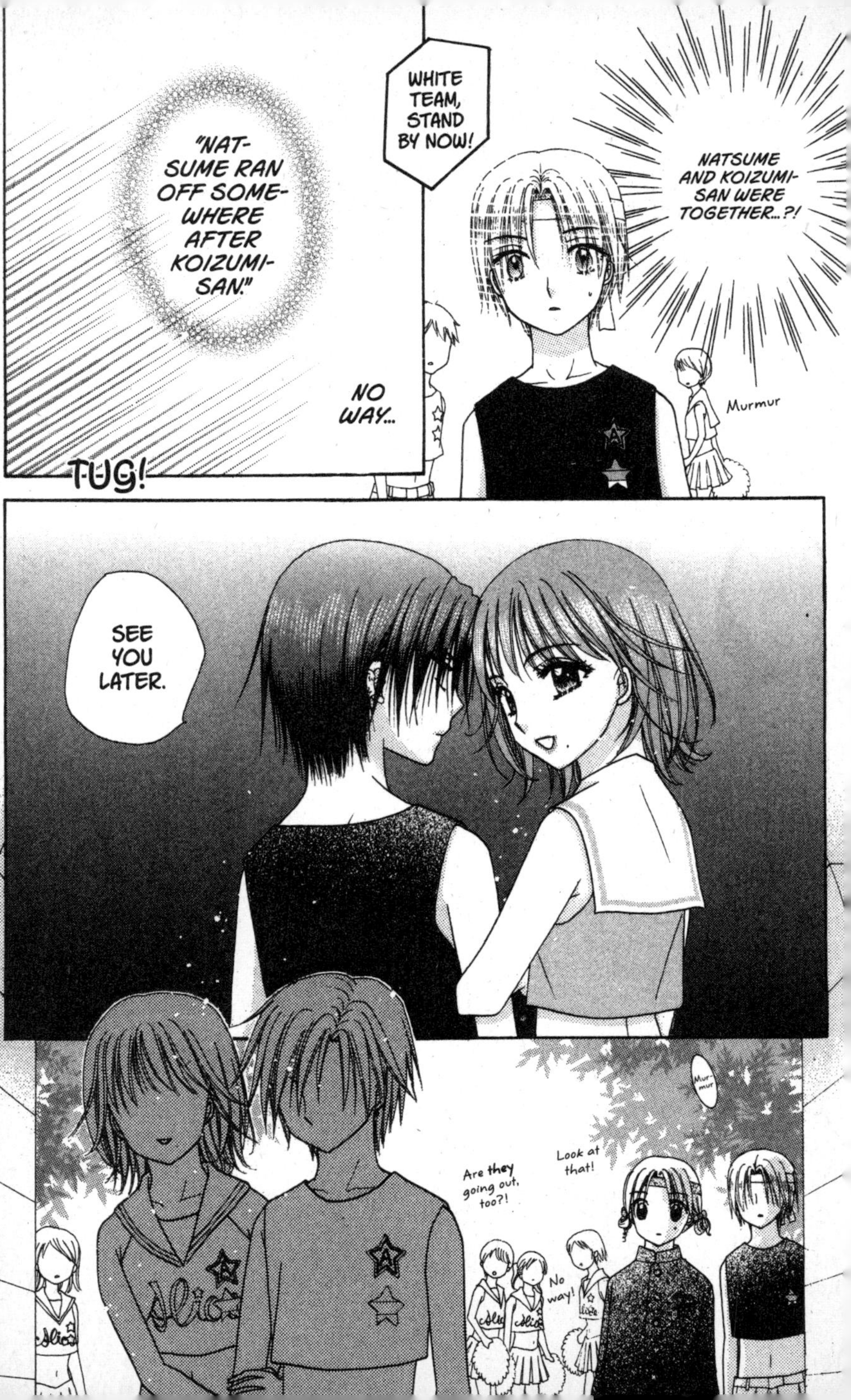
WHITE TEAM, STAND BY NOW!
NATSUME AND KOIZUMI-SAN WERE TOGETHER...?!
Murmur
"NATSUME RAN OFF SOMEWHERE AFTER KOIZUMI-SAN."
NO WAY...
TUG!
SEE YOU LATER.
Mur-mur
Look at that!
Are they going out, too?!
No way!

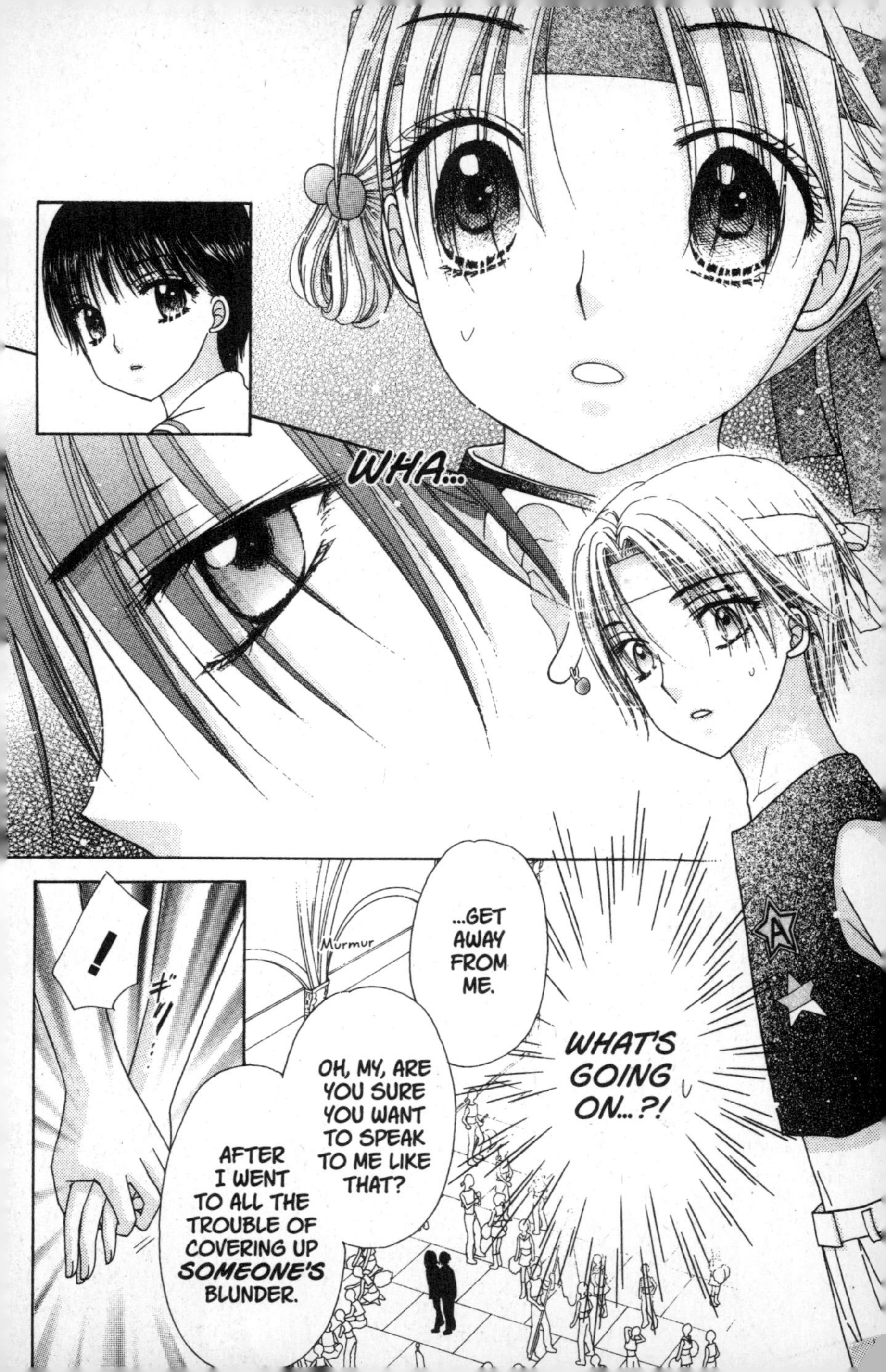
WHA...
...GET AWAY FROM ME.
Murmur
WHAT'S GOING ON...?!
OH, MY, ARE YOU SURE YOU WANT TO SPEAK TO ME LIKE THAT?
AFTER I WENT TO ALL THE TROUBLE OF COVERING UP *SOMEONE'S* BLUNDER.
!
ギリ

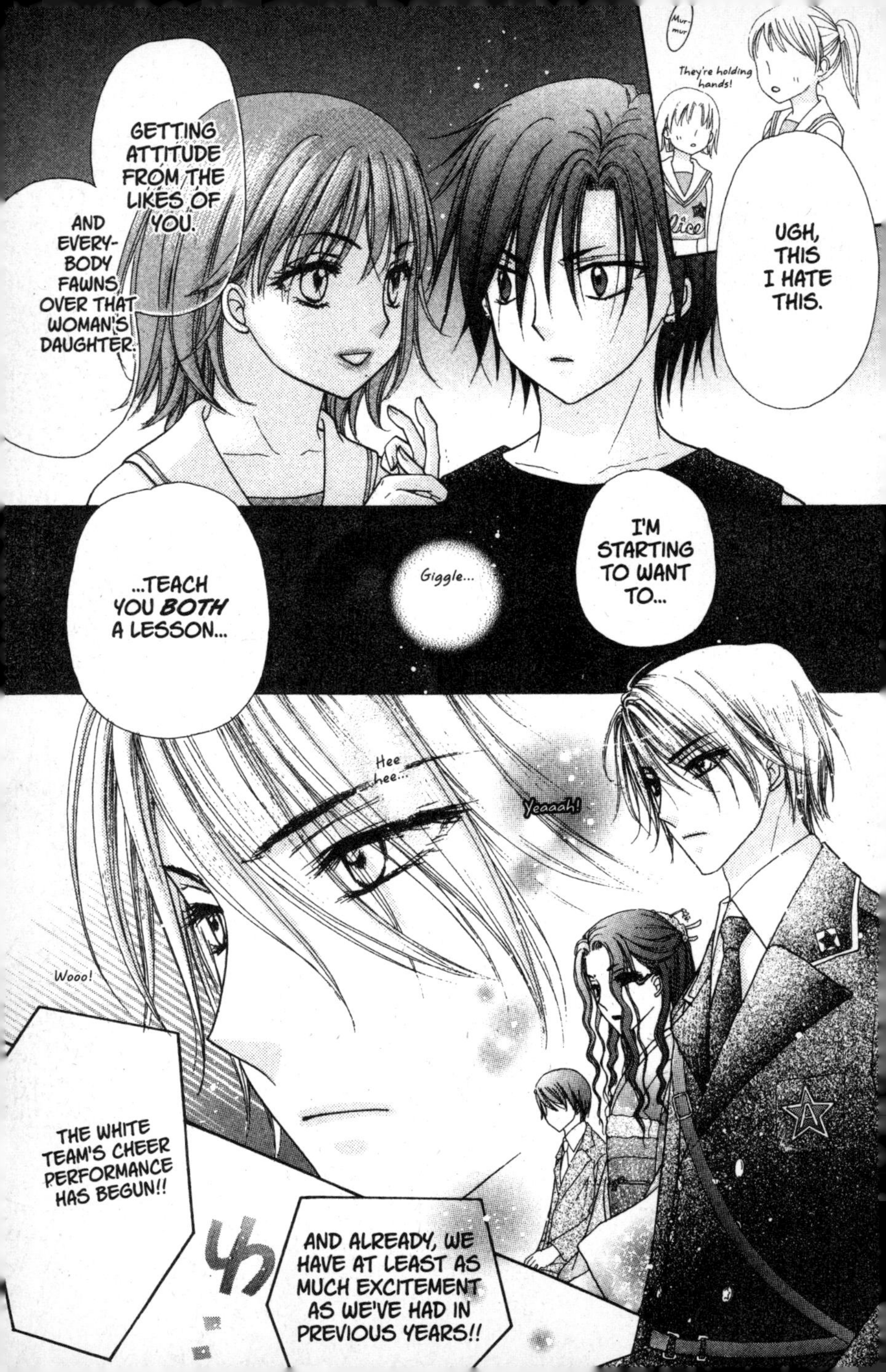
Mur-mur
They're holding hands!
UGH, THIS I HATE THIS.
GETTING ATTITUDE FROM THE LIKES OF YOU.
AND EVERY-BODY FAWNS OVER THAT WOMAN'S DAUGHTER.
I'M STARTING TO WANT TO...
Giggle...
...TEACH YOU BOTH A LESSON...
Hee hee...
Yeaaah!
Wooo!
THE WHITE TEAM'S CHEER PERFORMANCE HAS BEGUN!!
AND ALREADY, WE HAVE AT LEAST AS MUCH EXCITEMENT AS WE'VE HAD IN PREVIOUS YEARS!!

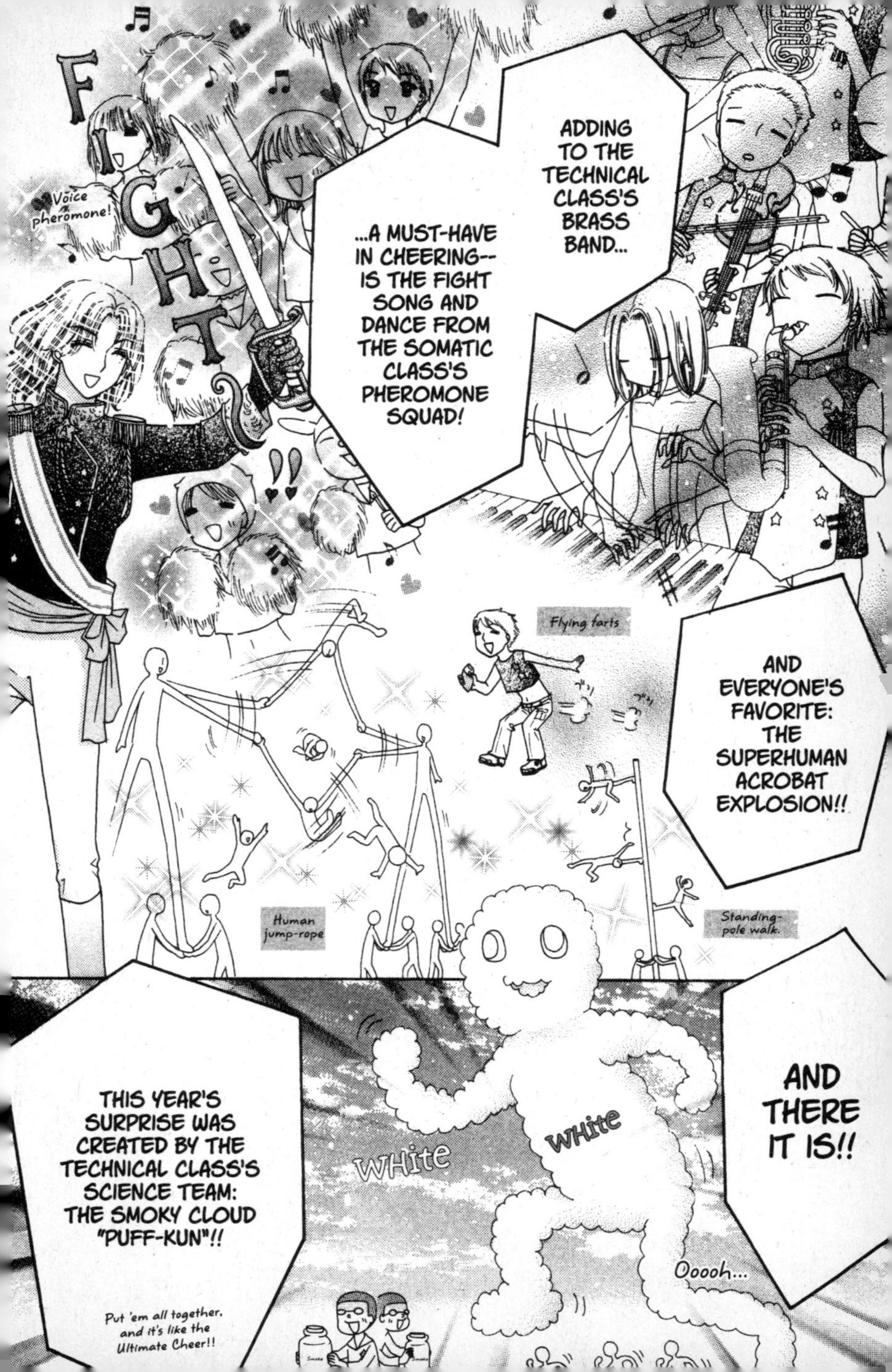
ADDING TO THE TECHNICAL CLASS'S BRASS BAND...
...A MUST-HAVE IN CHEERING-- IS THE FIGHT SONG AND DANCE FROM THE SOMATIC CLASS'S PHEROMONE SQUAD!
FIGHT!!
Voice pheromone!
AND EVERYONE'S FAVORITE: THE SUPERHUMAN ACROBAT EXPLOSION!!
Flying farts
Standing-pole walk.
Human jump-rope
AND THERE IT IS!!
THIS YEAR'S SURPRISE WAS CREATED BY THE TECHNICAL CLASS'S SCIENCE TEAM: THE SMOKY CLOUD "PUFF-KUN"!!
WHITE
WHITE
Ooooh...
Put 'em all together, and it's like the Ultimate Cheer!!

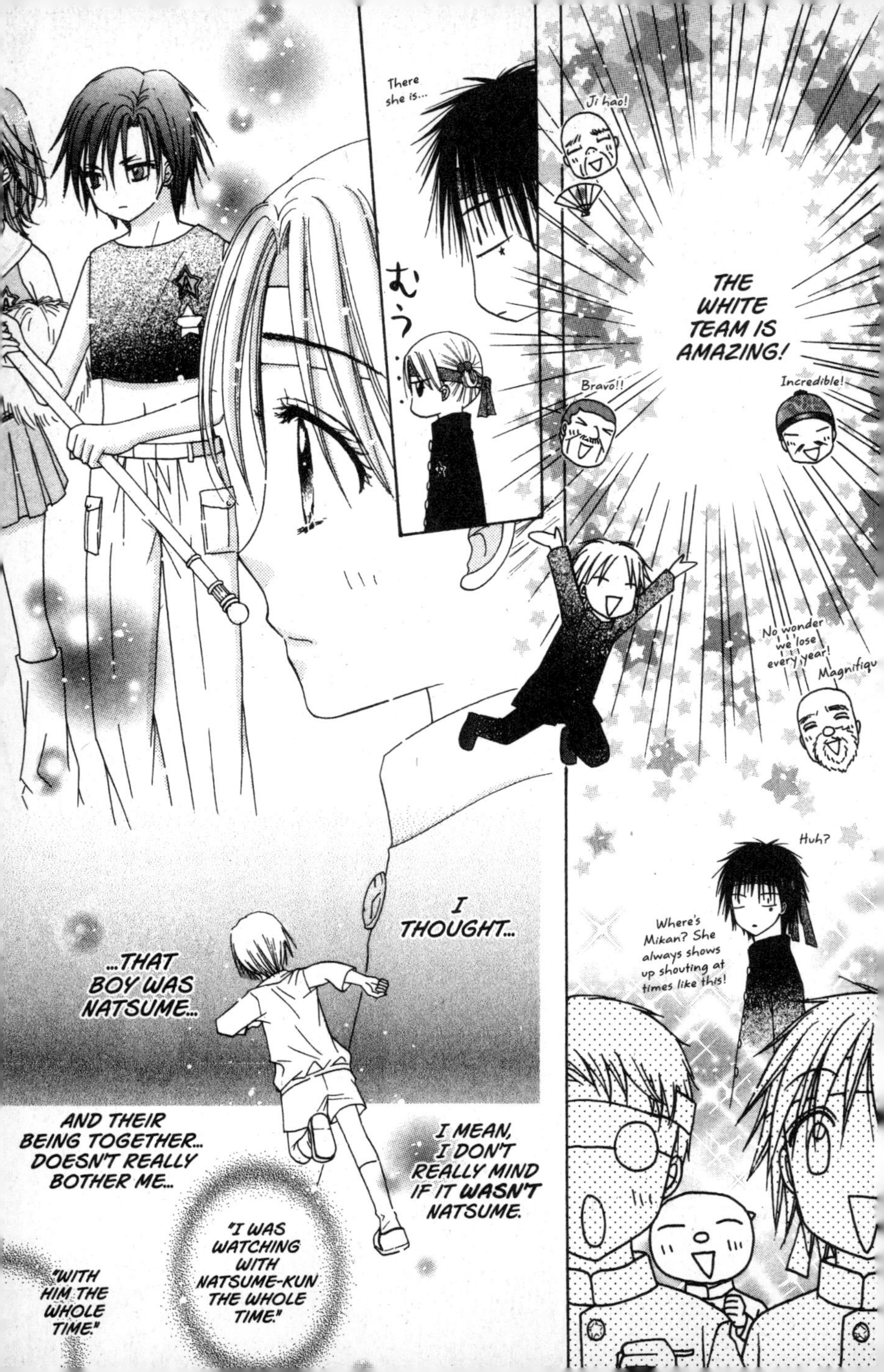
Ji hao!
THE WHITE TEAM IS AMAZING!
Incredible!
Bravo!!
No wonder we lose every year!
Magnifiqu
There she is...
むう
Huh?
Where's Mikan? She always shows up shouting at times like this!
I THOUGHT...
...THAT BOY WAS NATSUME...
I MEAN, I DON'T REALLY MIND IF IT WASN'T NATSUME.
AND THEIR BEING TOGETHER... DOESN'T REALLY BOTHER ME...
"I WAS WATCHING WITH NATSUME-KUN THE WHOLE TIME."
"WITH HIM THE WHOLE TIME."

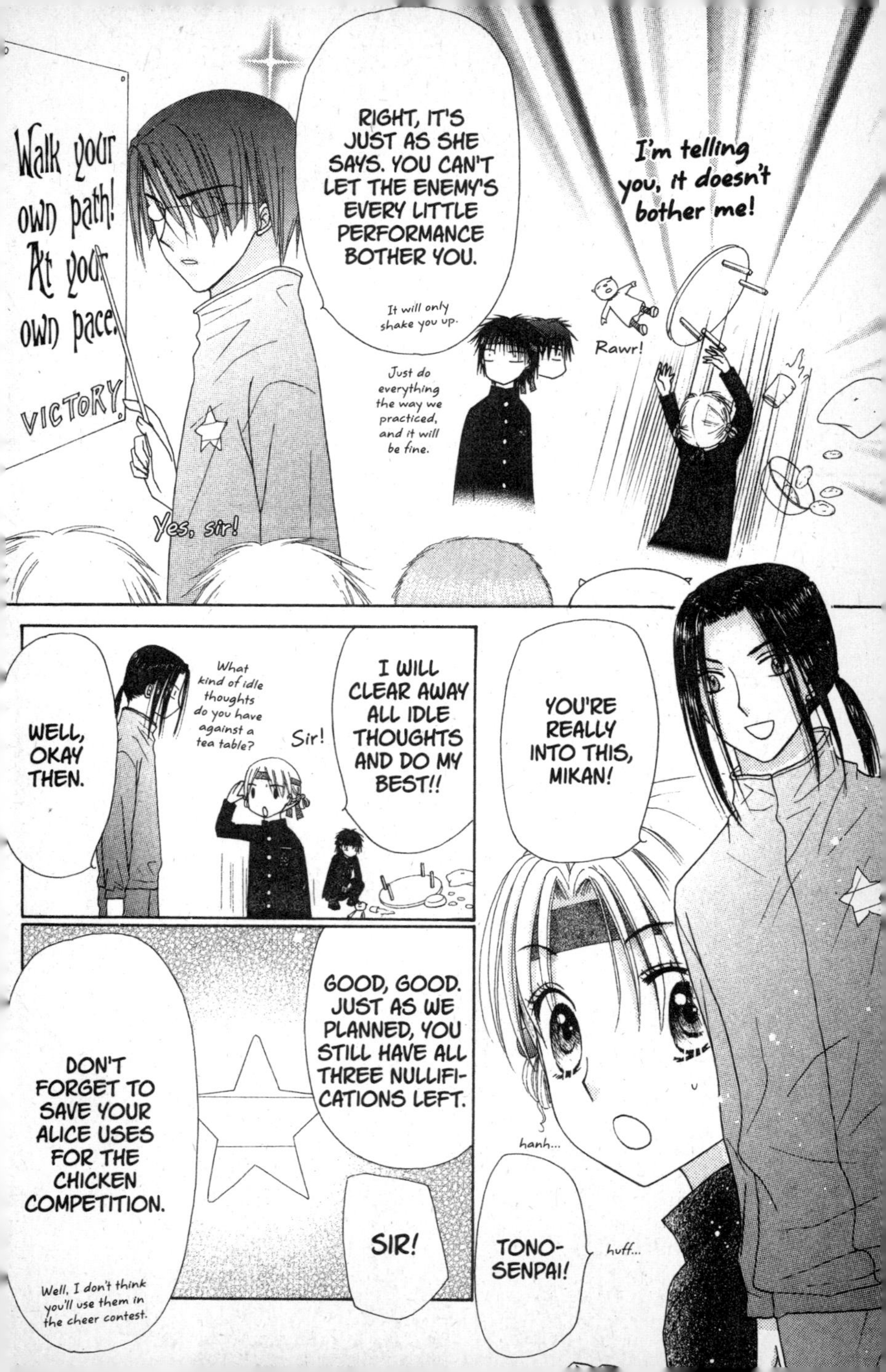
I'm telling you, it doesn't bother me!
Rawr!
RIGHT, IT'S JUST AS SHE SAYS. YOU CAN'T LET THE ENEMY'S EVERY LITTLE PERFORMANCE BOTHER YOU.
It will only shake you up.
Just do everything the way we practiced, and it will be fine.
Walk your own path! At your own pace.
VICTORY
Yes, sir!
YOU'RE REALLY INTO THIS, MIKAN!
hanh...
TONO-SENPAI!
huff...
I WILL CLEAR AWAY ALL IDLE THOUGHTS AND DO MY BEST!!
Sir!
What kind of idle thoughts do you have against a tea table?
WELL, OKAY THEN.
GOOD, GOOD. JUST AS WE PLANNED, YOU STILL HAVE ALL THREE NULLIFICATIONS LEFT.
SIR!
DON'T FORGET TO SAVE YOUR ALICE USES FOR THE CHICKEN COMPETITION.
Well, I don't think you'll use them in the cheer contest.

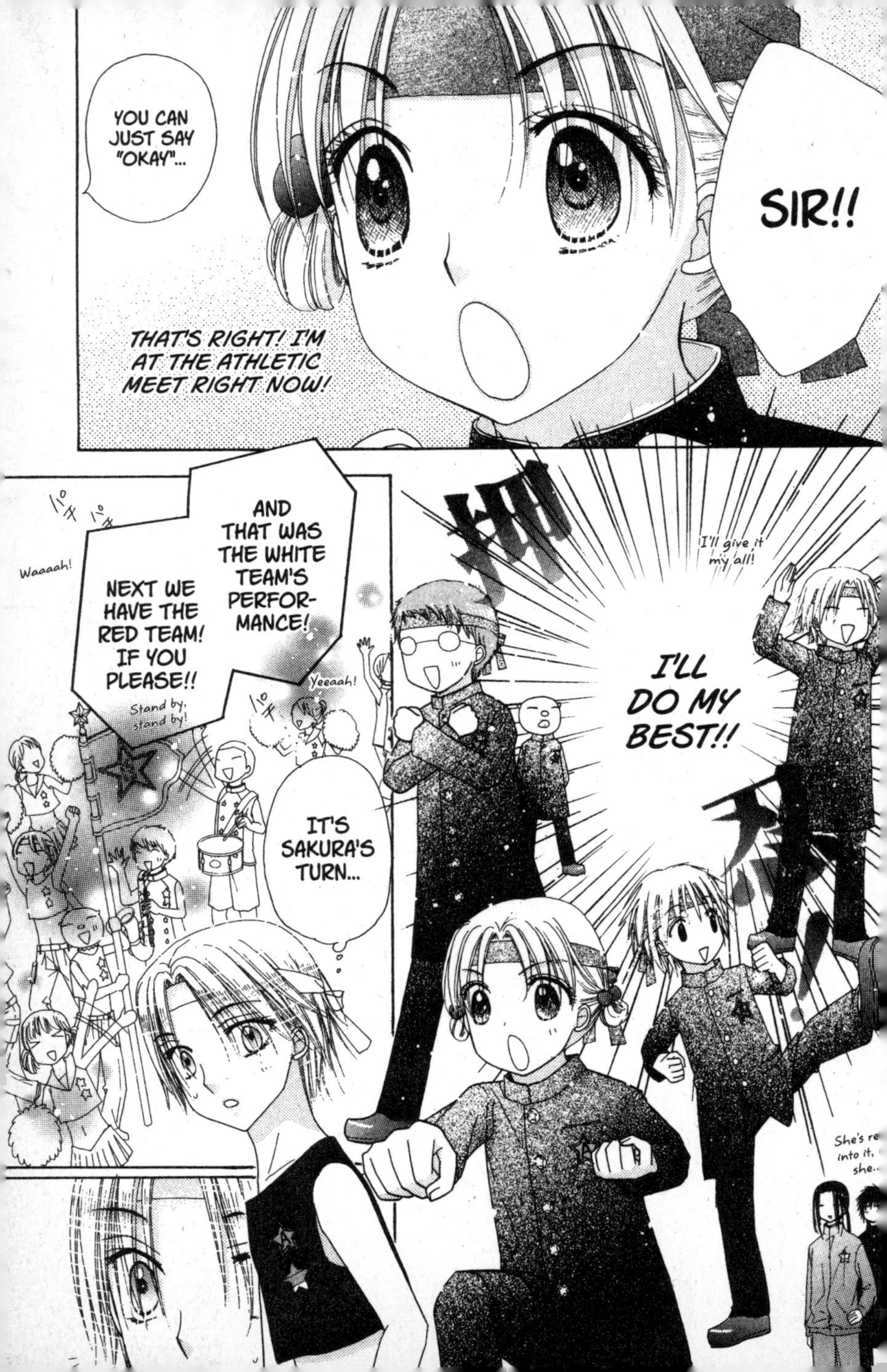
SIR!!
YOU CAN JUST SAY "OKAY"...
THAT'S RIGHT! I'M AT THE ATHLETIC MEET RIGHT NOW!
I'll give it my all!
I'LL DO MY BEST!!
AND THAT WAS THE WHITE TEAM'S PERFORMANCE!
NEXT WE HAVE THE RED TEAM! IF YOU PLEASE!!
パチ パチ
Waaaah!
Yeeaah!
Stand by, stand by!
IT'S SAKURA'S TURN...

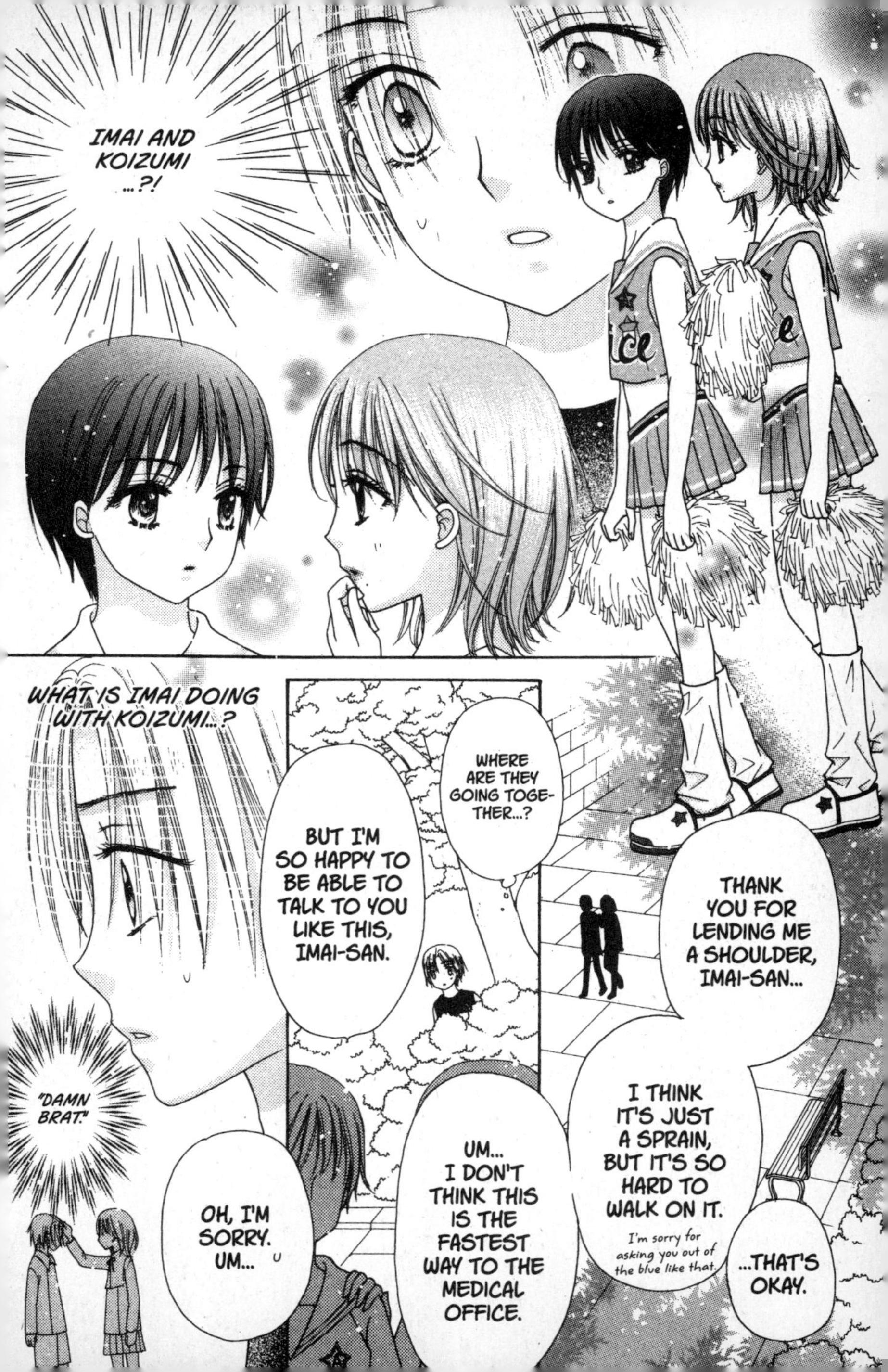
IMAI AND KOIZUMI ...?!
THANK YOU FOR LENDING ME A SHOULDER, IMAI-SAN...
I THINK IT'S JUST A SPRAIN, BUT IT'S SO HARD TO WALK ON IT.
I'm sorry for asking you out of the blue like that.
...THAT'S OKAY.
UM... I DON'T THINK THIS IS THE FASTEST WAY TO THE MEDICAL OFFICE.
WHERE ARE THEY GOING TOGE-THER...?
BUT I'M SO HAPPY TO BE ABLE TO TALK TO YOU LIKE THIS, IMAI-SAN.
WHAT IS IMAI DOING WITH KOIZUMI...?
"DAMN BRAT."
OH, I'M SORRY. UM...

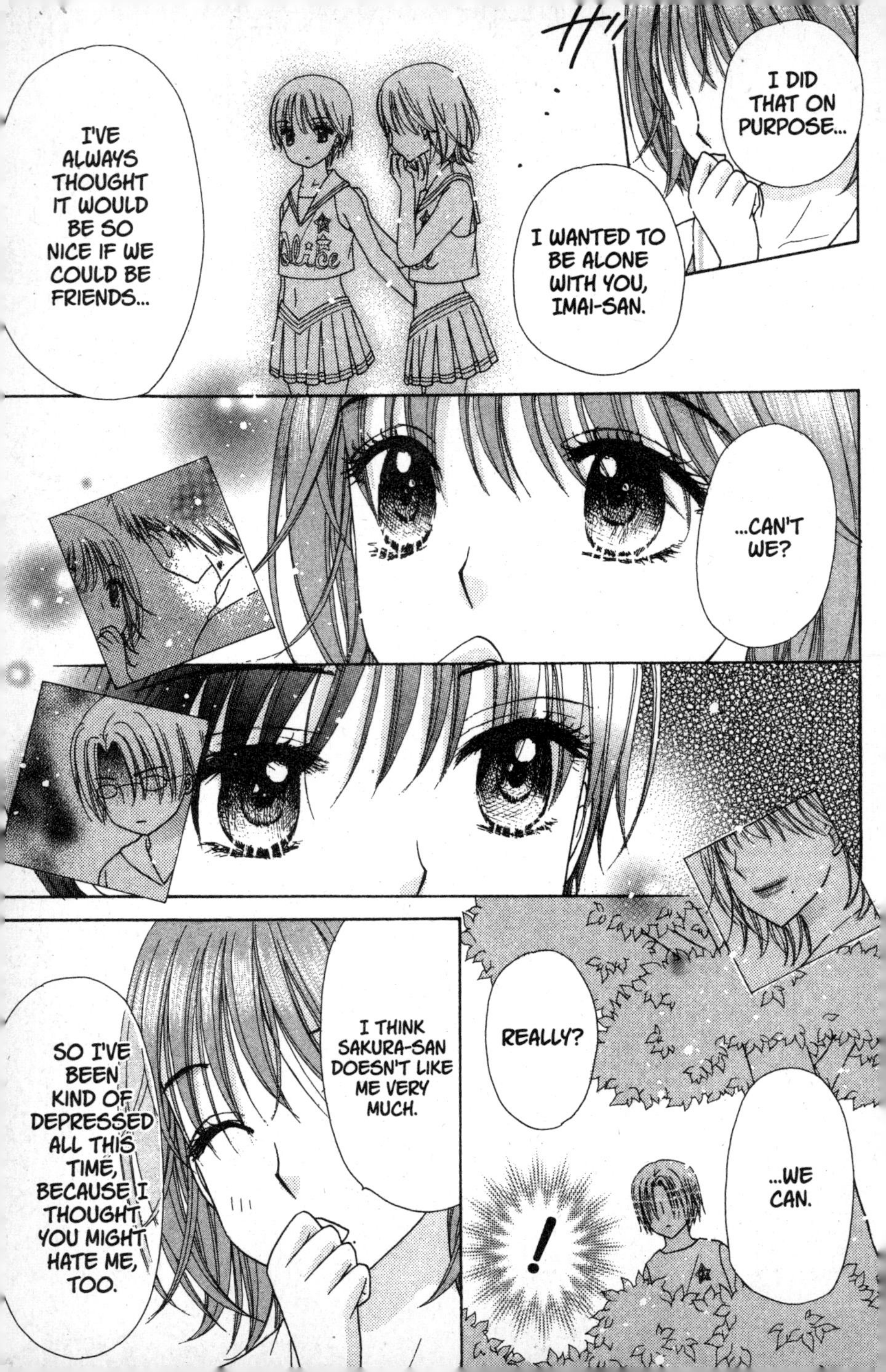

I DID THAT ON PURPOSE...
I WANTED TO BE ALONE WITH YOU, IMAI-SAN.
I'VE ALWAYS THOUGHT IT WOULD BE SO NICE IF WE COULD BE FRIENDS...
...CAN'T WE?
...WE CAN.
!
REALLY?
I THINK SAKURA-SAN DOESN'T LIKE ME VERY MUCH.
SO I'VE BEEN KIND OF DEPRESSED ALL THIS TIME, BECAUSE I THOUGHT YOU MIGHT HATE ME, TOO.

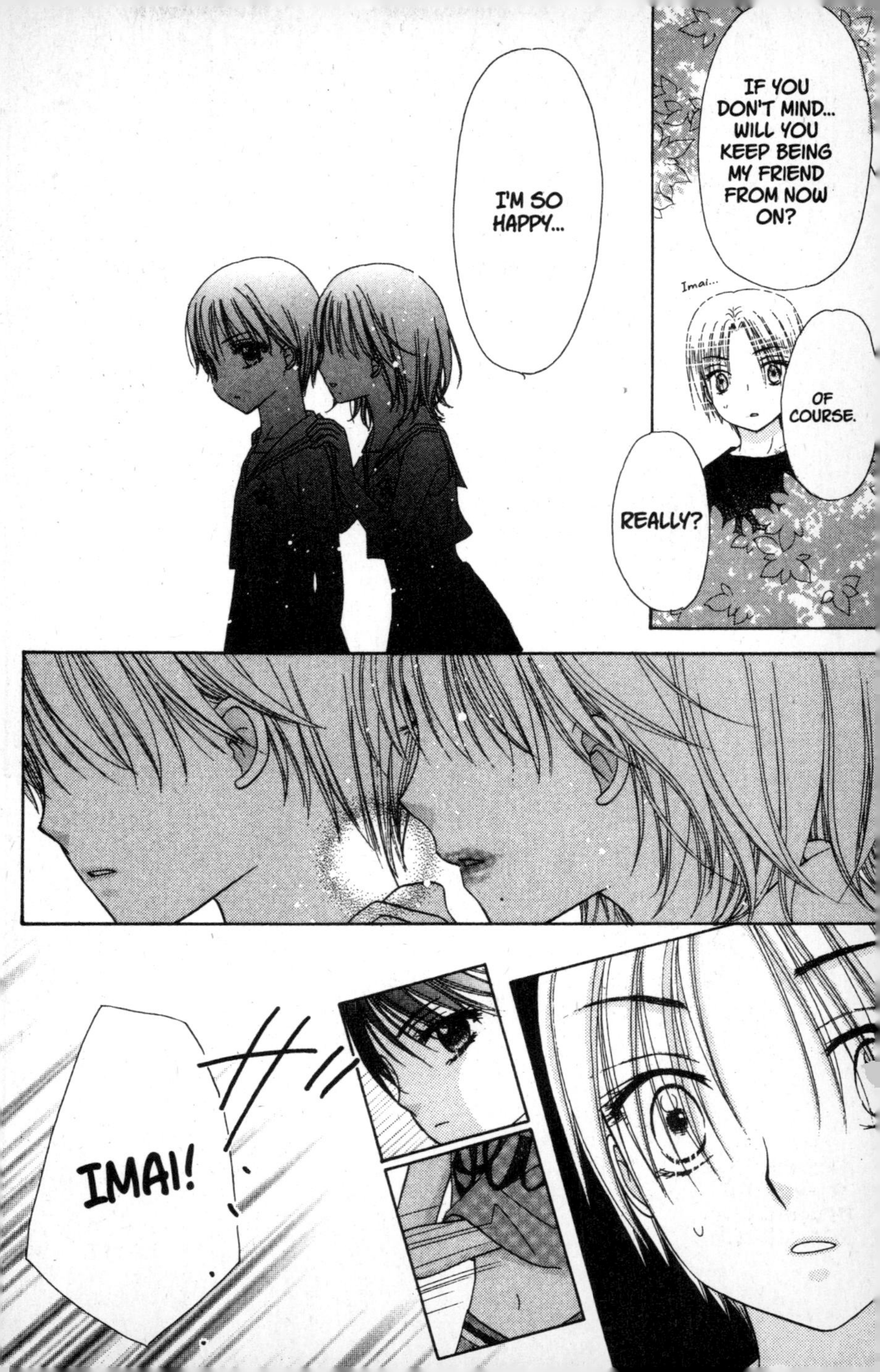
IF YOU DON'T MIND... WILL YOU KEEP BEING MY FRIEND FROM NOW ON?
Imai...
OF COURSE.
REALLY?
I'M SO HAPPY...
IMAI!

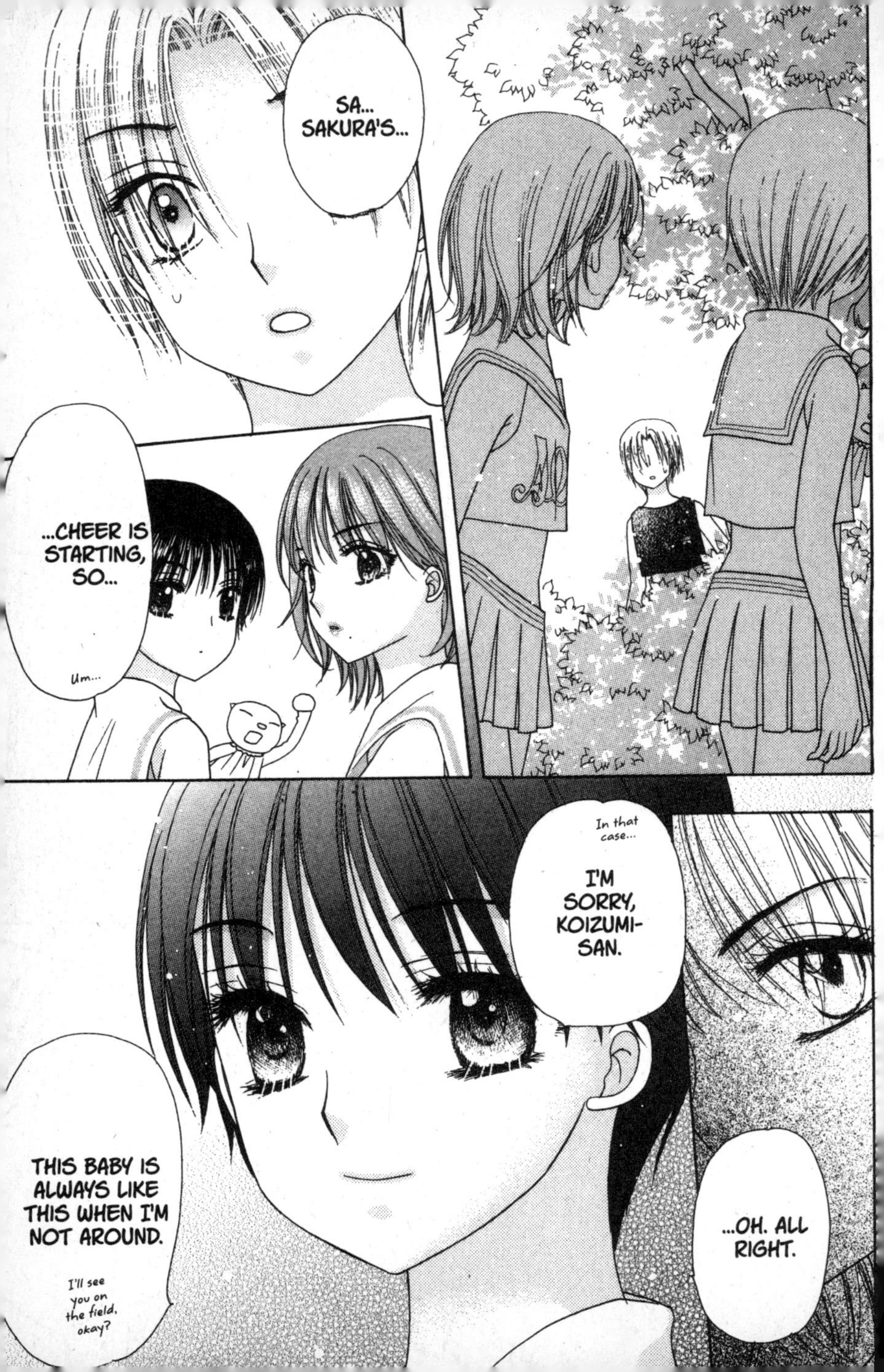
SA... SAKURA'S...
...CHEER IS STARTING, SO...
Um...
In that case...
I'M SORRY, KOIZUMI-SAN.
THIS BABY IS ALWAYS LIKE THIS WHEN I'M NOT AROUND.
I'll see you on the field, okay?
...OH. ALL RIGHT.

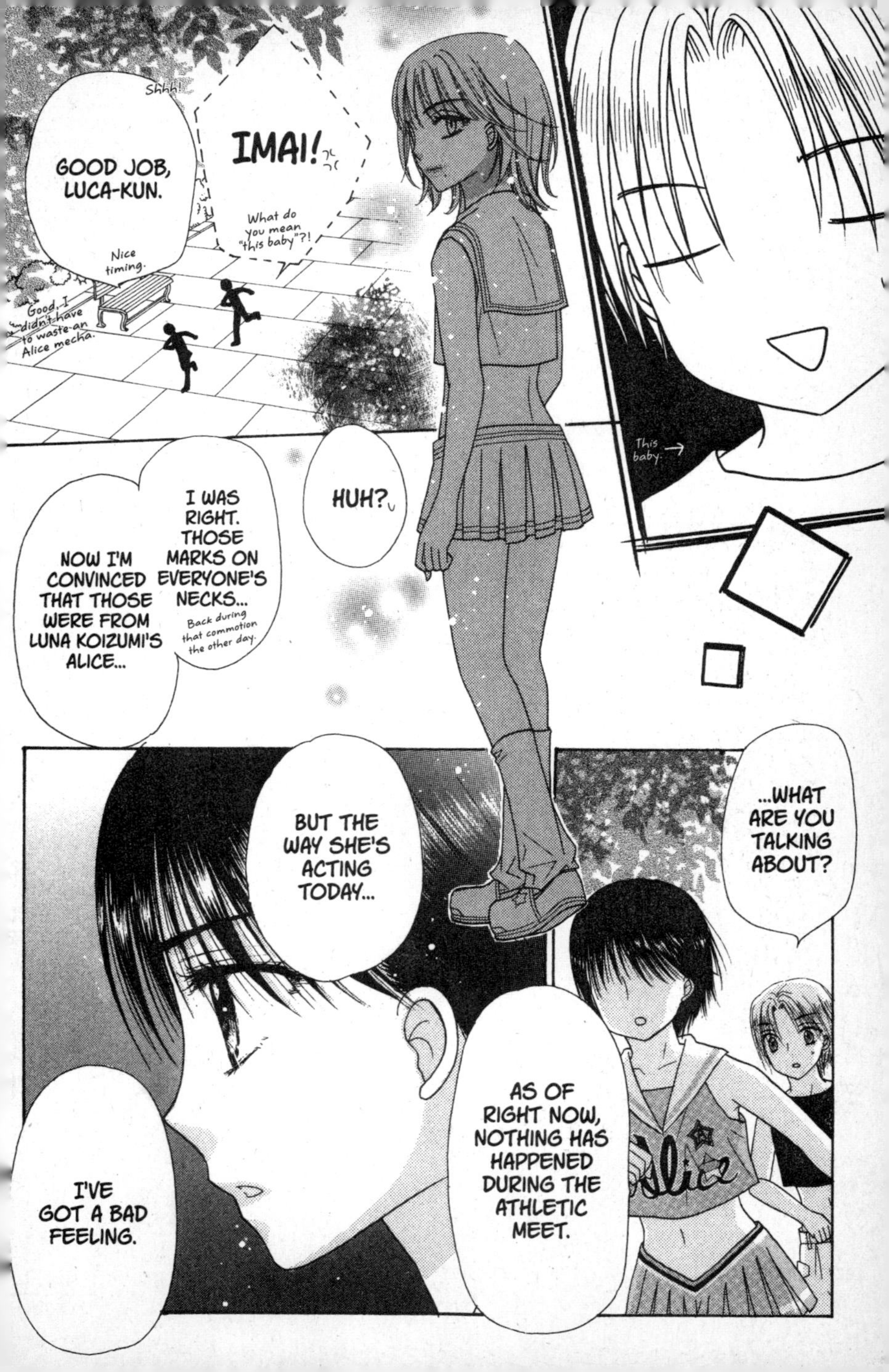
This baby. →
IMAI!
What do you mean "this baby"?!
Shhh!
GOOD JOB, LUCA-KUN.
Nice timing.
Good, I didn't have to waste an Alice mecha.
HUH?
I WAS RIGHT. THOSE MARKS ON EVERYONE'S NECKS...
Back during that commotion the other day.
NOW I'M CONVINCED THAT THOSE WERE FROM LUNA KOIZUMI'S ALICE...
...WHAT ARE YOU TALKING ABOUT?
AS OF RIGHT NOW, NOTHING HAS HAPPENED DURING THE ATHLETIC MEET.
BUT THE WAY SHE'S ACTING TODAY...
I'VE GOT A BAD FEELING.

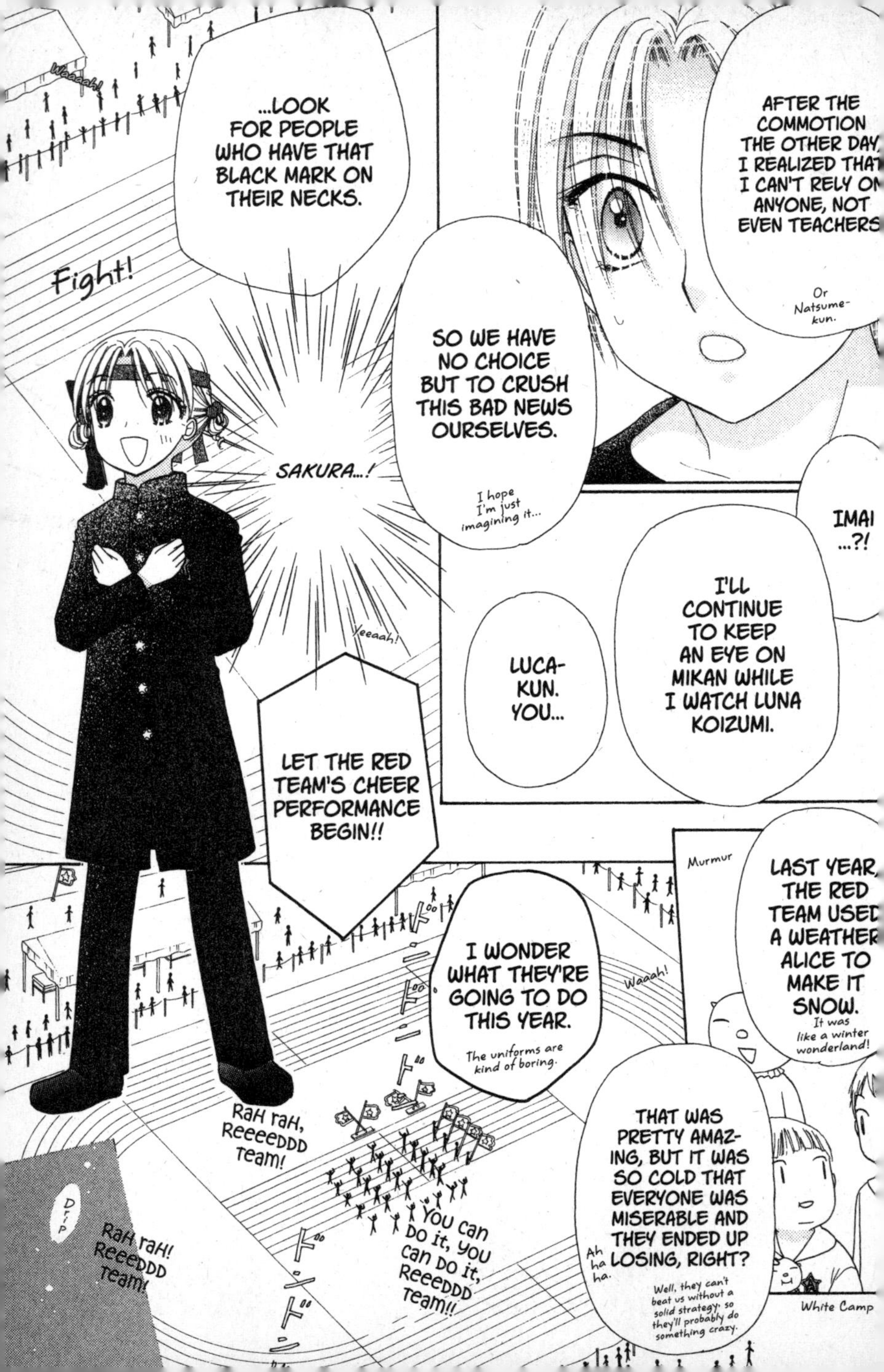
AFTER THE COMMOTION THE OTHER DAY, I REALIZED THAT I CAN'T RELY ON ANYONE, NOT EVEN TEACHERS
Or Natsume-kun.
SO WE HAVE NO CHOICE BUT TO CRUSH THIS BAD NEWS OURSELVES.
I hope I'm just imagining it...
...LOOK FOR PEOPLE WHO HAVE THAT BLACK MARK ON THEIR NECKS.
IMAI ...?!
I'LL CONTINUE TO KEEP AN EYE ON MIKAN WHILE I WATCH LUNA KOIZUMI.
LUCA-KUN. YOU...
Waaaah!
Fight!
SAKURA...!
Yeeaah!
LET THE RED TEAM'S CHEER PERFORMANCE BEGIN!!
Murmur
LAST YEAR, THE RED TEAM USED A WEATHER ALICE TO MAKE IT SNOW.
It was like a winter wonderland!
I WONDER WHAT THEY'RE GOING TO DO THIS YEAR.
The uniforms are kind of boring.
Waaah!
THAT WAS PRETTY AMAZING, BUT IT WAS SO COLD THAT EVERYONE WAS MISERABLE AND THEY ENDED UP LOSING, RIGHT?
Ah ha ha.
Well, they can't beat us without a solid strategy, so they'll probably do something crazy.
White Camp
Rah rah, Reeeeddd team!
You can do it, you can do it, Reeeddd team!!
Drip
Rah rah! Reeeddd team!

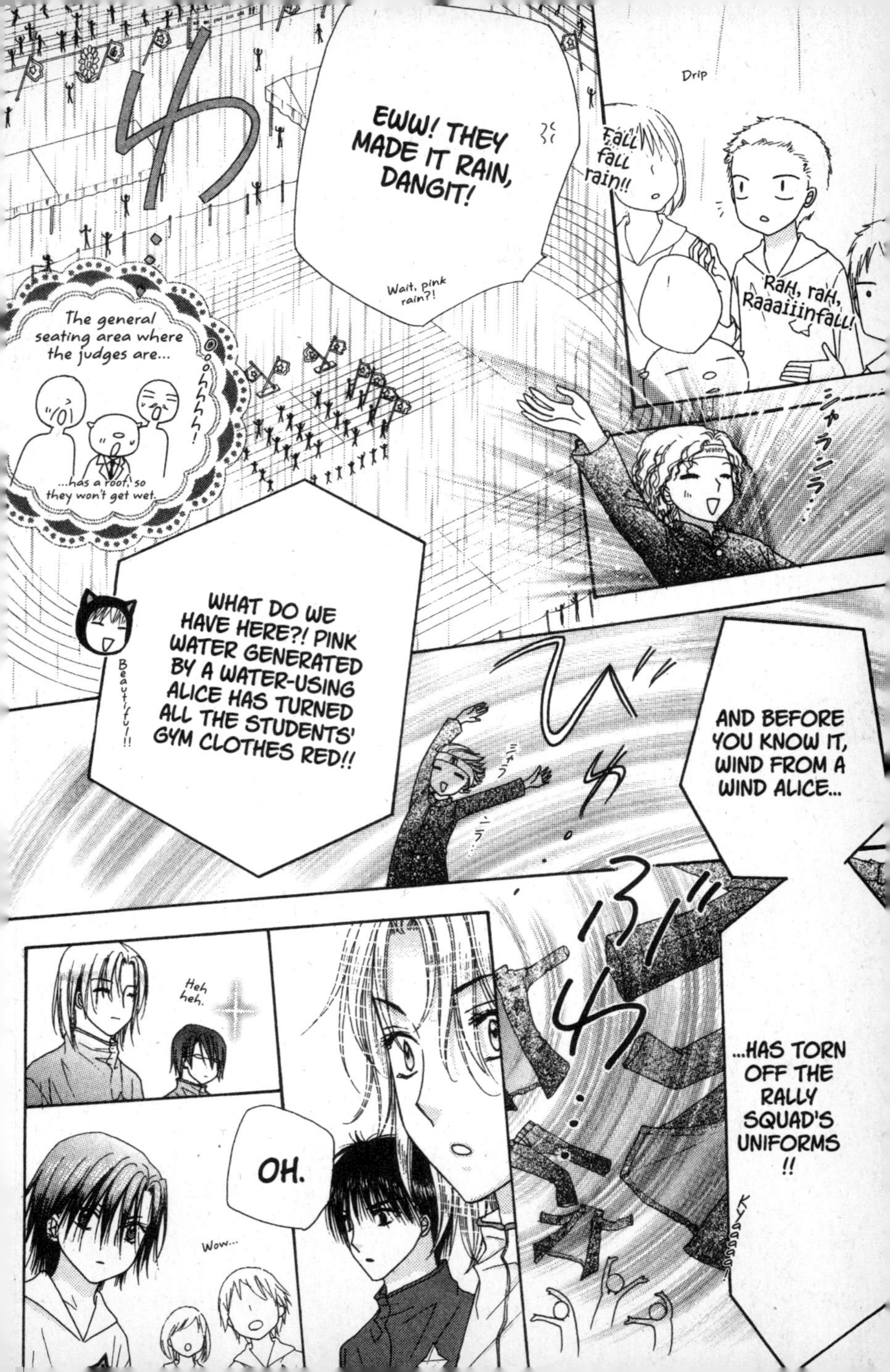

Drip
Fall fall rain!!
Rah, rah, Raaaiiinfall!
EWW! THEY MADE IT RAIN, DANGIT!
Wait, pink rain?!
The general seating area where the judges are...
Oohhhh!
...has a roof, so they won't get wet.
WHAT DO WE HAVE HERE?! PINK WATER GENERATED BY A WATER-USING ALICE HAS TURNED ALL THE STUDENTS' GYM CLOTHES RED!!
Beautiful!!
AND BEFORE YOU KNOW IT, WIND FROM A WIND ALICE...
...HAS TORN OFF THE RALLY SQUAD'S UNIFORMS!!
Kyaaaaa!
Heh heh.
OH.
Wow...

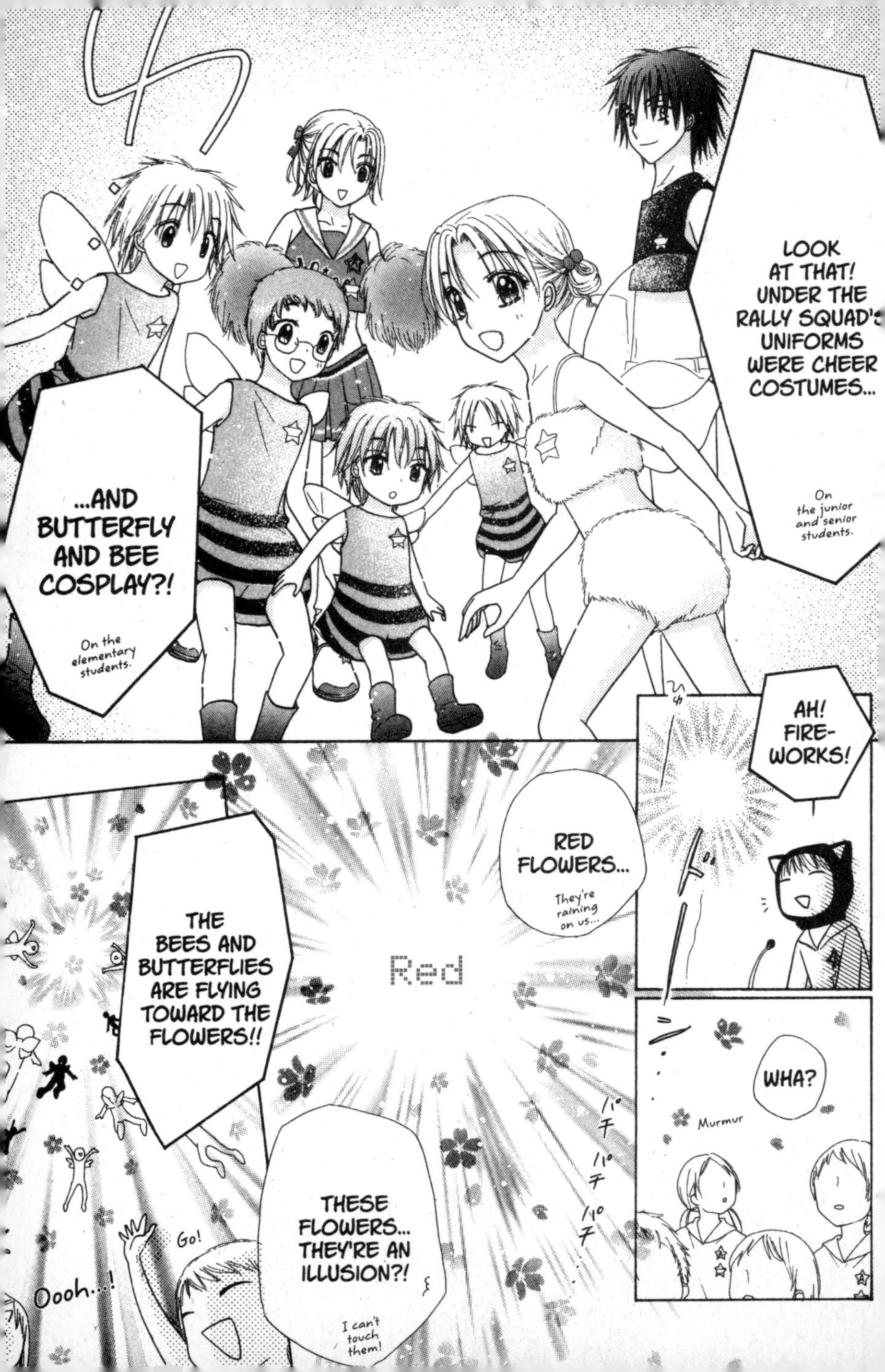
LOOK AT THAT! UNDER THE RALLY SQUAD'S UNIFORMS WERE CHEER COSTUMES...
On the junior and senior students.
...AND BUTTERFLY AND BEE COSPLAY?!
On the elementary students.
AH! FIRE-WORKS!
WHA?
Murmur
RED FLOWERS...
They're raining on us...
Red
THE BEES AND BUTTERFLIES ARE FLYING TOWARD THE FLOWERS!!
THESE FLOWERS... THEY'RE AN ILLUSION?!
I can't touch them!
Go!
Oooh...!

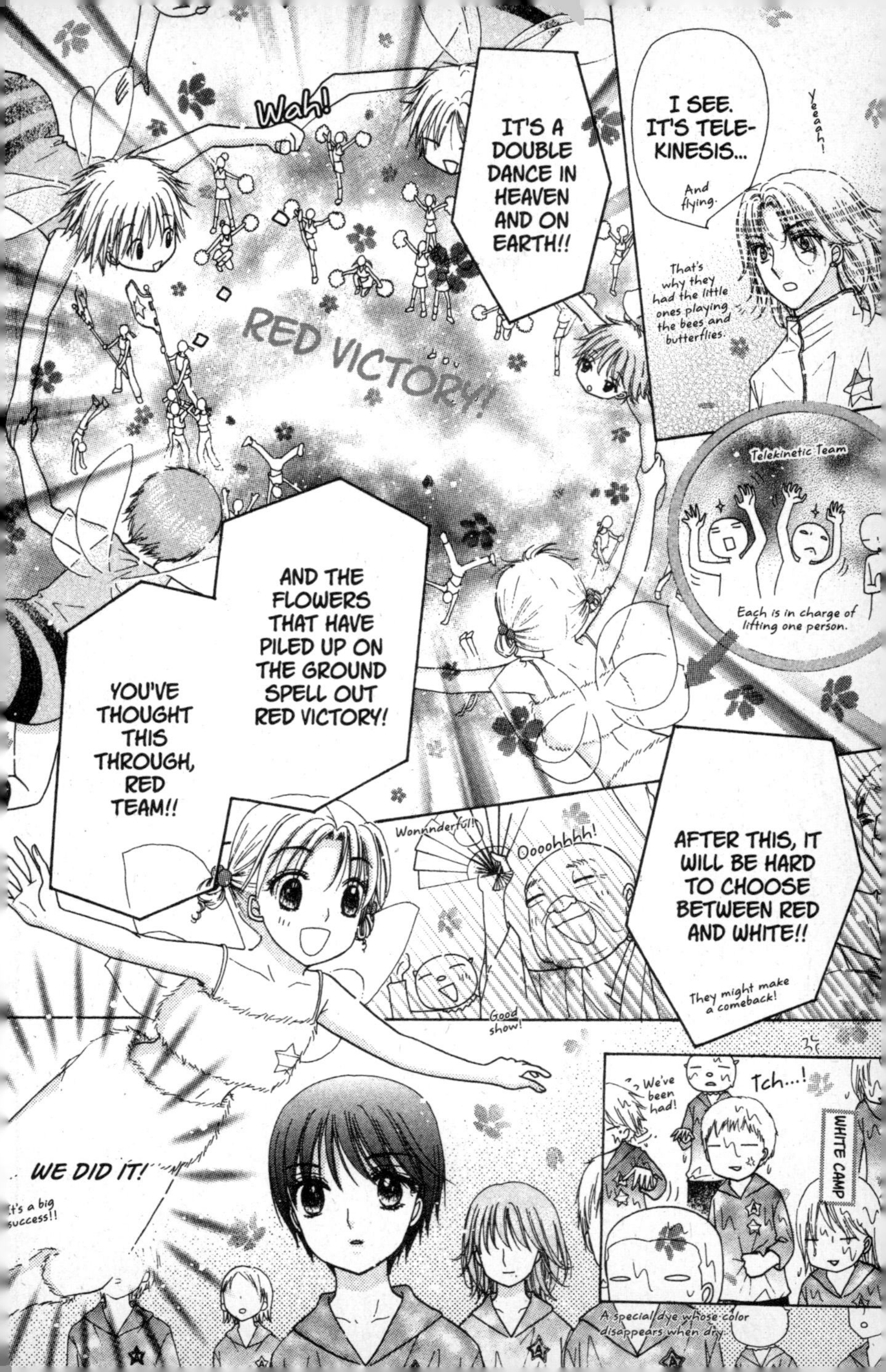
Yeeaah!
I SEE. IT'S TELE-KINESIS...
And flying.
That's why they had the little ones playing the bees and butterflies.
IT'S A DOUBLE DANCE IN HEAVEN AND ON EARTH!!
Wah!
RED VICTORY!
Telekinetic Team
Each is in charge of lifting one person.
AND THE FLOWERS THAT HAVE PILED UP ON THE GROUND SPELL OUT RED VICTORY!
YOU'VE THOUGHT THIS THROUGH, RED TEAM!!
AFTER THIS, IT WILL BE HARD TO CHOOSE BETWEEN RED AND WHITE!!
They might make a comeback!
Oooohhhh!
Wonnnderful!!
Good show!
Tch...!
We've been had!
WHITE CAMP
...WE DID IT!
It's a big success!!
A special dye whose color disappears when dry.

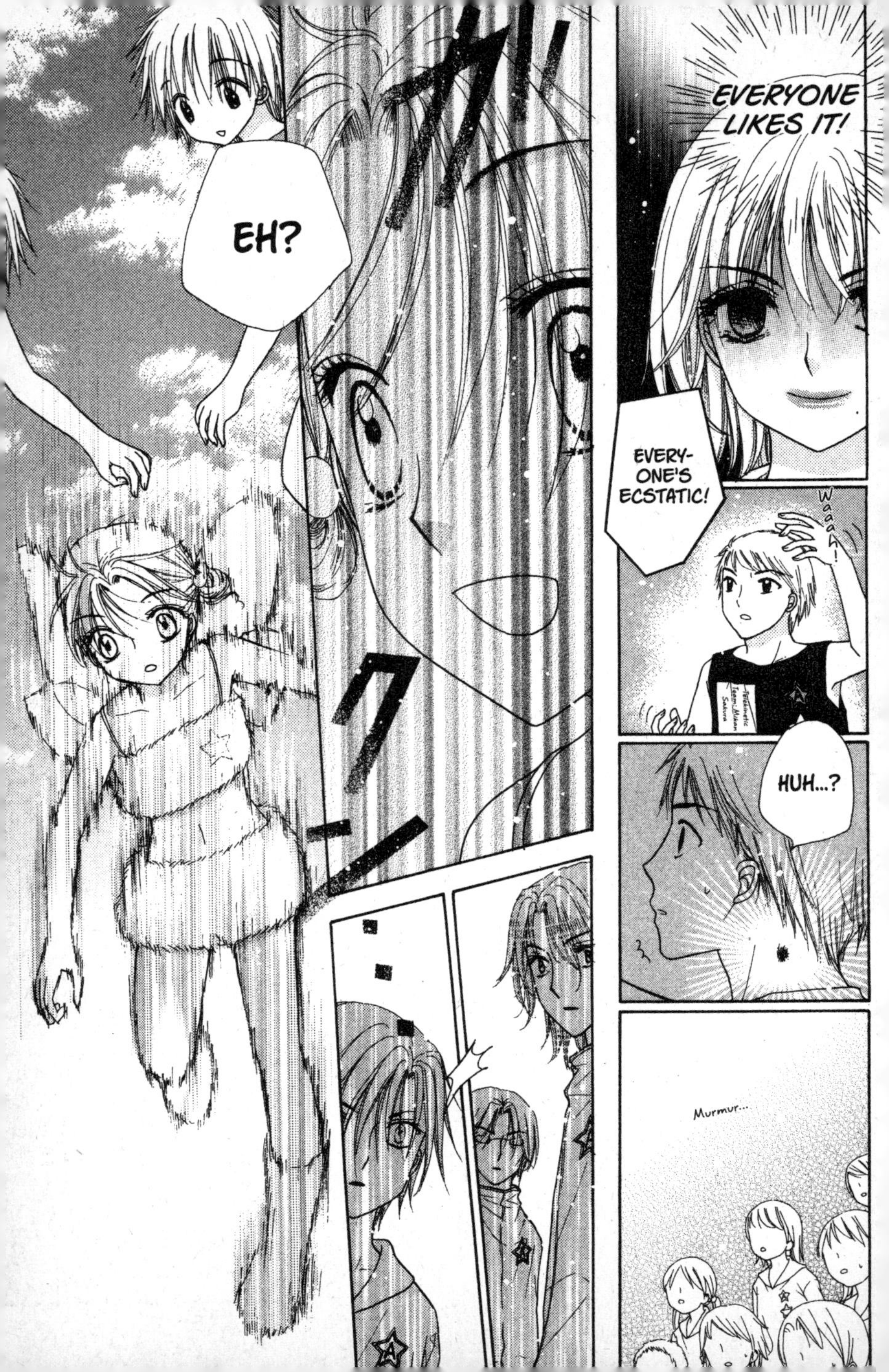
EVERYONE LIKES IT!
EVERY-ONE'S ECSTATIC!
Waaah!
HUH...?
Murmur...
EH?

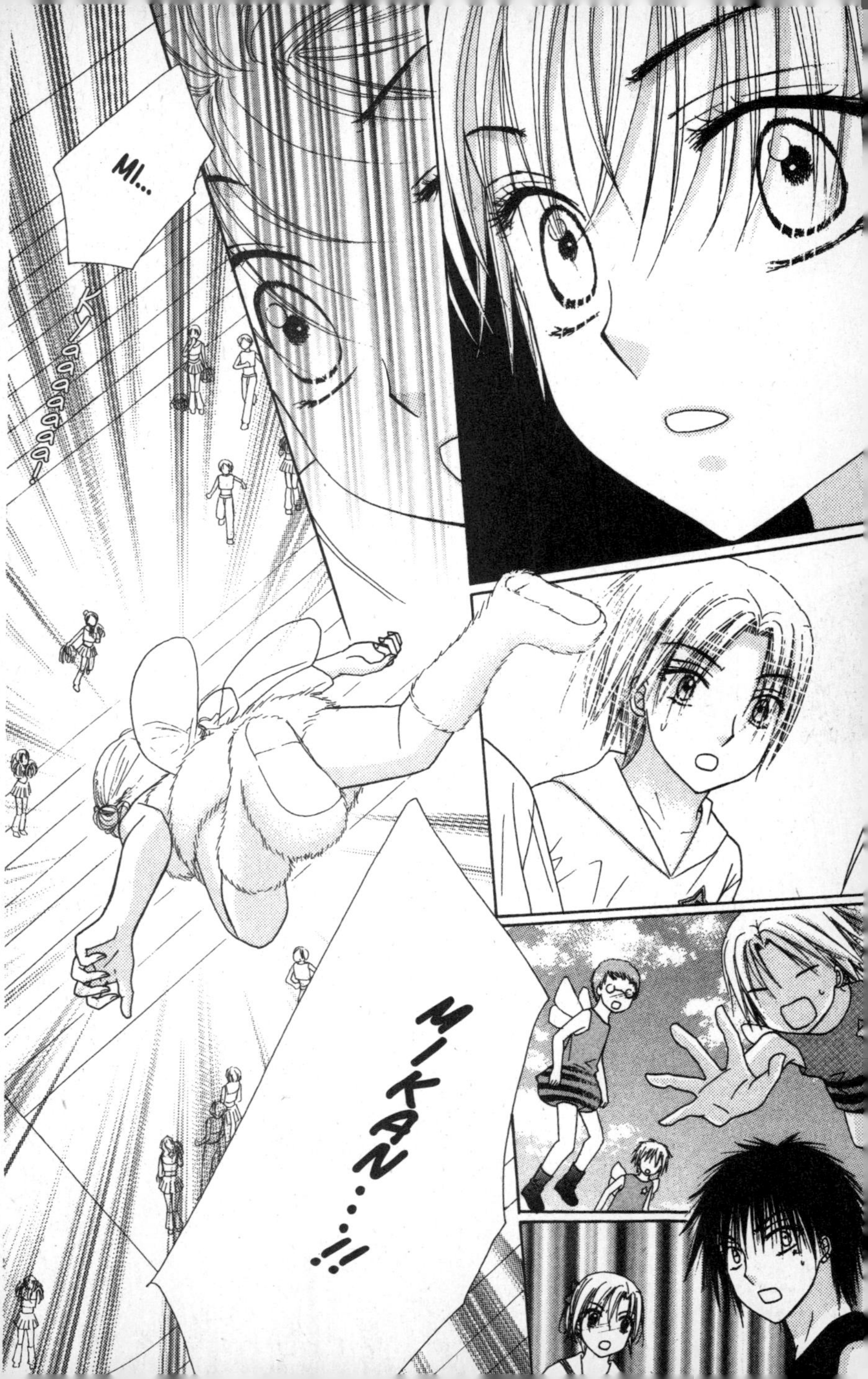

MI...
KYAAAAAAAAAAA!
MIKAN...!!!

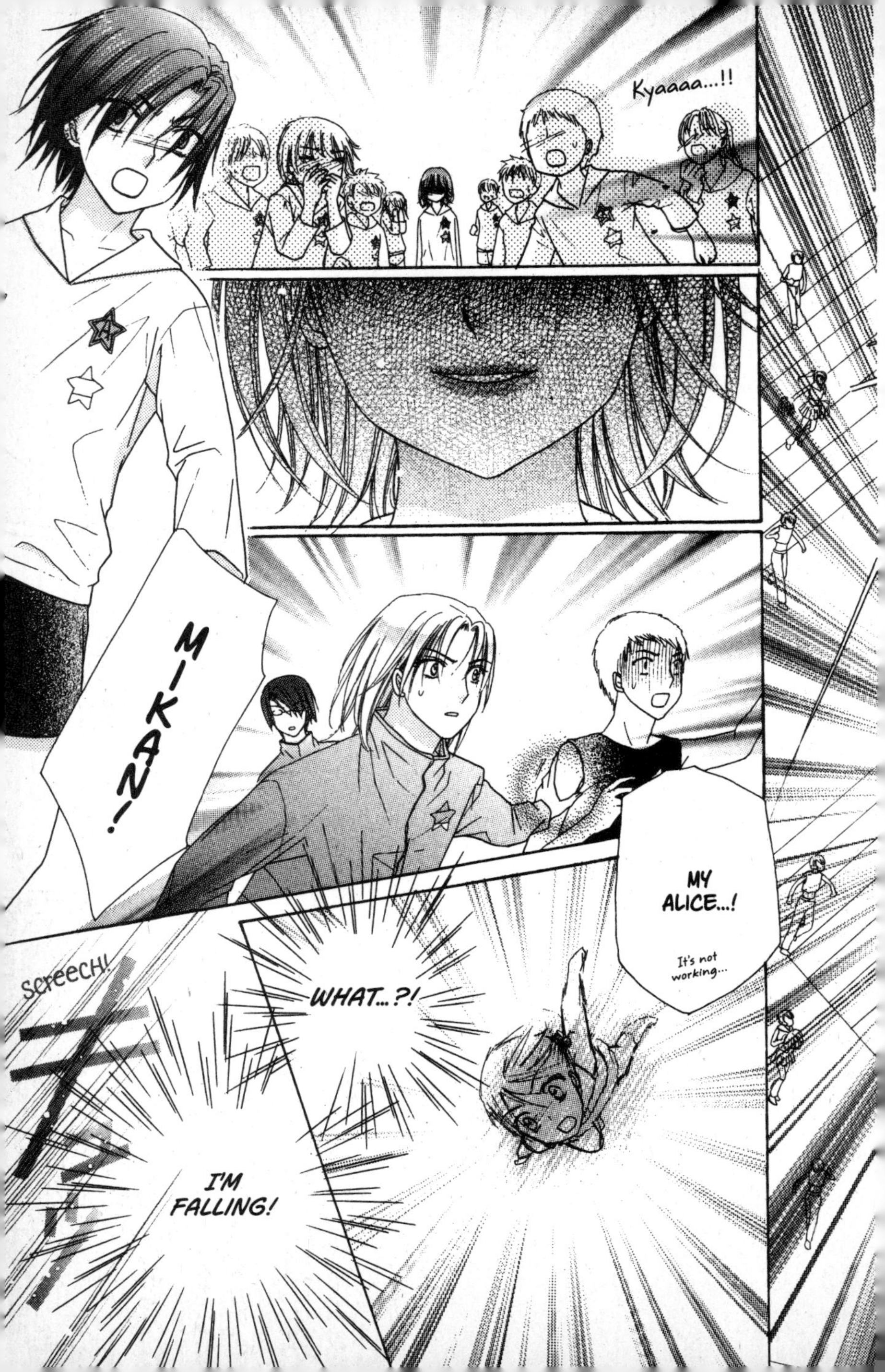
Kyaaaa...!!
MY ALICE...!
It's not working...
MIKAN!
WHAT...?!
I'M FALLING!
SCREECH!

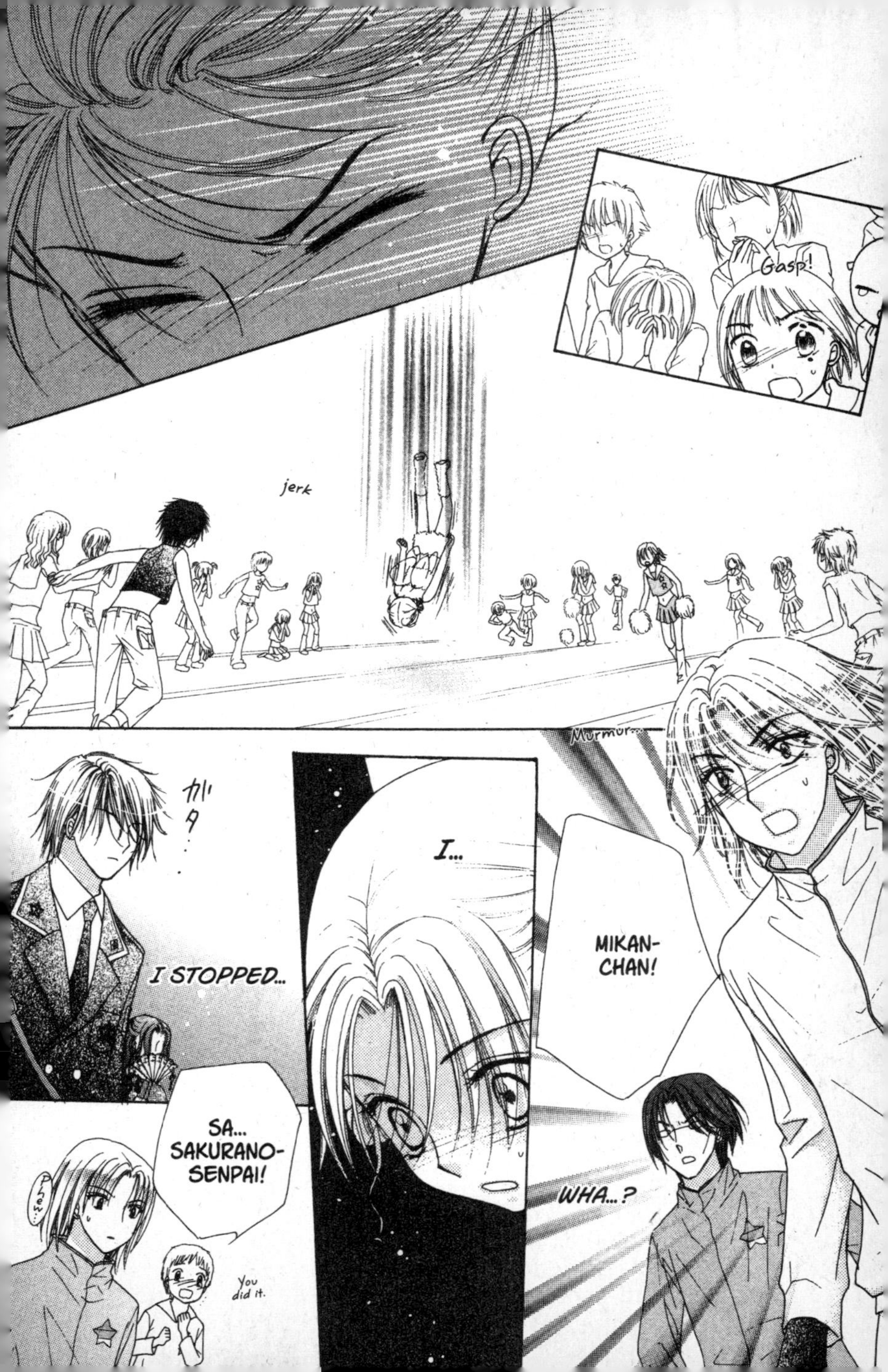
Gasp!
jerk
Murmur...
MIKAN-CHAN!
WHA...?
I...
ガタ...
I STOPPED...
SA... SAKURANO-SENPAI!
Phew...
You did it.

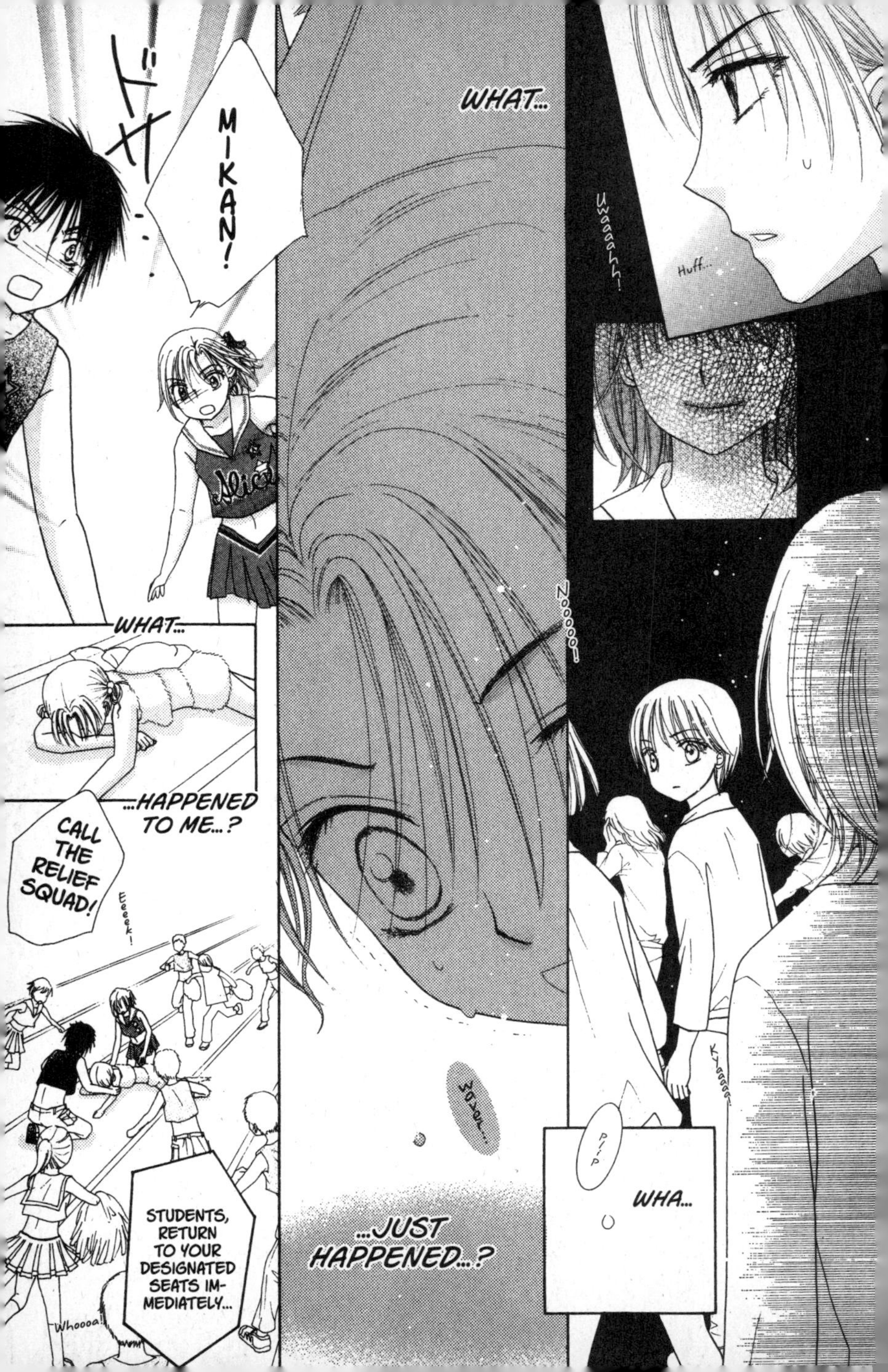

Uwaaaahh!
Huff...
Noooooo!
Kyaaaa...
WHA...
WHAT...
...JUST HAPPENED...?
ドサ
MIKAN!
WHAT...
...HAPPENED TO ME...?
CALL THE RELIEF SQUAD!
Eeeek!
STUDENTS, RETURN TO YOUR DESIGNATED SEATS IM- MEDIATELY...
Whoooa!

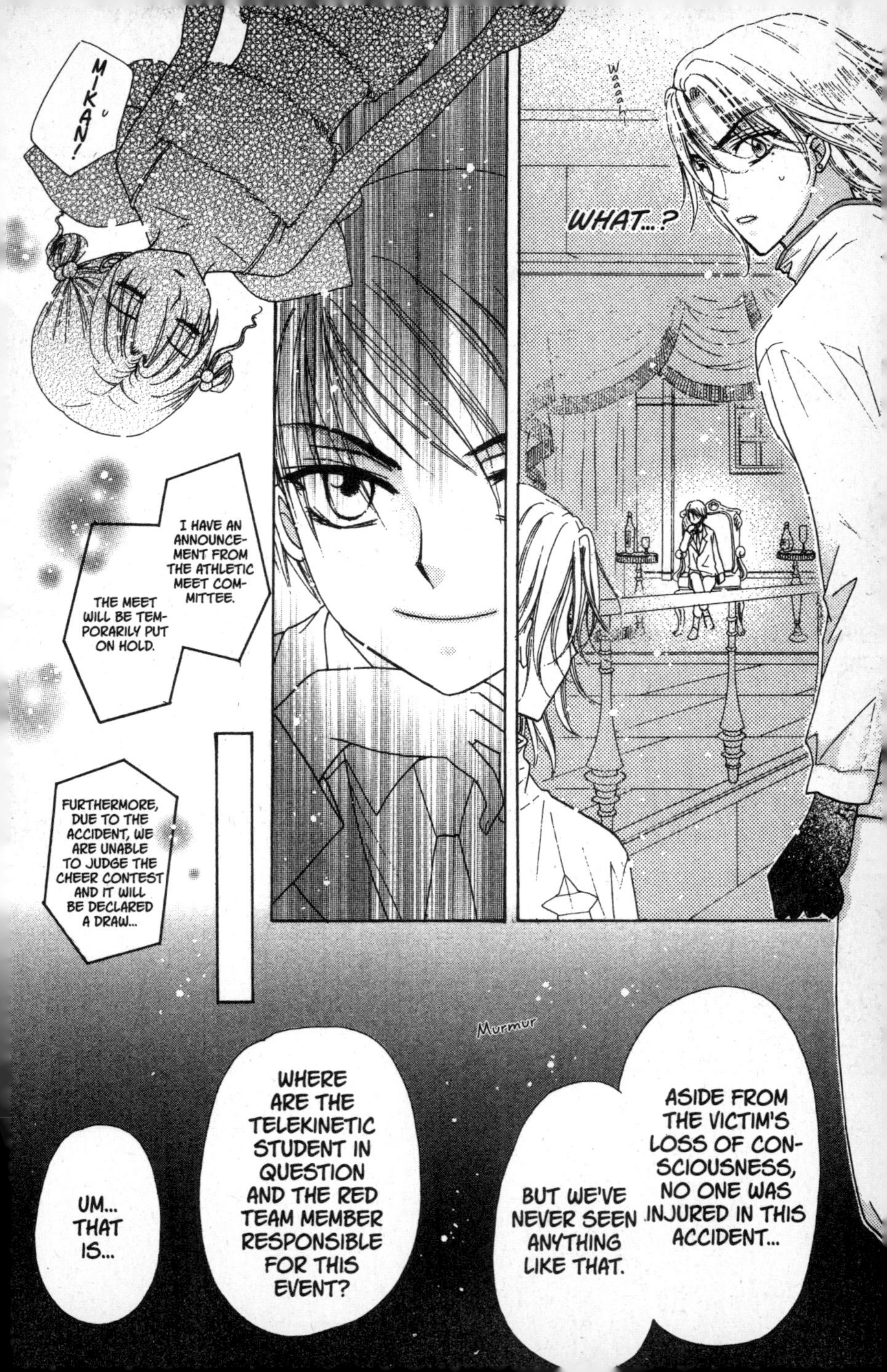

Waaaah
WHAT...?
MIKAN!
I HAVE AN ANNOUNCEMENT FROM THE ATHLETIC MEET COMMITTEE.
THE MEET WILL BE TEMPORARILY PUT ON HOLD.
FURTHERMORE, DUE TO THE ACCIDENT, WE ARE UNABLE TO JUDGE THE CHEER CONTEST AND IT WILL BE DECLARED A DRAW...
ASIDE FROM THE VICTIM'S LOSS OF CONSCIOUSNESS, NO ONE WAS INJURED IN THIS ACCIDENT...
BUT WE'VE NEVER SEEN ANYTHING LIKE THAT.
Murmur
WHERE ARE THE TELEKINETIC STUDENT IN QUESTION AND THE RED TEAM MEMBER RESPONSIBLE FOR THIS EVENT?
UM... THAT IS...

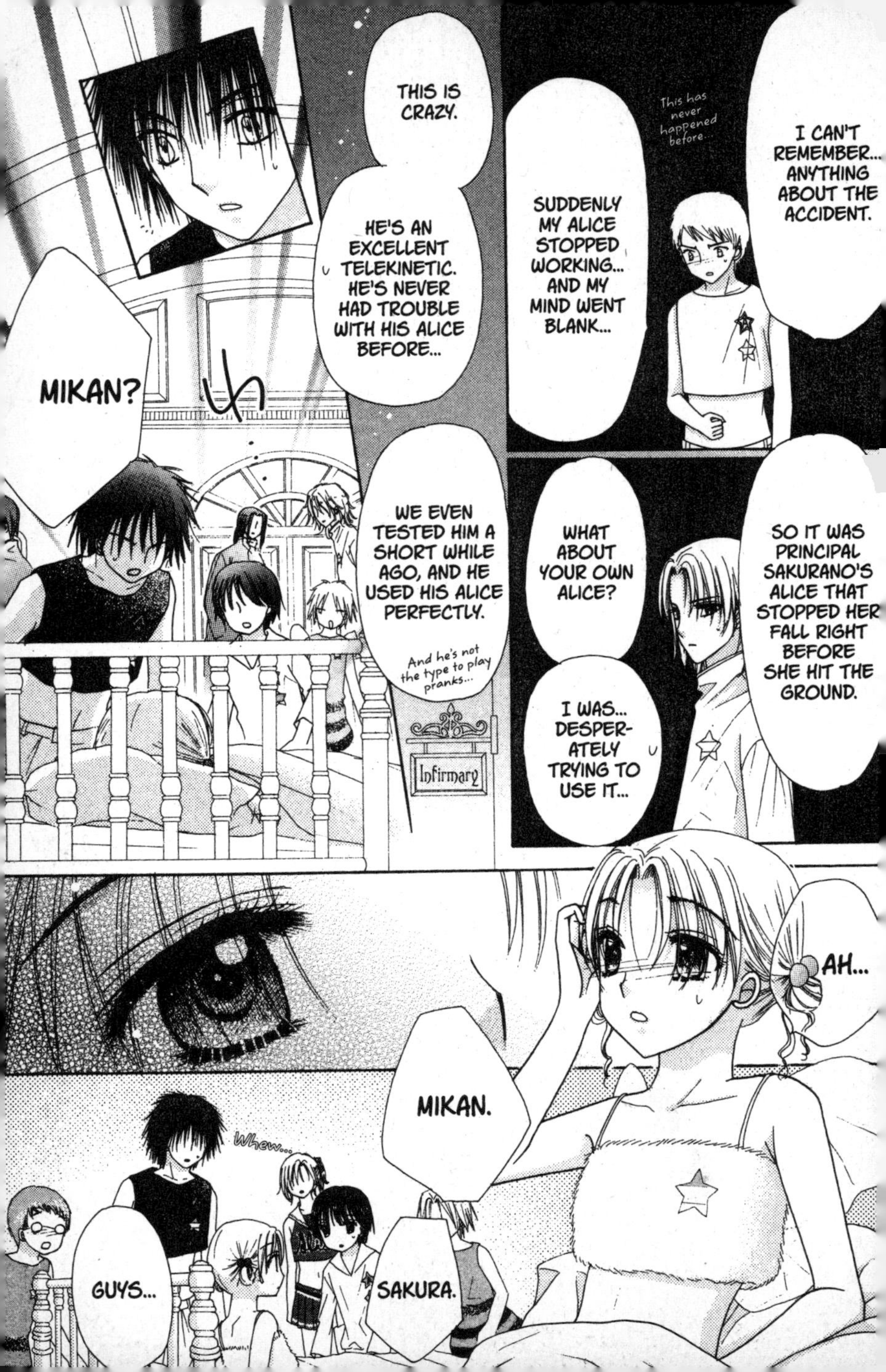
I CAN'T REMEMBER... ANYTHING ABOUT THE ACCIDENT.
This has never happened before...
SUDDENLY MY ALICE STOPPED WORKING... AND MY MIND WENT BLANK...
SO IT WAS PRINCIPAL SAKURANO'S ALICE THAT STOPPED HER FALL RIGHT BEFORE SHE HIT THE GROUND.
WHAT ABOUT YOUR OWN ALICE?
I WAS... DESPER-ATELY TRYING TO USE IT...
THIS IS CRAZY.
HE'S AN EXCELLENT TELEKINETIC. HE'S NEVER HAD TROUBLE WITH HIS ALICE BEFORE...
WE EVEN TESTED HIM A SHORT WHILE AGO, AND HE USED HIS ALICE PERFECTLY.
And he's not the type to play pranks...
MIKAN?
Infirmary
AH...
MIKAN.
Whew...
SAKURA.
GUYS...

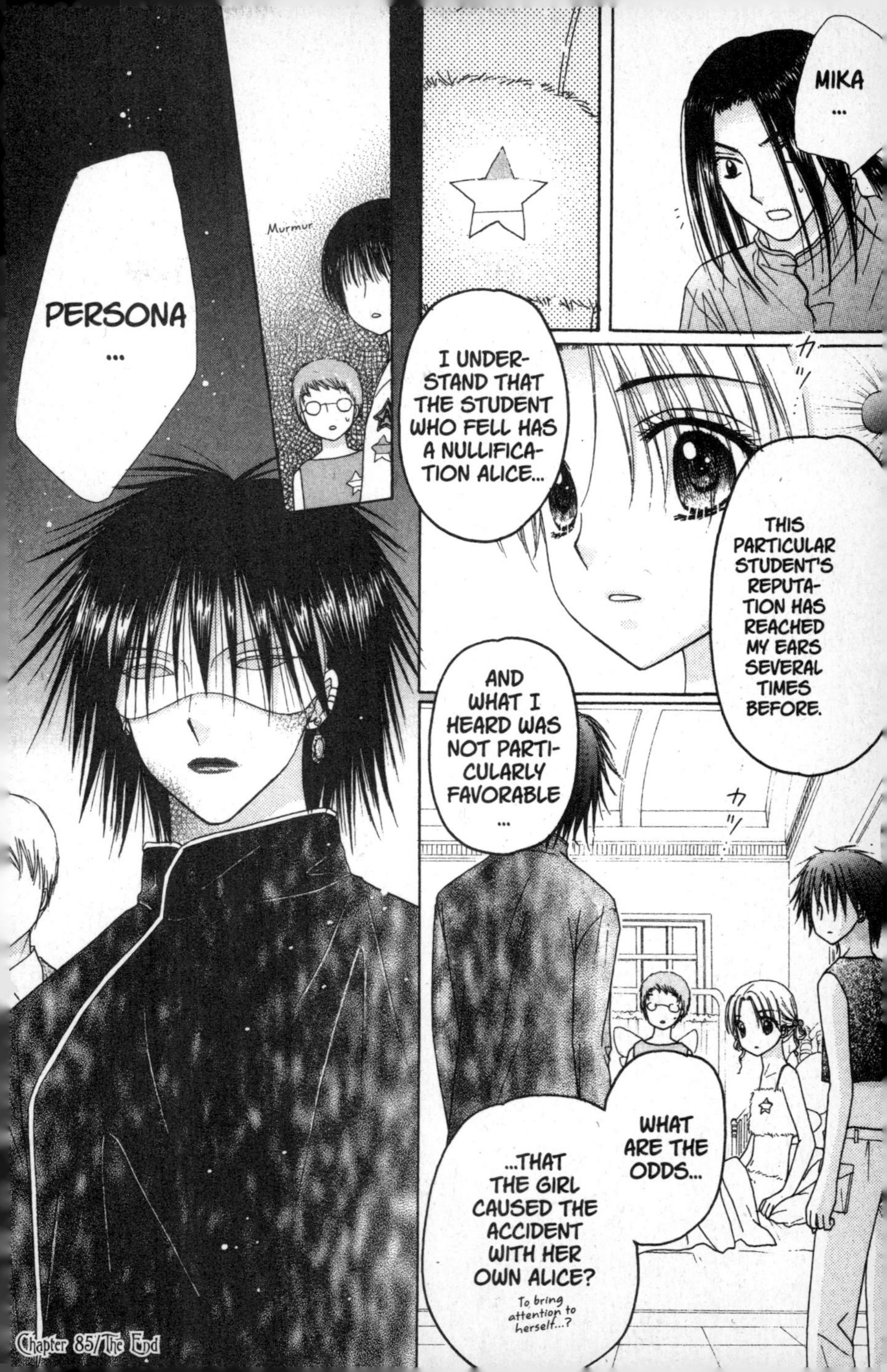
MIKA ...
I UNDERSTAND THAT THE STUDENT WHO FELL HAS A NULLIFICATION ALICE...
カツ
THIS PARTICULAR STUDENT'S REPUTATION HAS REACHED MY EARS SEVERAL TIMES BEFORE.
AND WHAT I HEARD WAS NOT PARTICULARLY FAVORABLE ...
カツ
WHAT ARE THE ODDS...
...THAT THE GIRL CAUSED THE ACCIDENT WITH HER OWN ALICE?
To bring attention to herself...?
Murmur
PERSONA ...
Chapter 85/The End

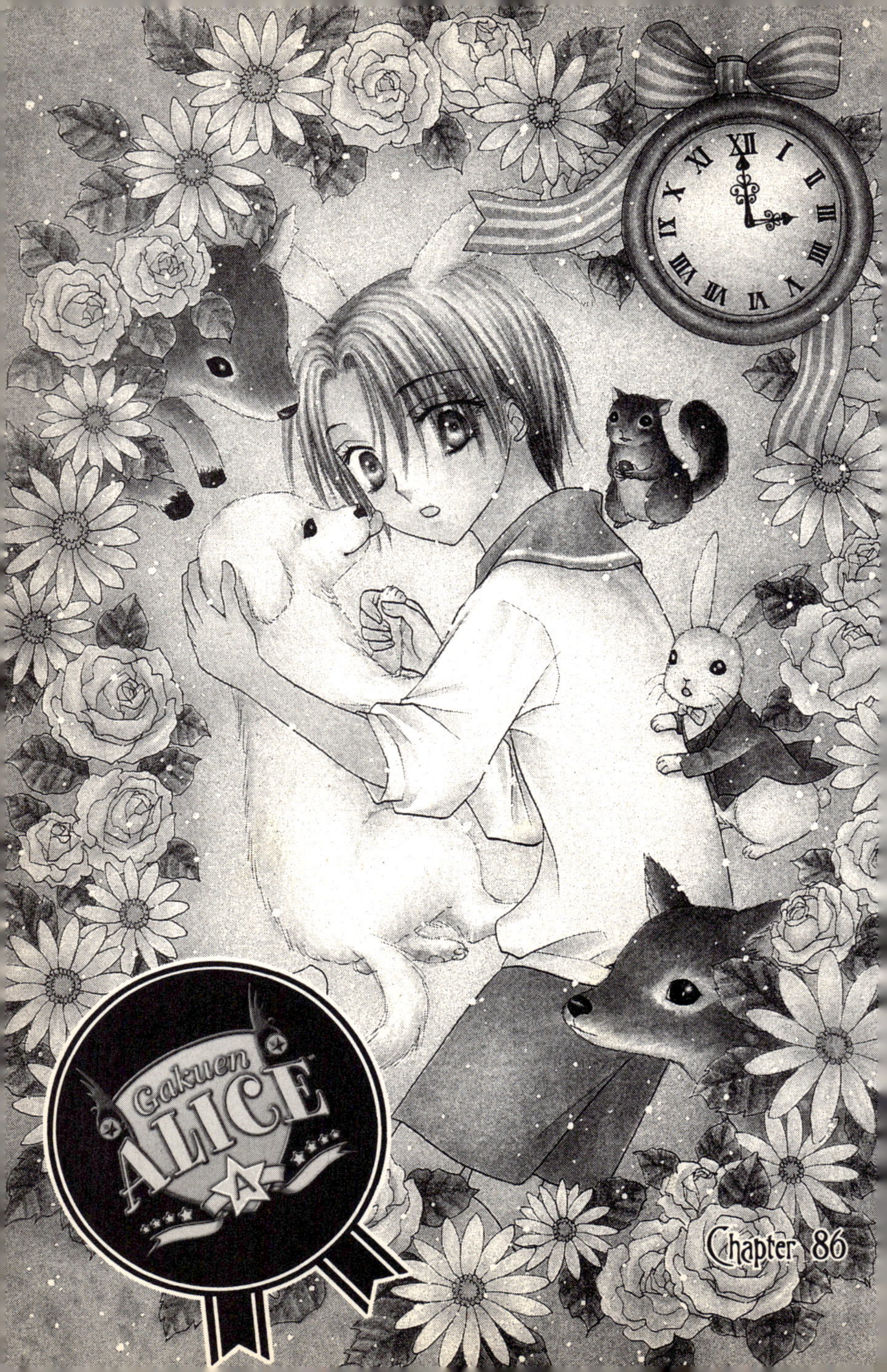
Gakuen ALICE
A
Chapter 86

Psychology Test Time (11)

Curly-san's Test

What is with this corner! Nothing could be more annoying.

Ugh!

	♡		❀	
	Natsume-kun ♡	You	Luca-kun ❀	Narumi-sensei ✦
	Mindreader, Foxeye	My family	Sakura-san?	Imai-san

...AND THERE YOU HAVE IT!

WELL, IT SEEMS LIKE IT'S GONNA BE BORING.

Nooooobody caaares...

About Curly's answers!

What?!

FOR ALL THE FUSS YOU WERE MAKING EARLIER, YOU'RE ALL ACTING RATHER INDIFFERENT, EVERYONE.

How sad and lonely!

Who you want to raise.	You	Who you want to kick around.	Who you want to be raised by.
(Who you want to serve.) Who you want to be kicked around by.	Who you want as a partner.	Who you want as a friend.	Your rival.

I MEAN, LOOK.

YOU TWO! SPEAKING OF ATTENTION, YOU BETTER WATCH YOUR BACK...!!

Check it!

It's so sad when people don't get any attention!

THE ONE THING WE DIDN'T EXPECT IS WHO SHE WANTS TO BE KICKED AROUND BY: MINDREADER AND FOXEYE...

WELL, IF SHE WANTS IT THAT BAD, WE'LL JUST HAVE TO GIVE HER WHAT SHE WANTS AND KICK HER AROUND.

Haaaa ha ha...

Rival, huh?

MISAKI-SENSEI HAD PREDICTABLE ANSWERS, TOO, BUT EVEN HE WAS MORE INTERESTING.

IT MIGHT BE A LITTLE BIT OF A SURPRISE THAT SHE WANTS MIKAN-CHAN FOR A FRIEND AND HOTARU-CHAN FOR A RIVAL.

IT'S LIKE, TOTALLY PREDICTABLE. THERE'S NOTHING NEW ABOUT IT.

So unoriginal.

PERSON SHE WANTS TO RAISE: NATSUME-KUN. PERSON SHE WANTS TO KICK AROUND: LUCA-KUN.

Then she wants to be raised by Naru and her partner is her family.

It's like her degree of freshness is zero.

NAH, THAT'S NOT A SURPRISE, EITHER. WE'RE SO BORED WITH HER!

Bwaah ha ha!

Orange

Mikan

Whatever happens is not my fault...   I kind of wonder what happened with them, so we'll go with Mindreader-kun next.

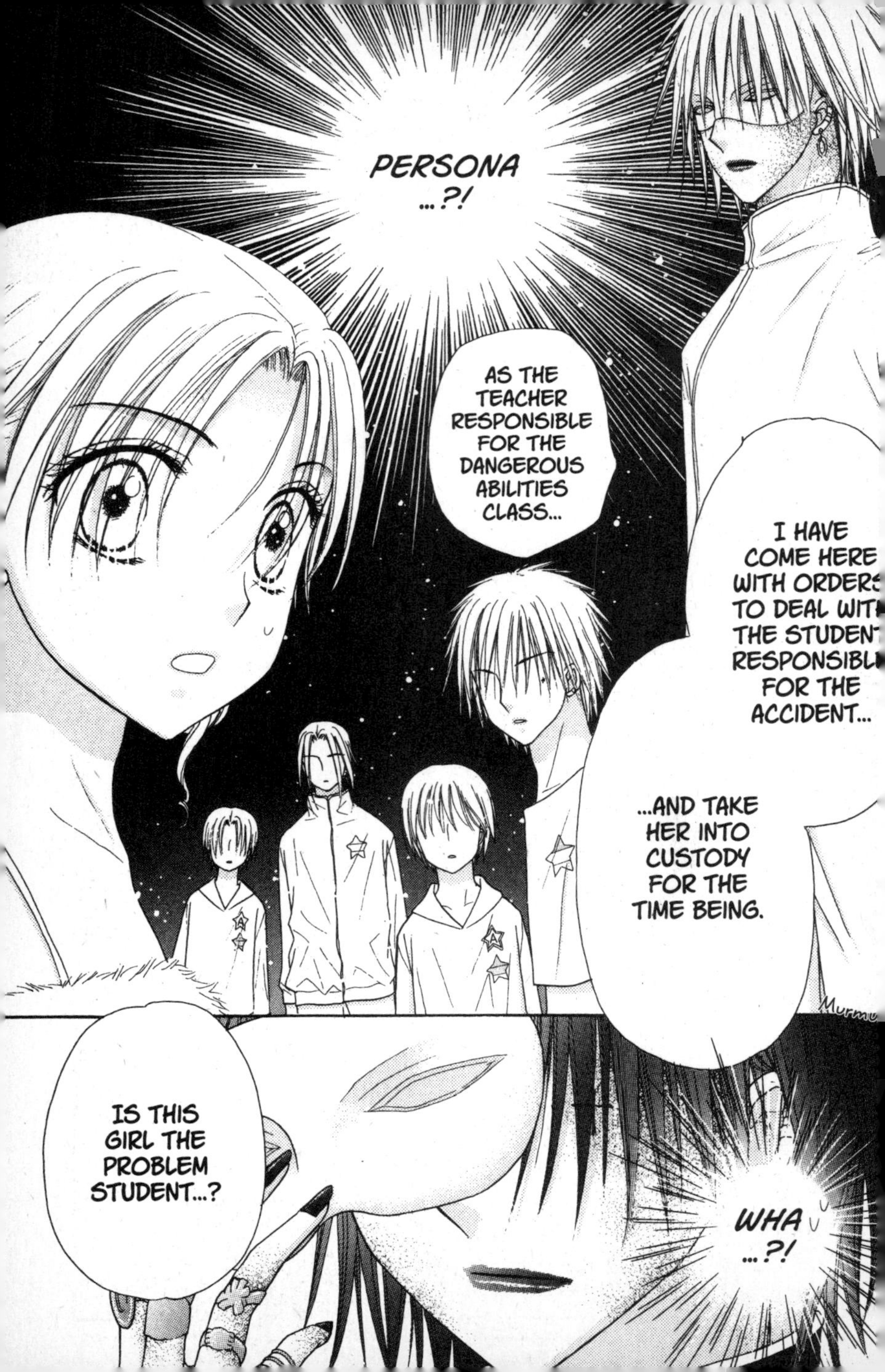
PERSONA ...?!
AS THE TEACHER RESPONSIBLE FOR THE DANGEROUS ABILITIES CLASS...
I HAVE COME HERE WITH ORDERS TO DEAL WITH THE STUDENT RESPONSIBLE FOR THE ACCIDENT...
...AND TAKE HER INTO CUSTODY FOR THE TIME BEING.
IS THIS GIRL THE PROBLEM STUDENT...?
WHA ...?!

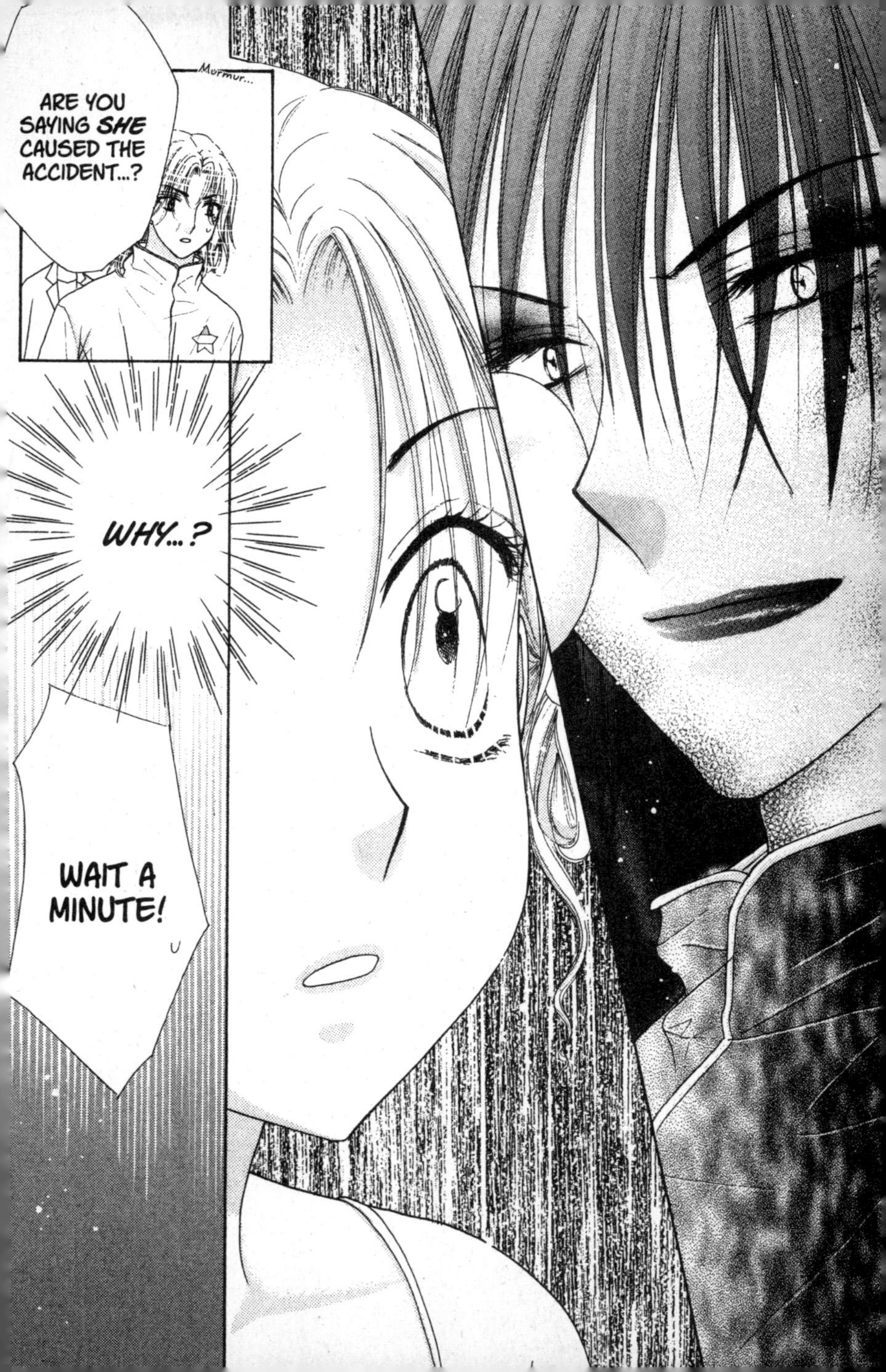
Murmur...
ARE YOU SAYING SHE CAUSED THE ACCIDENT...?
WHY...?
WAIT A MINUTE!

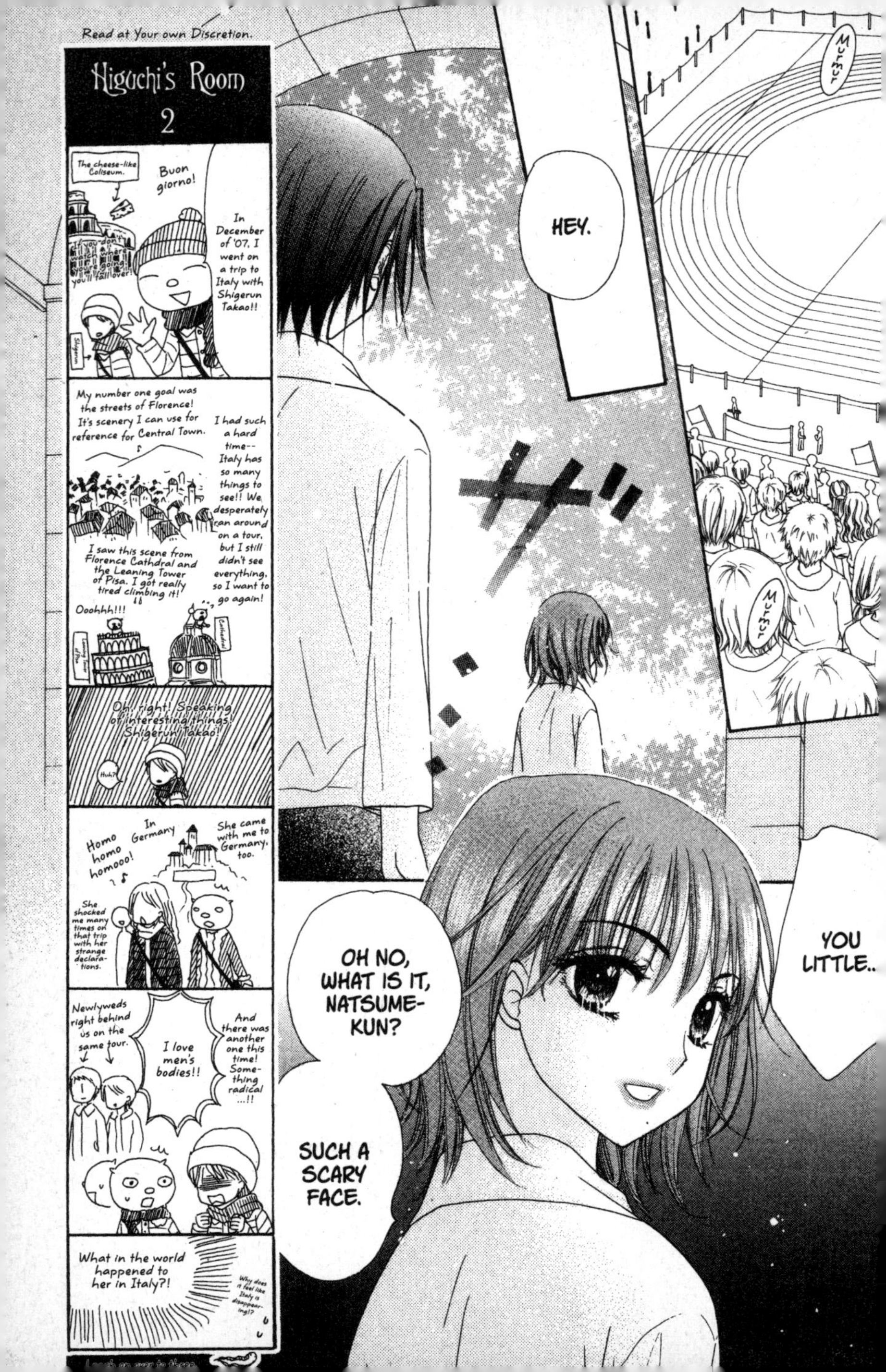
Read at Your own Discretion.
Higuchi's Room 2
The cheese-like Coliseum.
Buon giorno!
In December of '07, I went on a trip to Italy with Shigerun Takao!!
If you don't watch where you're going, you'll fall over!
Shigerun
My number one goal was the streets of Florence! It's scenery I can use for reference for Central Town.
I had such a hard time-- Italy has so many things to see!! We desperately ran around on a tour, but I still didn't see everything, so I want to go again!
I saw this scene from Florence Cathdral and the Leaning Tower of Pisa. I got really tired climbing it!
Ooohhh!!!
Leaning Tower of Pisa
Cathedral
Oh, right! Speaking of interesting things! Shigerun Takao!
Huh?
Homo homo homooo!
In Germany
She came with me to Germany, too.
She shocked me many times on that trip with her strange declarations.
Newlyweds right behind us on the same tour.
I love men's bodies!!
And there was another one this time! Something radical ...!!
What in the world happened to her in Italy?!
Why does it feel like Italy is disappearing!?
Murmur
HEY.
Murmur
YOU LITTLE..
OH NO, WHAT IS IT, NATSUME-KUN?
SUCH A SCARY FACE.

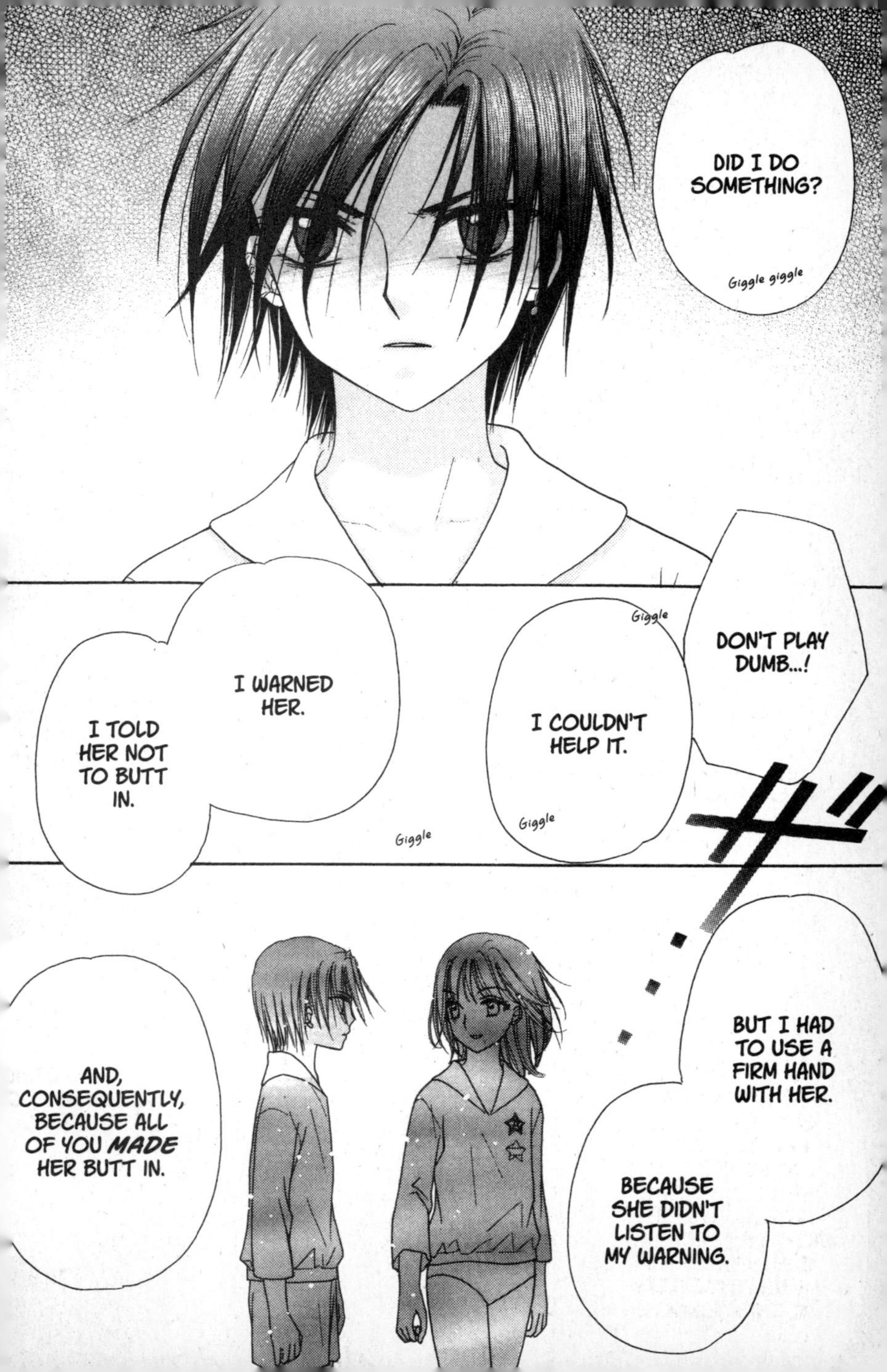
DID I DO SOMETHING?
Giggle giggle
DON'T PLAY DUMB...!
Giggle
I COULDN'T HELP IT.
Giggle
I WARNED HER.
I TOLD HER NOT TO BUTT IN.
Giggle
ザッ
BUT I HAD TO USE A FIRM HAND WITH HER.
BECAUSE SHE DIDN'T LISTEN TO MY WARNING.
AND, CONSEQUENTLY, BECAUSE ALL OF YOU *MADE* HER BUTT IN.

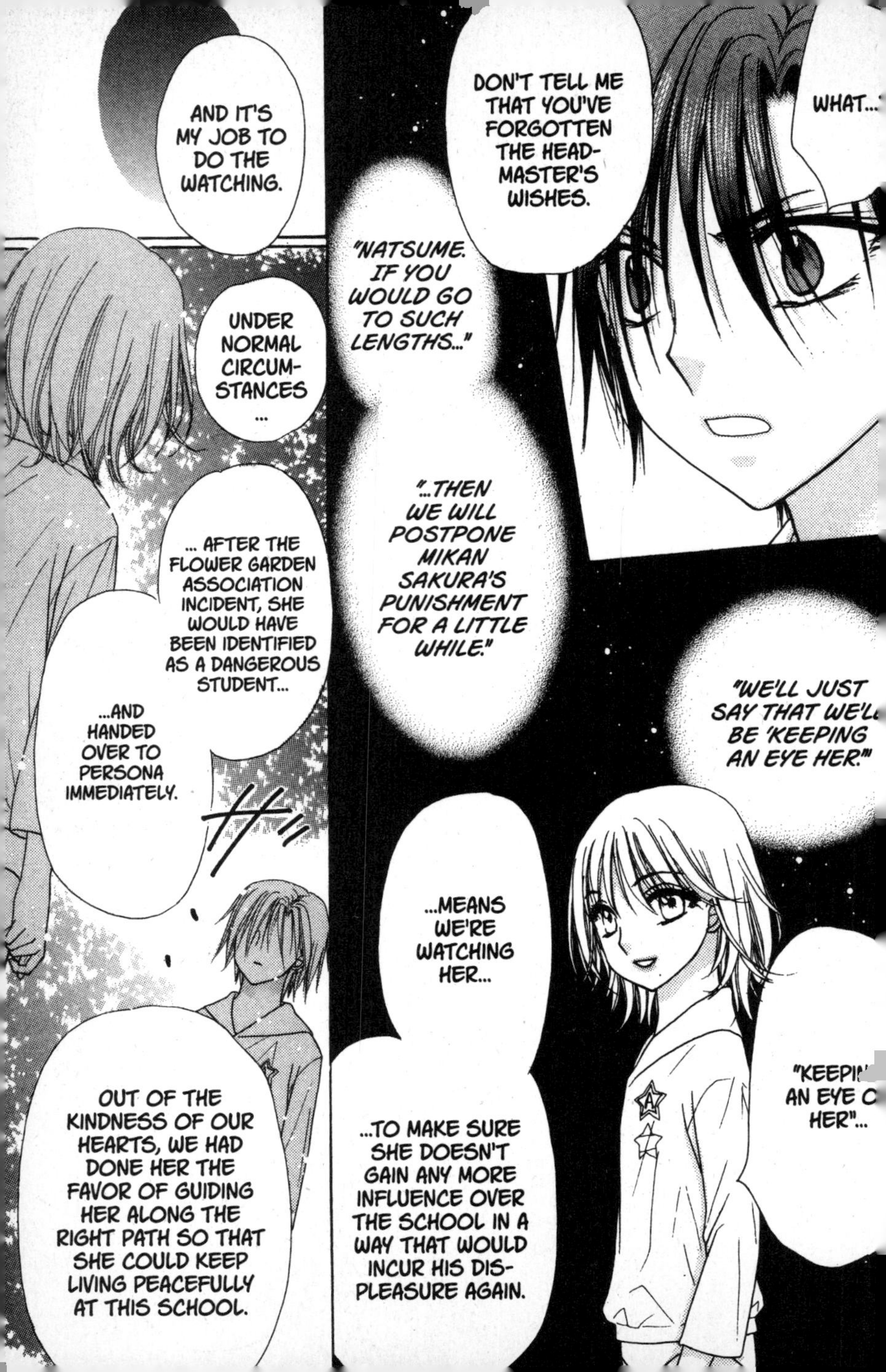
WHAT...
DON'T TELL ME THAT YOU'VE FORGOTTEN THE HEAD-MASTER'S WISHES.
"NATSUME. IF YOU WOULD GO TO SUCH LENGTHS..."
"...THEN WE WILL POSTPONE MIKAN SAKURA'S PUNISHMENT FOR A LITTLE WHILE."
"WE'LL JUST SAY THAT WE'LL BE 'KEEPING AN EYE HER.'"
"KEEPIN AN EYE O HER"...
...MEANS WE'RE WATCHING HER...
...TO MAKE SURE SHE DOESN'T GAIN ANY MORE INFLUENCE OVER THE SCHOOL IN A WAY THAT WOULD INCUR HIS DIS-PLEASURE AGAIN.
AND IT'S MY JOB TO DO THE WATCHING.
UNDER NORMAL CIRCUM-STANCES ...
... AFTER THE FLOWER GARDEN ASSOCIATION INCIDENT, SHE WOULD HAVE BEEN IDENTIFIED AS A DANGEROUS STUDENT...
...AND HANDED OVER TO PERSONA IMMEDIATELY.
OUT OF THE KINDNESS OF OUR HEARTS, WE HAD DONE HER THE FAVOR OF GUIDING HER ALONG THE RIGHT PATH SO THAT SHE COULD KEEP LIVING PEACEFULLY AT THIS SCHOOL.

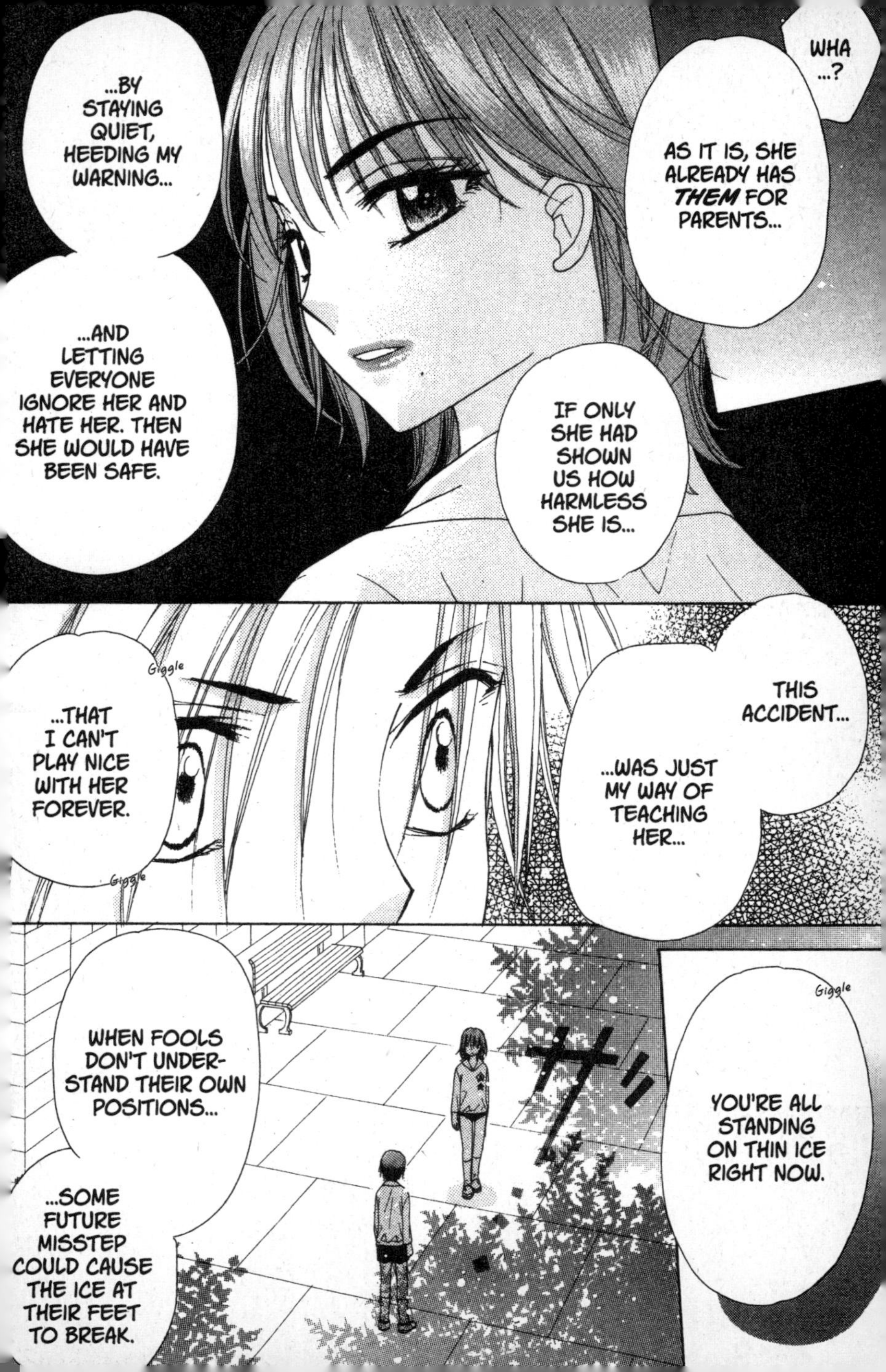
WHA...?
AS IT IS, SHE ALREADY HAS *THEM* FOR PARENTS...
IF ONLY SHE HAD SHOWN US HOW HARMLESS SHE IS...
...BY STAYING QUIET, HEEDING MY WARNING...
...AND LETTING EVERYONE IGNORE HER AND HATE HER. THEN SHE WOULD HAVE BEEN SAFE.
THIS ACCIDENT...
...WAS JUST MY WAY OF TEACHING HER...
Giggle
...THAT I CAN'T PLAY NICE WITH HER FOREVER.
Giggle
Giggle
YOU'RE ALL STANDING ON THIN ICE RIGHT NOW.
WHEN FOOLS DON'T UNDER-STAND THEIR OWN POSITIONS...
...SOME FUTURE MISSTEP COULD CAUSE THE ICE AT THEIR FEET TO BREAK.

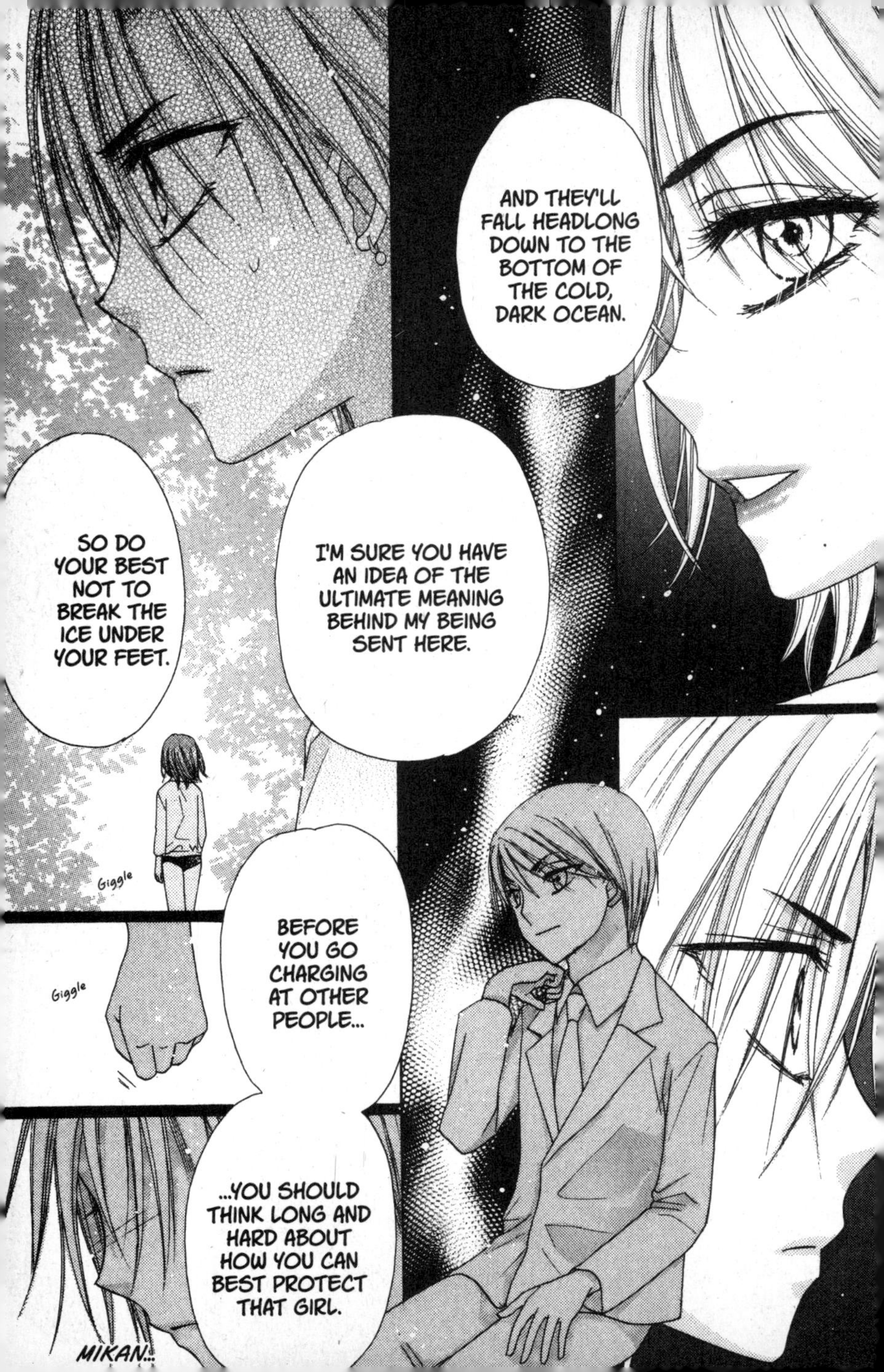
AND THEY'LL FALL HEADLONG DOWN TO THE BOTTOM OF THE COLD, DARK OCEAN.
I'M SURE YOU HAVE AN IDEA OF THE ULTIMATE MEANING BEHIND MY BEING SENT HERE.
SO DO YOUR BEST NOT TO BREAK THE ICE UNDER YOUR FEET.
Giggle
Giggle
BEFORE YOU GO CHARGING AT OTHER PEOPLE...
...YOU SHOULD THINK LONG AND HARD ABOUT HOW YOU CAN BEST PROTECT THAT GIRL.
MIKAN...

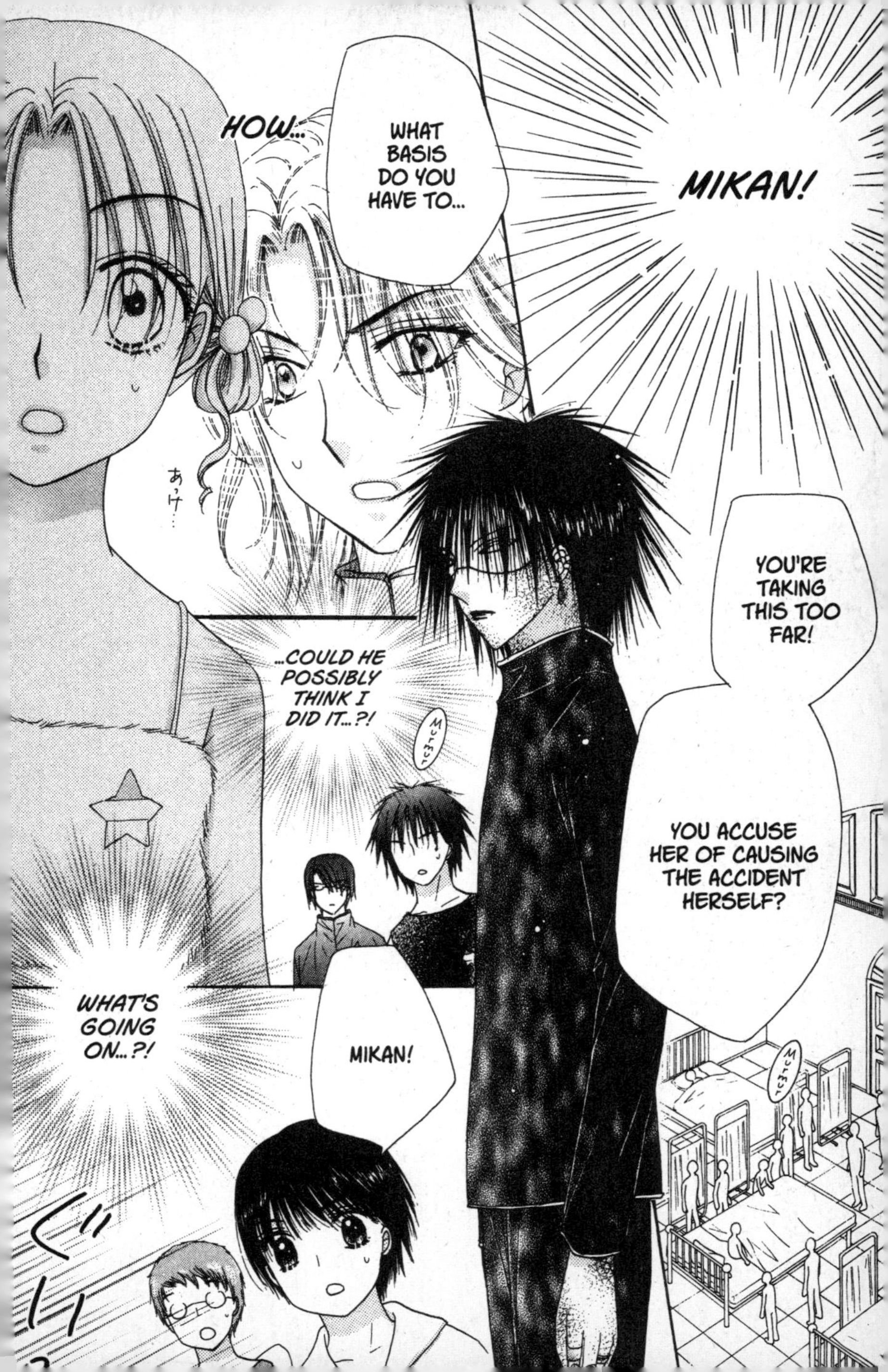
MIKAN!
WHAT BASIS DO YOU HAVE TO...
HOW...
YOU'RE TAKING THIS TOO FAR!
YOU ACCUSE HER OF CAUSING THE ACCIDENT HERSELF?
Murmur
...COULD HE POSSIBLY THINK I DID IT...?!
Murmur
MIKAN!
WHAT'S GOING ON...?!

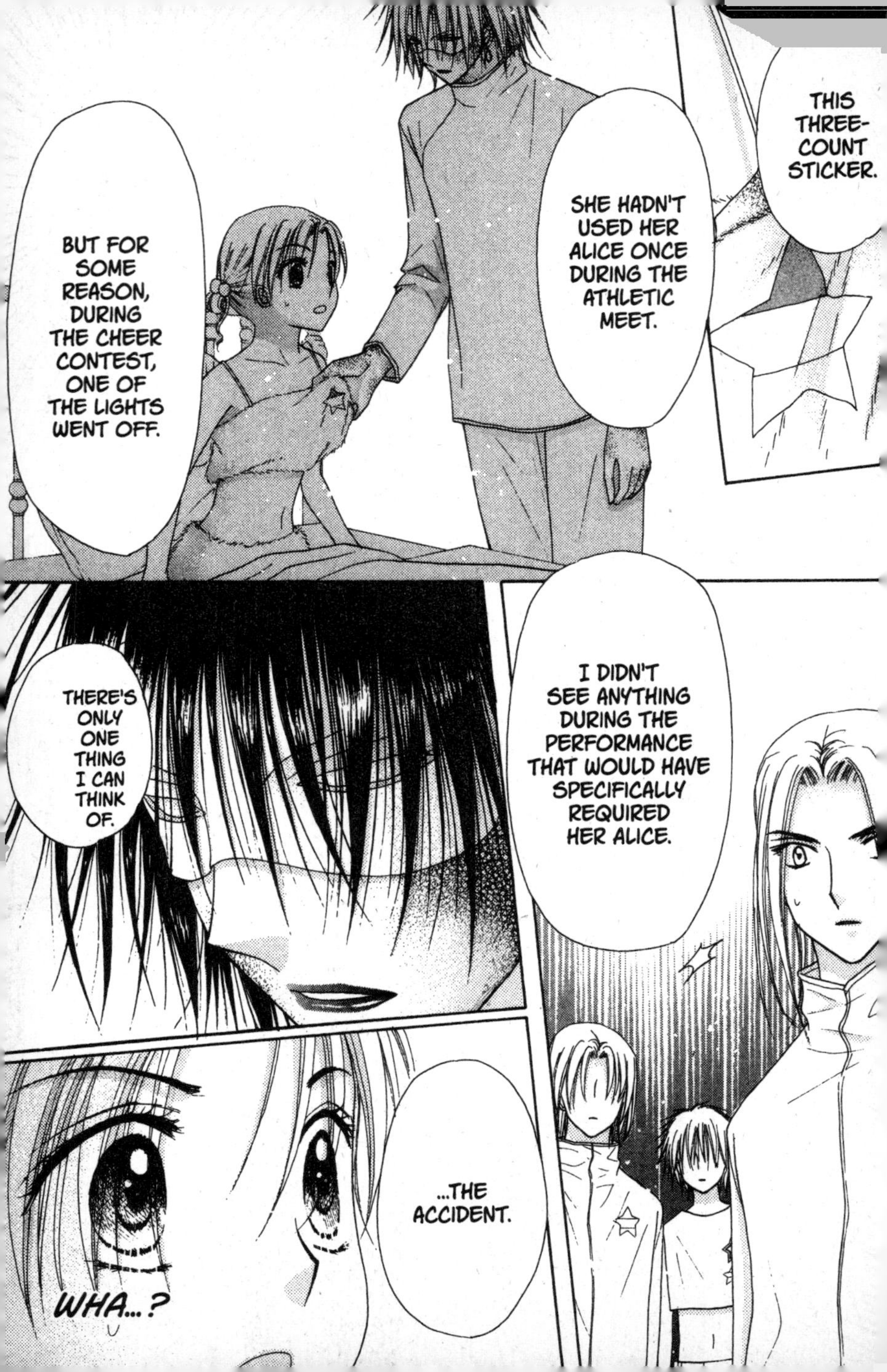
THIS THREE-COUNT STICKER.
SHE HADN'T USED HER ALICE ONCE DURING THE ATHLETIC MEET.
BUT FOR SOME REASON, DURING THE CHEER CONTEST, ONE OF THE LIGHTS WENT OFF.
I DIDN'T SEE ANYTHING DURING THE PERFORMANCE THAT WOULD HAVE SPECIFICALLY REQUIRED HER ALICE.
THERE'S ONLY ONE THING I CAN THINK OF.
...THE ACCIDENT.
WHA...?

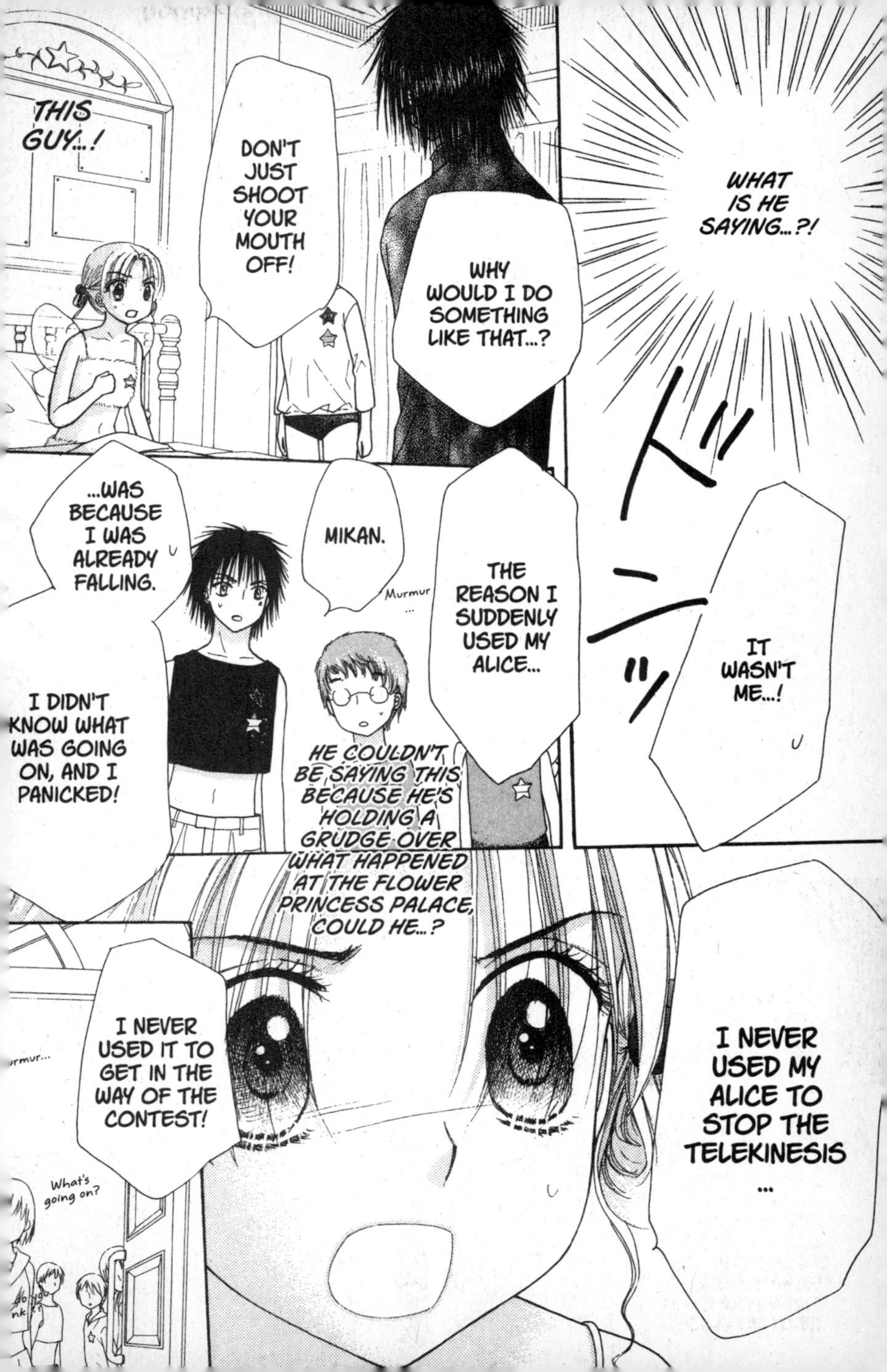
WHAT IS HE SAYING...?!
IT WASN'T ME...!
WHY WOULD I DO SOMETHING LIKE THAT...?
DON'T JUST SHOOT YOUR MOUTH OFF!
THIS GUY...!
THE REASON I SUDDENLY USED MY ALICE...
MIKAN.
Murmur...
...WAS BECAUSE I WAS ALREADY FALLING.
HE COULDN'T BE SAYING THIS BECAUSE HE'S HOLDING A GRUDGE OVER WHAT HAPPENED AT THE FLOWER PRINCESS PALACE, COULD HE...?
I DIDN'T KNOW WHAT WAS GOING ON, AND I PANICKED!
I NEVER USED MY ALICE TO STOP THE TELEKINESIS...
I NEVER USED IT TO GET IN THE WAY OF THE CONTEST!
What's going on?

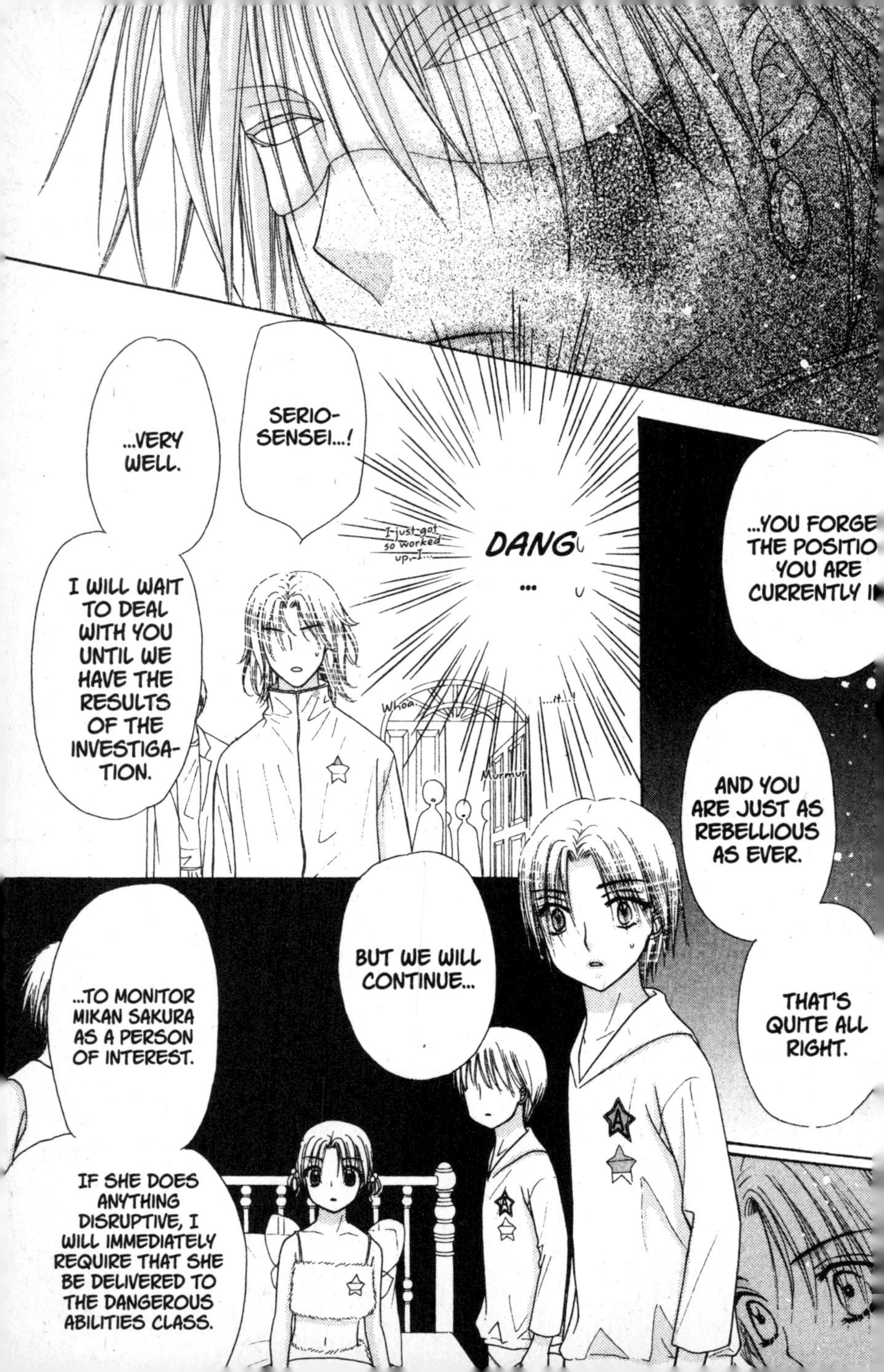

...YOU FORGE THE POSITIO YOU ARE CURRENTLY I
AND YOU ARE JUST AS REBELLIOUS AS EVER.
THAT'S QUITE ALL RIGHT.
DANG ...
...it..!
Murmur
Whoa..
I just got so worked up, I...
SERIO-SENSEI...!
...VERY WELL.
I WILL WAIT TO DEAL WITH YOU UNTIL WE HAVE THE RESULTS OF THE INVESTIGA-TION.
BUT WE WILL CONTINUE...
...TO MONITOR MIKAN SAKURA AS A PERSON OF INTEREST.
IF SHE DOES ANYTHING DISRUPTIVE, I WILL IMMEDIATELY REQUIRE THAT SHE BE DELIVERED TO THE DANGEROUS ABILITIES CLASS.

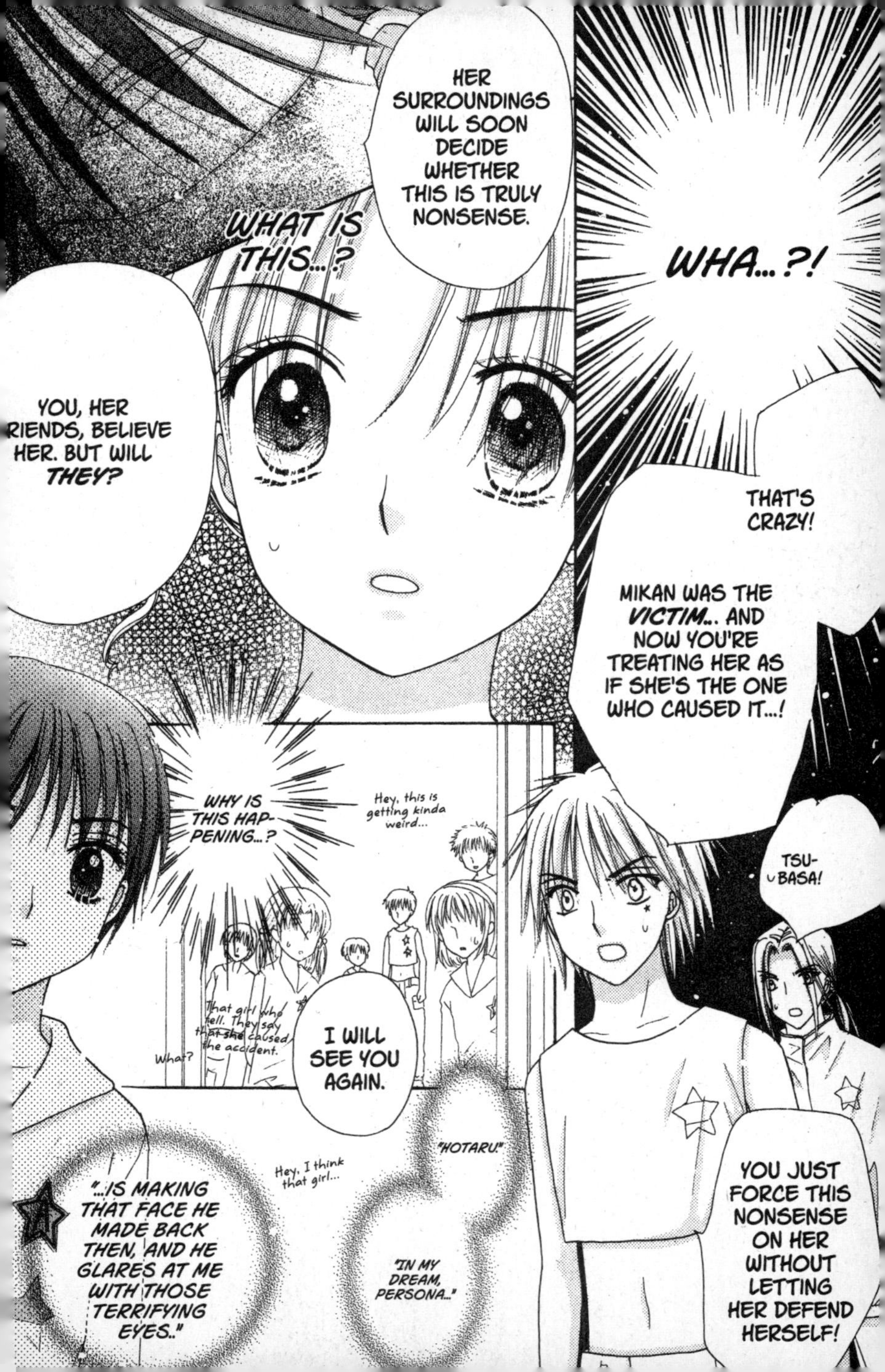

WHA...?!
HER SURROUNDINGS WILL SOON DECIDE WHETHER THIS IS TRULY NONSENSE.
WHAT IS THIS...?
YOU, HER RIENDS, BELIEVE HER. BUT WILL THEY?
THAT'S CRAZY!
MIKAN WAS THE VICTIM... AND NOW YOU'RE TREATING HER AS IF SHE'S THE ONE WHO CAUSED IT...!
TSU-BASA!
YOU JUST FORCE THIS NONSENSE ON HER WITHOUT LETTING HER DEFEND HERSELF!
Hey, this is getting kinda weird...
WHY IS THIS HAP-PENING...?
That girl who fell. They say that she caused the accident.
What?
I WILL SEE YOU AGAIN.
"HOTARU."
Hey, I think that girl...
"IN MY DREAM, PERSONA..."
"...IS MAKING THAT FACE HE MADE BACK THEN, AND HE GLARES AT ME WITH THOSE TERRIFYING EYES."

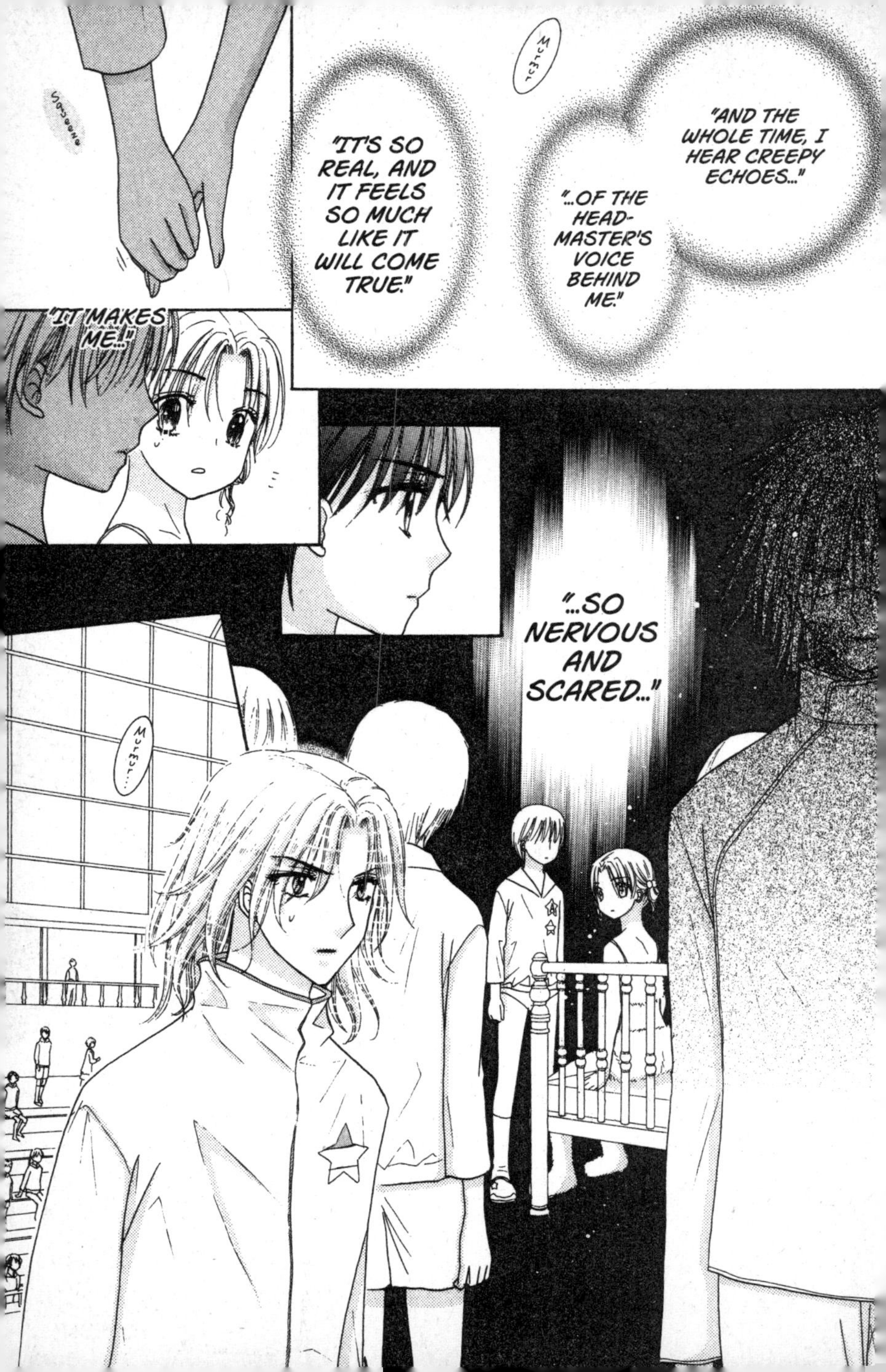
Murmur
"AND THE WHOLE TIME, I HEAR CREEPY ECHOES..."
"...OF THE HEAD-MASTER'S VOICE BEHIND ME."
"IT'S SO REAL, AND IT FEELS SO MUCH LIKE IT WILL COME TRUE."
Squeeze
"IT MAKES ME...!"
"...SO NERVOUS AND SCARED..."
Murmur...

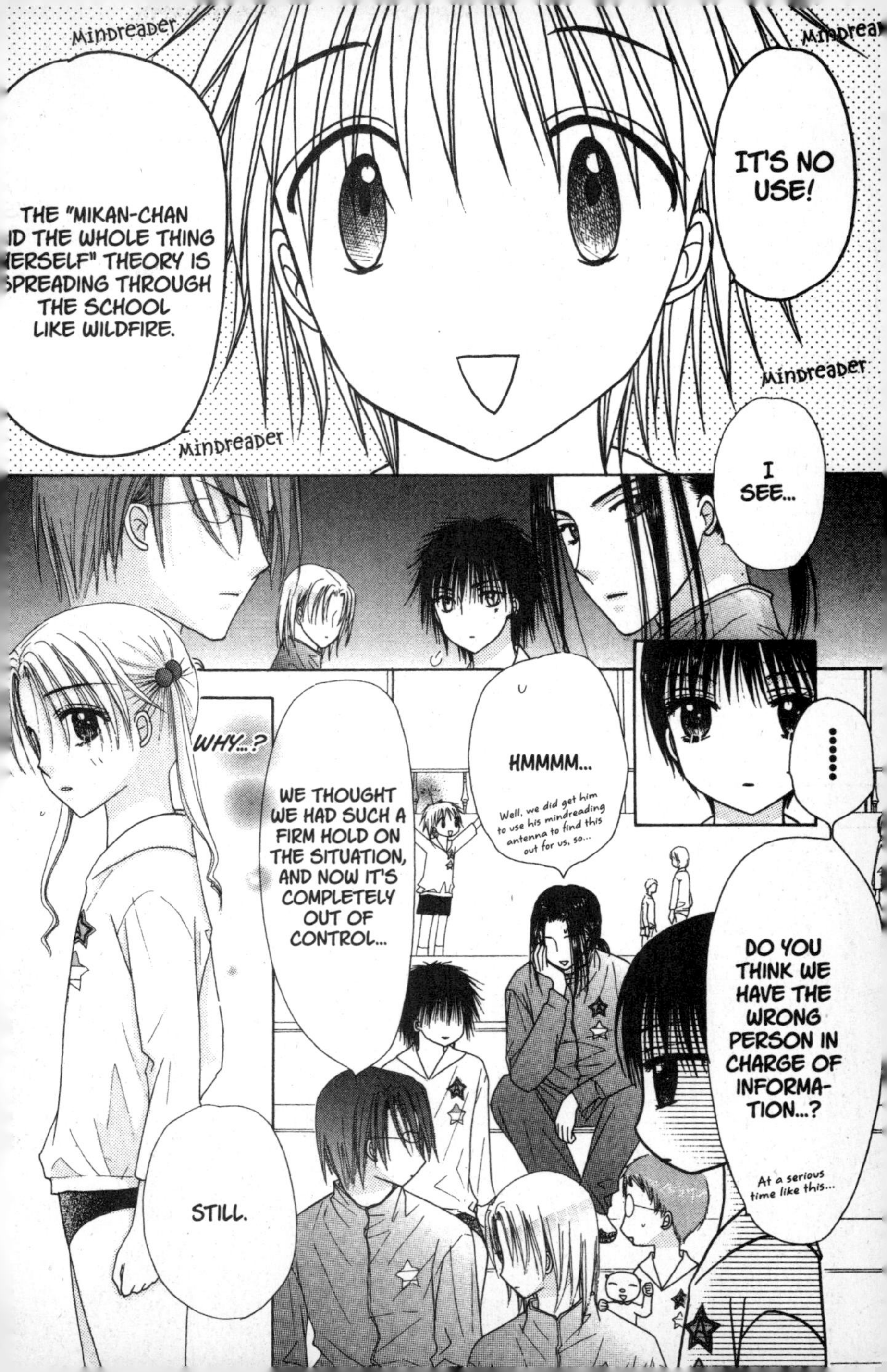
Mindreader
Mindreader
IT'S NO USE!
THE "MIKAN-CHAN
ID THE WHOLE THING
IERSELF" THEORY IS
SPREADING THROUGH
THE SCHOOL
LIKE WILDFIRE.
Mindreader
Mindreader
I SEE...
......
HMMMM...
Well, we did get him to use his mindreading antenna to find this out for us, so...
WE THOUGHT WE HAD SUCH A FIRM HOLD ON THE SITUATION, AND NOW IT'S COMPLETELY OUT OF CONTROL...
WHY...?
DO YOU THINK WE HAVE THE WRONG PERSON IN CHARGE OF INFORMATION...?
At a serious time like this...
STILL.

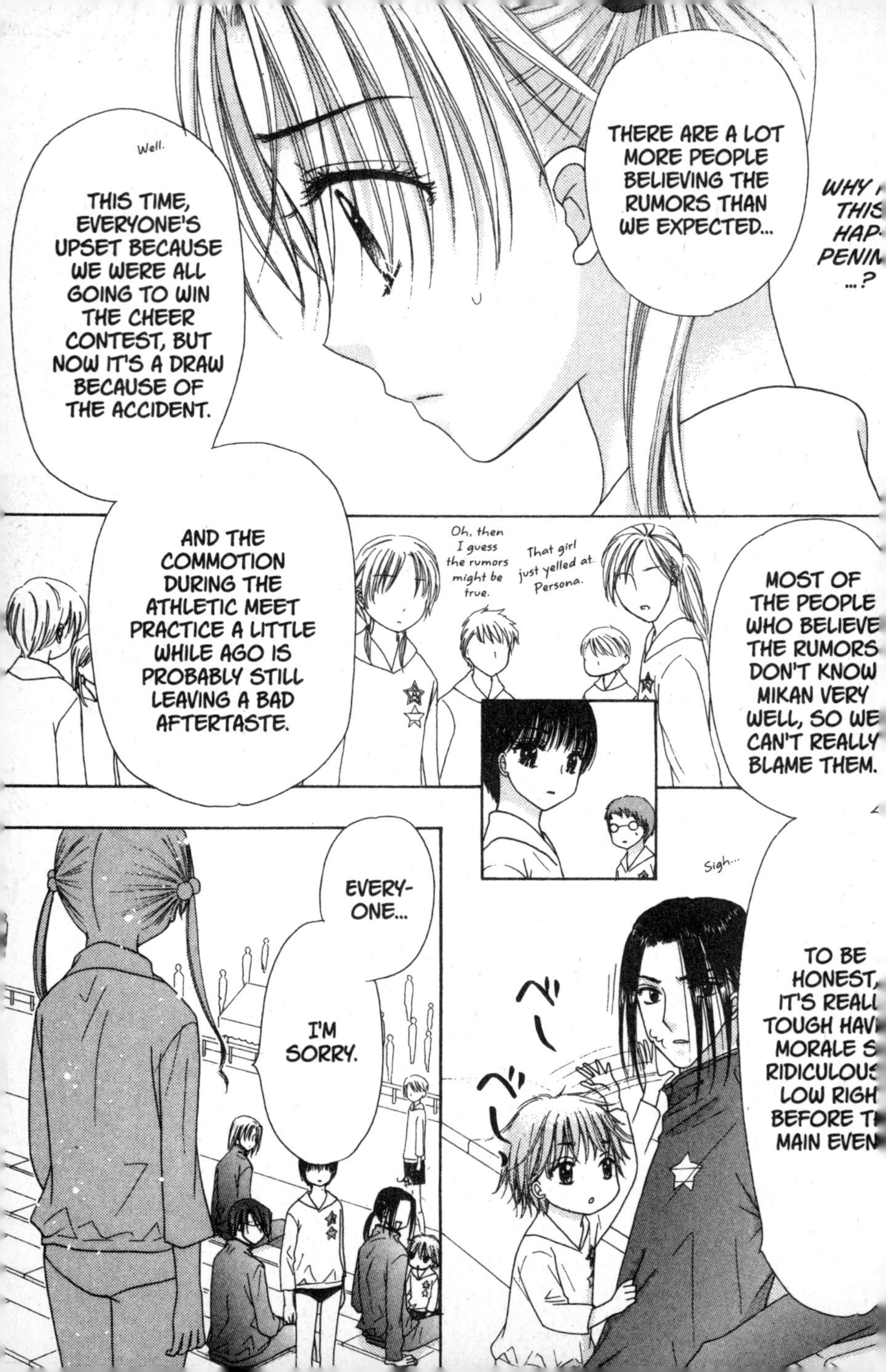

WHY I THIS HAP- PENIN ...?
THERE ARE A LOT MORE PEOPLE BELIEVING THE RUMORS THAN WE EXPECTED...
Well.
THIS TIME, EVERYONE'S UPSET BECAUSE WE WERE ALL GOING TO WIN THE CHEER CONTEST, BUT NOW IT'S A DRAW BECAUSE OF THE ACCIDENT.
MOST OF THE PEOPLE WHO BELIEVE THE RUMORS DON'T KNOW MIKAN VERY WELL, SO WE CAN'T REALLY BLAME THEM.
That girl just yelled at Persona.
Oh, then I guess the rumors might be true.
AND THE COMMOTION DURING THE ATHLETIC MEET PRACTICE A LITTLE WHILE AGO IS PROBABLY STILL LEAVING A BAD AFTERTASTE.
Sigh...
TO BE HONEST, IT'S REALL TOUGH HAVI MORALE S RIDICULOUS LOW RIGH BEFORE T MAIN EVEN
べし
べし
EVERY- ONE...
I'M SORRY.

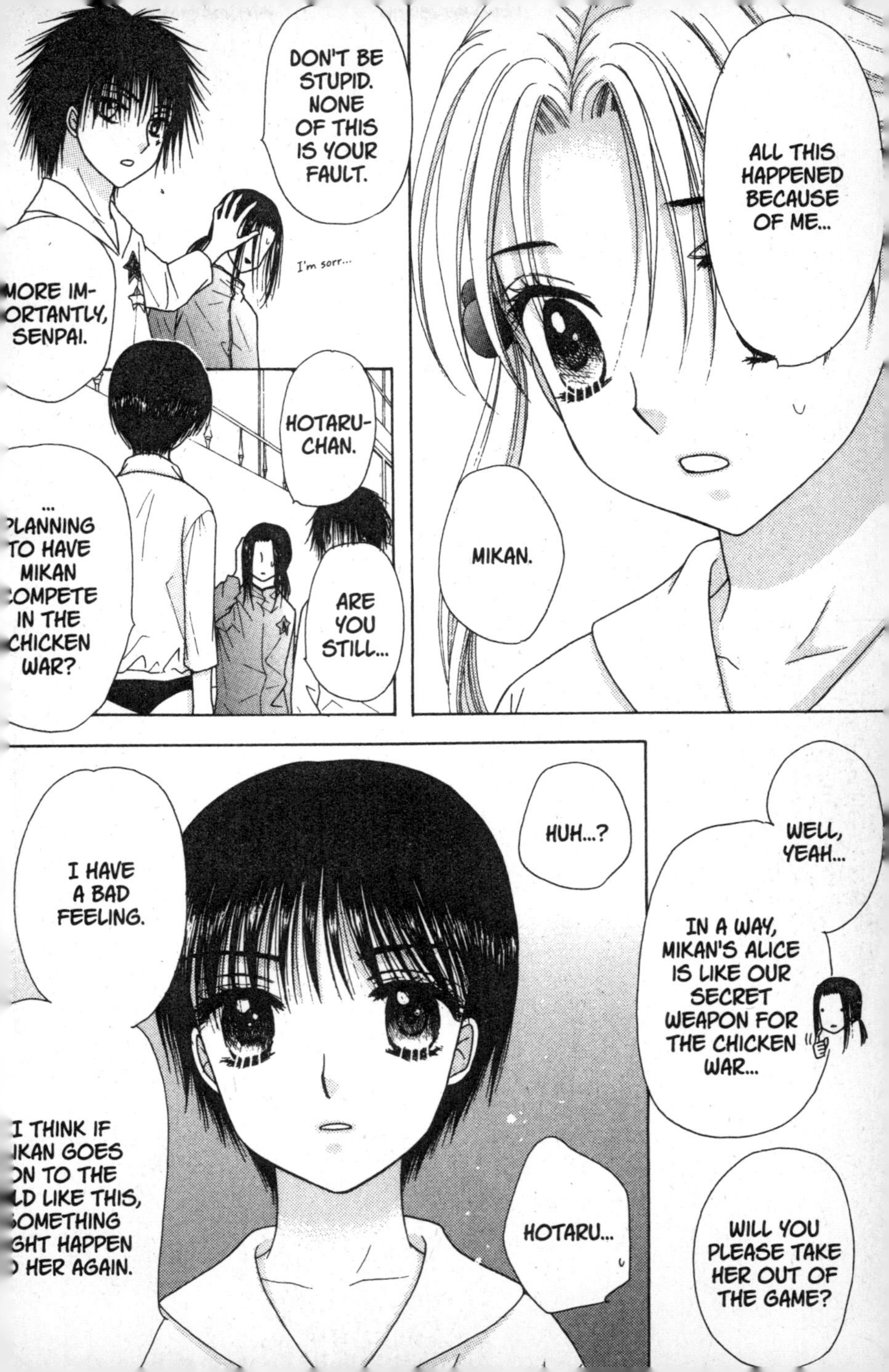
ALL THIS HAPPENED BECAUSE OF ME...
MIKAN.
DON'T BE STUPID. NONE OF THIS IS YOUR FAULT.
I'm sorr...
MORE IM-ORTANTLY, SENPAI.
HOTARU-CHAN.
ARE YOU STILL...
... LANNING TO HAVE MIKAN OMPETE IN THE CHICKEN WAR?
HUH...?
WELL, YEAH...
IN A WAY, MIKAN'S ALICE IS LIKE OUR SECRET WEAPON FOR THE CHICKEN WAR...
I HAVE A BAD FEELING.
I THINK IF IKAN GOES ON TO THE LD LIKE THIS, OMETHING GHT HAPPEN O HER AGAIN.
WILL YOU PLEASE TAKE HER OUT OF THE GAME?
HOTARU...

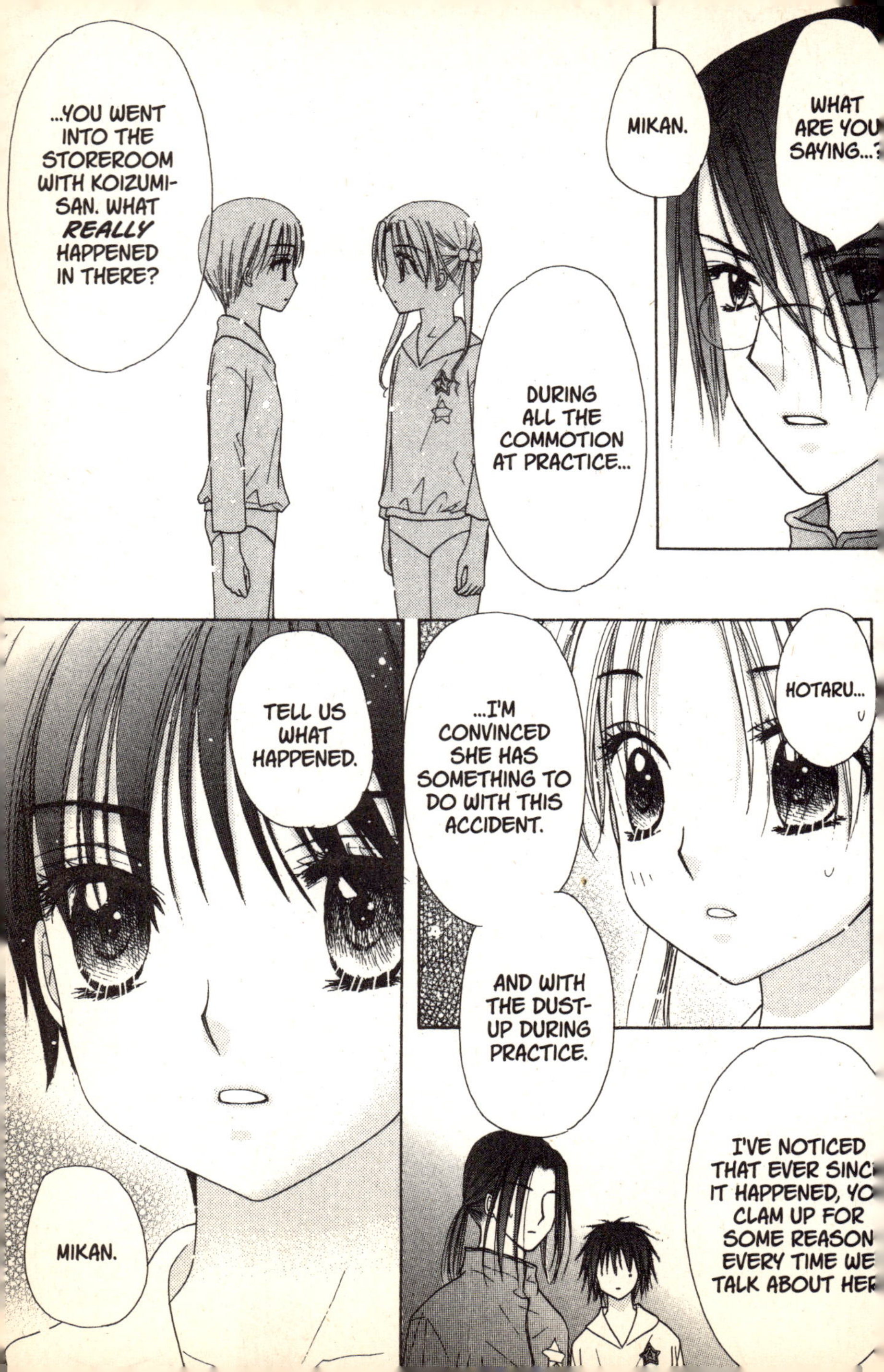
WHAT ARE YOU SAYING...
MIKAN.
DURING ALL THE COMMOTION AT PRACTICE...
...YOU WENT INTO THE STOREROOM WITH KOIZUMI-SAN. WHAT *REALLY* HAPPENED IN THERE?
HOTARU...
...I'M CONVINCED SHE HAS SOMETHING TO DO WITH THIS ACCIDENT.
AND WITH THE DUST-UP DURING PRACTICE.
I'VE NOTICED THAT EVER SINC IT HAPPENED, YO CLAM UP FOR SOME REASON EVERY TIME WE TALK ABOUT HE
TELL US WHAT HAPPENED.
MIKAN.

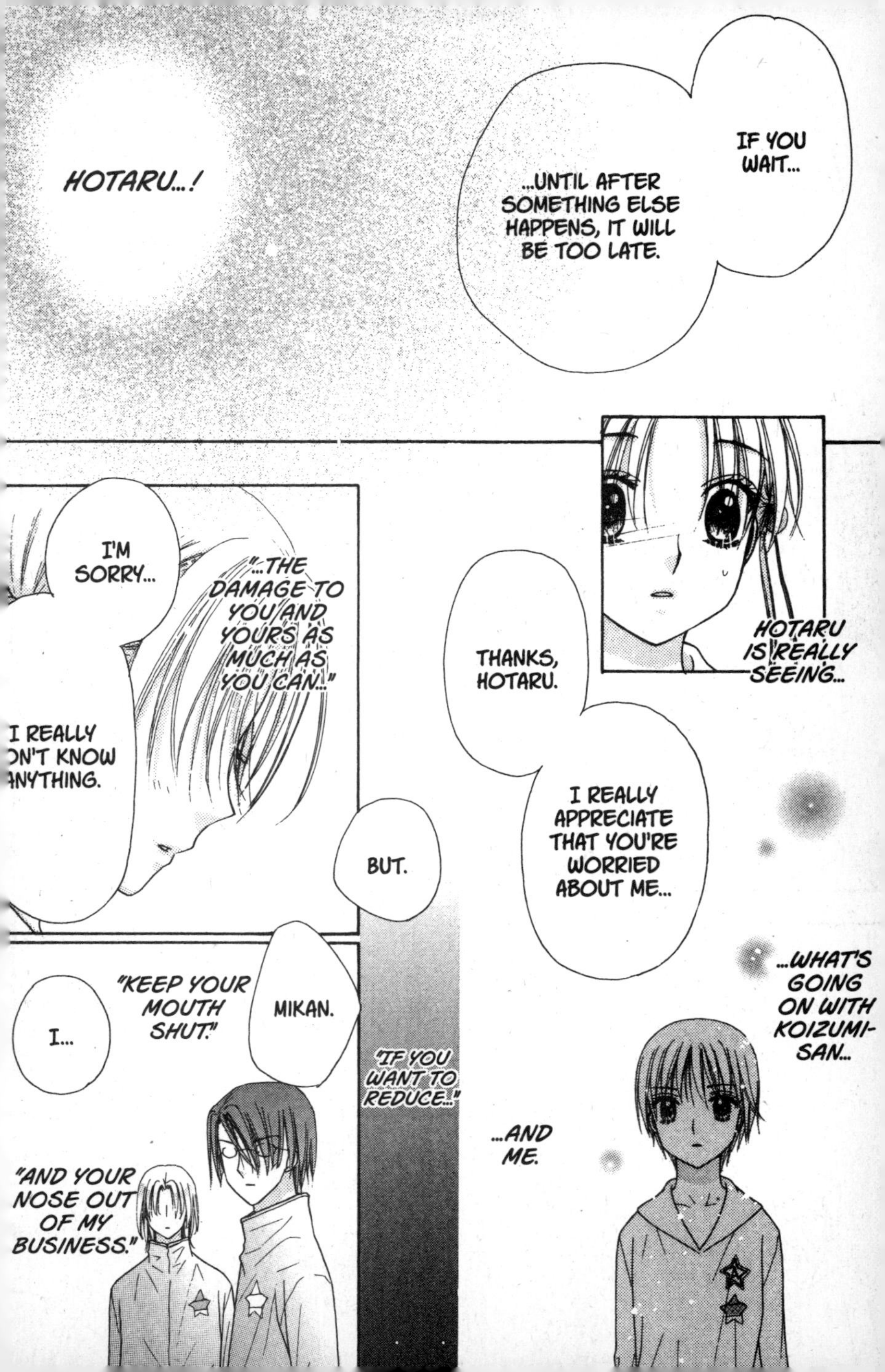
IF YOU WAIT...
...UNTIL AFTER SOMETHING ELSE HAPPENS, IT WILL BE TOO LATE.
HOTARU...!
HOTARU IS REALLY SEEING...
THANKS, HOTARU.
I REALLY APPRECIATE THAT YOU'RE WORRIED ABOUT ME...
...WHAT'S GOING ON WITH KOIZUMI-SAN...
...AND ME.
"IF YOU WANT TO REDUCE..."
I'M SORRY...
"...THE DAMAGE TO YOU AND YOURS AS MUCH AS YOU CAN..."
I REALLY ON'T KNOW NYTHING.
BUT.
MIKAN.
"KEEP YOUR MOUTH SHUT."
I...
"AND YOUR NOSE OUT OF MY BUSINESS."

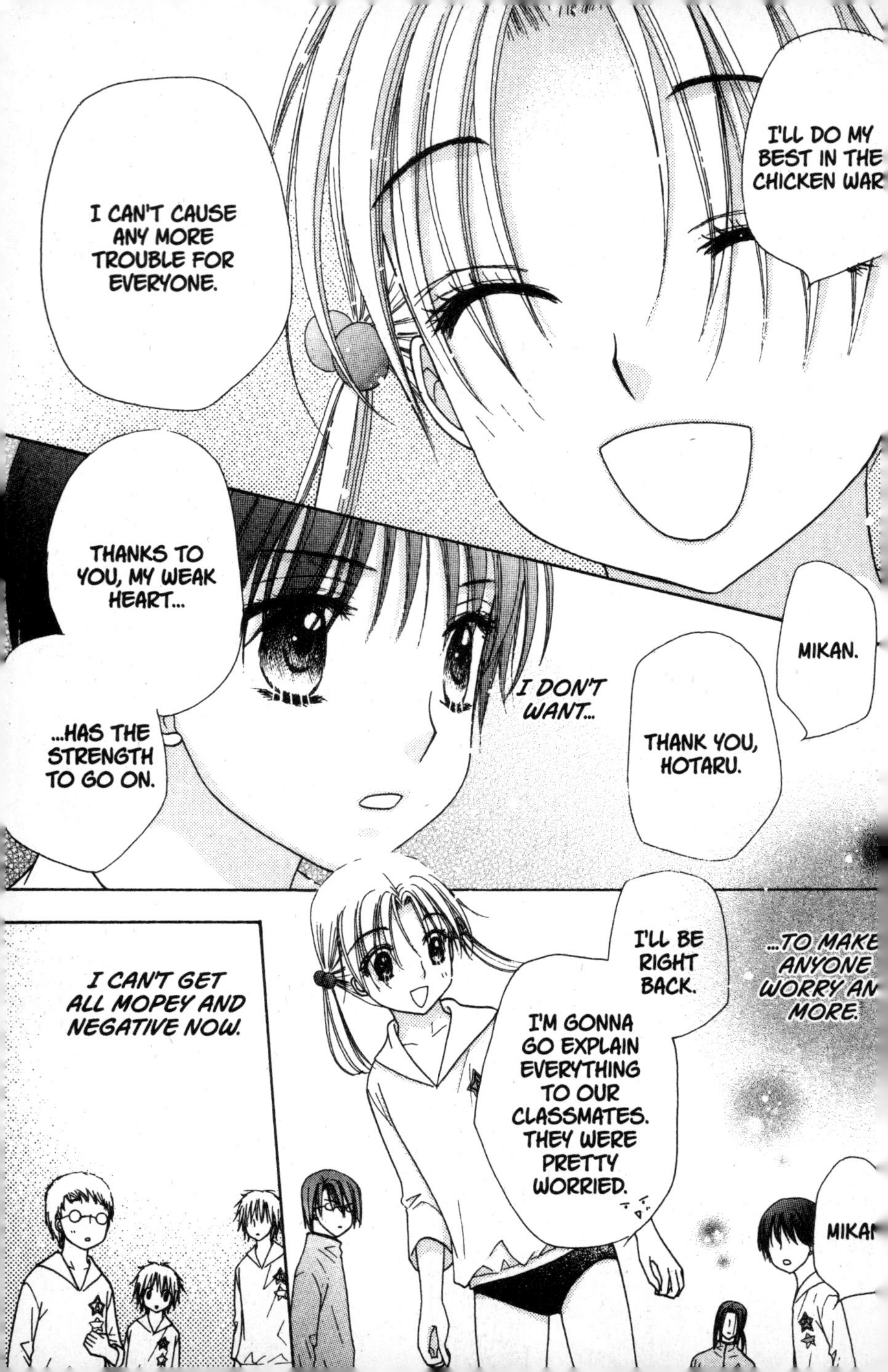
I'LL DO MY BEST IN THE CHICKEN WAR
I CAN'T CAUSE ANY MORE TROUBLE FOR EVERYONE.
MIKAN.
THANK YOU, HOTARU.
I DON'T WANT...
THANKS TO YOU, MY WEAK HEART...
...HAS THE STRENGTH TO GO ON.
...TO MAKE ANYONE WORRY AN MORE.
MIKA
I'LL BE RIGHT BACK.
I'M GONNA GO EXPLAIN EVERYTHING TO OUR CLASSMATES. THEY WERE PRETTY WORRIED.
I CAN'T GET ALL MOPEY AND NEGATIVE NOW.

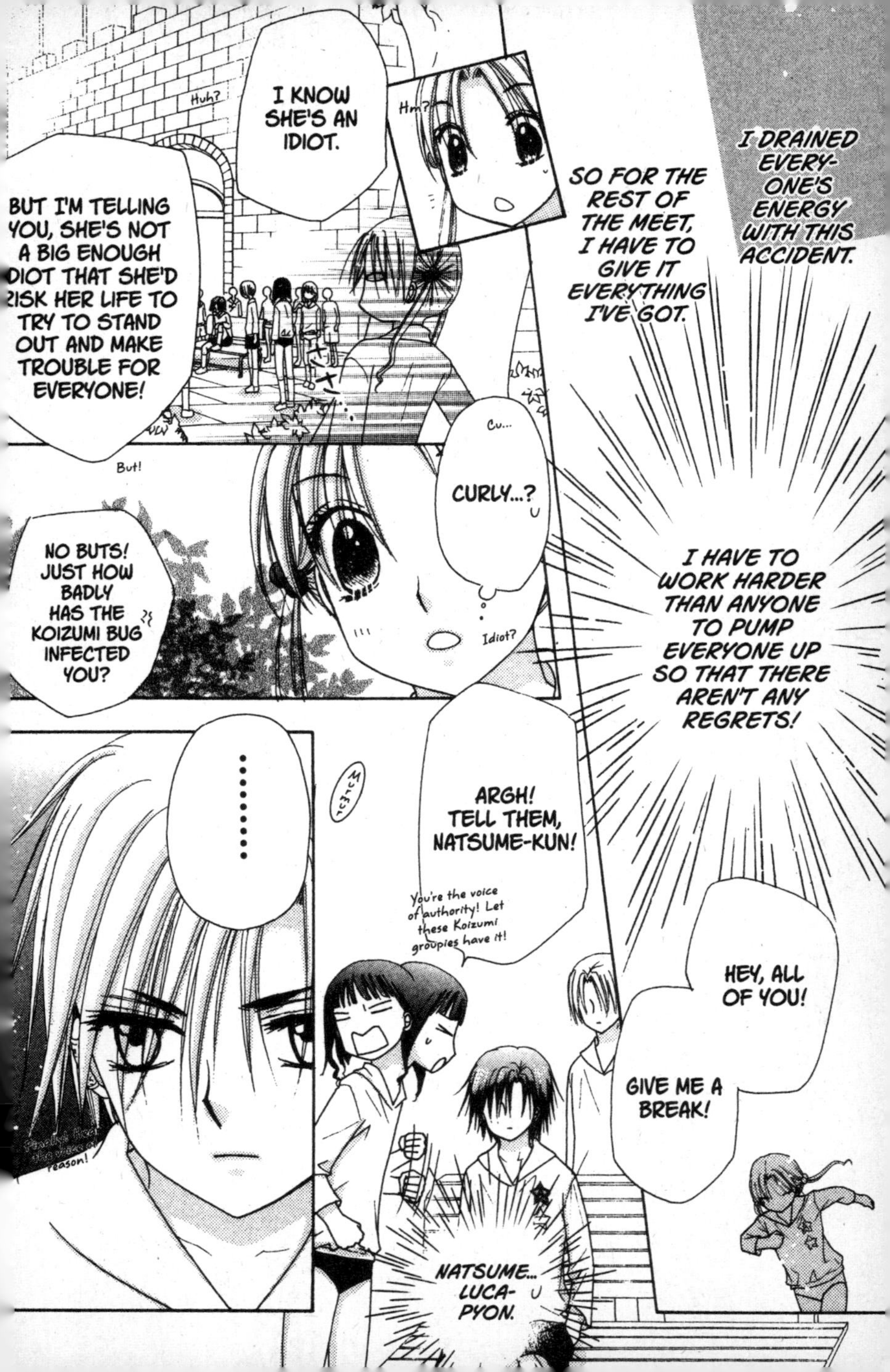
I DRAINED EVERY-ONE'S ENERGY WITH THIS ACCIDENT.
SO FOR THE REST OF THE MEET, I HAVE TO GIVE IT EVERYTHING I'VE GOT.
Hm?
I KNOW SHE'S AN IDIOT.
Huh?
BUT I'M TELLING YOU, SHE'S NOT A BIG ENOUGH IDIOT THAT SHE'D RISK HER LIFE TO TRY TO STAND OUT AND MAKE TROUBLE FOR EVERYONE!
I HAVE TO WORK HARDER THAN ANYONE TO PUMP EVERYONE UP SO THAT THERE AREN'T ANY REGRETS!
Cu...
CURLY...?
Idiot?
But!
NO BUTS! JUST HOW BADLY HAS THE KOIZUMI BUG INFECTED YOU?
HEY, ALL OF YOU!
GIVE ME A BREAK!
ARGH! TELL THEM, NATSUME-KUN!
You're the voice of authority! Let these Koizumi groupies have it!
Mutter
....
Finally! Here's the voice of reason!
NATSUME... LUCA-PYON.

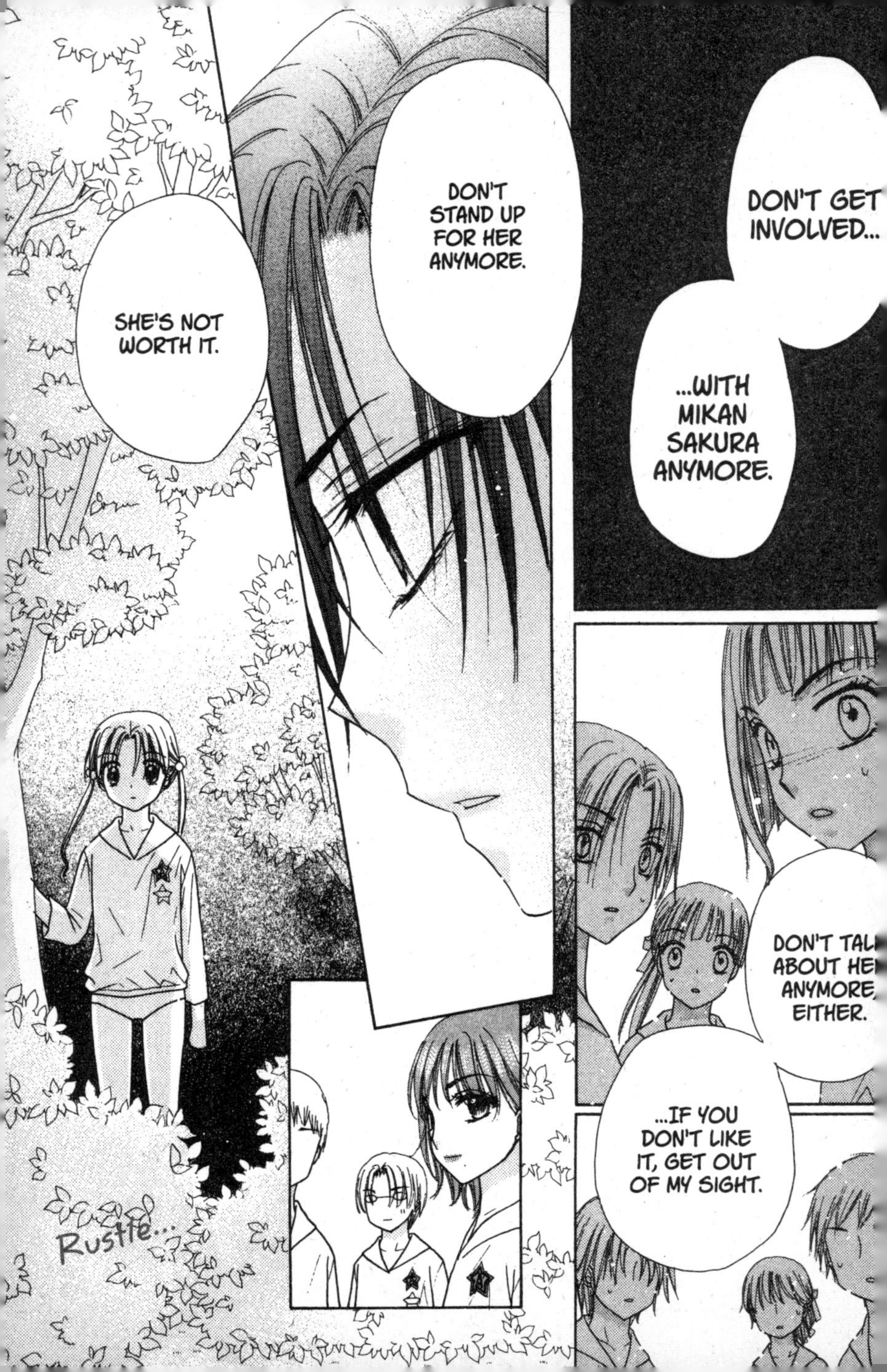
DON'T GET INVOLVED...
...WITH MIKAN SAKURA ANYMORE.
DON'T TAL ABOUT HE ANYMORE, EITHER.
...IF YOU DON'T LIKE IT, GET OUT OF MY SIGHT.
DON'T STAND UP FOR HER ANYMORE.
SHE'S NOT WORTH IT.
Rustle...

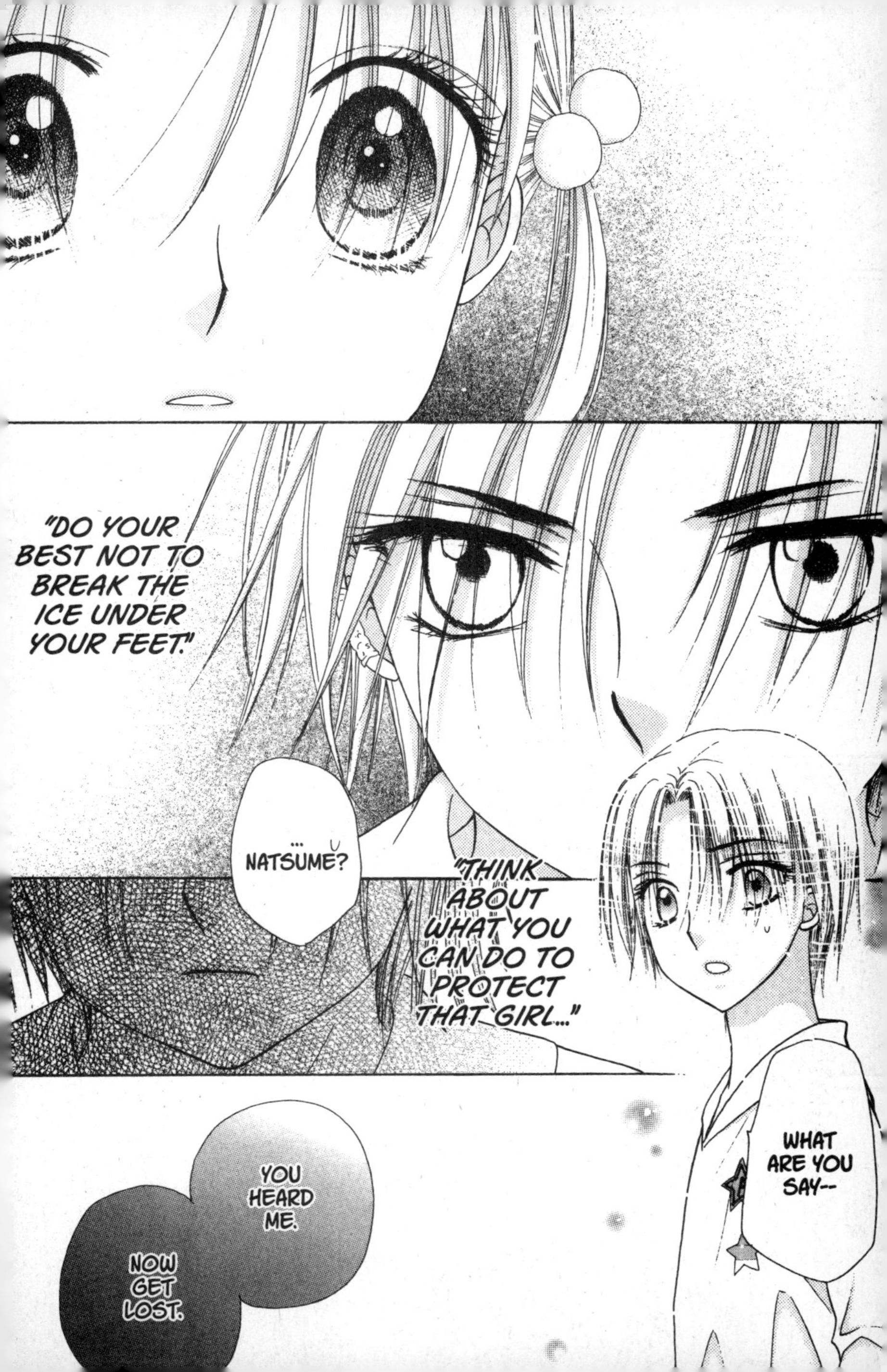
"DO YOUR BEST NOT TO BREAK THE ICE UNDER YOUR FEET."
"THINK ABOUT WHAT YOU CAN DO TO PROTECT THAT GIRL..."
... NATSUME?
WHAT ARE YOU SAY--
YOU HEARD ME.
NOW GET LOST.

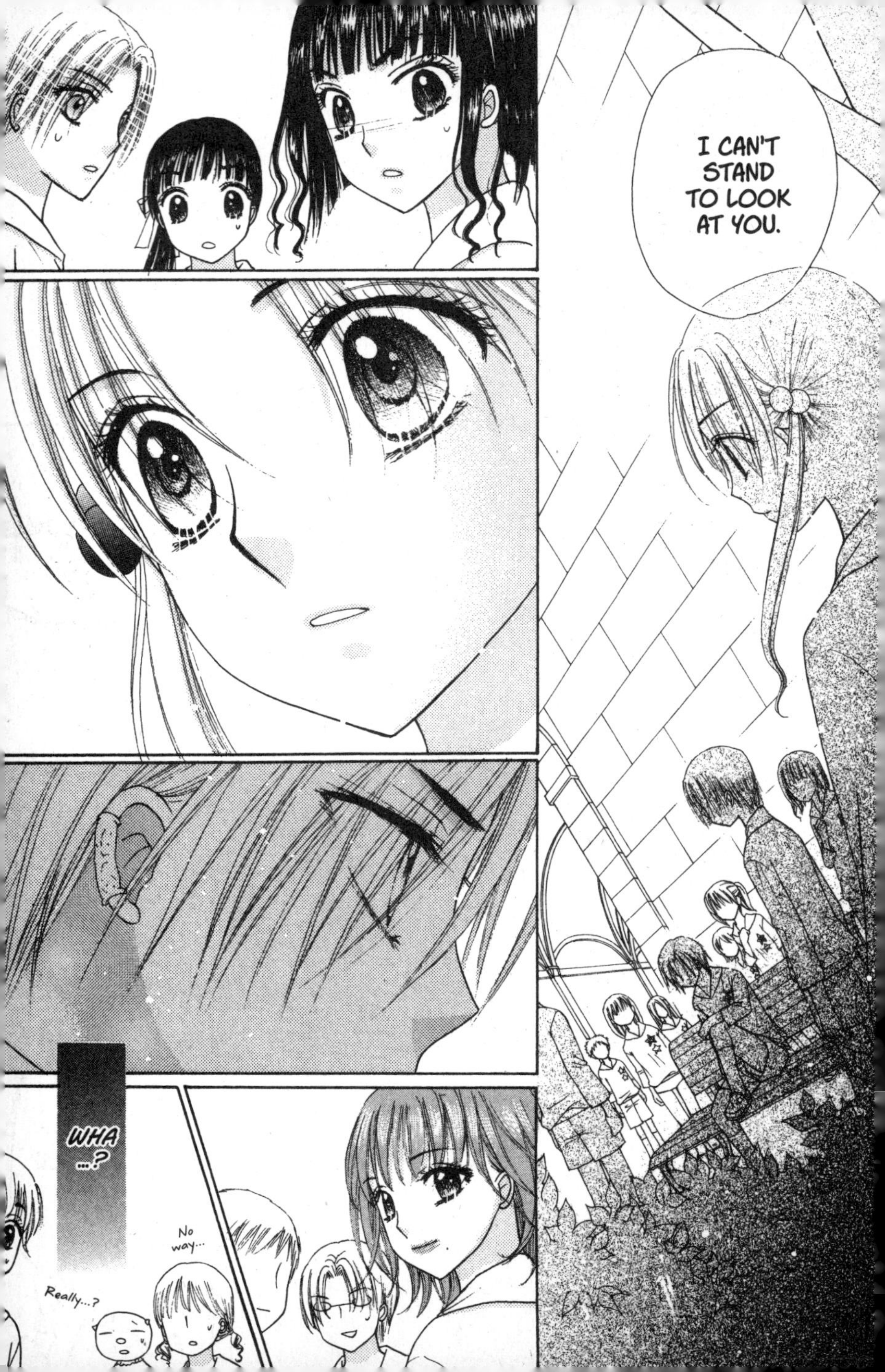
I CAN'T STAND TO LOOK AT YOU.
WHA ...?
No way...
Really...?

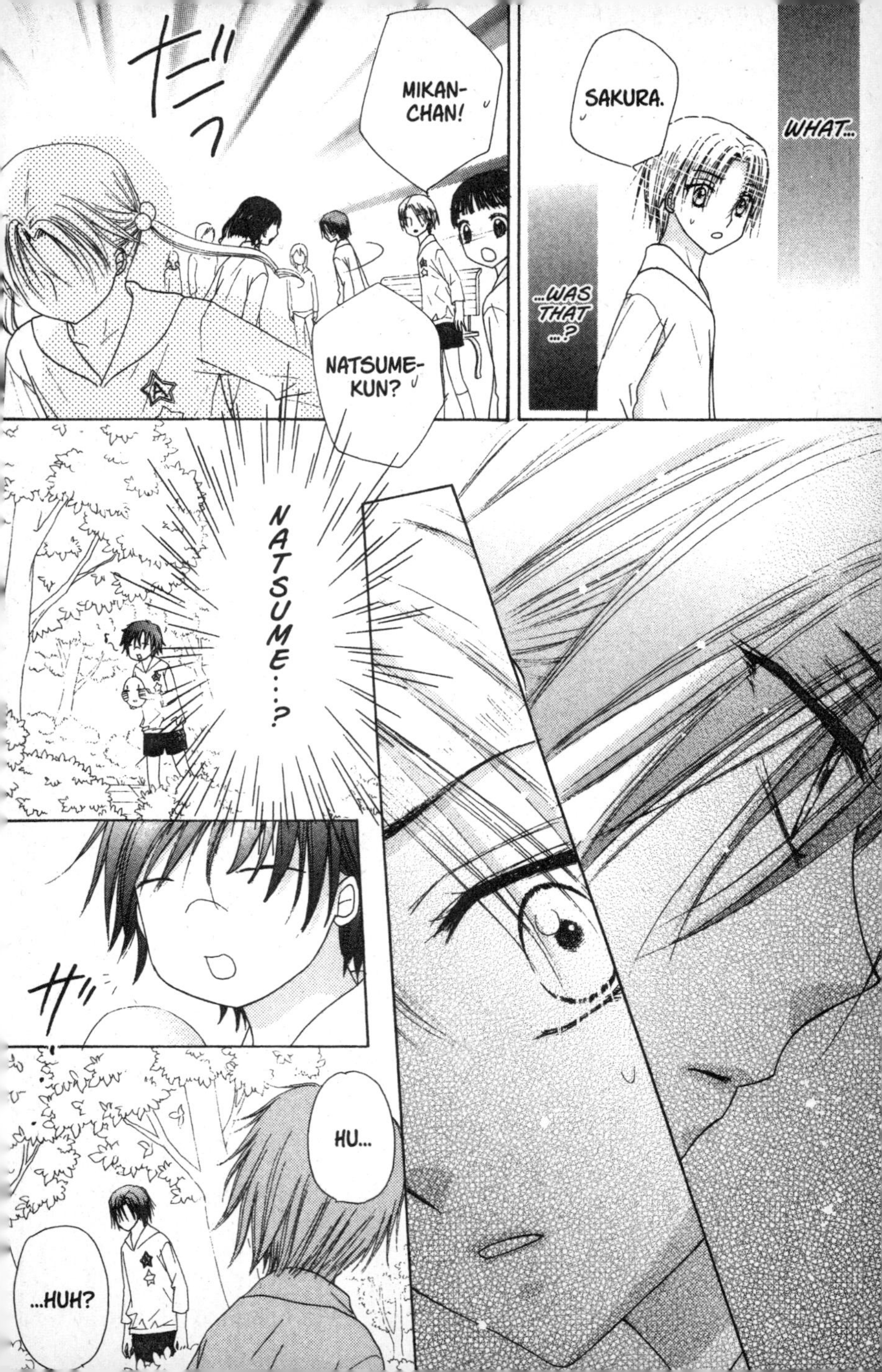
WHAT...
...WAS THAT ...?
SAKURA.
MIKAN-CHAN!
NATSUME-KUN?
NATSUME...?
HU...
...HUH?

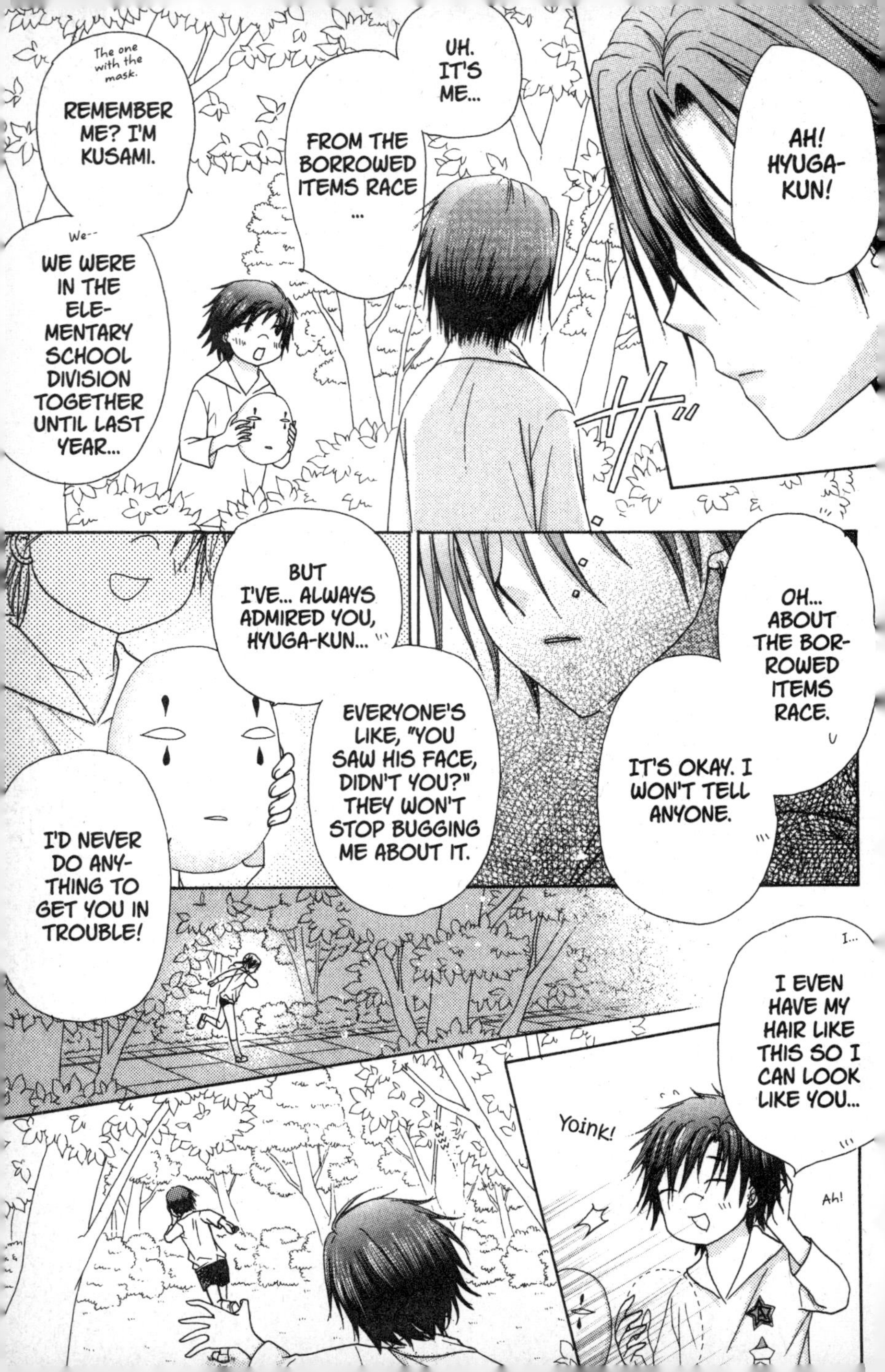
AH! HYUGA-KUN!
UH. IT'S ME...
FROM THE BORROWED ITEMS RACE ...
REMEMBER ME? I'M KUSAMI.
The one with the mask.
We--
WE WERE IN THE ELE-MENTARY SCHOOL DIVISION TOGETHER UNTIL LAST YEAR...
OH... ABOUT THE BOR-ROWED ITEMS RACE.
IT'S OKAY. I WON'T TELL ANYONE.
EVERYONE'S LIKE, "YOU SAW HIS FACE, DIDN'T YOU?" THEY WON'T STOP BUGGING ME ABOUT IT.
I'D NEVER DO ANY-THING TO GET YOU IN TROUBLE!
BUT I'VE... ALWAYS ADMIRED YOU, HYUGA-KUN...
I...
I EVEN HAVE MY HAIR LIKE THIS SO I CAN LOOK LIKE YOU...
Ah!
Yoink!

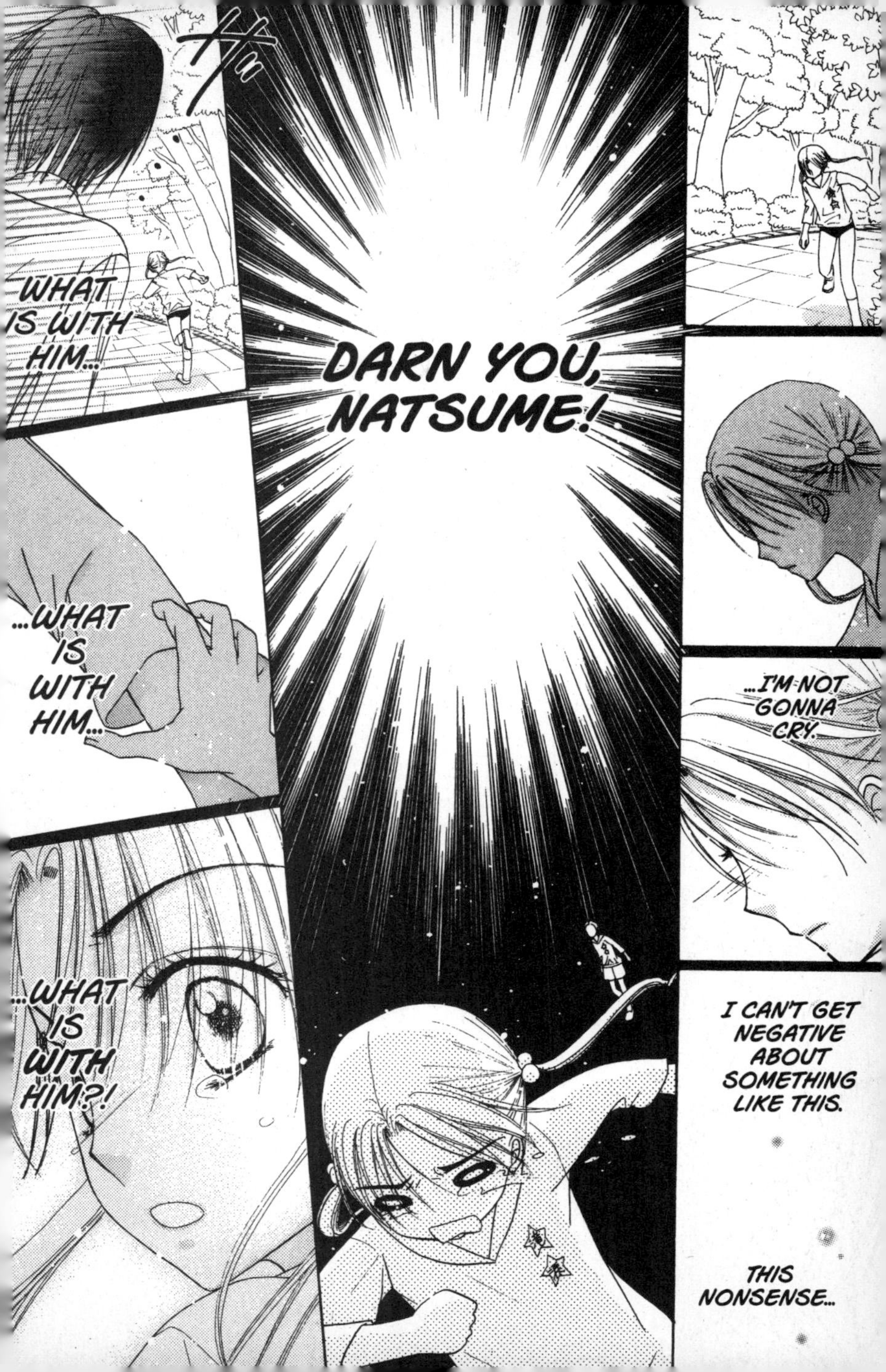
...I'M NOT GONNA CRY.
I CAN'T GET NEGATIVE ABOUT SOMETHING LIKE THIS.
THIS NONSENSE...
DARN YOU, NATSUME!
WHAT IS WITH HIM...
...WHAT IS WITH HIM...
...WHAT IS WITH HIM?!

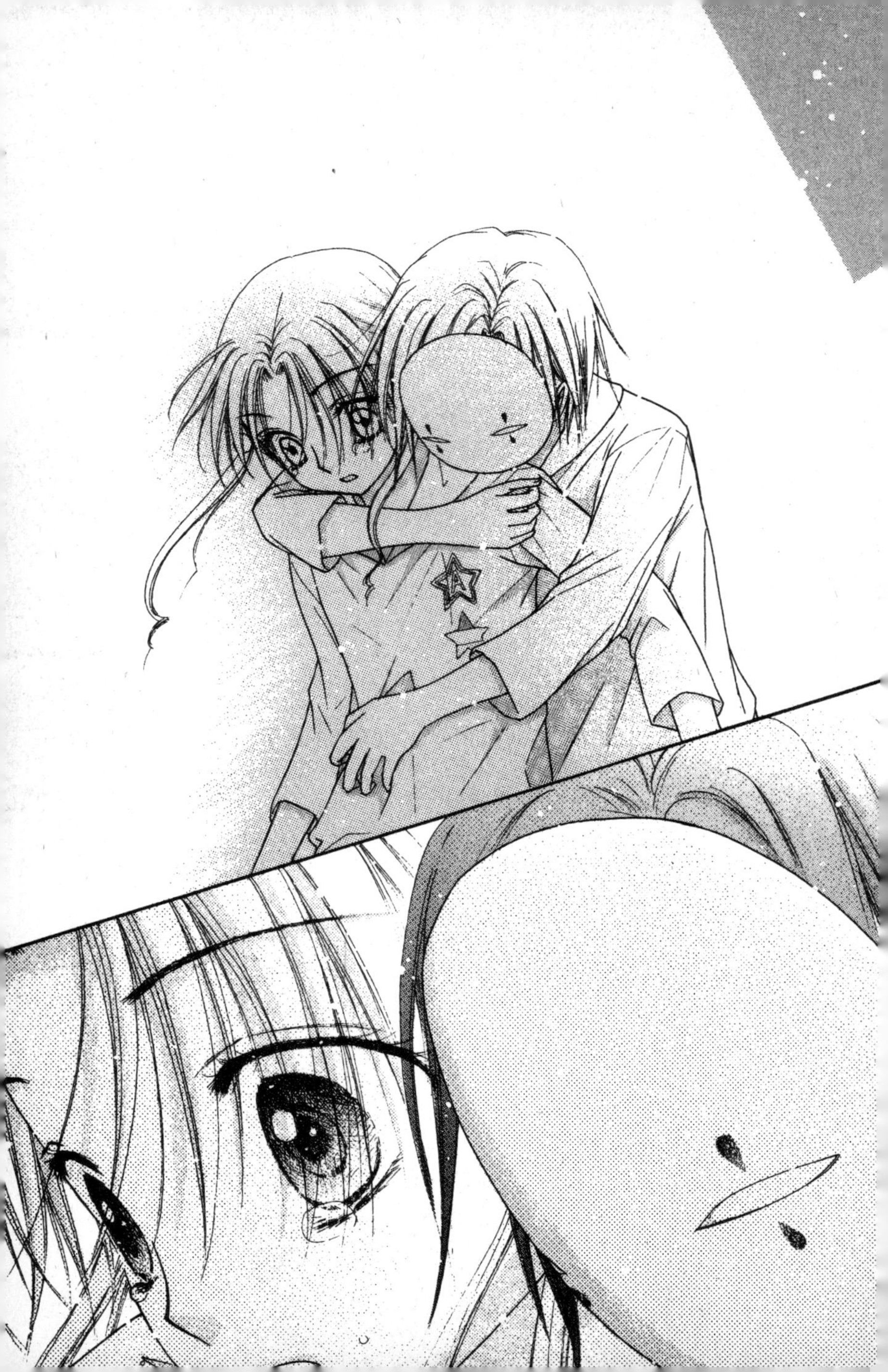

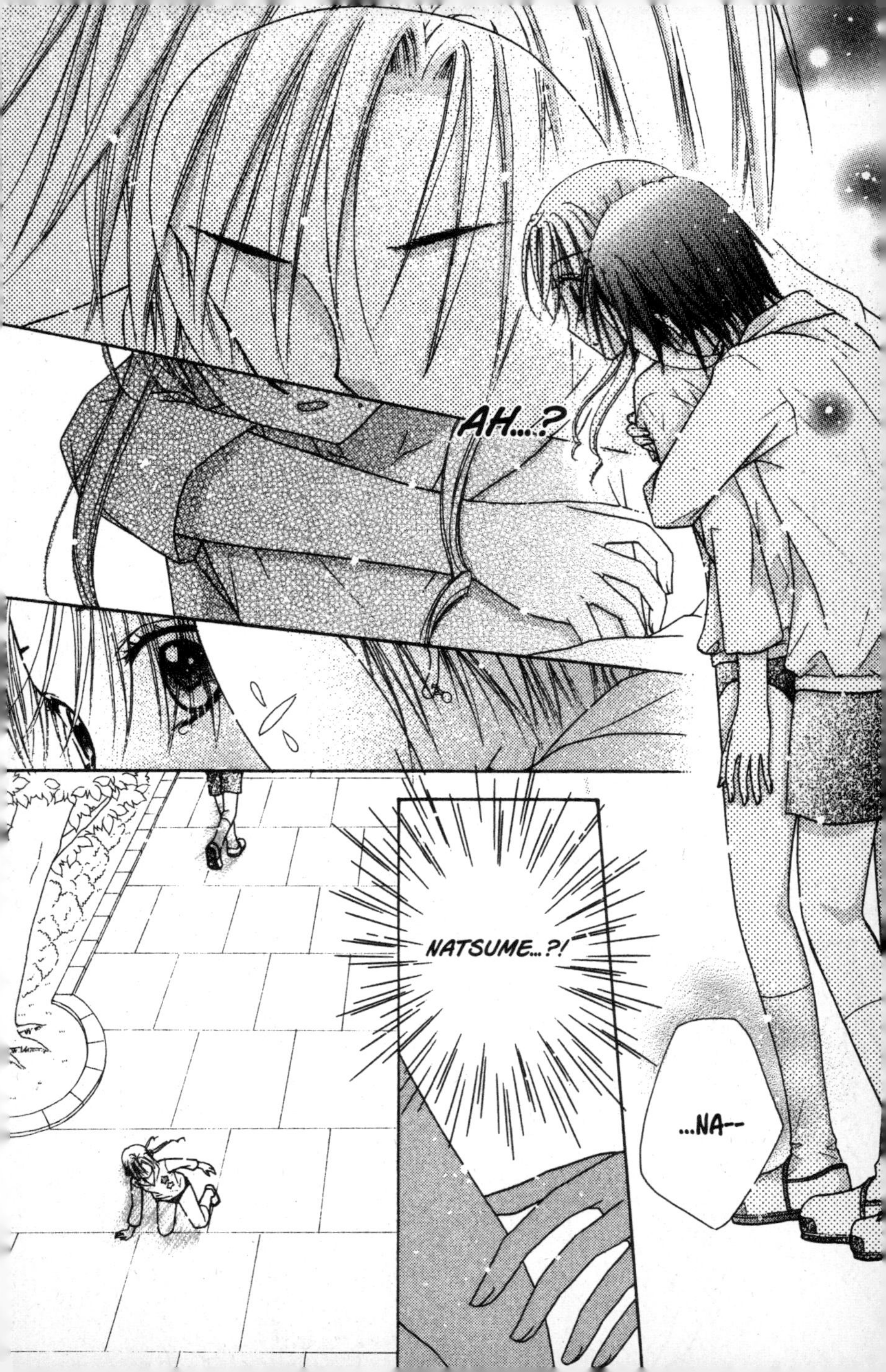
AH...?
...NA--
NATSUME...?!

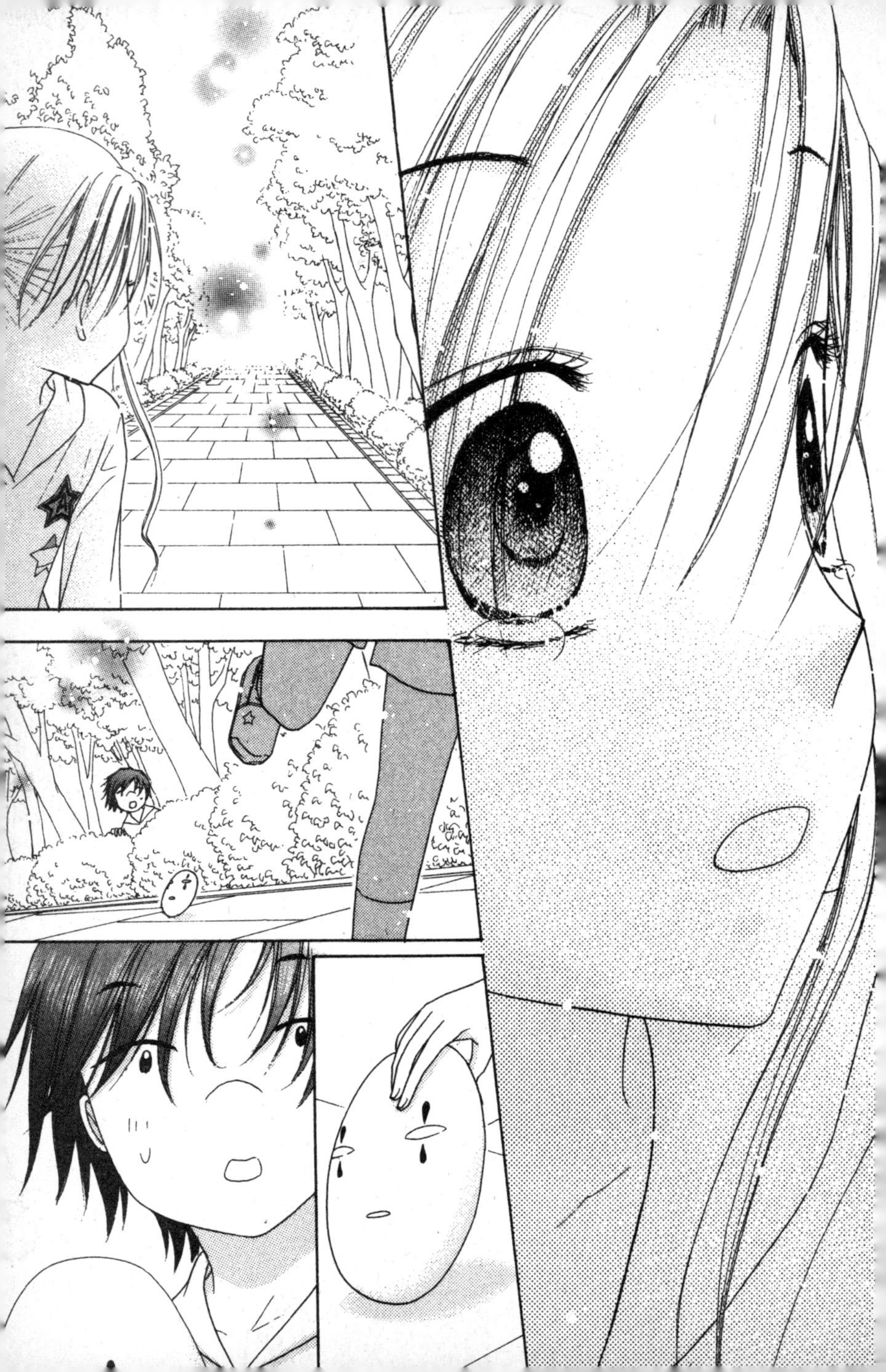

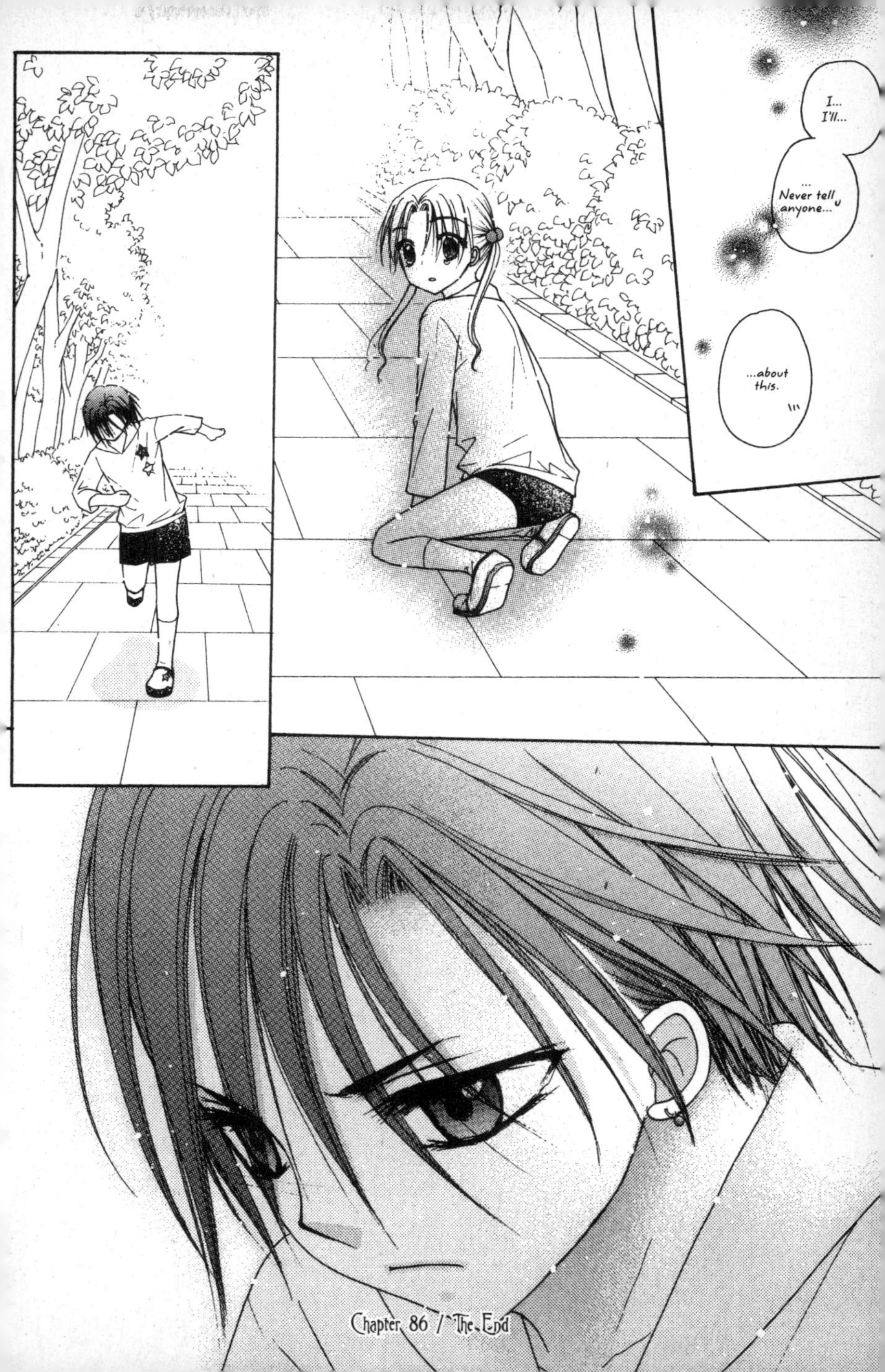
I... I'll...
... Never tell anyone...
...about this.
Chapter 86 / The End

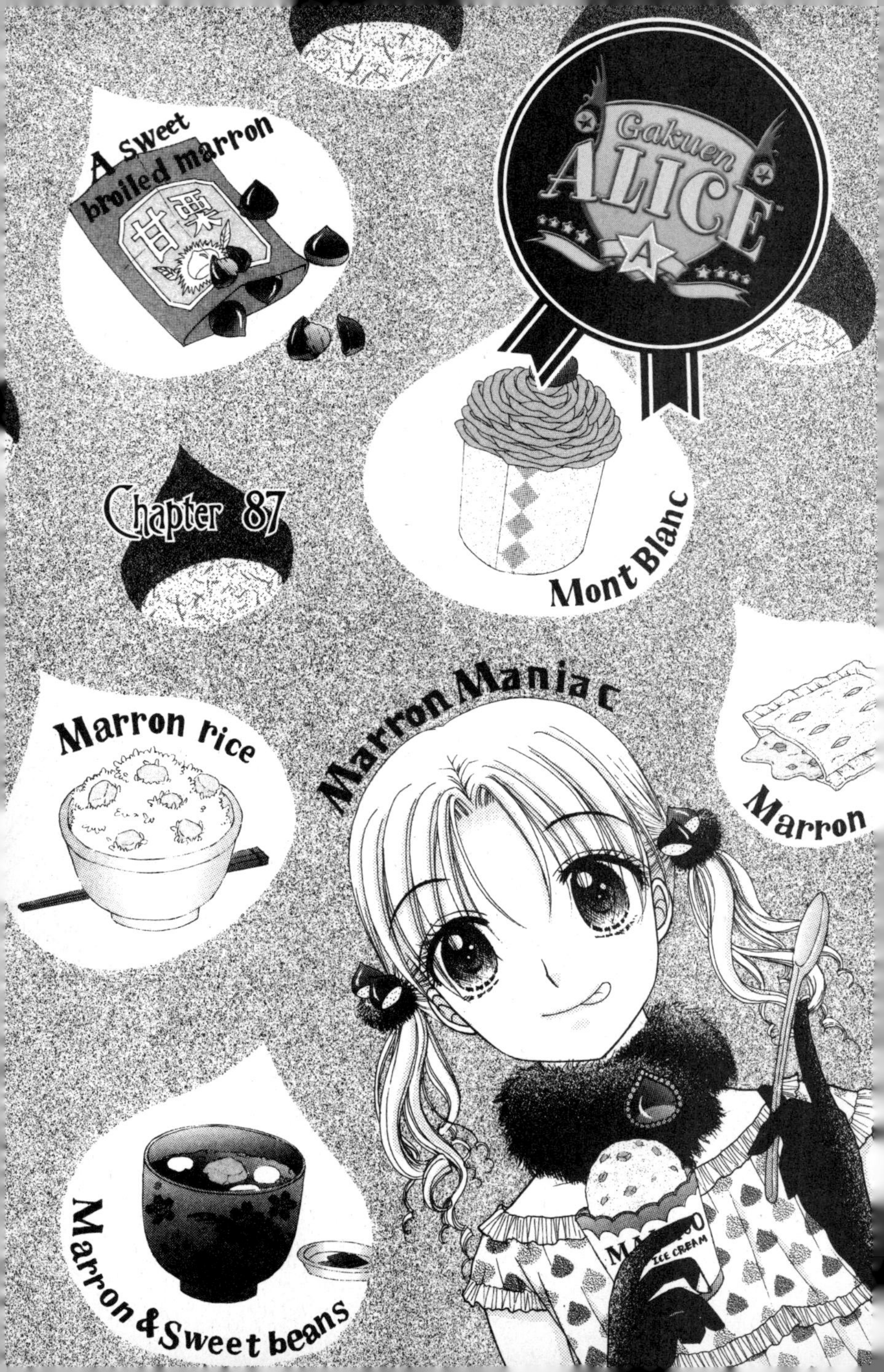
Gakuen ALICE
A sweet broiled marron
甘栗
Chapter 87
Mont Blanc
Marron Maniac
Marron rice
Marron
Marron & Sweet beans

WHICH ONE IS THE REAL NATSUME...?

THE ONE WEARING THE MASK DURING THE BORROWED ITEMS RACE...

WHAT'S GOING ON?

IT DOESN'T MAKE SENSE...

AND JUST NOW...

...OR THE NATSUME WITH THE COLD EYES A FEW MINUTES AGO?

IS THERE SOME REASON THAT NATSUME...

...HAS TO TREAT ME LIKE THAT...

...AND HIDE THE REAL NATSUME UNDER A MASK...?

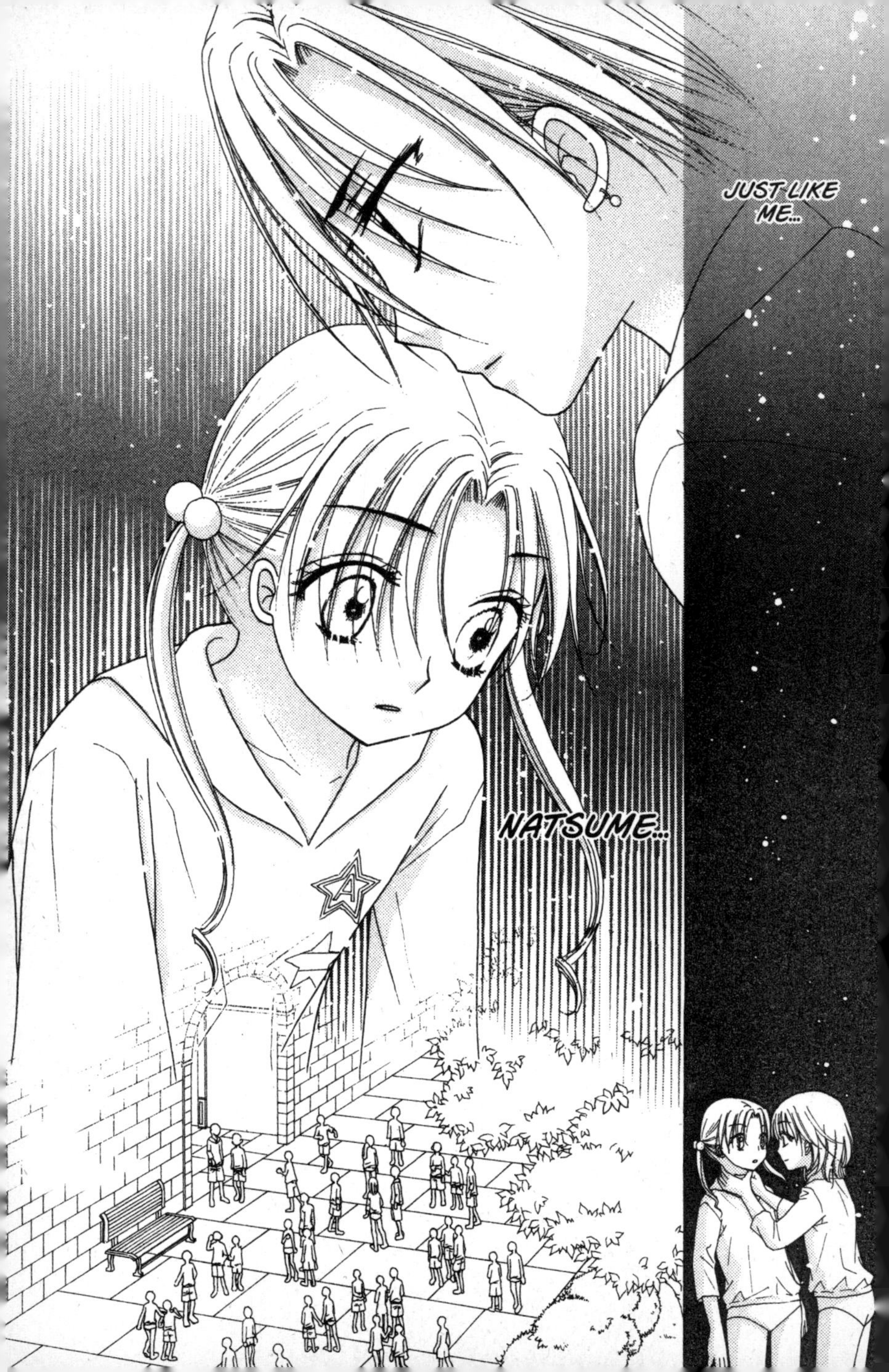
JUST LIKE ME...
NATSUME...

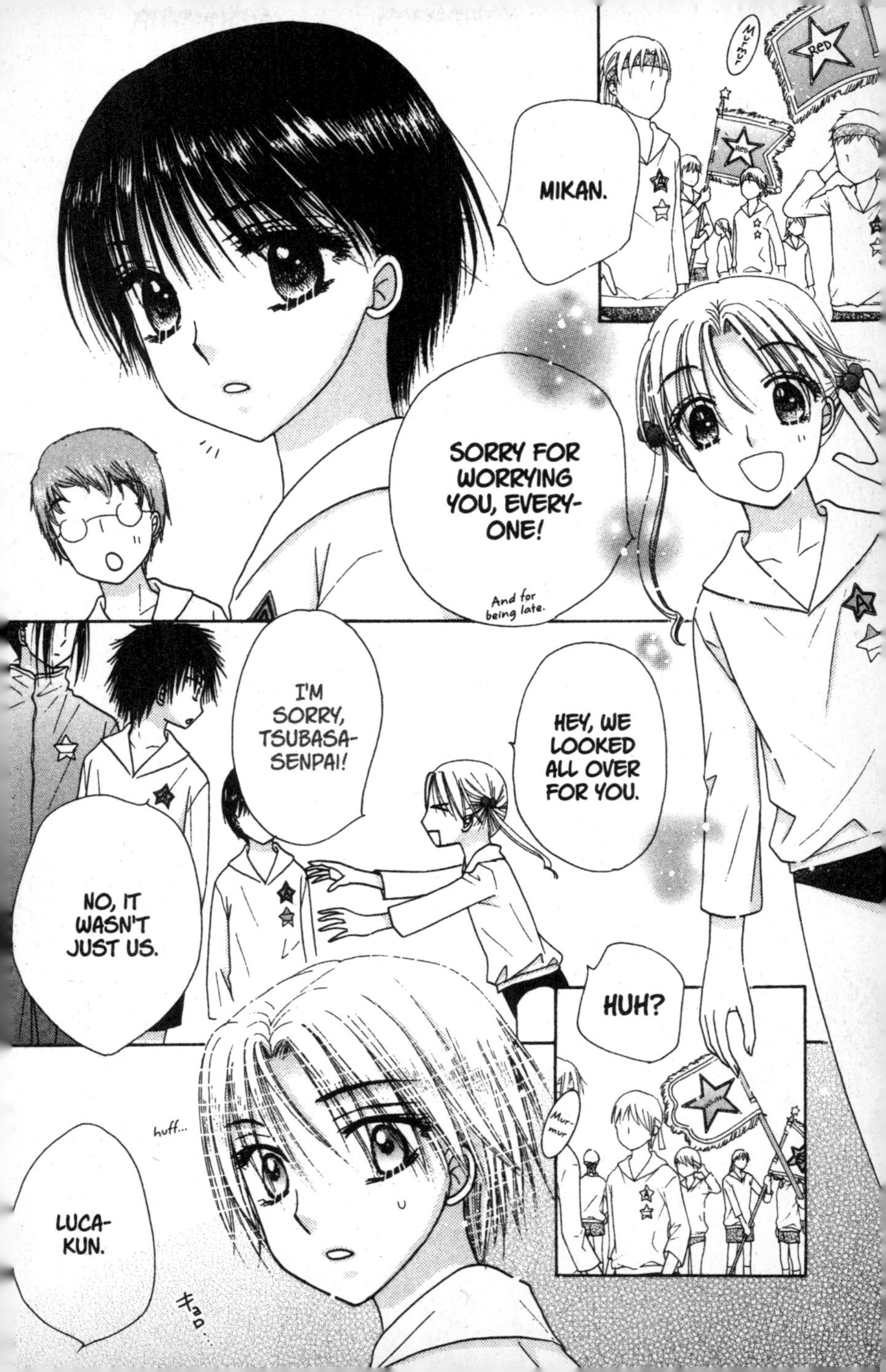
Murmur
MIKAN.
SORRY FOR WORRYING YOU, EVERY-ONE!
And for being late.
HEY, WE LOOKED ALL OVER FOR YOU.
I'M SORRY, TSUBASA-SENPAI!
NO, IT WASN'T JUST US.
HUH?
Mur-mur
huff...
LUCA-KUN.
キョロ...

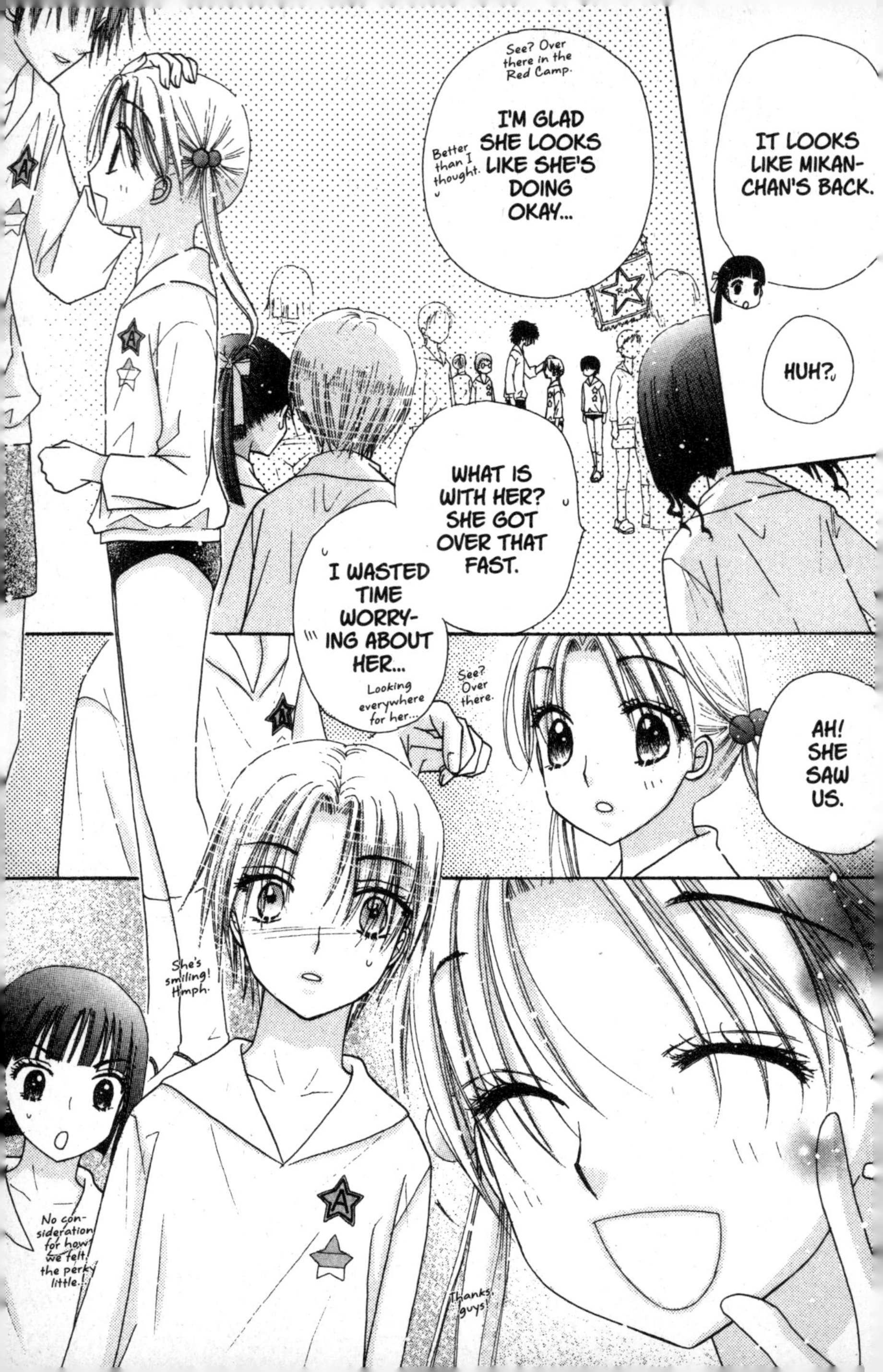
IT LOOKS LIKE MIKAN-CHAN'S BACK.
HUH?
See? Over there in the Red Camp.
I'M GLAD SHE LOOKS LIKE SHE'S DOING OKAY...
Better than I thought.
WHAT IS WITH HER? SHE GOT OVER THAT FAST.
I WASTED TIME WORRY-ING ABOUT HER...
Looking everywhere for her...
AH! SHE SAW US.
See? Over there.
Thanks, guys!
She's smiling! Hmph.
No con-sideration for how we felt, the perky little..!

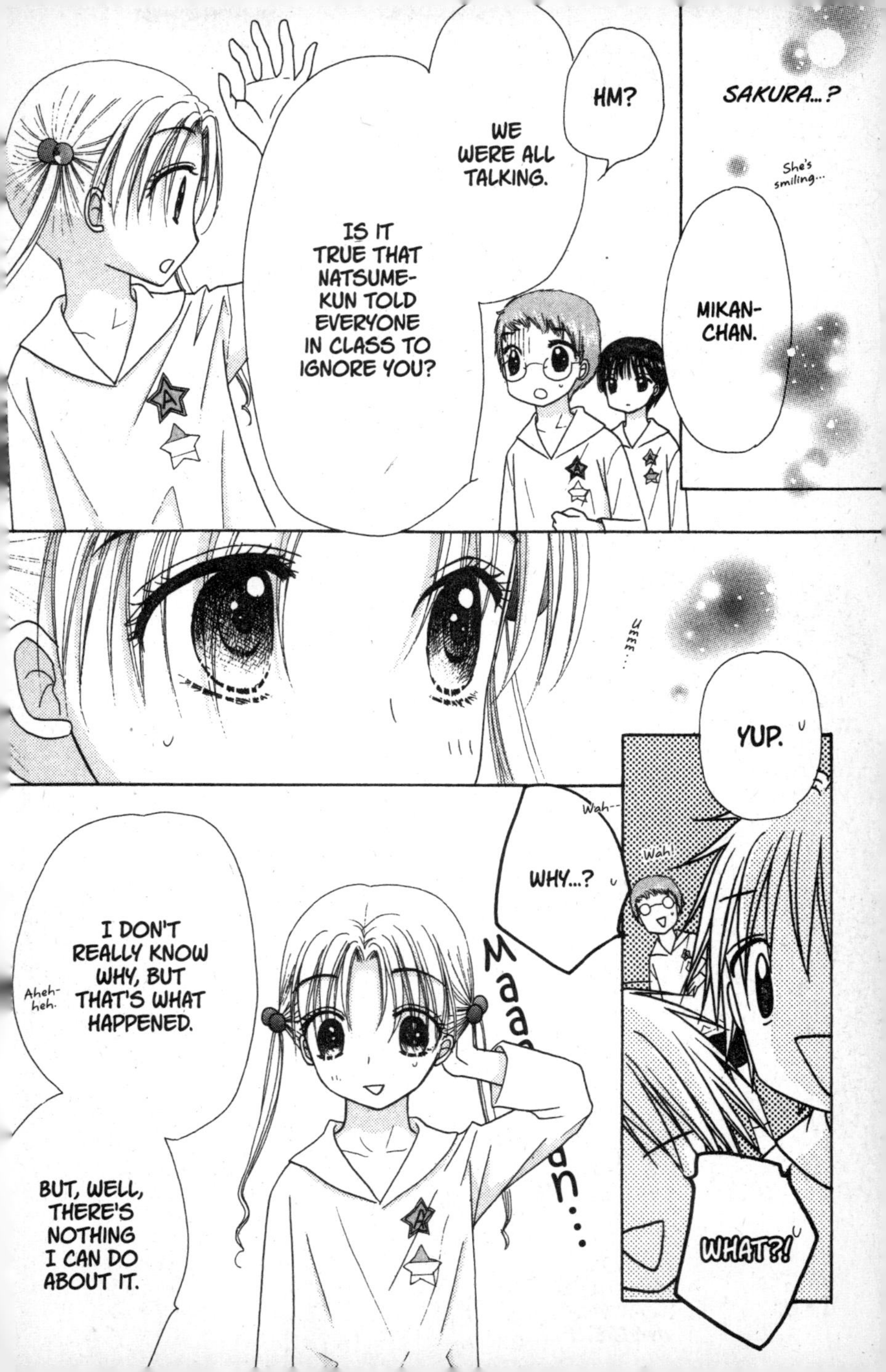
SAKURA...?
She's smiling...
MIKAN-CHAN.
HM?
WE WERE ALL TALKING.
IS IT TRUE THAT NATSUME-KUN TOLD EVERYONE IN CLASS TO IGNORE YOU?
Ummm...
YUP.
Wah--
WHY...?
Wah!
WHAT?!
Maaan...
I DON'T REALLY KNOW WHY, BUT THAT'S WHAT HAPPENED.
Aheh-heh.
BUT, WELL, THERE'S NOTHING I CAN DO ABOUT IT.

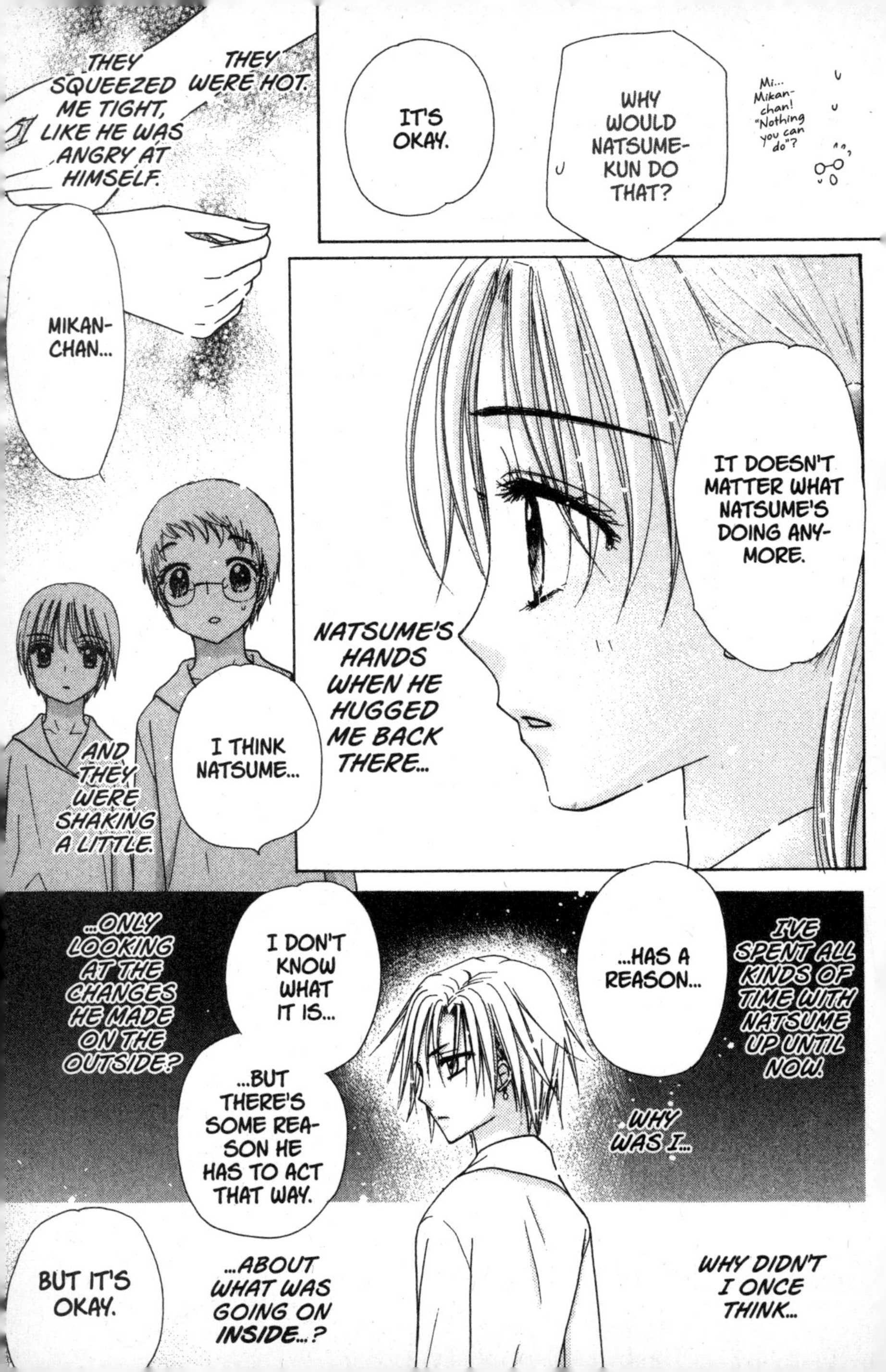
Mi... Mikan-chan! "Nothing you can do"?
WHY WOULD NATSUME-KUN DO THAT?
IT'S OKAY.
IT DOESN'T MATTER WHAT NATSUME'S DOING ANYMORE.
NATSUME'S HANDS WHEN HE HUGGED ME BACK THERE...
THEY WERE HOT.
THEY SQUEEZED ME TIGHT, LIKE HE WAS ANGRY AT HIMSELF.
MIKAN-CHAN...
AND THEY WERE SHAKING A LITTLE.
I THINK NATSUME...
I'VE SPENT ALL KINDS OF TIME WITH NATSUME UP UNTIL NOW.
...HAS A REASON...
WHY WAS I...
I DON'T KNOW WHAT IT IS...
...ONLY LOOKING AT THE CHANGES HE MADE ON THE OUTSIDE?
...BUT THERE'S SOME REASON HE HAS TO ACT THAT WAY.
WHY DIDN'T I ONCE THINK...
...ABOUT WHAT WAS GOING ON INSIDE...?
BUT IT'S OKAY.

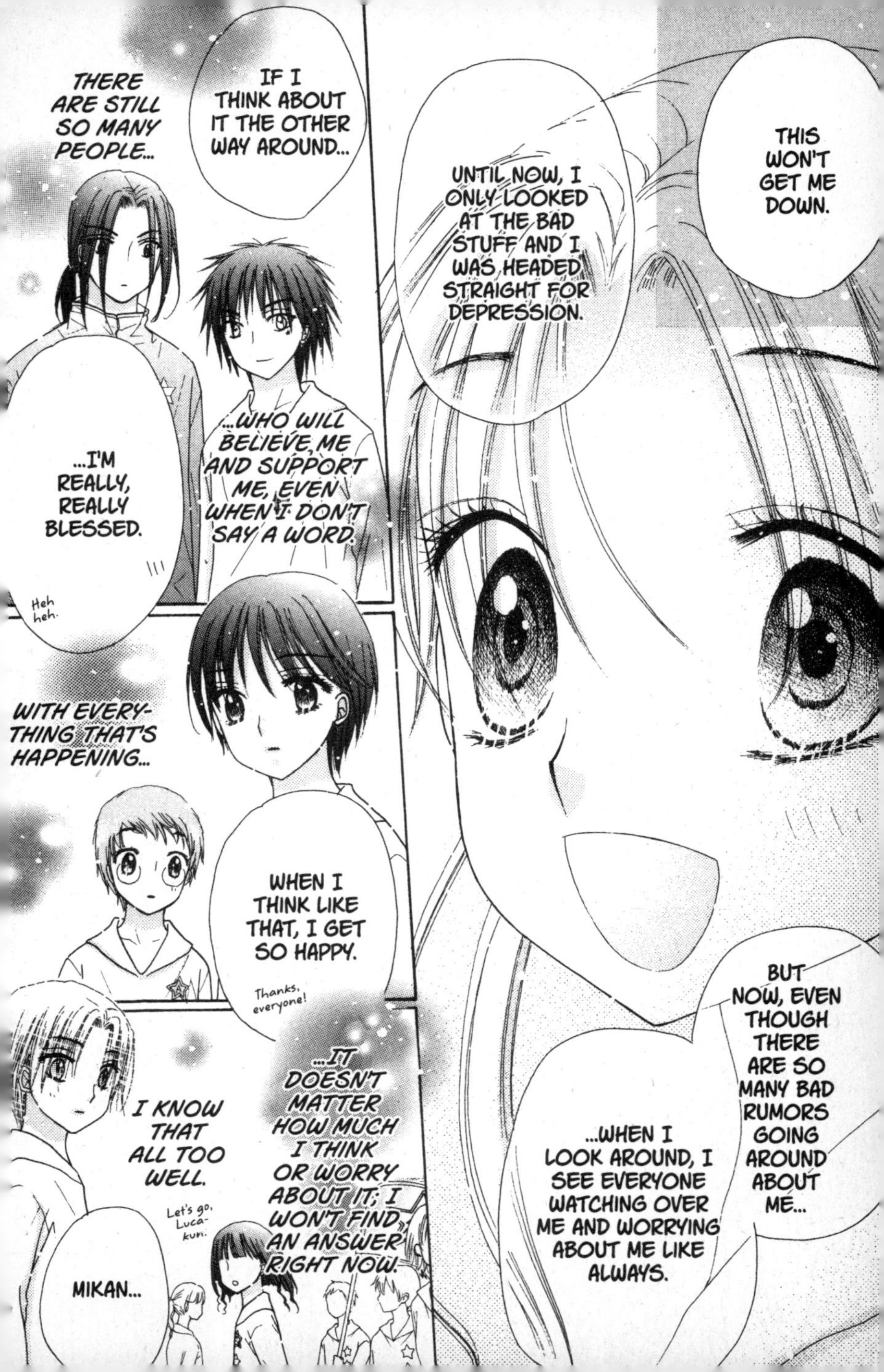
THIS WON'T GET ME DOWN.
UNTIL NOW, I ONLY LOOKED AT THE BAD STUFF AND I WAS HEADED STRAIGHT FOR DEPRESSION.
BUT NOW, EVEN THOUGH THERE ARE SO MANY BAD RUMORS GOING AROUND ABOUT ME...
...WHEN I LOOK AROUND, I SEE EVERYONE WATCHING OVER ME AND WORRYING ABOUT ME LIKE ALWAYS.
IF I THINK ABOUT IT THE OTHER WAY AROUND...
THERE ARE STILL SO MANY PEOPLE...
...WHO WILL BELIEVE ME AND SUPPORT ME, EVEN WHEN I DON'T SAY A WORD.
...I'M REALLY, REALLY BLESSED.
Heh heh.
WHEN I THINK LIKE THAT, I GET SO HAPPY.
Thanks, everyone!
WITH EVERY-THING THAT'S HAPPENING...
...IT DOESN'T MATTER HOW MUCH I THINK OR WORRY ABOUT IT; I WON'T FIND AN ANSWER RIGHT NOW.
I KNOW THAT ALL TOO WELL.
Let's go, Luca-kun.
MIKAN...

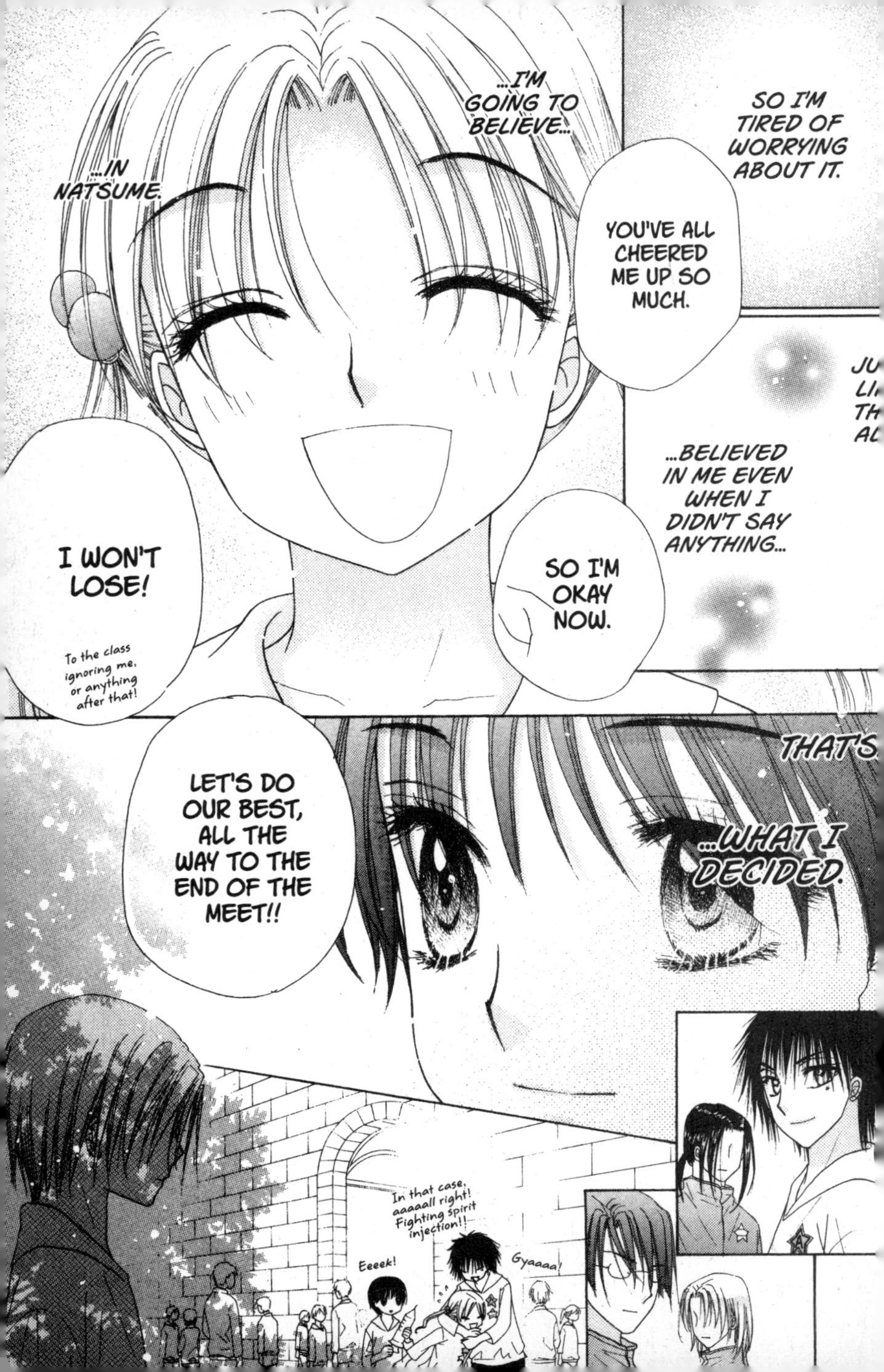

SO I'M TIRED OF WORRYING ABOUT IT.
...I'M GOING TO BELIEVE...
...IN NATSUME.
YOU'VE ALL CHEERED ME UP SO MUCH.
...BELIEVED IN ME EVEN WHEN I DIDN'T SAY ANYTHING...
SO I'M OKAY NOW.
I WON'T LOSE!
To the class ignoring me, or anything after that!
THAT'S
...WHAT I DECIDED.
LET'S DO OUR BEST, ALL THE WAY TO THE END OF THE MEET!!
In that case, aaaaall right! Fighting spirit injection!!
Gyaaaa!
Eeeek!

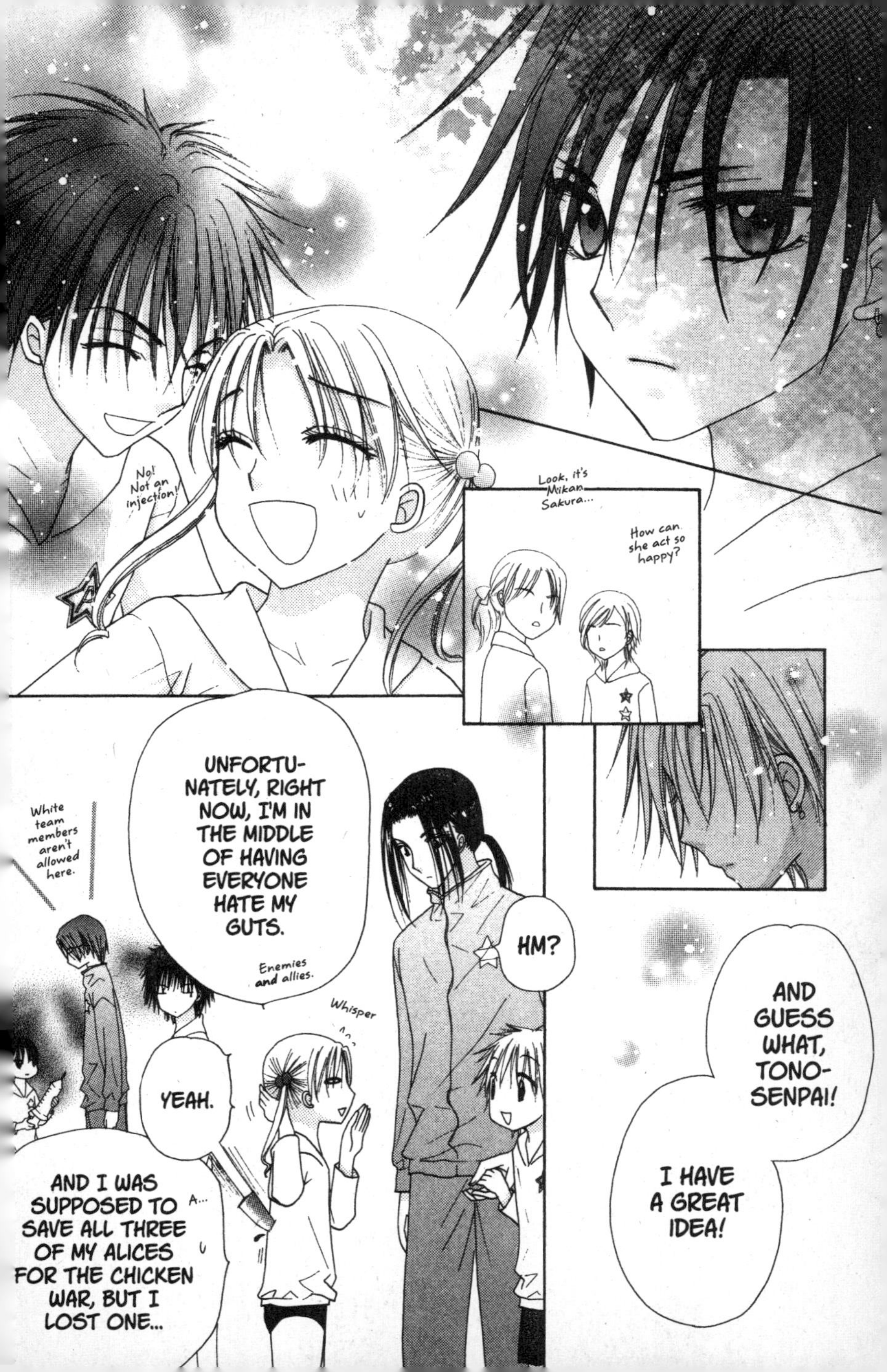
No! Not an injection!
Look, it's Mikan Sakura...
How can she act so happy?
AND GUESS WHAT, TONO-SENPAI!
I HAVE A GREAT IDEA!
HM?
UNFORTU-NATELY, RIGHT NOW, I'M IN THE MIDDLE OF HAVING EVERYONE HATE MY GUTS.
White team members aren't allowed here.
Enemies and allies.
Whisper
YEAH.
AND I WAS SUPPOSED TO SAVE ALL THREE OF MY ALICES FOR THE CHICKEN WAR, BUT I LOST ONE...
A...

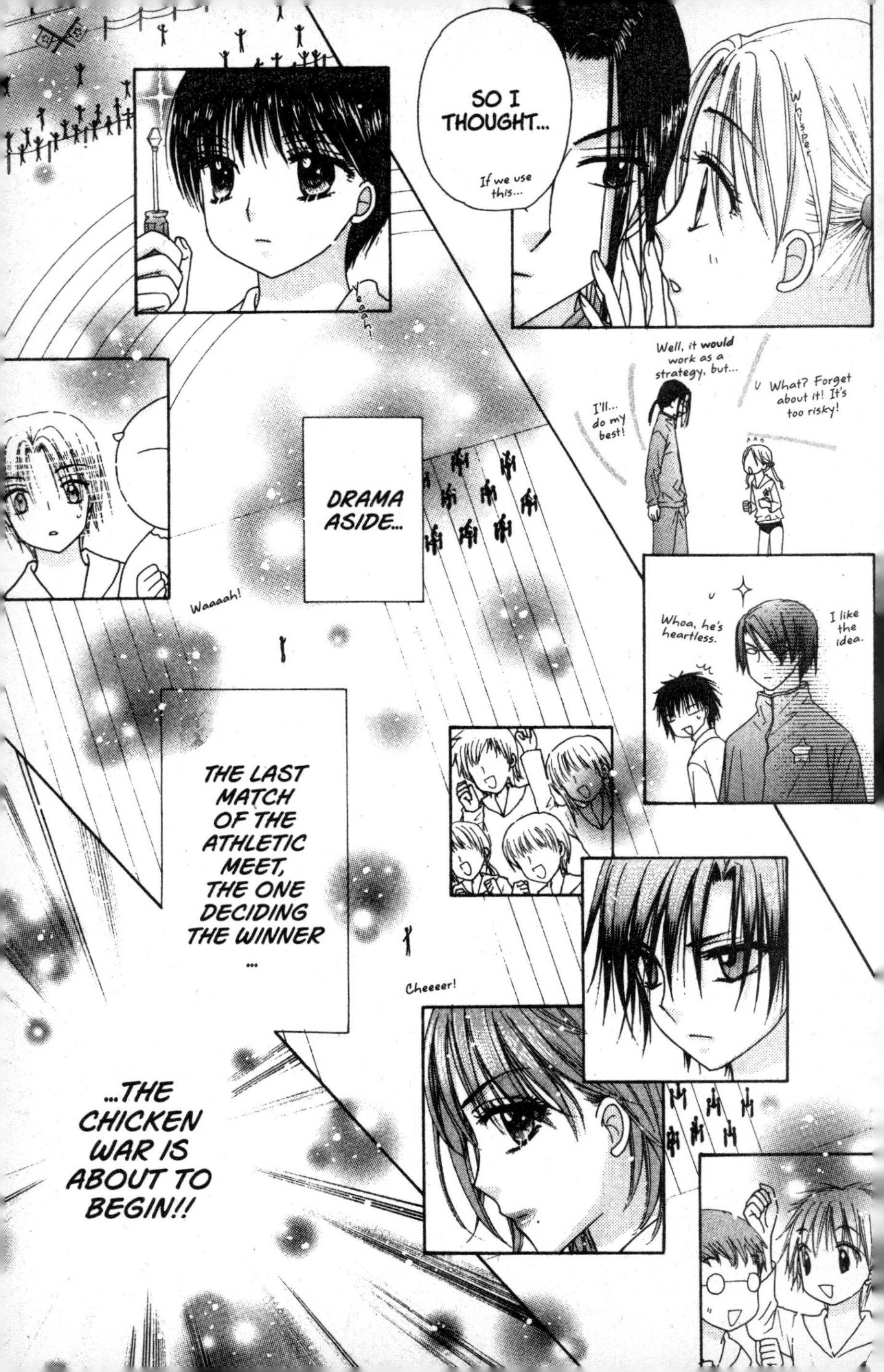
SO I THOUGHT...
If we use this...
Whisper
Yeaah!
Well, it would work as a strategy, but...
What? Forget about it! It's too risky!
I'll... do my best!
I like the idea.
Whoa, he's heartless.
DRAMA ASIDE...
Waaaah!
THE LAST MATCH OF THE ATHLETIC MEET, THE ONE DECIDING THE WINNER ...
Cheeeer!
...THE CHICKEN WAR IS ABOUT TO BEGIN!!

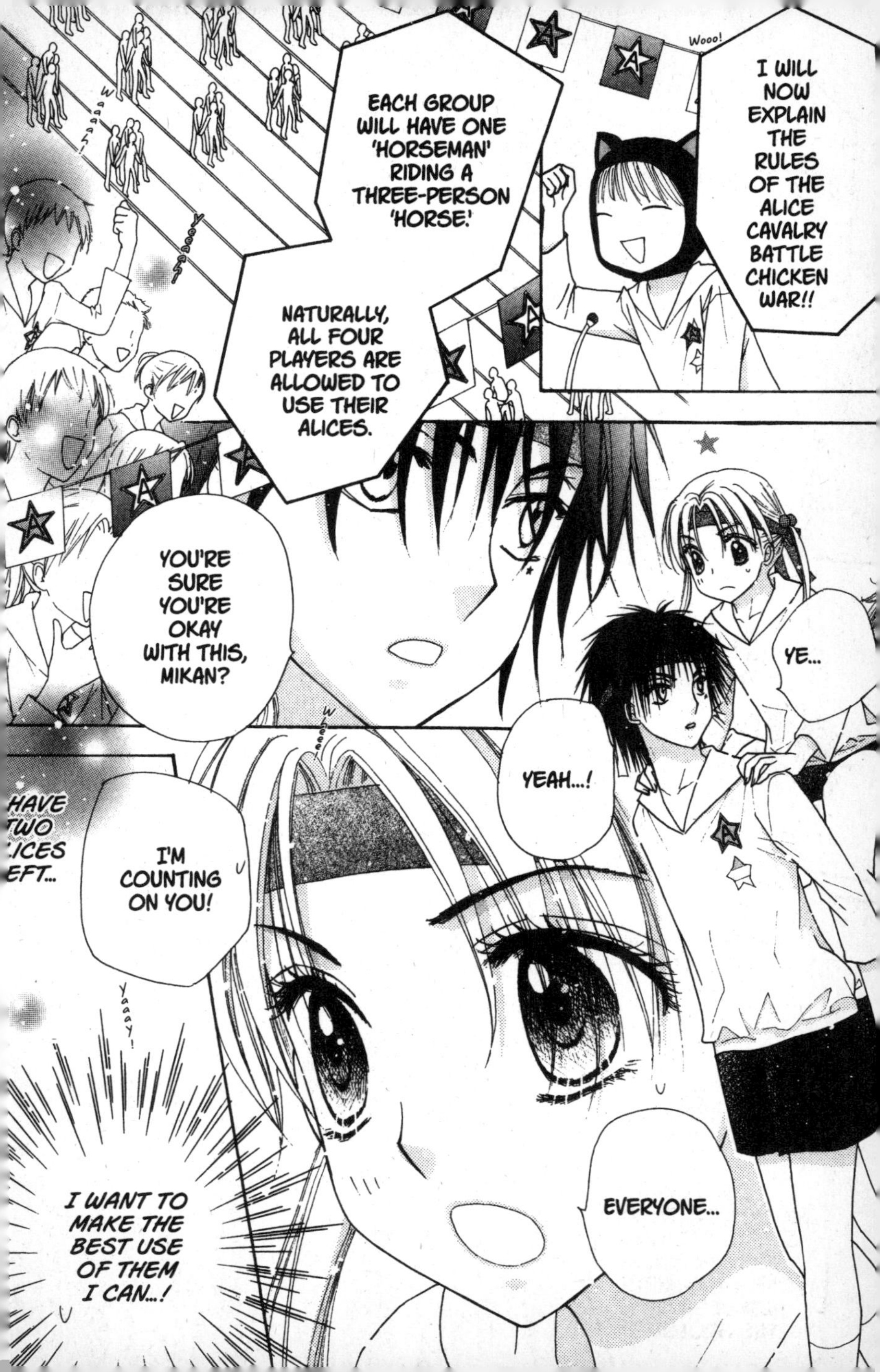
Wooo!
I WILL NOW EXPLAIN THE RULES OF THE ALICE CAVALRY BATTLE CHICKEN WAR!!
EACH GROUP WILL HAVE ONE 'HORSEMAN' RIDING A THREE-PERSON 'HORSE.'
NATURALLY, ALL FOUR PLAYERS ARE ALLOWED TO USE THEIR ALICES.
YE...
YOU'RE SURE YOU'RE OKAY WITH THIS, MIKAN?
YEAH...!
EVERYONE...
I'M COUNTING ON YOU!
HAVE TWO ICES EFT...
Yaaay!
I WANT TO MAKE THE BEST USE OF THEM I CAN...!

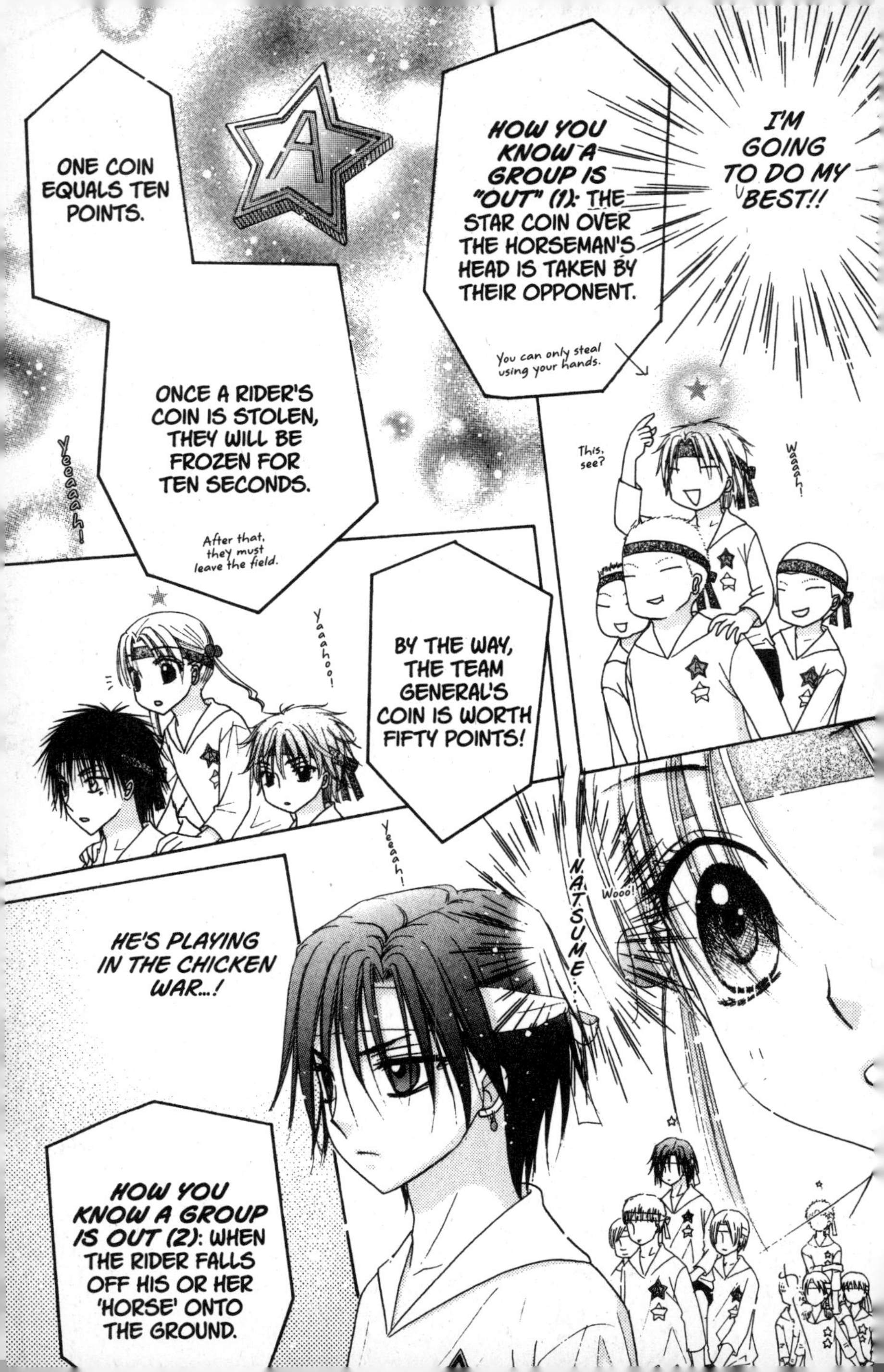
I'M GOING TO DO MY BEST!!
HOW YOU KNOW A GROUP IS "OUT" (1): THE STAR COIN OVER THE HORSEMAN'S HEAD IS TAKEN BY THEIR OPPONENT.
You can only steal using your hands.
ONE COIN EQUALS TEN POINTS.
ONCE A RIDER'S COIN IS STOLEN, THEY WILL BE FROZEN FOR TEN SECONDS.
After that, they must leave the field.
Yeeaaah!
Waaaah!
This, see?
BY THE WAY, THE TEAM GENERAL'S COIN IS WORTH FIFTY POINTS!
Yaaahoo!
NATSUME...
Wooo!
Yeeaah!
HE'S PLAYING IN THE CHICKEN WAR...!
HOW YOU KNOW A GROUP IS OUT (2): WHEN THE RIDER FALLS OFF HIS OR HER 'HORSE' ONTO THE GROUND.

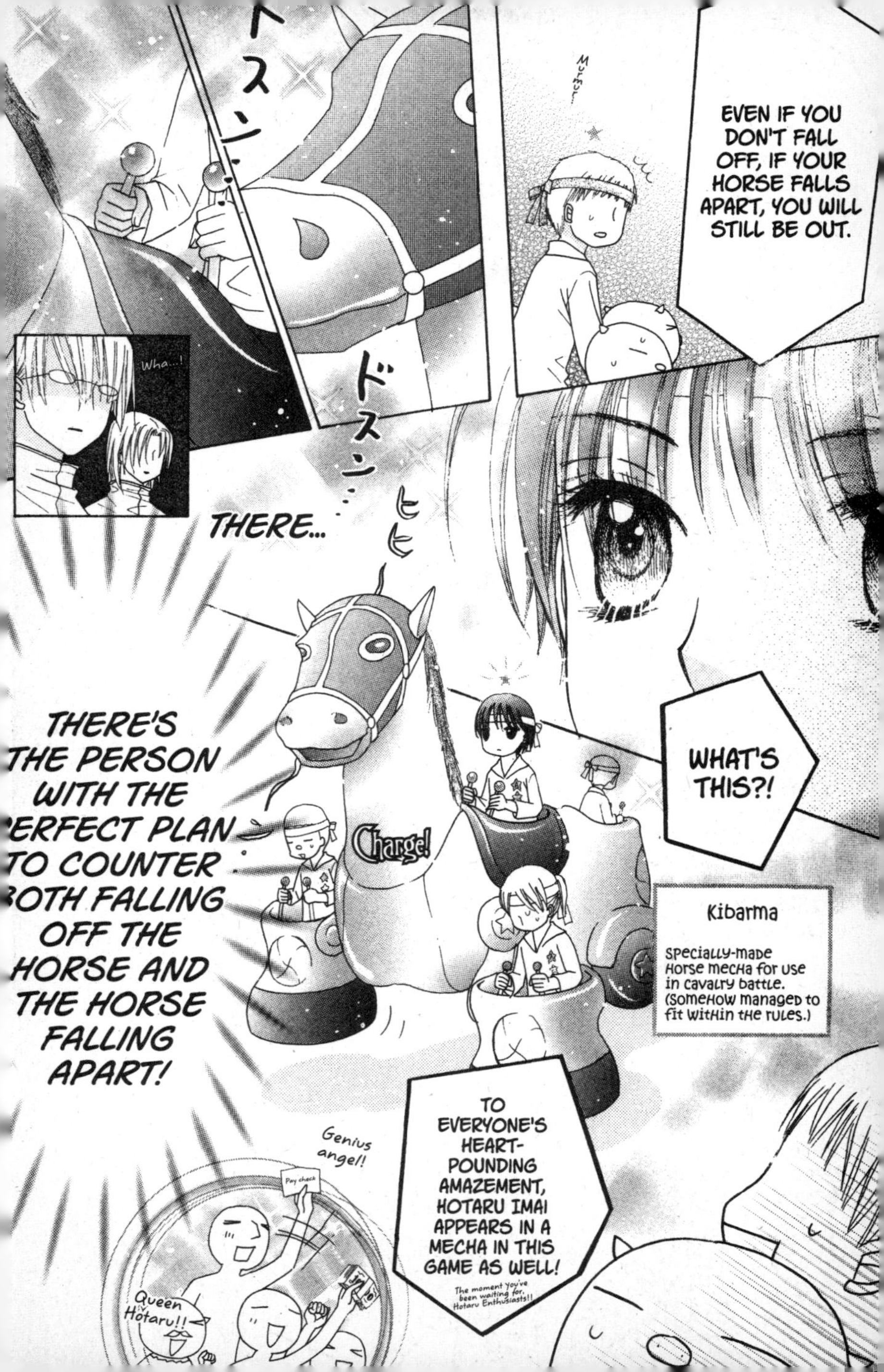
Murmur...
EVEN IF YOU DON'T FALL OFF, IF YOUR HORSE FALLS APART, YOU WILL STILL BE OUT.
ヘスン…
Wha...!
ドスン…
THERE...
ヒヒ
WHAT'S THIS?!
THERE'S THE PERSON WITH THE PERFECT PLAN TO COUNTER BOTH FALLING OFF THE HORSE AND THE HORSE FALLING APART!
Charge!
Kibarma
Specially-made horse mecha for use in cavalry battle. (Somehow managed to fit within the rules.)
TO EVERYONE'S HEART-POUNDING AMAZEMENT, HOTARU IMAI APPEARS IN A MECHA IN THIS GAME AS WELL!
The moment you've been waiting for, Hotaru Enthusiasts!!
Genius angel!
Pay check
Queen Hotaru!!

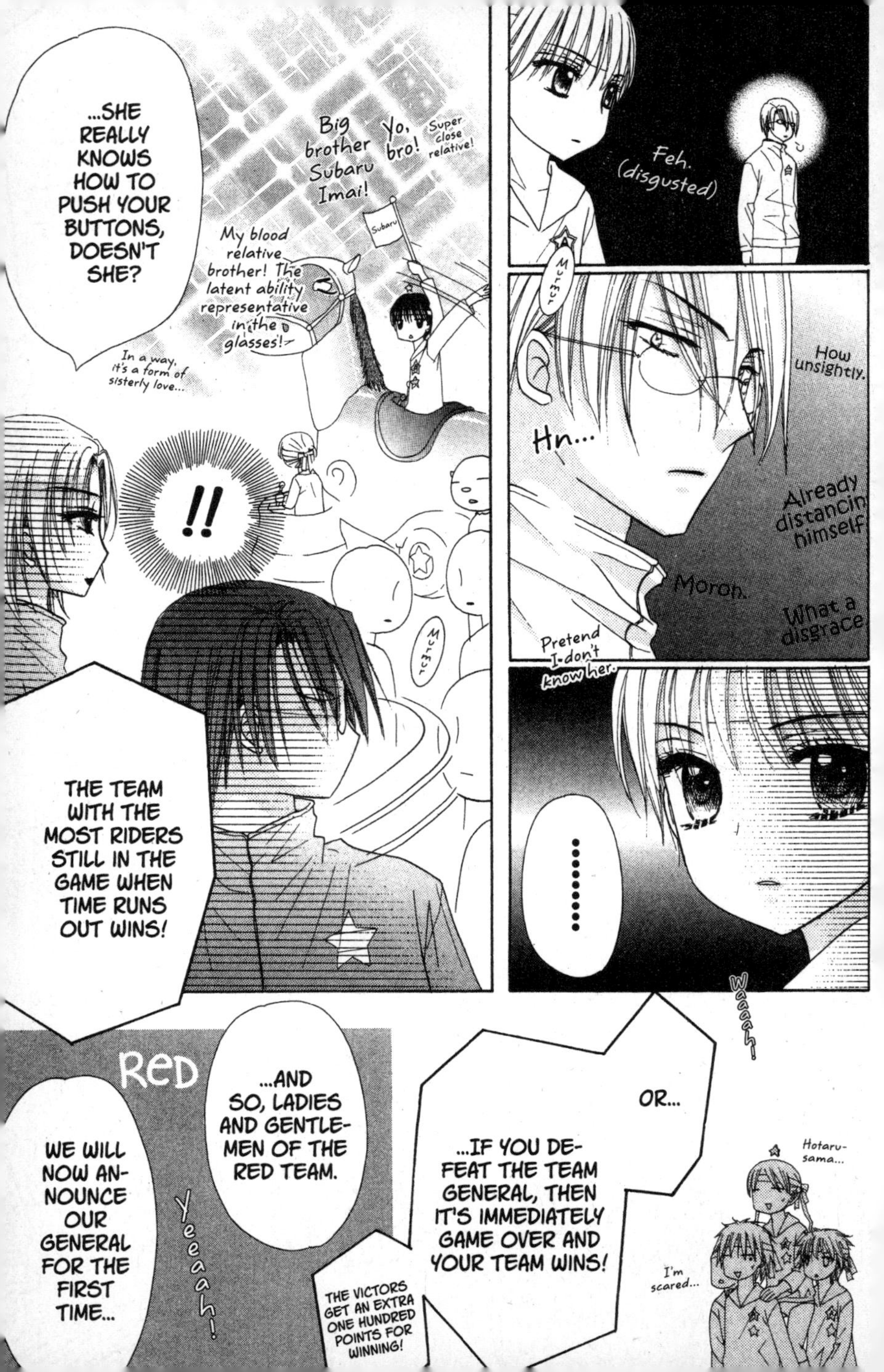
Feh. (disgusted)
Murmur
Hn...
How unsightly.
Already distancing himself
Moron.
What a disgrace
Pretend I don't know her.
....
...SHE REALLY KNOWS HOW TO PUSH YOUR BUTTONS, DOESN'T SHE?
Super close relative!
Yo, bro!
Big brother Subaru Imai!
Subaru
My blood relative brother! The latent ability representative in the glasses!
In a way, it's a form of sisterly love...
!!
Murmur
THE TEAM WITH THE MOST RIDERS STILL IN THE GAME WHEN TIME RUNS OUT WINS!
Waaaah!
OR...
...IF YOU DEFEAT THE TEAM GENERAL, THEN IT'S IMMEDIATELY GAME OVER AND YOUR TEAM WINS!
THE VICTORS GET AN EXTRA ONE HUNDRED POINTS FOR WINNING!
Hotaru-sama...
I'm scared...
RED
...AND SO, LADIES AND GENTLEMEN OF THE RED TEAM.
WE WILL NOW ANNOUNCE OUR GENERAL FOR THE FIRST TIME...
Yeeaah!

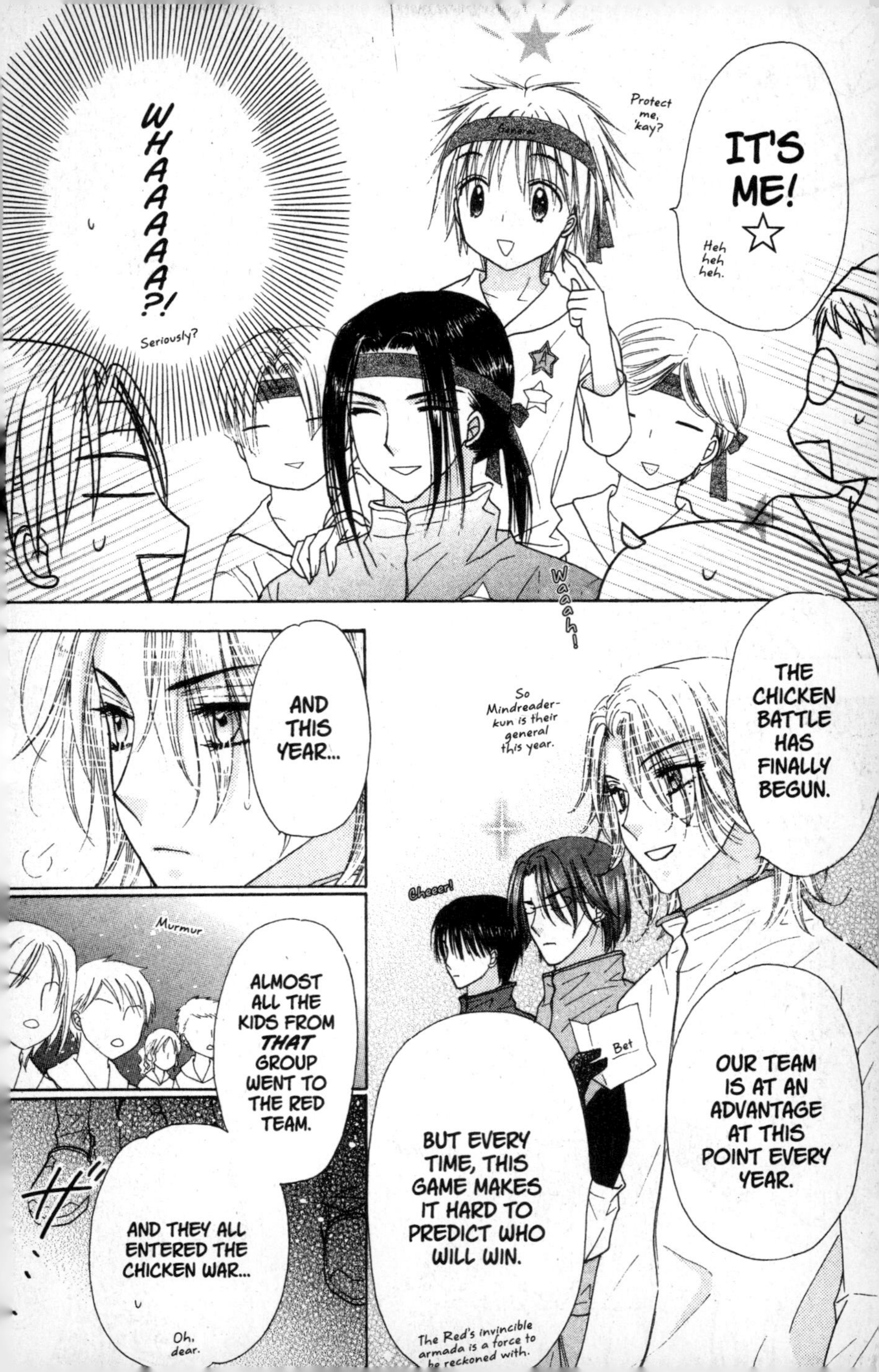
IT'S ME! ☆
Heh heh heh.
Protect me, 'kay?
General
WHAAAAAA?!
Seriously?
Waaah!
THE CHICKEN BATTLE HAS FINALLY BEGUN.
So Mindreader-kun is their general this year.
Cheeer!
OUR TEAM IS AT AN ADVANTAGE AT THIS POINT EVERY YEAR.
Bet
BUT EVERY TIME, THIS GAME MAKES IT HARD TO PREDICT WHO WILL WIN.
The Red's invincible armada is a force to be reckoned with.
AND THIS YEAR...
Murmur
ALMOST ALL THE KIDS FROM *THAT* GROUP WENT TO THE RED TEAM.
AND THEY ALL ENTERED THE CHICKEN WAR...
Oh, dear.

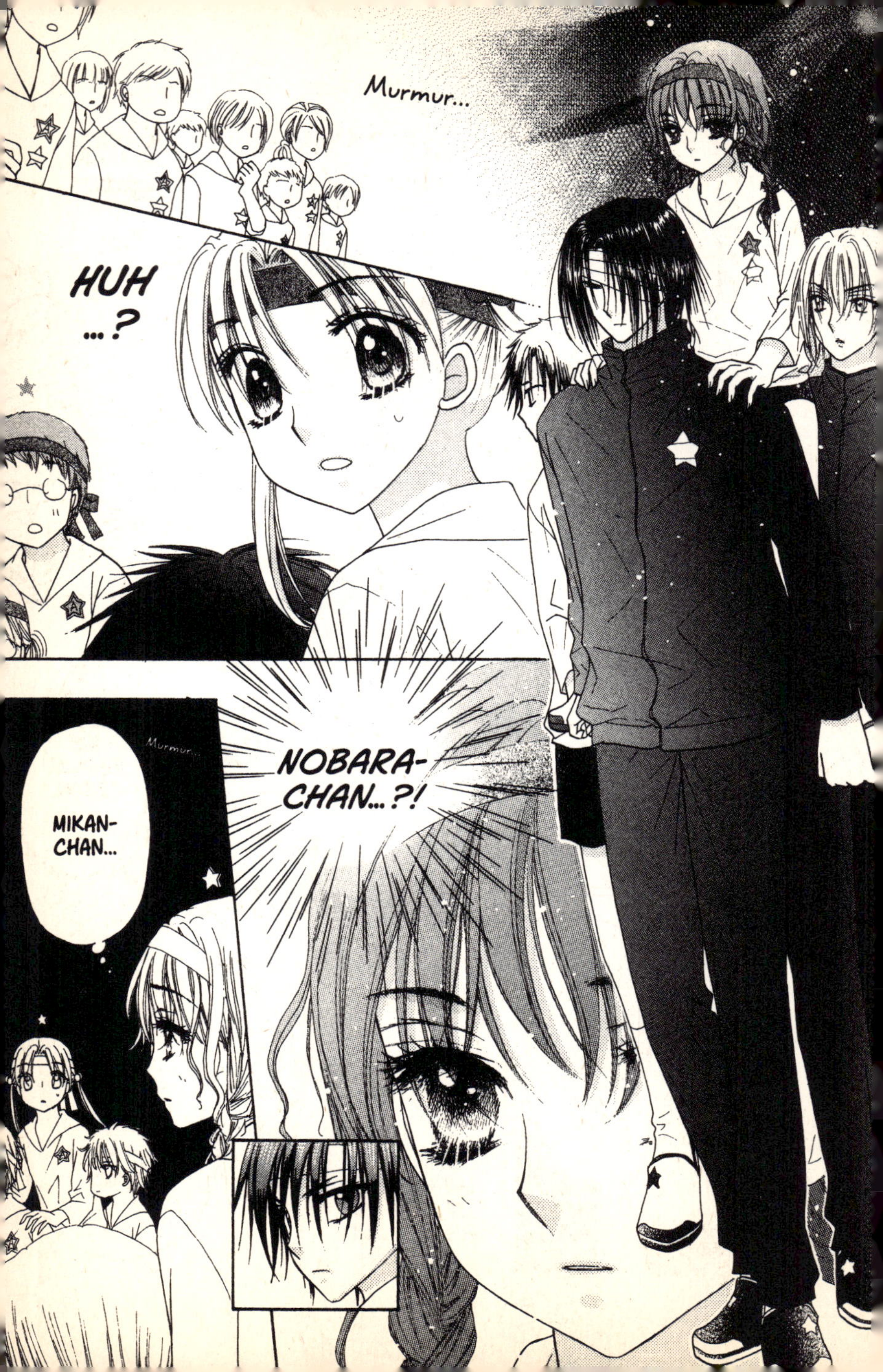
Murmur...
HUH ...?
NOBARA-CHAN...?!
Murmur...
MIKAN-CHAN...

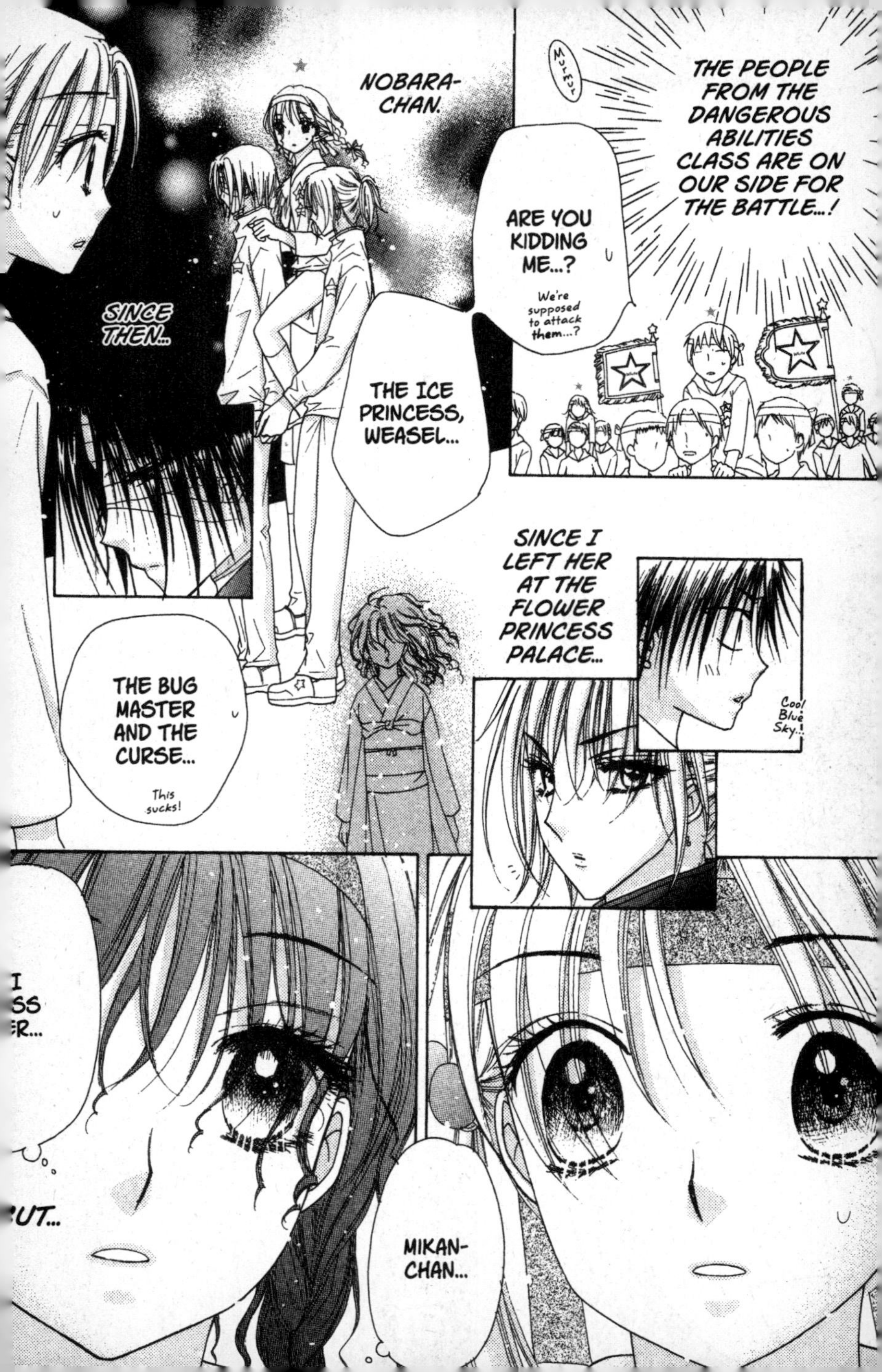
THE PEOPLE FROM THE DANGEROUS ABILITIES CLASS ARE ON OUR SIDE FOR THE BATTLE...!
Murmur
ARE YOU KIDDING ME...?
We're supposed to attack them...?
NOBARA-CHAN.
THE ICE PRINCESS, WEASEL...
SINCE THEN...
THE BUG MASTER AND THE CURSE...
This sucks!
SINCE I LEFT HER AT THE FLOWER PRINCESS PALACE...
Cool Blue Sky..!
MIKAN-CHAN...
I
SS
ER...
UT...

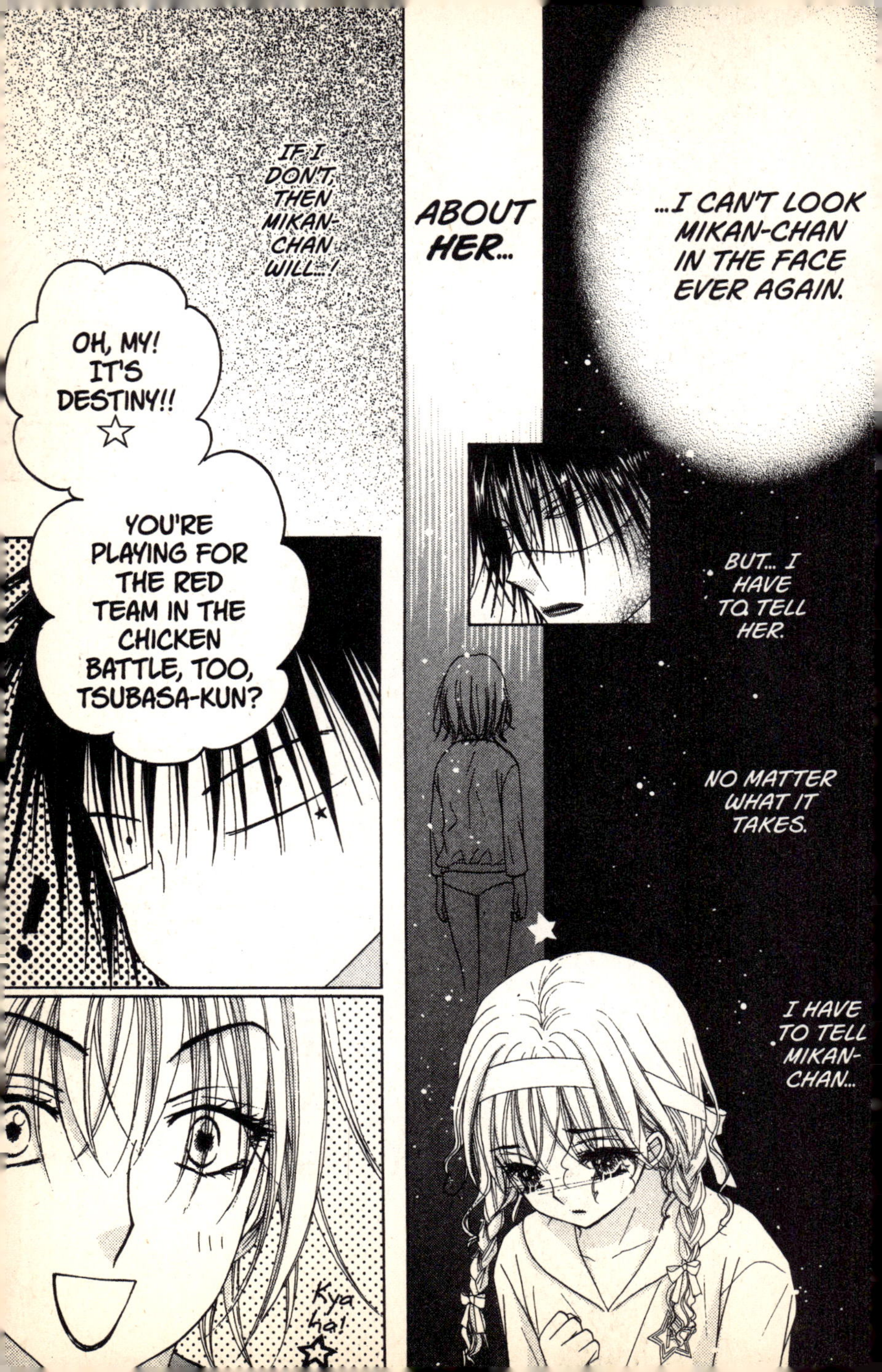
...I CAN'T LOOK MIKAN-CHAN IN THE FACE EVER AGAIN.
ABOUT HER...
BUT... I HAVE TO TELL HER.
NO MATTER WHAT IT TAKES.
I HAVE TO TELL MIKAN-CHAN...
IF I DON'T, THEN MIKAN-CHAN WILL...!
OH, MY! IT'S DESTINY!! ☆
YOU'RE PLAYING FOR THE RED TEAM IN THE CHICKEN BATTLE, TOO, TSUBASA-KUN?
Kya ha!

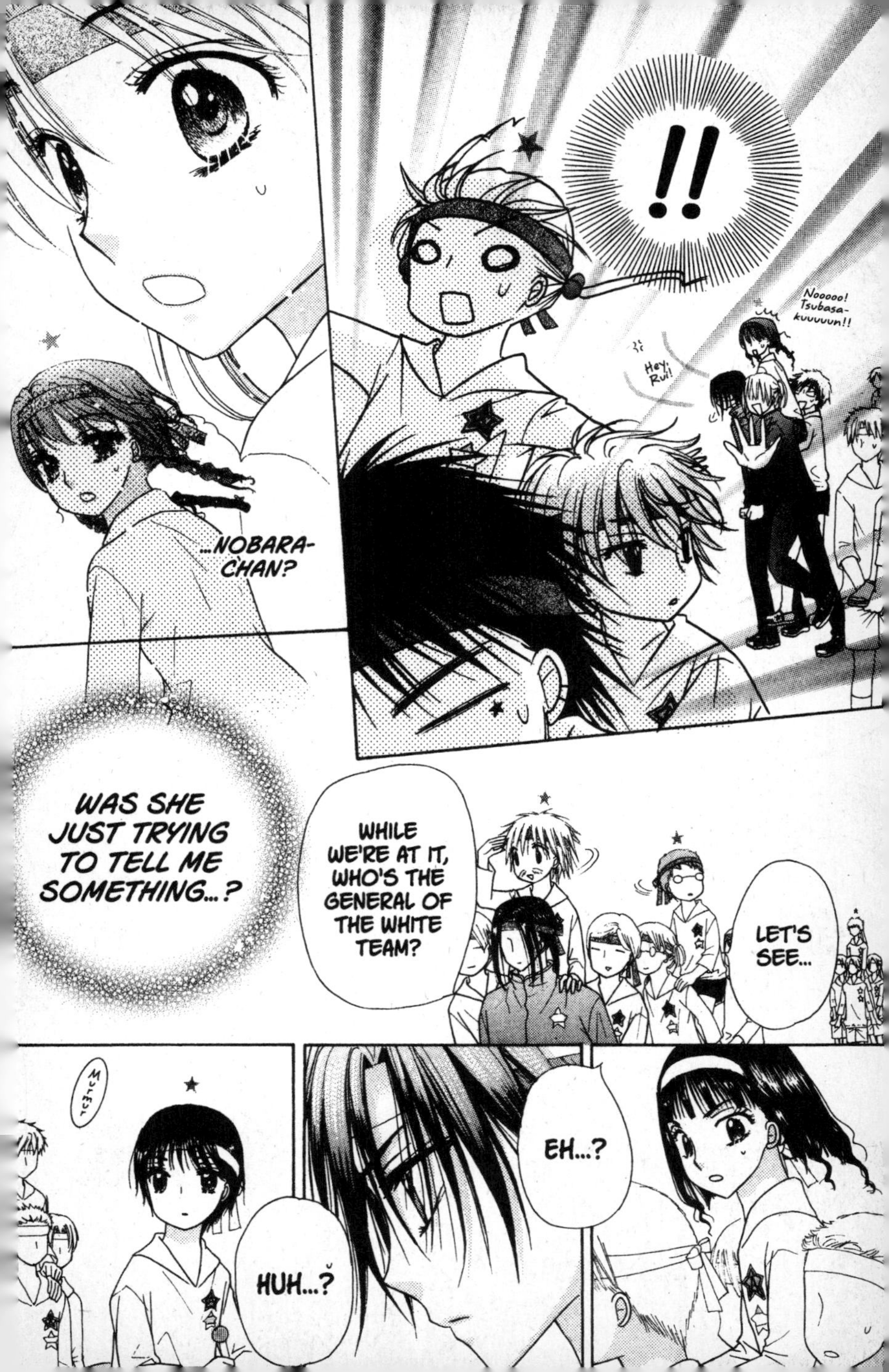
!!
Nooooo! Tsubasa-kuuuuun!!
Hey, Rui!
...NOBARA-CHAN?
WHILE WE'RE AT IT, WHO'S THE GENERAL OF THE WHITE TEAM?
LET'S SEE...
WAS SHE JUST TRYING TO TELL ME SOMETHING...?
EH...?
Murmur
HUH...?

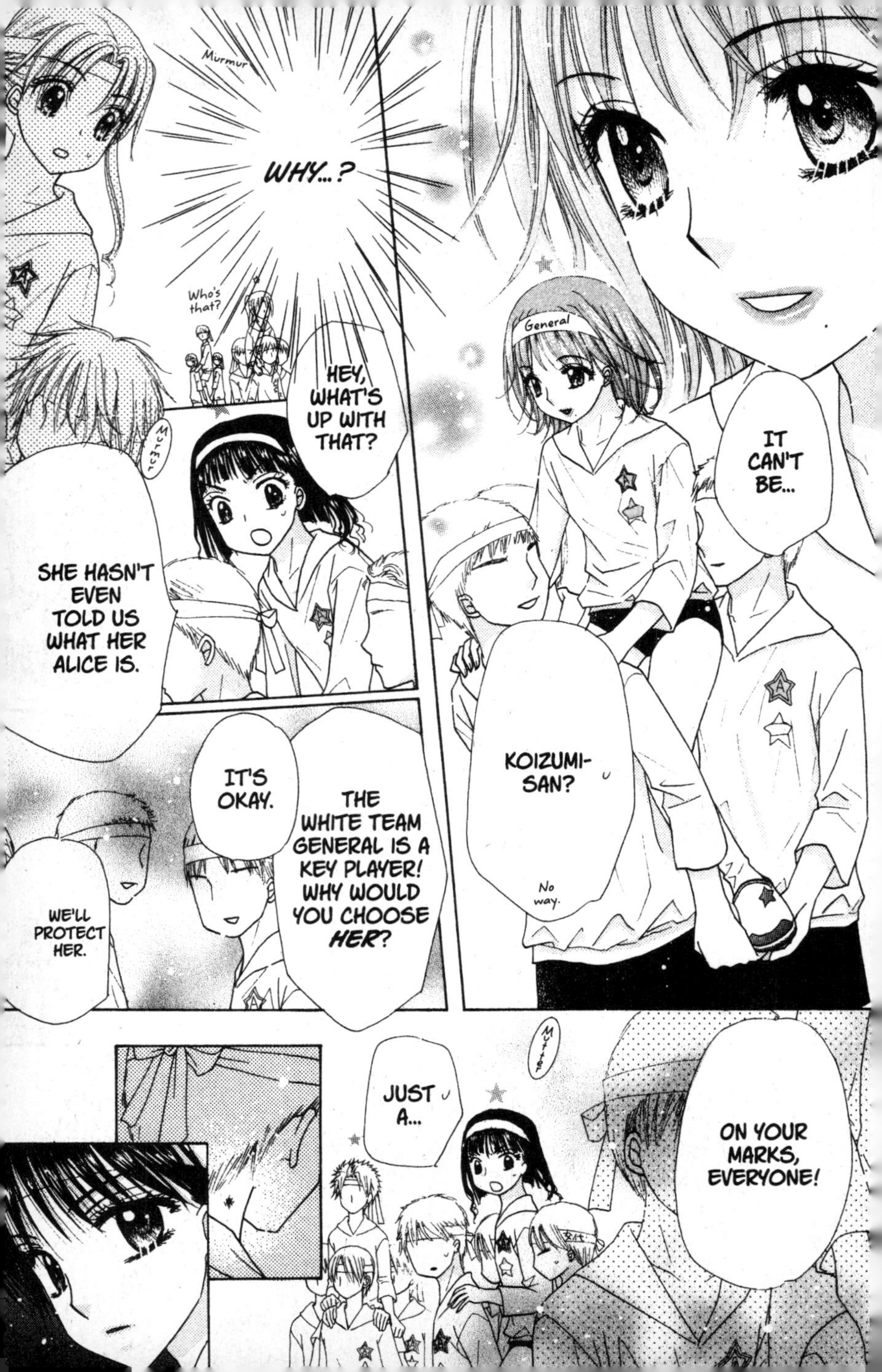
IT CAN'T BE...
WHY...?
Murmur
Who's that?
HEY, WHAT'S UP WITH THAT?
Murmur
SHE HASN'T EVEN TOLD US WHAT HER ALICE IS.
General
KOIZUMI-SAN?
No way.
THE WHITE TEAM GENERAL IS A KEY PLAYER! WHY WOULD YOU CHOOSE *HER*?
IT'S OKAY.
WE'LL PROTECT HER.
ON YOUR MARKS, EVERYONE!
Mutter
JUST A...

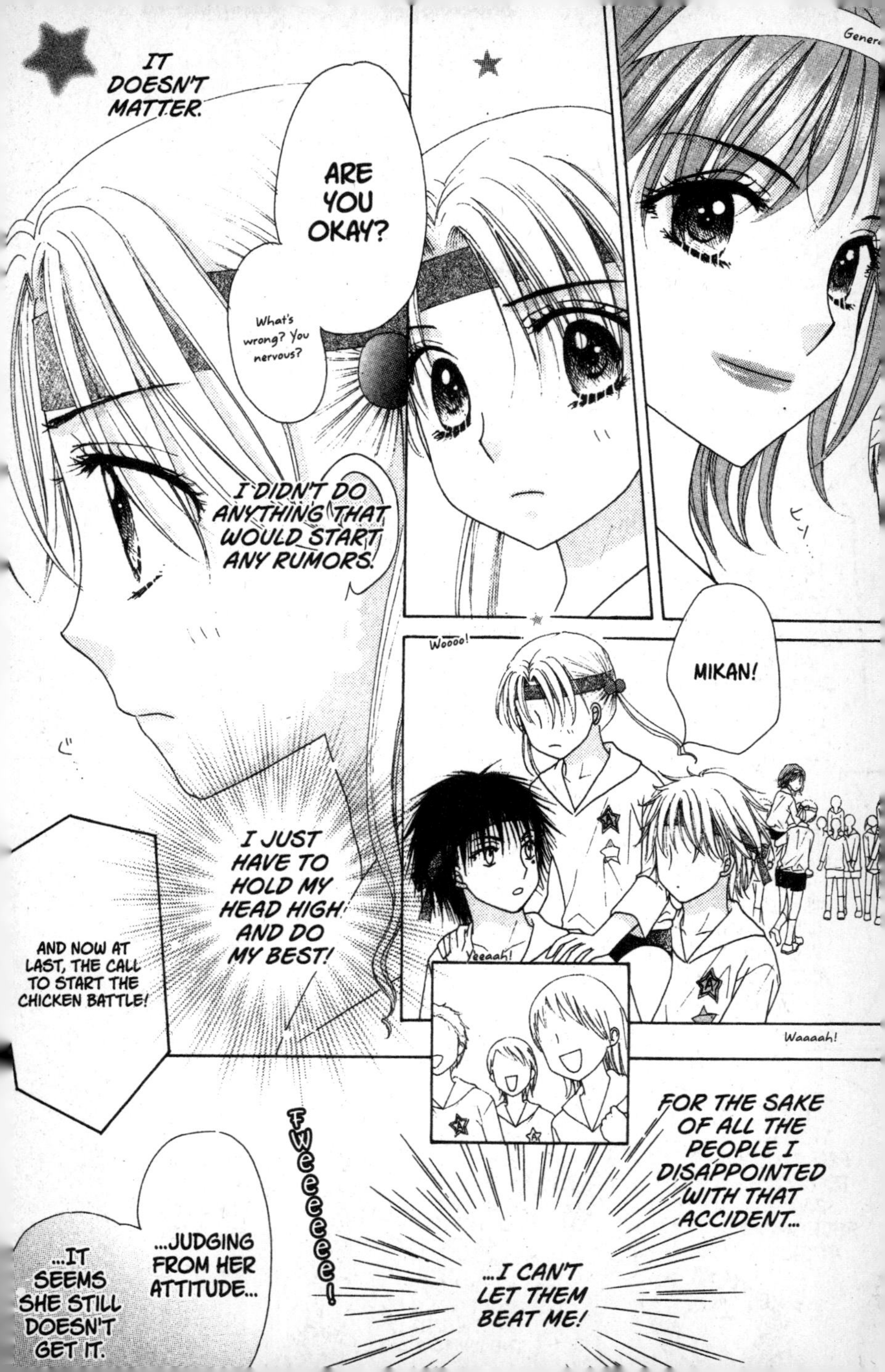
ARE YOU OKAY?
What's wrong? You nervous?
IT DOESN'T MATTER.
I DIDN'T DO ANYTHING THAT WOULD START ANY RUMORS.
I JUST HAVE TO HOLD MY HEAD HIGH AND DO MY BEST!
MIKAN!
Woooo!
Yeeaah!
Waaaah!
FOR THE SAKE OF ALL THE PEOPLE I DISAPPOINTED WITH THAT ACCIDENT...
...I CAN'T LET THEM BEAT ME!
AND NOW AT LAST, THE CALL TO START THE CHICKEN BATTLE!
Fweeeeee!
...JUDGING FROM HER ATTITUDE...
...IT SEEMS SHE STILL DOESN'T GET IT.

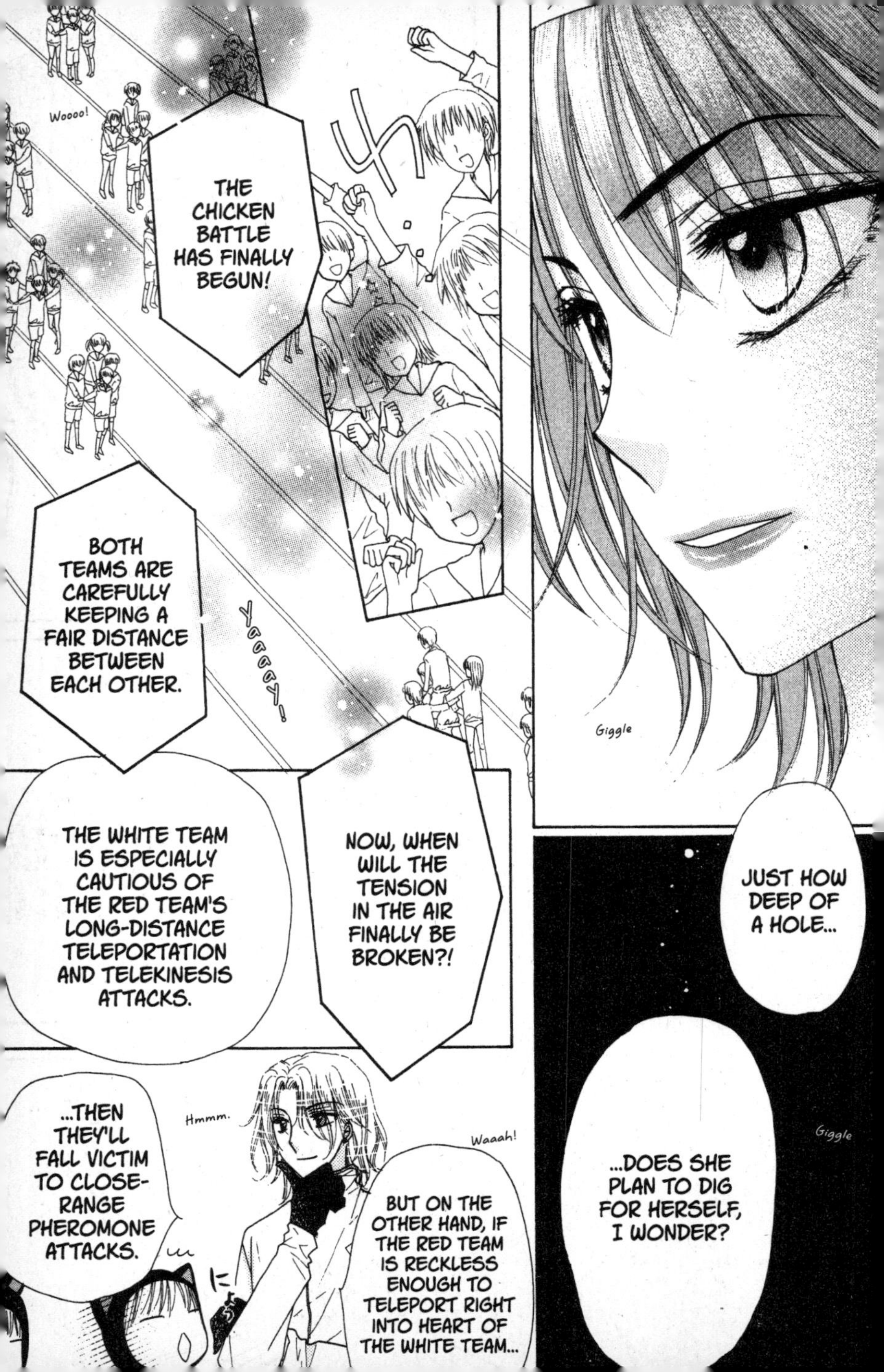
Giggle
JUST HOW DEEP OF A HOLE...
Giggle
...DOES SHE PLAN TO DIG FOR HERSELF, I WONDER?
THE CHICKEN BATTLE HAS FINALLY BEGUN!
Woooo!
BOTH TEAMS ARE CAREFULLY KEEPING A FAIR DISTANCE BETWEEN EACH OTHER.
Yaaaay!
NOW, WHEN WILL THE TENSION IN THE AIR FINALLY BE BROKEN?!
THE WHITE TEAM IS ESPECIALLY CAUTIOUS OF THE RED TEAM'S LONG-DISTANCE TELEPORTATION AND TELEKINESIS ATTACKS.
Waaah!
BUT ON THE OTHER HAND, IF THE RED TEAM IS RECKLESS ENOUGH TO TELEPORT RIGHT INTO HEART OF THE WHITE TEAM...
Hmmm.
...THEN THEY'LL FALL VICTIM TO CLOSE-RANGE PHEROMONE ATTACKS.

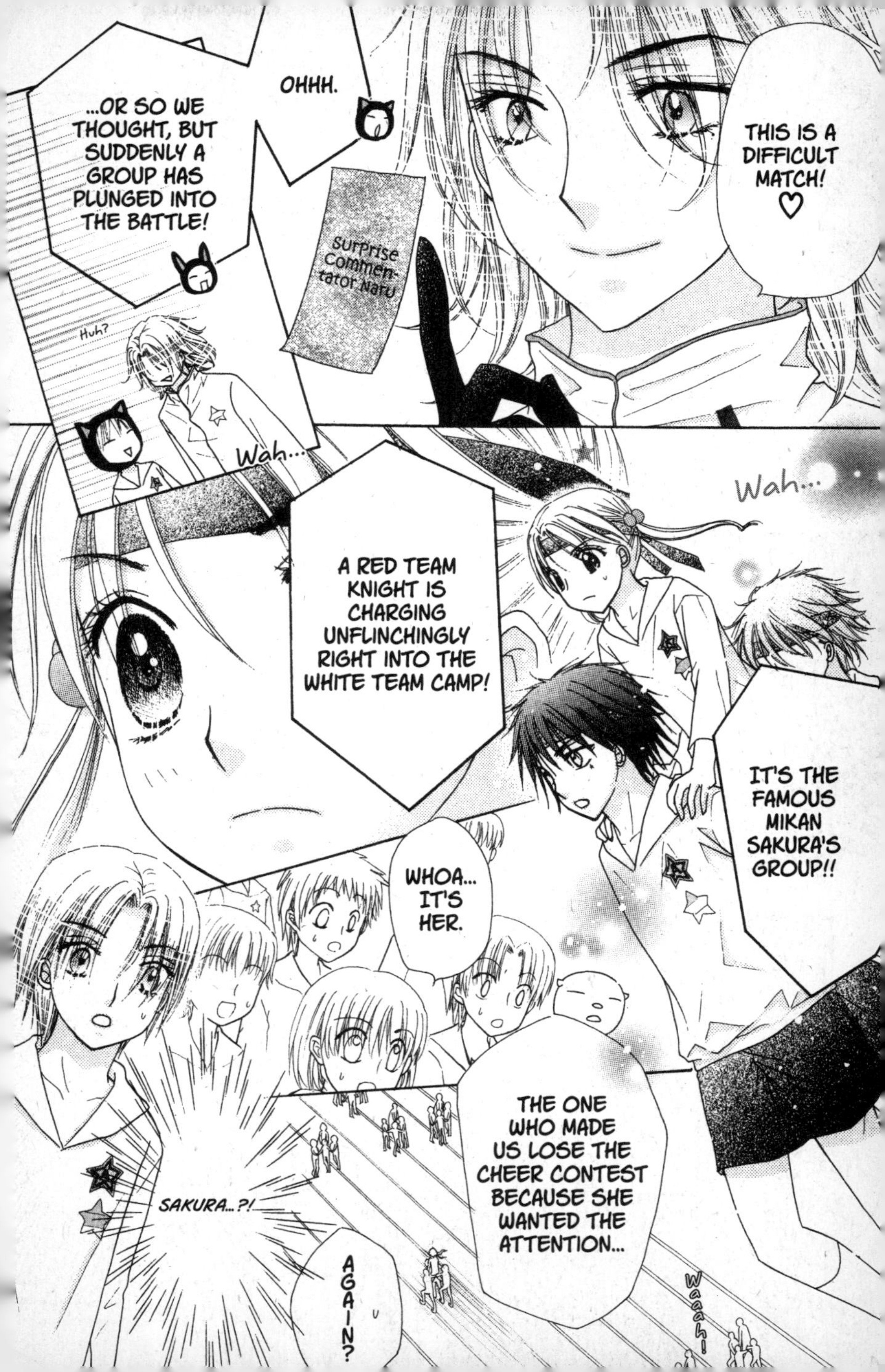
THIS IS A DIFFICULT MATCH! ♡
Surprise Commentator Naru
OHHH.
...OR SO WE THOUGHT, BUT SUDDENLY A GROUP HAS PLUNGED INTO THE BATTLE!
Huh?
Wah...
Wah...
IT'S THE FAMOUS MIKAN SAKURA'S GROUP!!
A RED TEAM KNIGHT IS CHARGING UNFLINCHINGLY RIGHT INTO THE WHITE TEAM CAMP!
WHOA... IT'S HER.
THE ONE WHO MADE US LOSE THE CHEER CONTEST BECAUSE SHE WANTED THE ATTENTION...
Waaah!
AGAIN?
SAKURA...?!

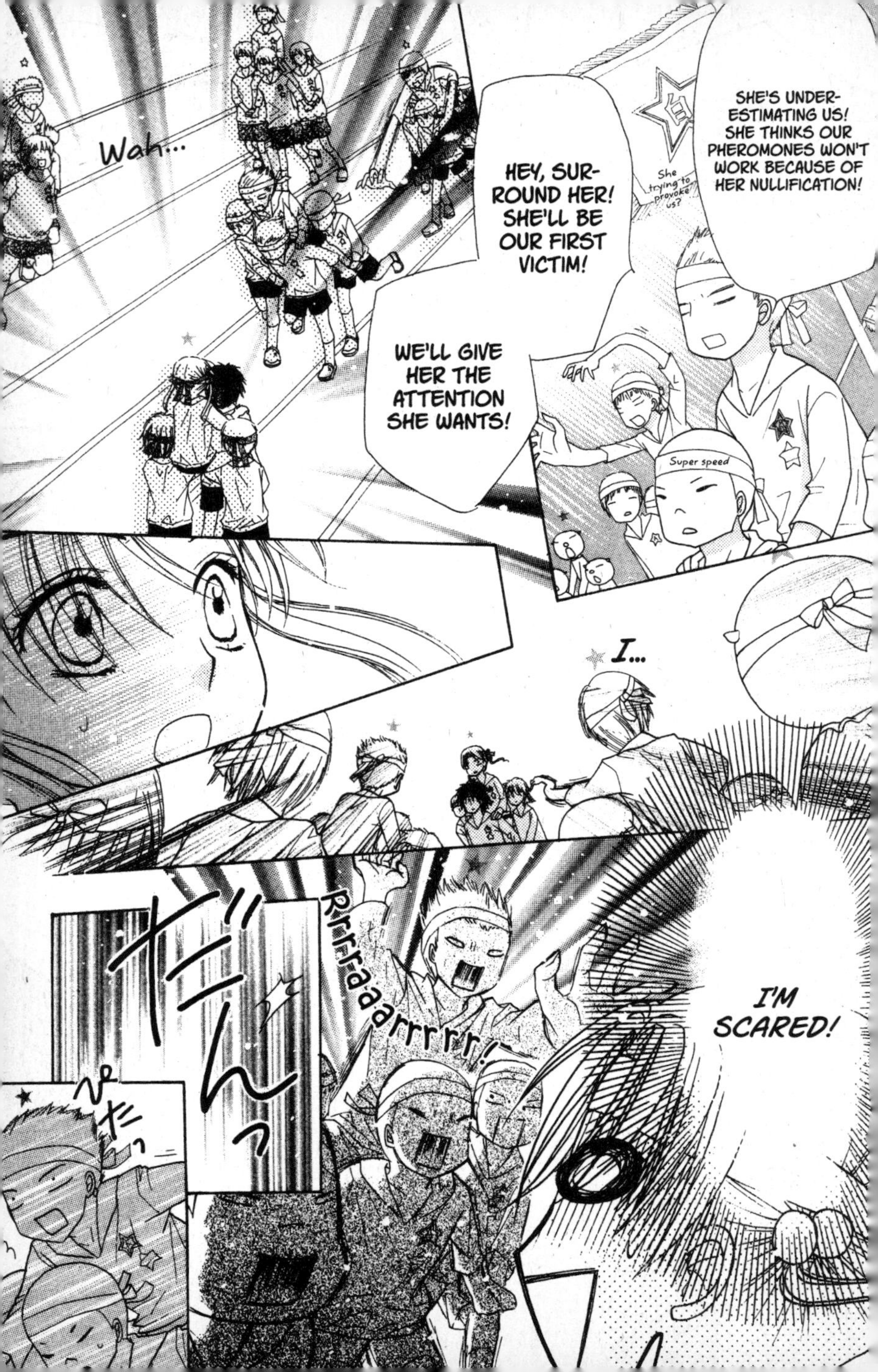
SHE'S UNDER-ESTIMATING US! SHE THINKS OUR PHEROMONES WON'T WORK BECAUSE OF HER NULLIFICATION!
She trying to provoke us?
HEY, SUR-ROUND HER! SHE'LL BE OUR FIRST VICTIM!
WE'LL GIVE HER THE ATTENTION SHE WANTS!
Super speed
Wah...
I...
I'M SCARED!
Rrrrraaarrrrr!
だんっ
ぴたっ

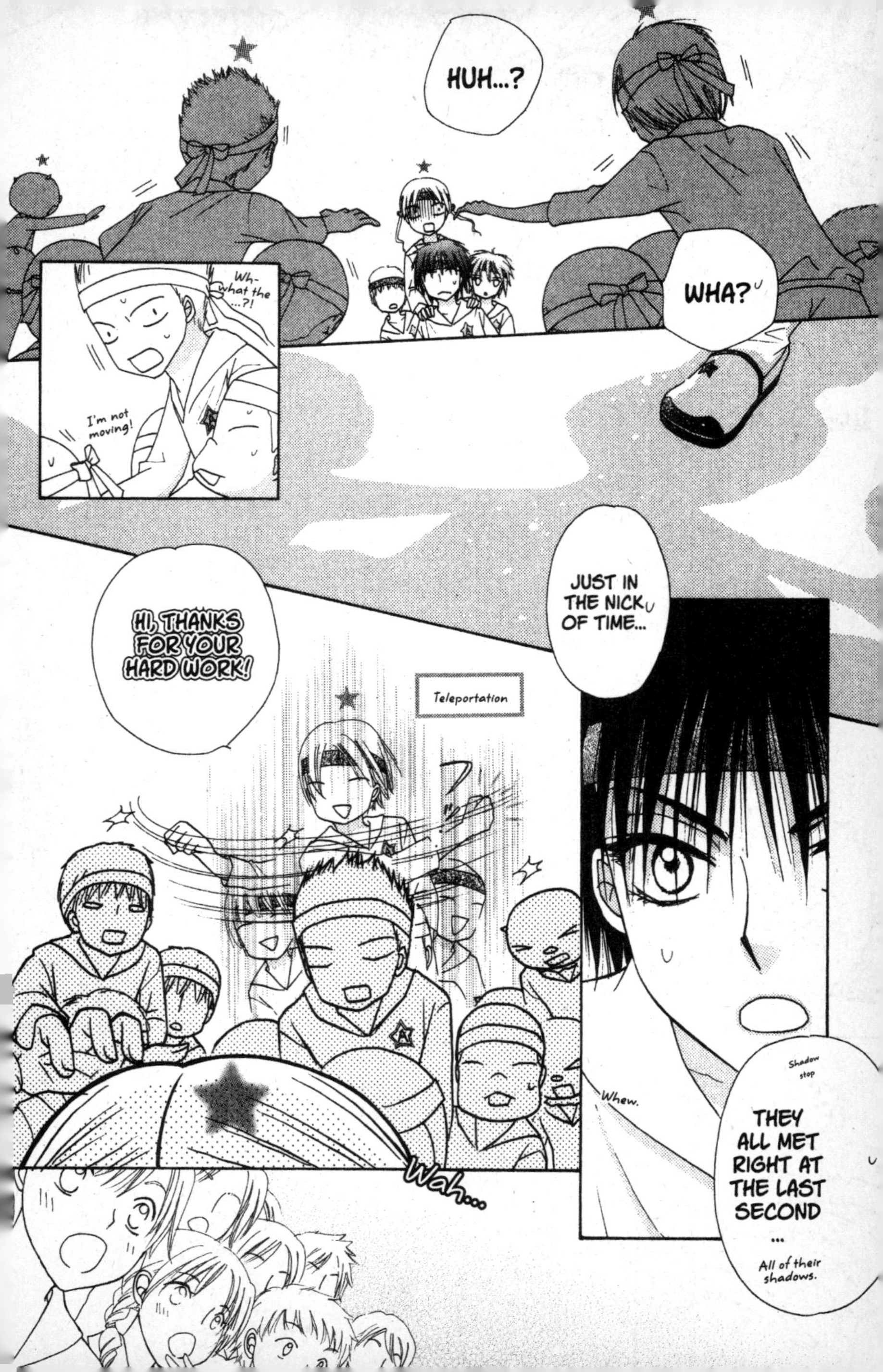
HUH...?
WHA?
Wh-what the ...?!
I'm not moving!
JUST IN THE NICK OF TIME...
Whew.
Shadow stop
THEY ALL MET RIGHT AT THE LAST SECOND ...
All of their shadows.
HI, THANKS FOR YOUR HARD WORK!
Teleportation
Wah...

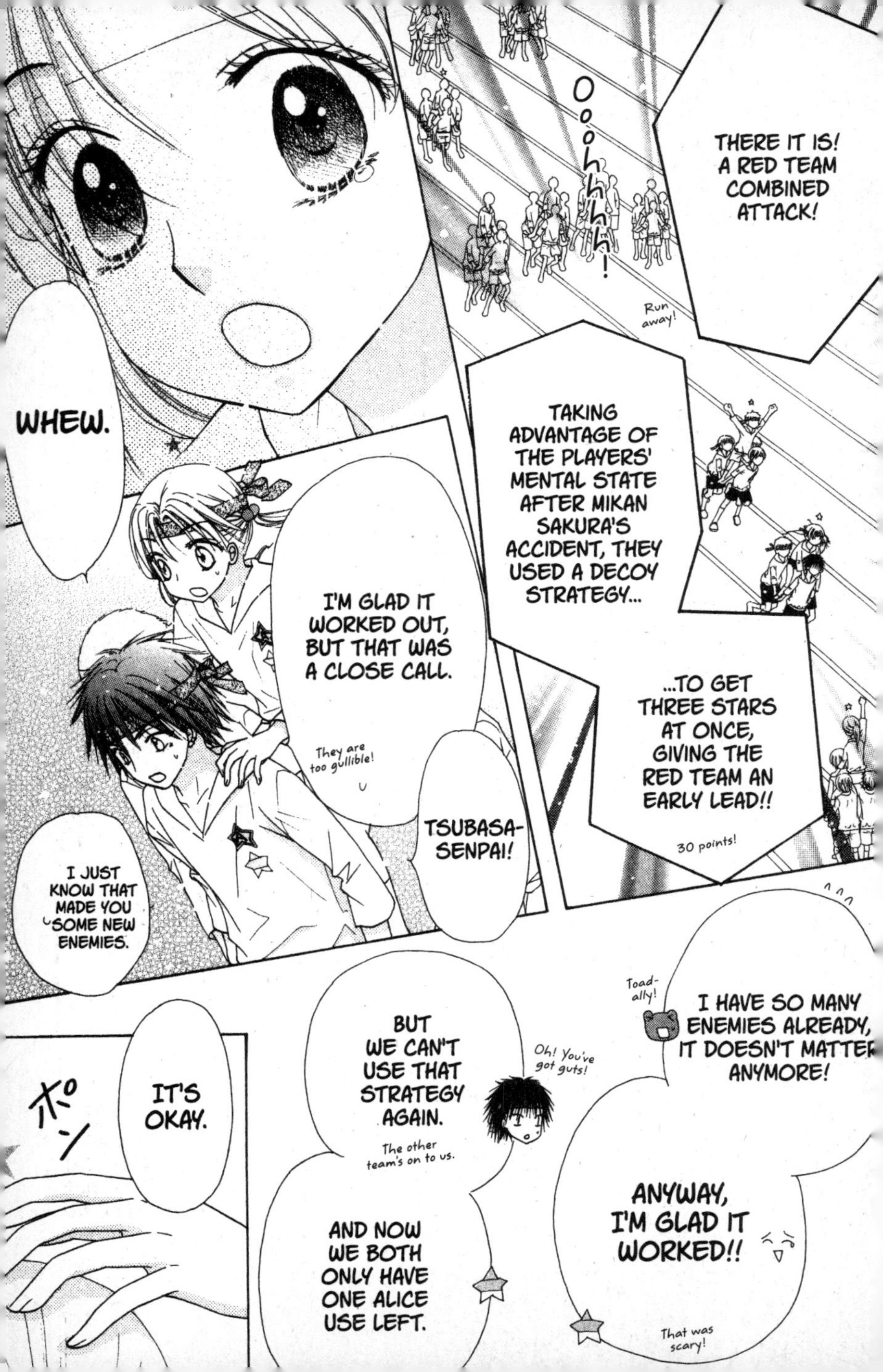
THERE IT IS! A RED TEAM COMBINED ATTACK!
Ooohhhhh!
Run away!
TAKING ADVANTAGE OF THE PLAYERS' MENTAL STATE AFTER MIKAN SAKURA'S ACCIDENT, THEY USED A DECOY STRATEGY...
...TO GET THREE STARS AT ONCE, GIVING THE RED TEAM AN EARLY LEAD!!
30 points!
WHEW.
I'M GLAD IT WORKED OUT, BUT THAT WAS A CLOSE CALL.
They are too gullible!
TSUBASA-SENPAI!
I JUST KNOW THAT MADE YOU SOME NEW ENEMIES.
I HAVE SO MANY ENEMIES ALREADY, IT DOESN'T MATTER ANYMORE!
Toad-ally!
ANYWAY, I'M GLAD IT WORKED!!
That was scary!
BUT WE CAN'T USE THAT STRATEGY AGAIN.
Oh! You've got guts!
The other team's on to us.
AND NOW WE BOTH ONLY HAVE ONE ALICE USE LEFT.
IT'S OKAY.
ポン

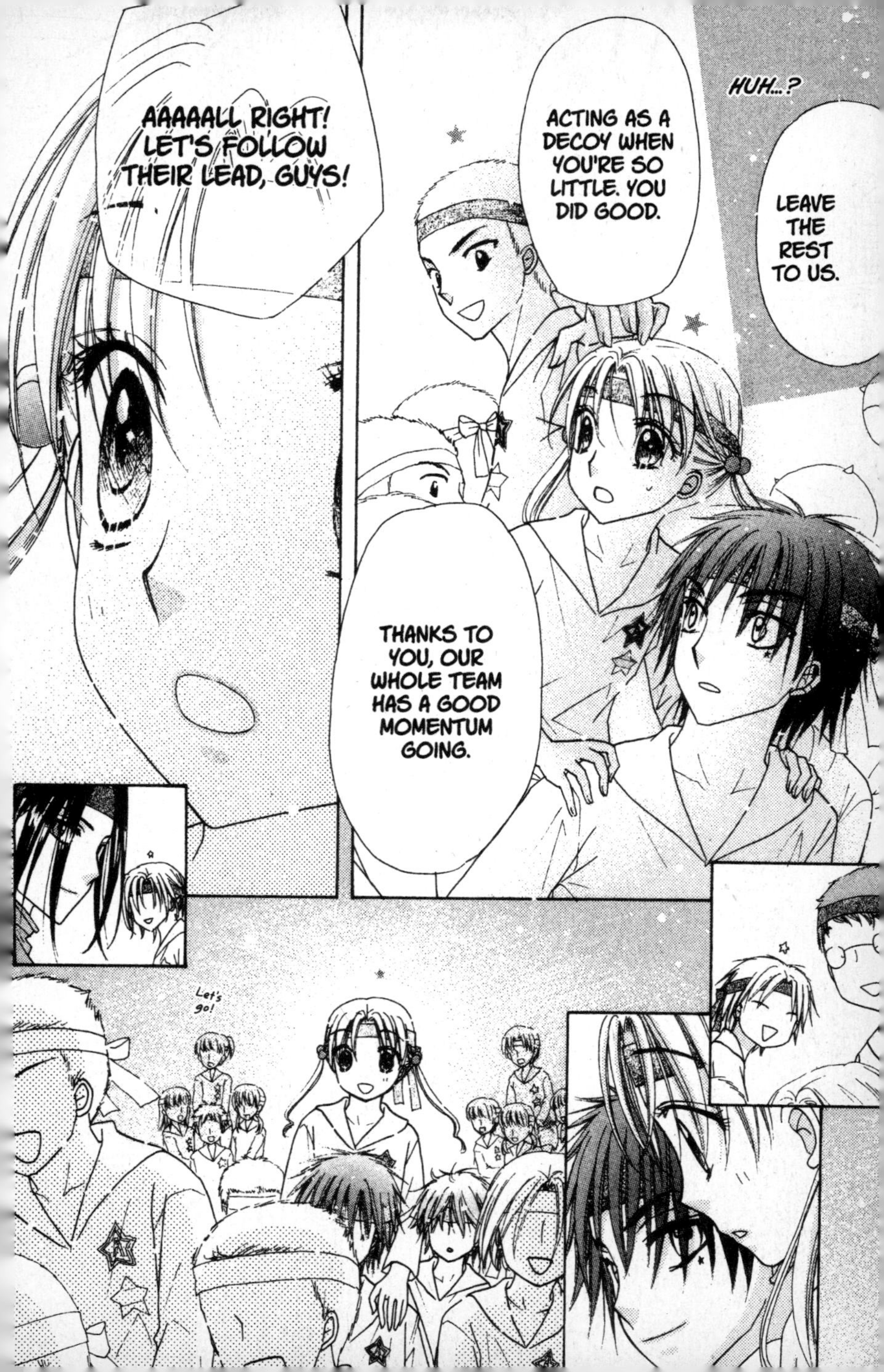
HUH...?
LEAVE THE REST TO US.
ACTING AS A DECOY WHEN YOU'RE SO LITTLE. YOU DID GOOD.
THANKS TO YOU, OUR WHOLE TEAM HAS A GOOD MOMENTUM GOING.
AAAAALL RIGHT! LET'S FOLLOW THEIR LEAD, GUYS!
Let's go!

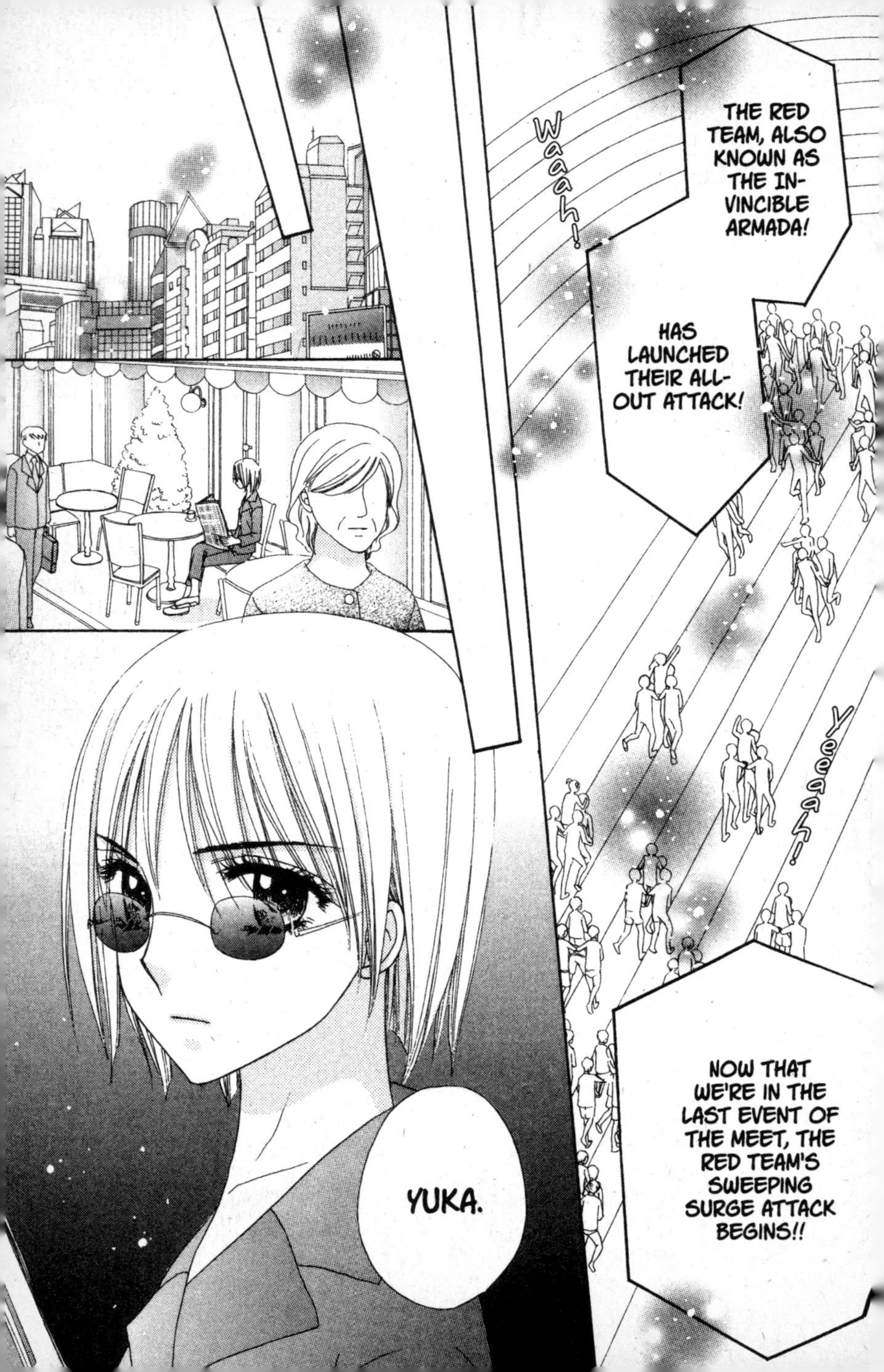
THE RED TEAM, ALSO KNOWN AS THE IN-VINCIBLE ARMADA!
Waaah!
HAS LAUNCHED THEIR ALL-OUT ATTACK!
Yeeaah!
NOW THAT WE'RE IN THE LAST EVENT OF THE MEET, THE RED TEAM'S SWEEPING SURGE ATTACK BEGINS!!
YUKA.

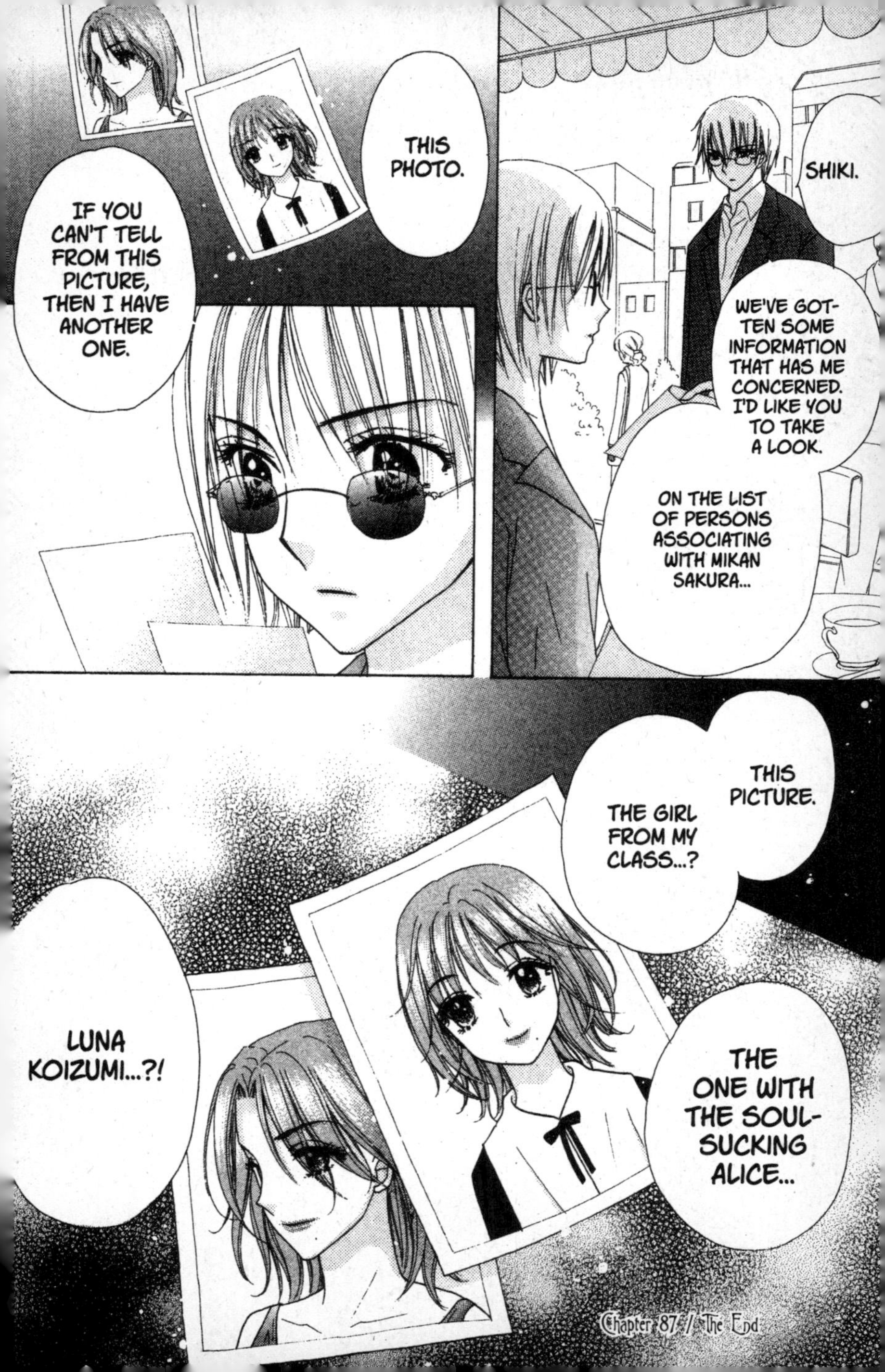
SHIKI.
WE'VE GOTTEN SOME INFORMATION THAT HAS ME CONCERNED. I'D LIKE YOU TO TAKE A LOOK.
ON THE LIST OF PERSONS ASSOCIATING WITH MIKAN SAKURA...
THIS PHOTO.
IF YOU CAN'T TELL FROM THIS PICTURE, THEN I HAVE ANOTHER ONE.
THIS PICTURE.
THE GIRL FROM MY CLASS...?
THE ONE WITH THE SOUL-SUCKING ALICE...
LUNA KOIZUMI...?!
Chapter 87 / The End

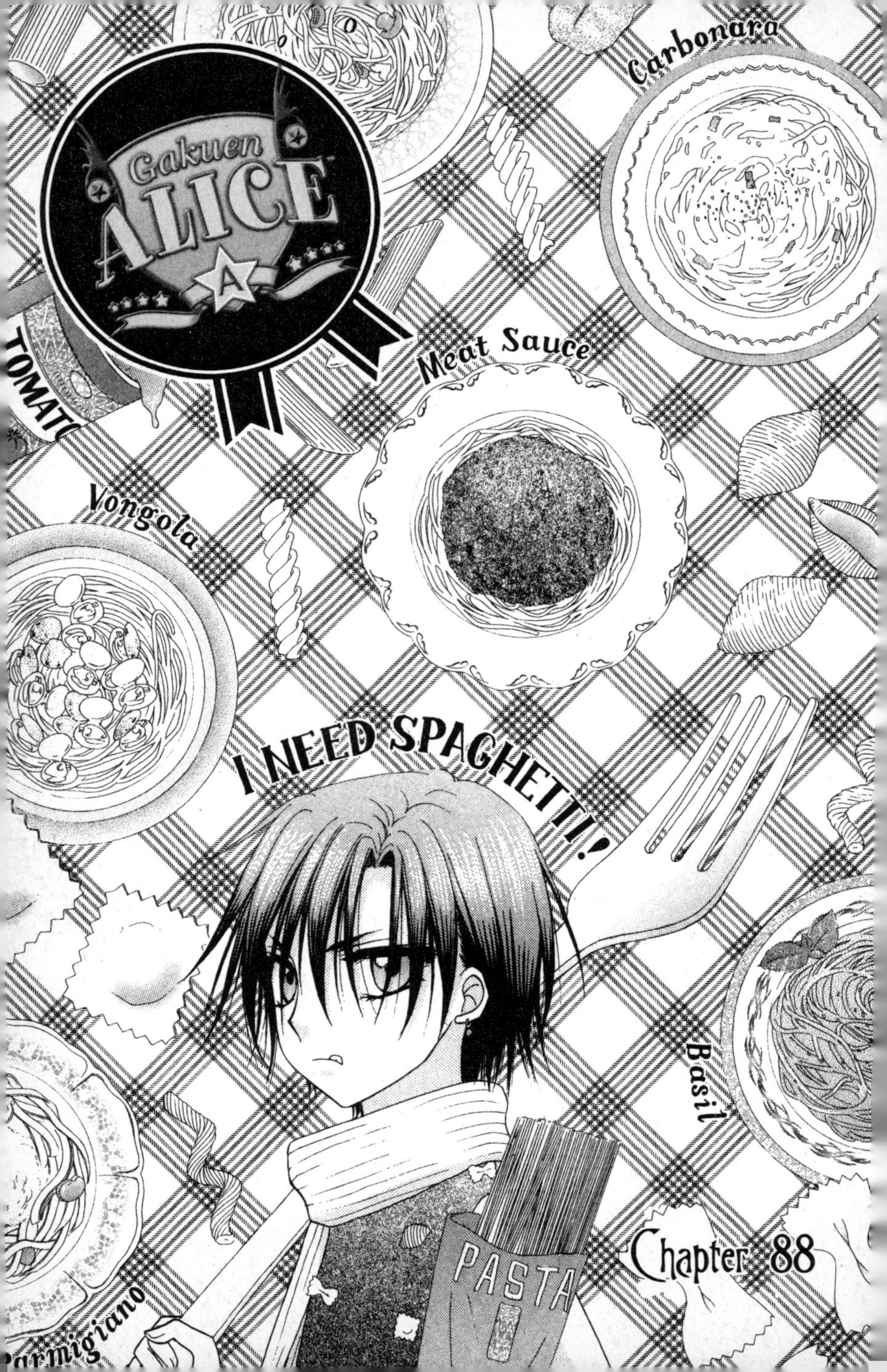
Carbonara
Gakuen ALICE
Meat Sauce
Vongola
I NEED SPAGHETTI!
Basil
Chapter 88
PASTA
Parmigiano

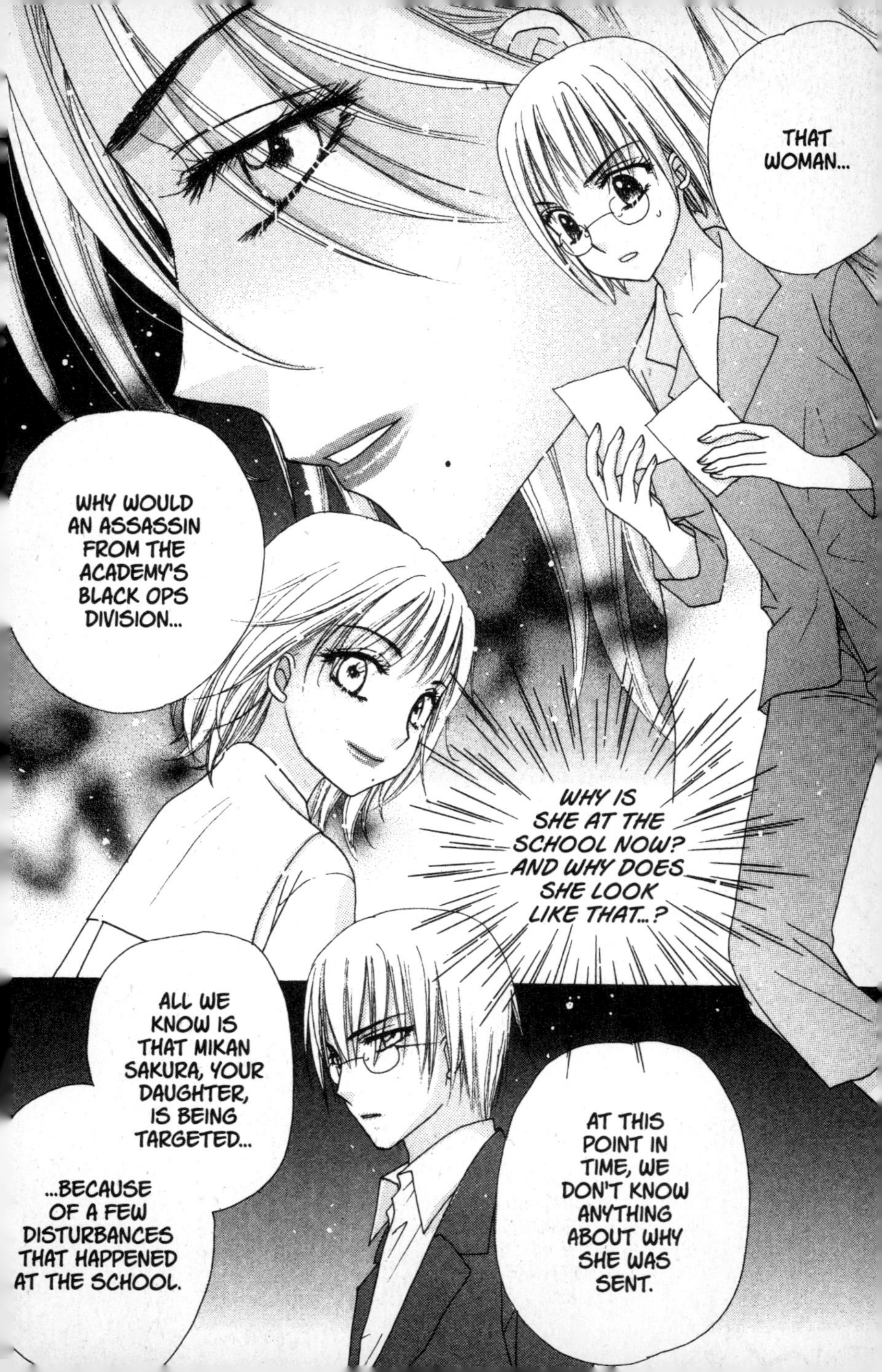
THAT WOMAN...
WHY WOULD AN ASSASSIN FROM THE ACADEMY'S BLACK OPS DIVISION...
WHY IS SHE AT THE SCHOOL NOW? AND WHY DOES SHE LOOK LIKE THAT...?
AT THIS POINT IN TIME, WE DON'T KNOW ANYTHING ABOUT WHY SHE WAS SENT.
ALL WE KNOW IS THAT MIKAN SAKURA, YOUR DAUGHTER, IS BEING TARGETED...
...BECAUSE OF A FEW DISTURBANCES THAT HAPPENED AT THE SCHOOL.

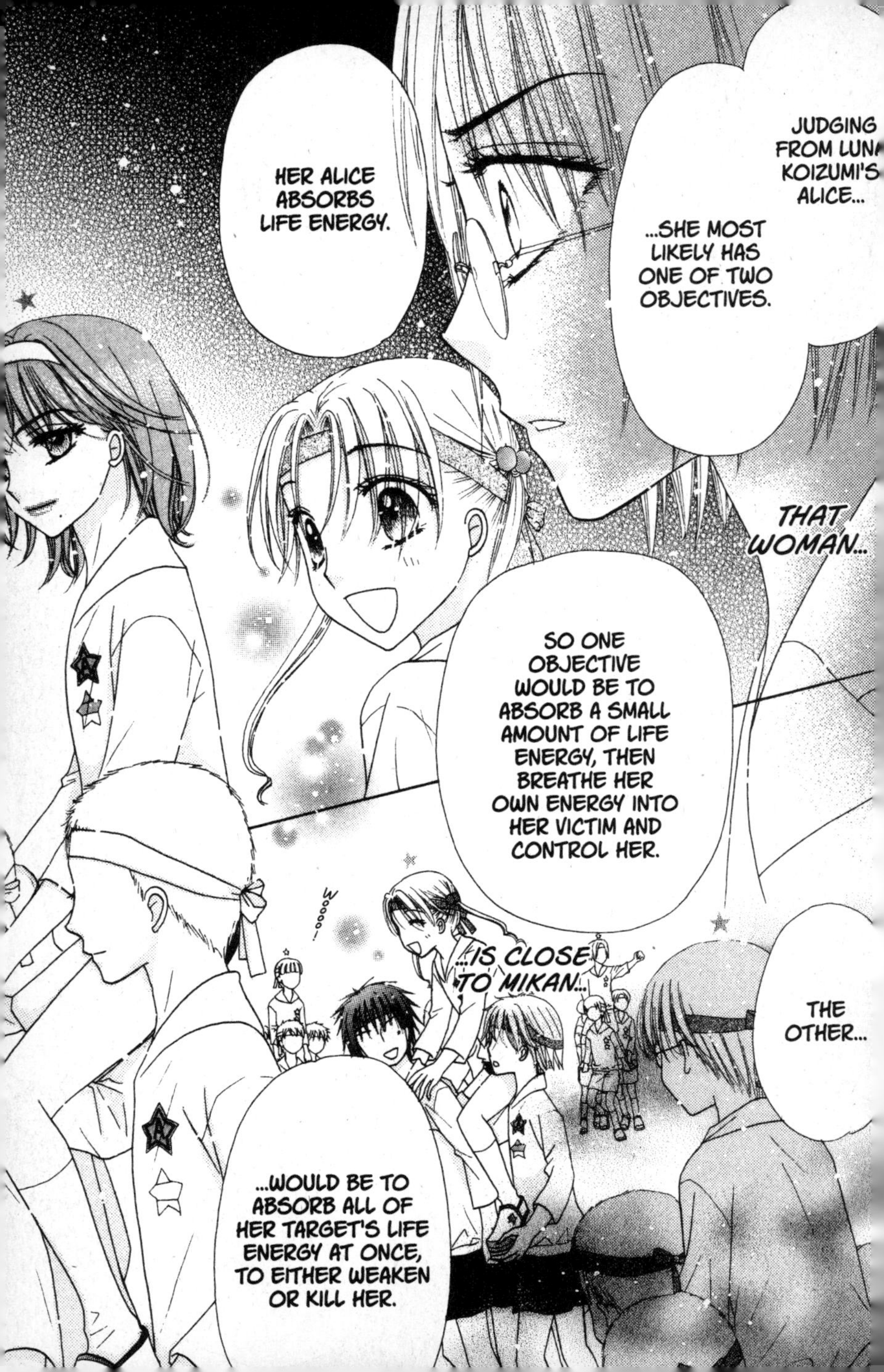

JUDGING FROM LUNA KOIZUMI'S ALICE...
...SHE MOST LIKELY HAS ONE OF TWO OBJECTIVES.
HER ALICE ABSORBS LIFE ENERGY.
THAT WOMAN...
SO ONE OBJECTIVE WOULD BE TO ABSORB A SMALL AMOUNT OF LIFE ENERGY, THEN BREATHE HER OWN ENERGY INTO HER VICTIM AND CONTROL HER.
...IS CLOSE TO MIKAN...
Woooo!
THE OTHER...
...WOULD BE TO ABSORB ALL OF HER TARGET'S LIFE ENERGY AT ONCE, TO EITHER WEAKEN OR KILL HER.

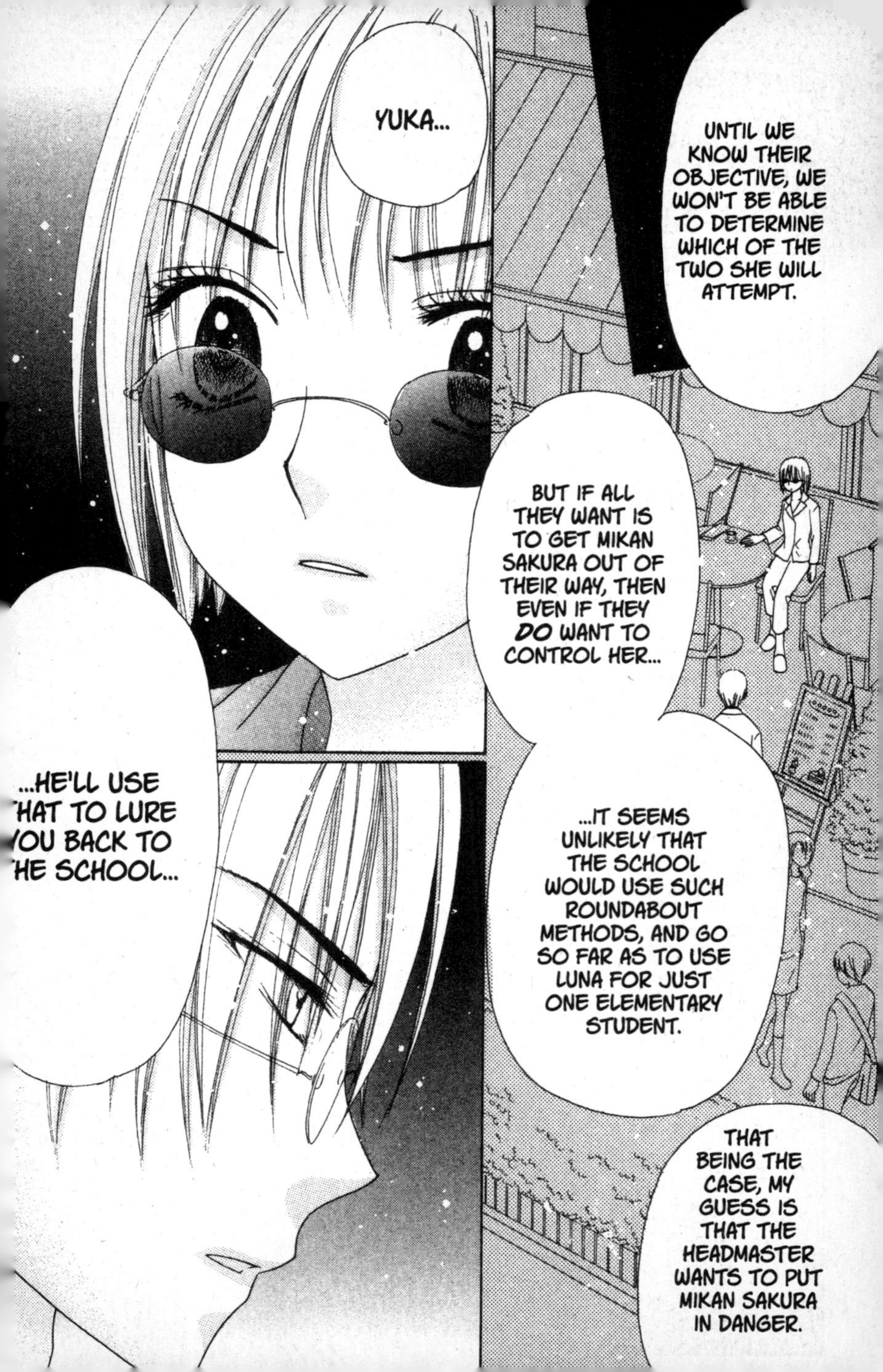
UNTIL WE KNOW THEIR OBJECTIVE, WE WON'T BE ABLE TO DETERMINE WHICH OF THE TWO SHE WILL ATTEMPT.
BUT IF ALL THEY WANT IS TO GET MIKAN SAKURA OUT OF THEIR WAY, THEN EVEN IF THEY *DO* WANT TO CONTROL HER...
...IT SEEMS UNLIKELY THAT THE SCHOOL WOULD USE SUCH ROUNDABOUT METHODS, AND GO SO FAR AS TO USE LUNA FOR JUST ONE ELEMENTARY STUDENT.
THAT BEING THE CASE, MY GUESS IS THAT THE HEADMASTER WANTS TO PUT MIKAN SAKURA IN DANGER.
YUKA...
...HE'LL USE THAT TO LURE YOU BACK TO THE SCHOOL...

Read at Your own Discretion.

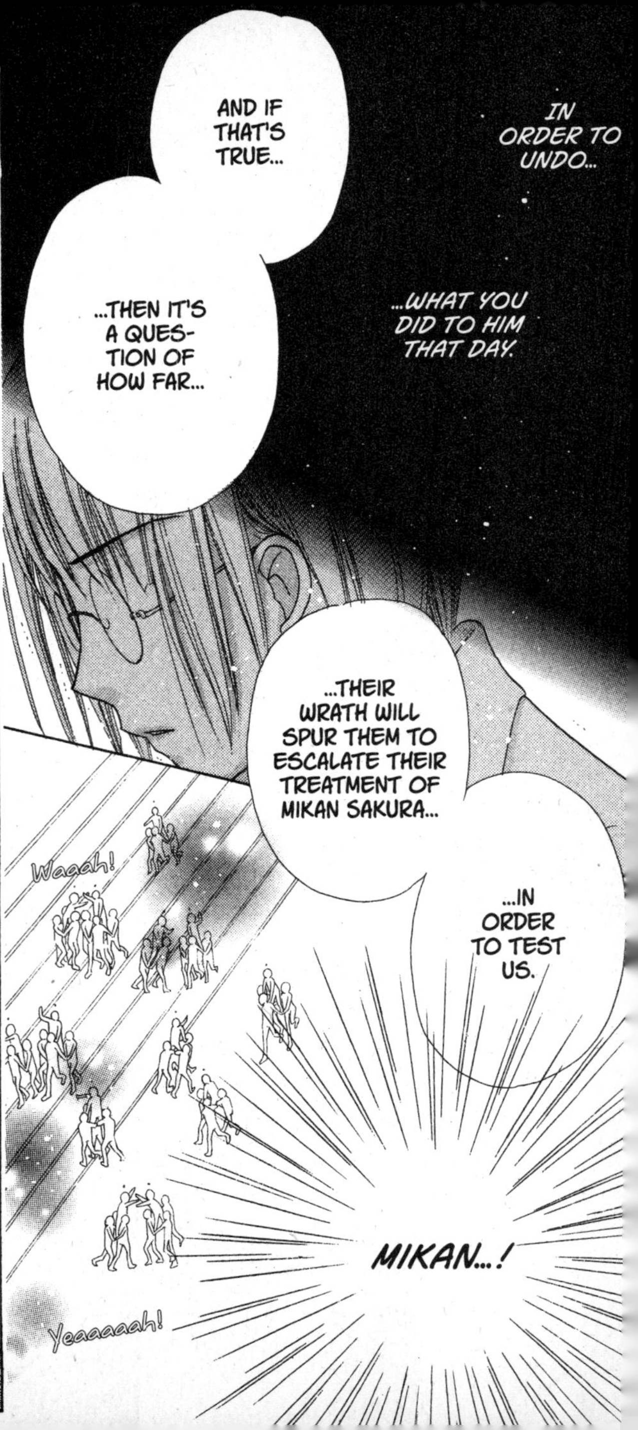

IN ORDER TO UNDO...
...WHAT YOU DID TO HIM THAT DAY.
AND IF THAT'S TRUE...
...THEN IT'S A QUES-TION OF HOW FAR...
...THEIR WRATH WILL SPUR THEM TO ESCALATE THEIR TREATMENT OF MIKAN SAKURA...
...IN ORDER TO TEST US.
Waaah!
MIKAN...!
Yeaaaaah!

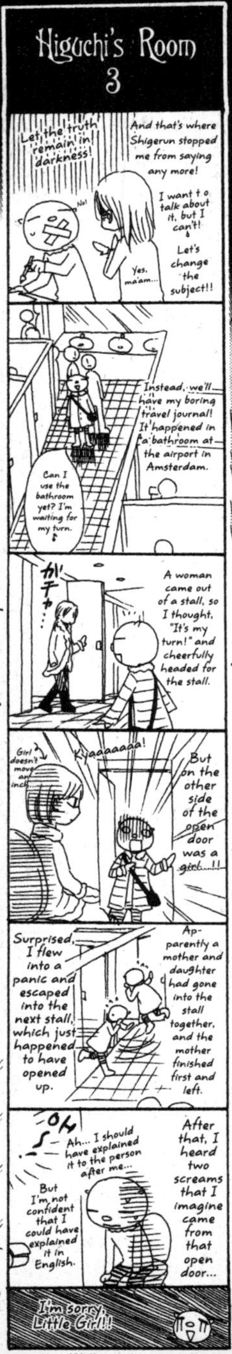

Higuchi's Room 3
Let the truth remain in darkness!
And that's where Shigerun stopped me from saying any more!
No!
I want to talk about it, but I can't!
Let's change the subject!!
Yes, ma'am...
Instead, we'll have my boring travel journal! It happened in a bathroom at the airport in Amsterdam.
Can I use the bathroom yet? I'm waiting for my turn.
A woman came out of a stall, so I thought, "It's my turn!" and cheerfully headed for the stall.
Kyaaaaaaa!
Girl doesn't move an inch...
But on the other side of the open door was a girl...!!
Surprised, I flew into a panic and escaped into the next stall, which just happened to have opened up.
Apparently a mother and daughter had gone into the stall together, and the mother finished first and left.
After that, I heard two screams that I imagine came from that open door...
Ah... I should have explained it to the person after me...
But I'm not confident that I could have explained it in English.
I'm sorry, Little Girl!!
The ending

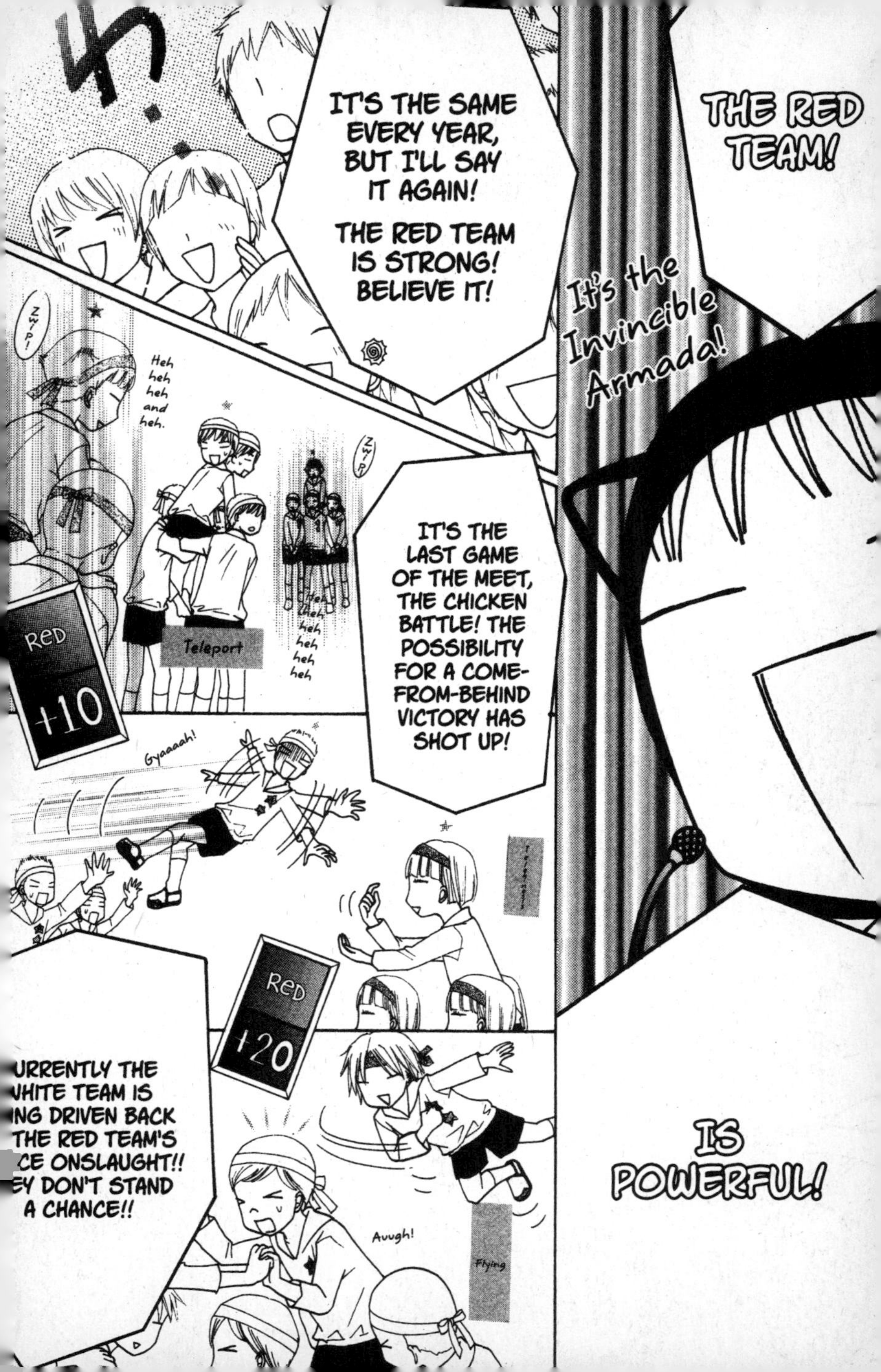
THE RED TEAM!
It's the Invincible Armada!
IS POWERFUL!
わ
IT'S THE SAME EVERY YEAR, BUT I'LL SAY IT AGAIN!
THE RED TEAM IS STRONG! BELIEVE IT!
ZWIP!
Heh heh heh and heh.
ZWIP!
Heh heh heh heh heh heh
Teleport
RED
+10
IT'S THE LAST GAME OF THE MEET, THE CHICKEN BATTLE! THE POSSIBILITY FOR A COME-FROM-BEHIND VICTORY HAS SHOT UP!
Gyaaaah!
RED
+20
URRENTLY THE WHITE TEAM IS NG DRIVEN BACK THE RED TEAM'S CE ONSLAUGHT!! EY DON'T STAND A CHANCE!!
Augh!
Flying

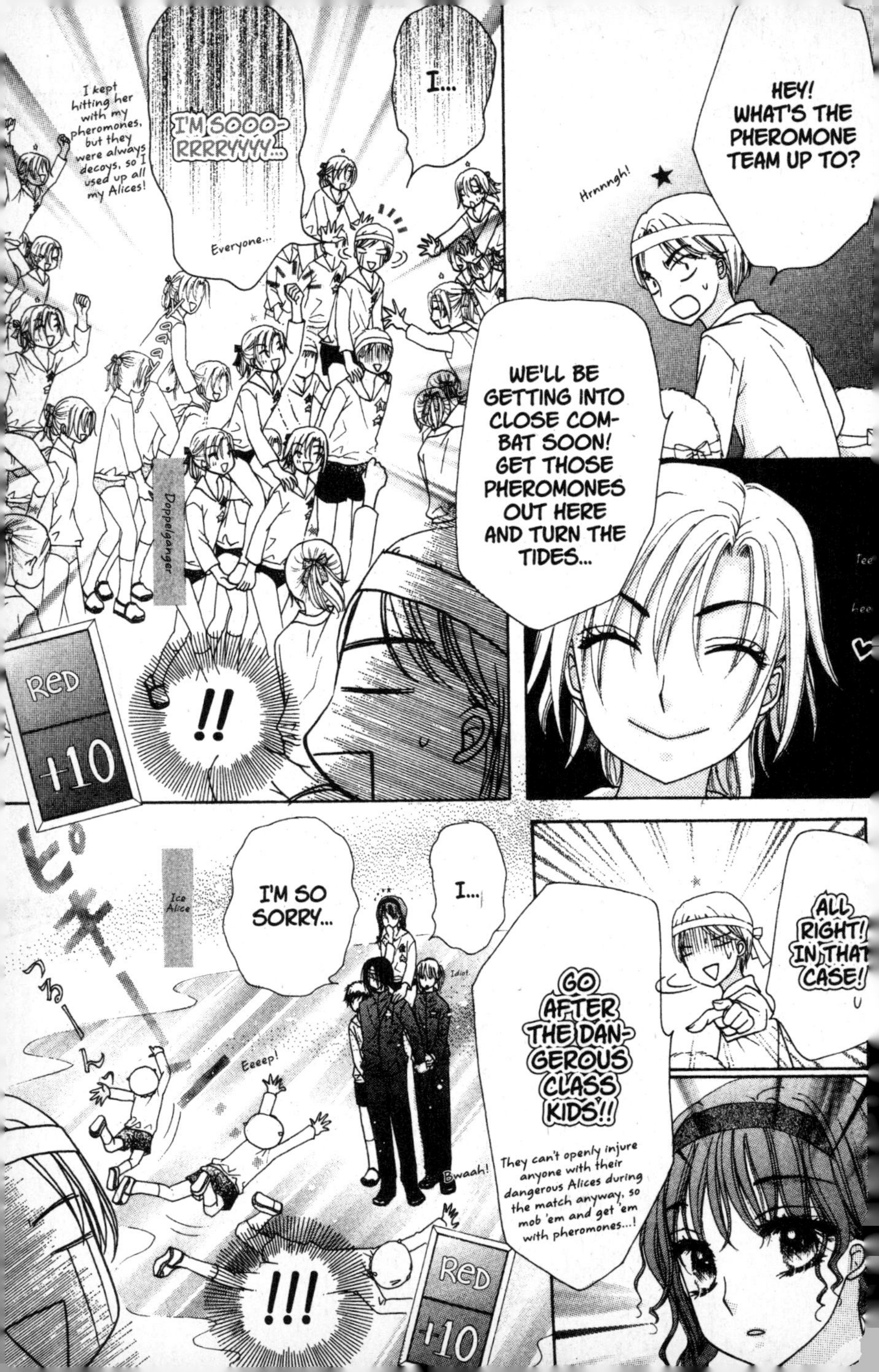
HEY! WHAT'S THE PHEROMONE TEAM UP TO?
Hrnnngh!
WE'LL BE GETTING INTO CLOSE COMBAT SOON! GET THOSE PHEROMONES OUT HERE AND TURN THE TIDES...
Tee hee
I...
I'M SOOOO-RRRRYYYY...
Everyone...
I kept hitting her with my pheromones, but they were always decoys, so I used up all my Alices!
Doppelganger
!!
RED
+10
ALL RIGHT! IN THAT CASE!
GO AFTER THE DANGEROUS CLASS KIDS!!
They can't openly injure anyone with their dangerous Alices during the match anyway, so mob 'em and get 'em with pheromones...!
I...
I'M SO SORRY...
Ice Alice
Idiot.
Eeeep!
Bwaah!
!!!
RED
+10

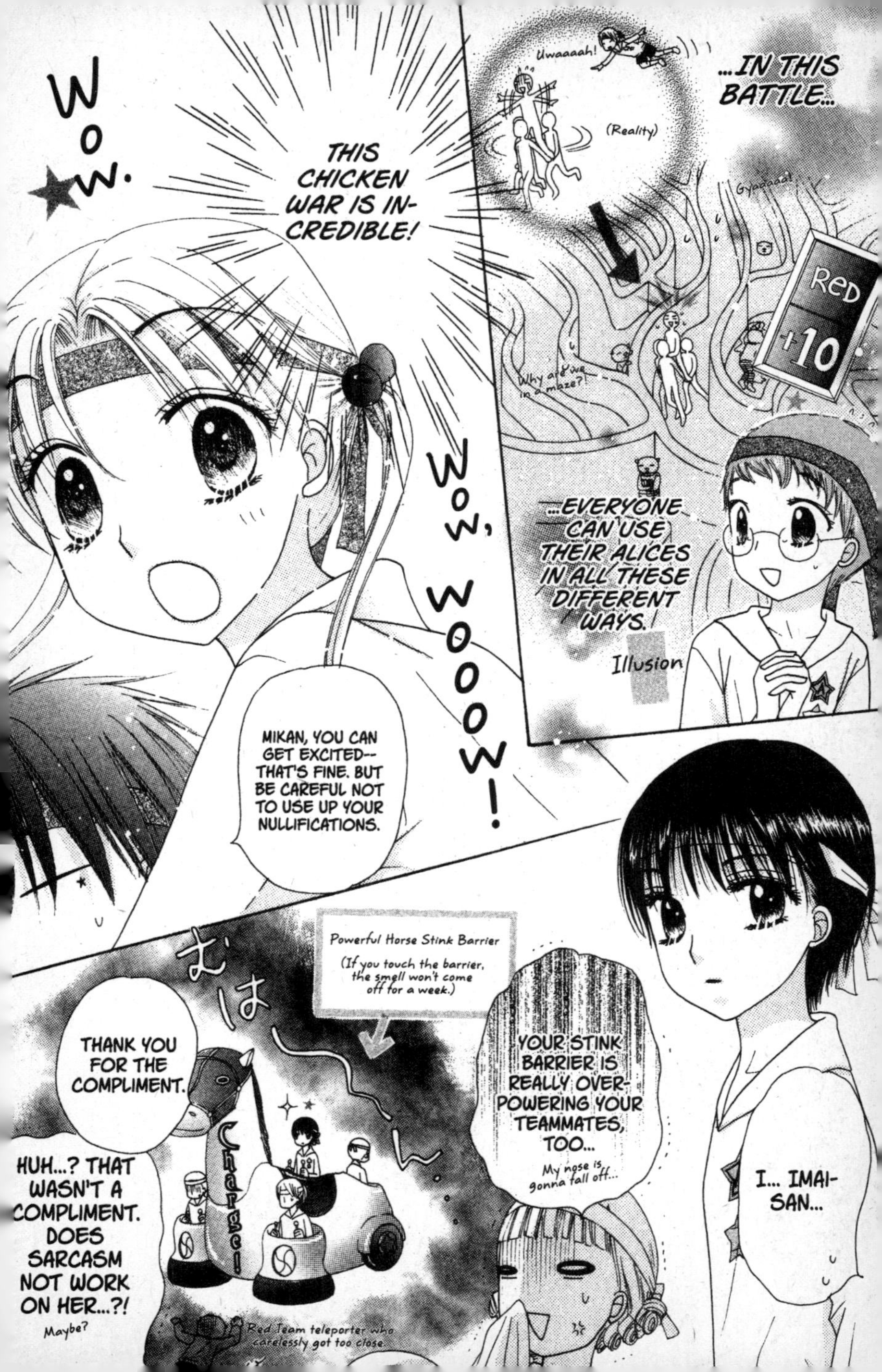

Uwaaaah!
(Reality)
...IN THIS BATTLE...
Gyaaaaa!
RED +10
Why are we in a maze?!
...EVERYONE CAN USE THEIR ALICES IN ALL THESE DIFFERENT WAYS.
Illusion
WOW.
THIS CHICKEN WAR IS IN-CREDIBLE!
WOW, WOOOOW!
MIKAN, YOU CAN GET EXCITED--THAT'S FINE. BUT BE CAREFUL NOT TO USE UP YOUR NULLIFICATIONS.
I... IMAI-SAN...
YOUR STINK BARRIER IS REALLY OVER-POWERING YOUR TEAMMATES, TOO...
My nose is gonna fall off...
Powerful Horse Stink Barrier
(If you touch the barrier, the smell won't come off for a week.)
THANK YOU FOR THE COMPLIMENT.
Charge!
HUH...? THAT WASN'T A COMPLIMENT. DOES SARCASM NOT WORK ON HER...?!
Maybe?
Red Team teleporter who carelessly got too close

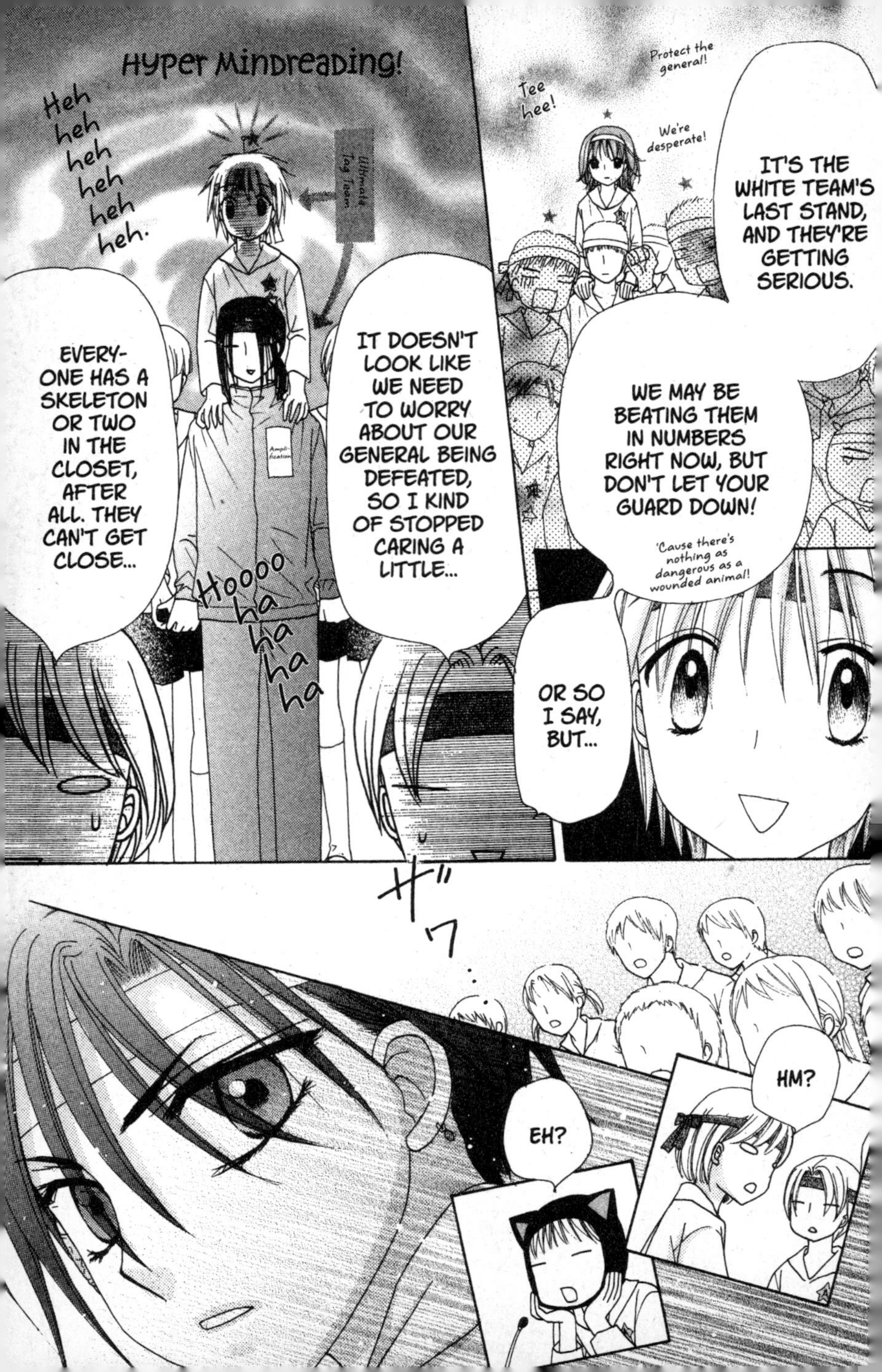
IT'S THE WHITE TEAM'S LAST STAND, AND THEY'RE GETTING SERIOUS.
Protect the general!
We're desperate!
Tee hee!
WE MAY BE BEATING THEM IN NUMBERS RIGHT NOW, BUT DON'T LET YOUR GUARD DOWN!
'Cause there's nothing as dangerous as a wounded animal!
OR SO I SAY, BUT...
Hyper Mindreading!
Ultimate Tag Team
Heh heh heh heh heh heh.
IT DOESN'T LOOK LIKE WE NEED TO WORRY ABOUT OUR GENERAL BEING DEFEATED, SO I KIND OF STOPPED CARING A LITTLE...
Amplification
EVERY-ONE HAS A SKELETON OR TWO IN THE CLOSET, AFTER ALL. THEY CAN'T GET CLOSE...
Hoooo ha ha ha ha ha
ザッ
HM?
EH?

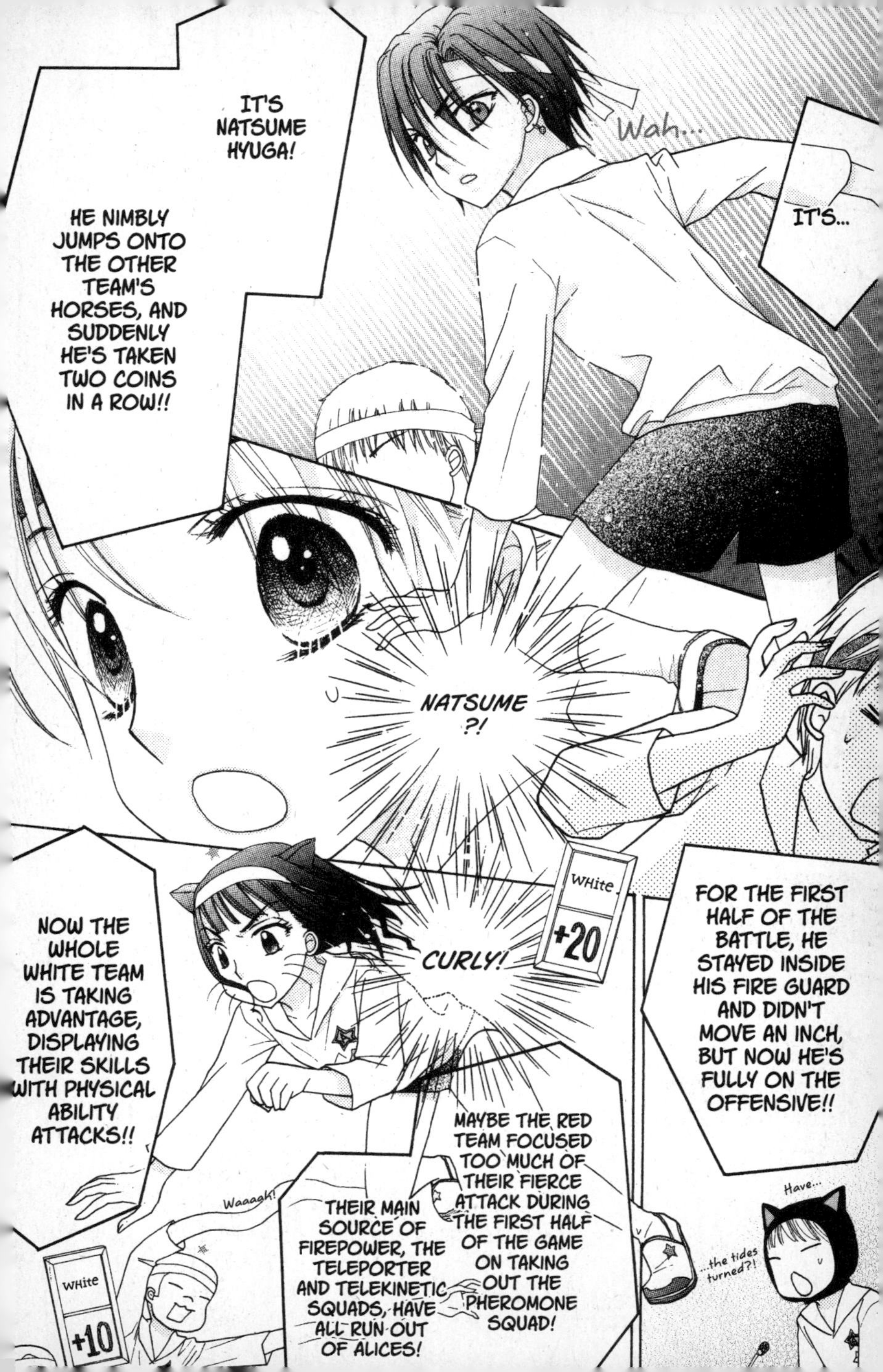
IT'S...
Wah...
IT'S NATSUME HYUGA!
HE NIMBLY JUMPS ONTO THE OTHER TEAM'S HORSES, AND SUDDENLY HE'S TAKEN TWO COINS IN A ROW!!
NATSUME ?!
FOR THE FIRST HALF OF THE BATTLE, HE STAYED INSIDE HIS FIRE GUARD AND DIDN'T MOVE AN INCH, BUT NOW HE'S FULLY ON THE OFFENSIVE!!
WHITE
+20
CURLY!
NOW THE WHOLE WHITE TEAM IS TAKING ADVANTAGE, DISPLAYING THEIR SKILLS WITH PHYSICAL ABILITY ATTACKS!!
Have...
...the tides turned?!
MAYBE THE RED TEAM FOCUSED TOO MUCH OF THEIR FIERCE ATTACK DURING THE FIRST HALF OF THE GAME ON TAKING OUT THE PHEROMONE SQUAD!
THEIR MAIN SOURCE OF FIREPOWER, THE TELEPORTER AND TELEKINETIC SQUADS, HAVE ALL RUN OUT OF ALICES!
Waaagh!
WHITE
+10

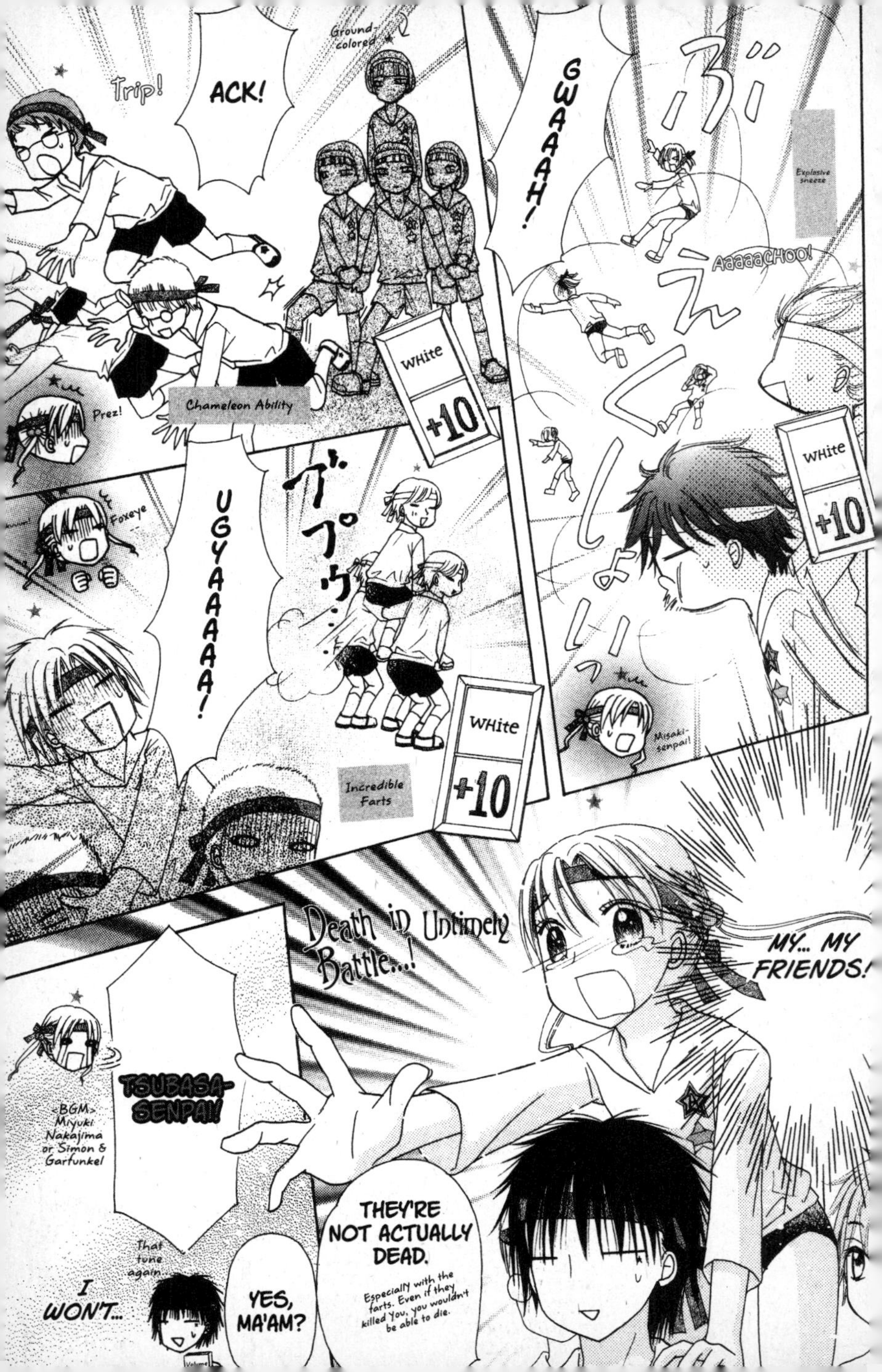
Explosive sneeze
AAAAACHOO!
GWAAAAH!
White +10
Misaki-senpai!
Ground-colored
ACK!
Trip!
Prez!
Chameleon Ability
White +10
UGYAAAAAAA!
Foxeye
Incredible Farts
White +10
MY... MY FRIENDS!
Death in Untimely Battle...!
TSUBASA-SENPAI!
<BGM> Miyuki Nakajima or Simon & Garfunkel
THEY'RE NOT ACTUALLY DEAD.
Especially with the farts. Even if they killed You, you wouldn't be able to die.
YES, MA'AM?
That tune again...
I WON'T...

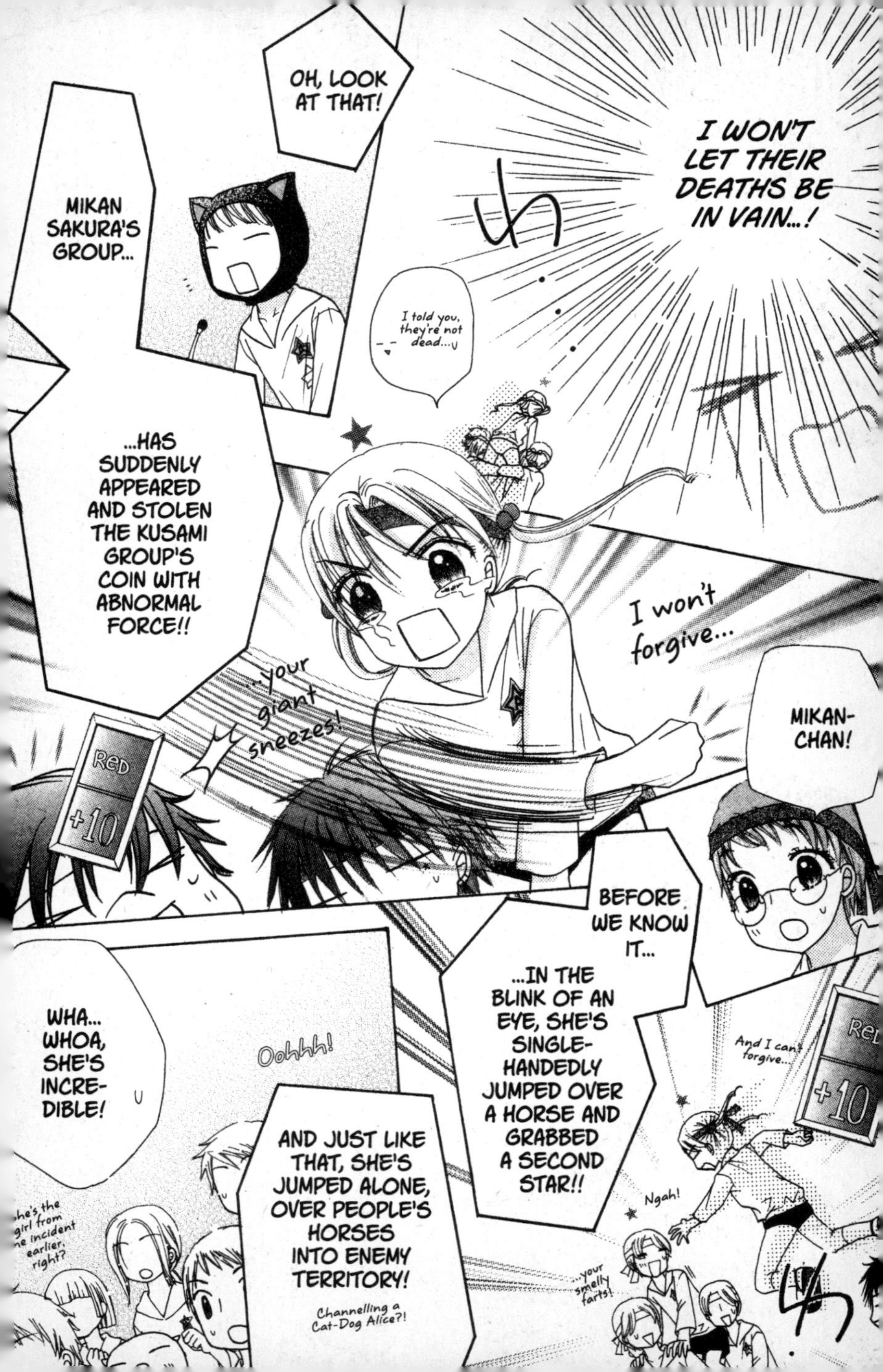
I WON'T LET THEIR DEATHS BE IN VAIN...!
I told you, they're not dead...
OH, LOOK AT THAT!
MIKAN SAKURA'S GROUP...
...HAS SUDDENLY APPEARED AND STOLEN THE KUSAMI GROUP'S COIN WITH ABNORMAL FORCE!!
I won't forgive...
...your giant sneezes!
RED
+10
MIKAN-CHAN!
BEFORE WE KNOW IT...
...IN THE BLINK OF AN EYE, SHE'S SINGLE-HANDEDLY JUMPED OVER A HORSE AND GRABBED A SECOND STAR!!
And I can't forgive...
...your smelly farts!
Ngah!
+10
WHA... WHOA, SHE'S INCREDIBLE!
Oohhh!
AND JUST LIKE THAT, SHE'S JUMPED ALONE, OVER PEOPLE'S HORSES INTO ENEMY TERRITORY!
Channelling a Cat-Dog Alice?!
he's the girl from ne incident earlier, right?

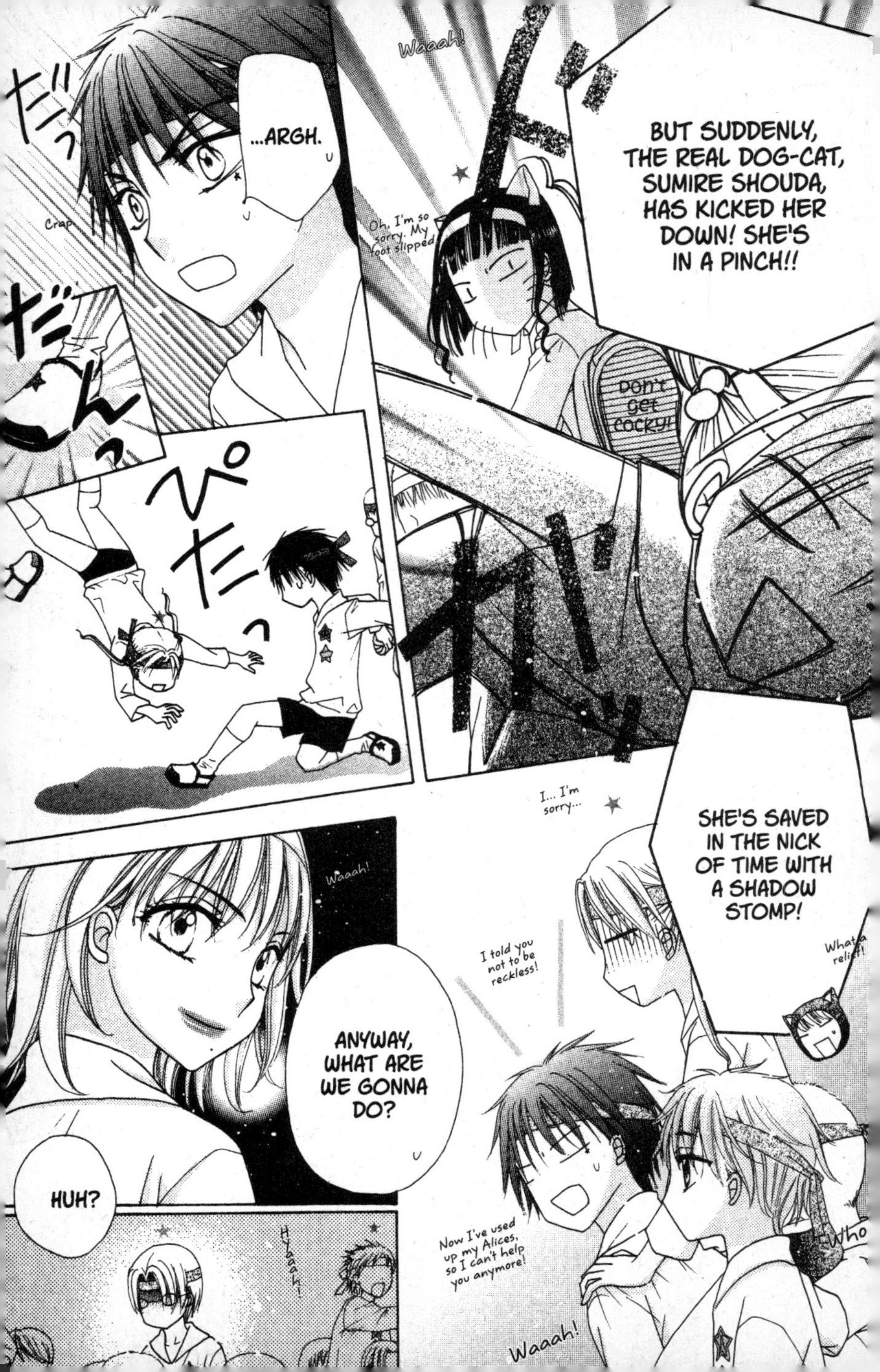

Waaah!
BUT SUDDENLY, THE REAL DOG-CAT, SUMIRE SHOUDA, HAS KICKED HER DOWN! SHE'S IN A PINCH!!
Oh, I'm so sorry. My foot slipped
Don't get cocky!!
...ARGH.
Crap
SHE'S SAVED IN THE NICK OF TIME WITH A SHADOW STOMP!
I... I'm sorry...
What a relief!
I told you not to be reckless!
Now I've used up my Alices, so I can't help you anymore!
Who
Waaah!
Waaah!
ANYWAY, WHAT ARE WE GONNA DO?
HUH?
Hyaaah!

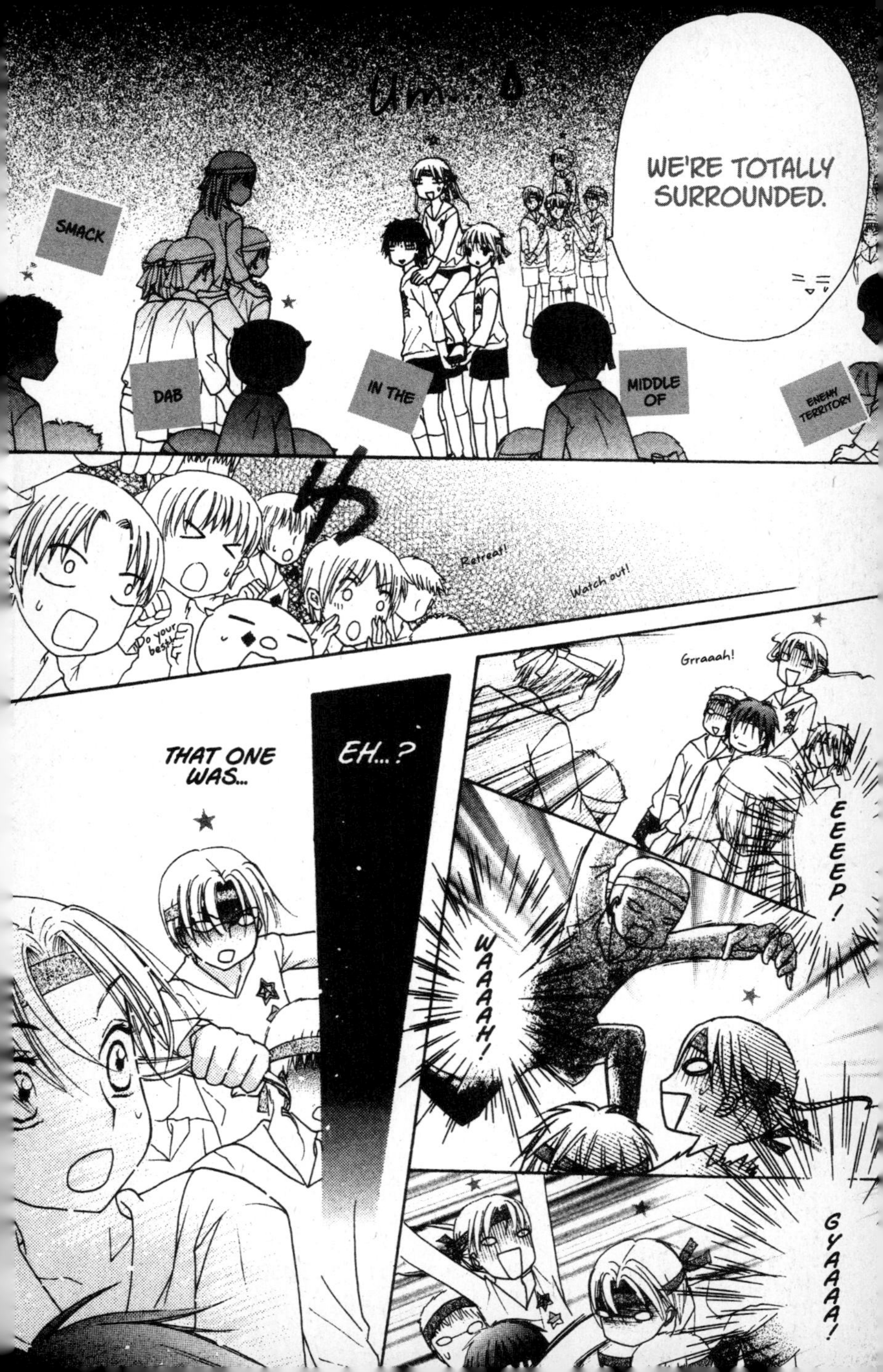

WE'RE TOTALLY SURROUNDED.
Um...
SMACK
DAB
IN THE
MIDDLE OF
ENEMY TERRITORY
Watch out!
Retreat!
Do your best!!
Grraaah!
EEEEP!
WAAAAH!
GYAAAAA!
EH...?
THAT ONE WAS...

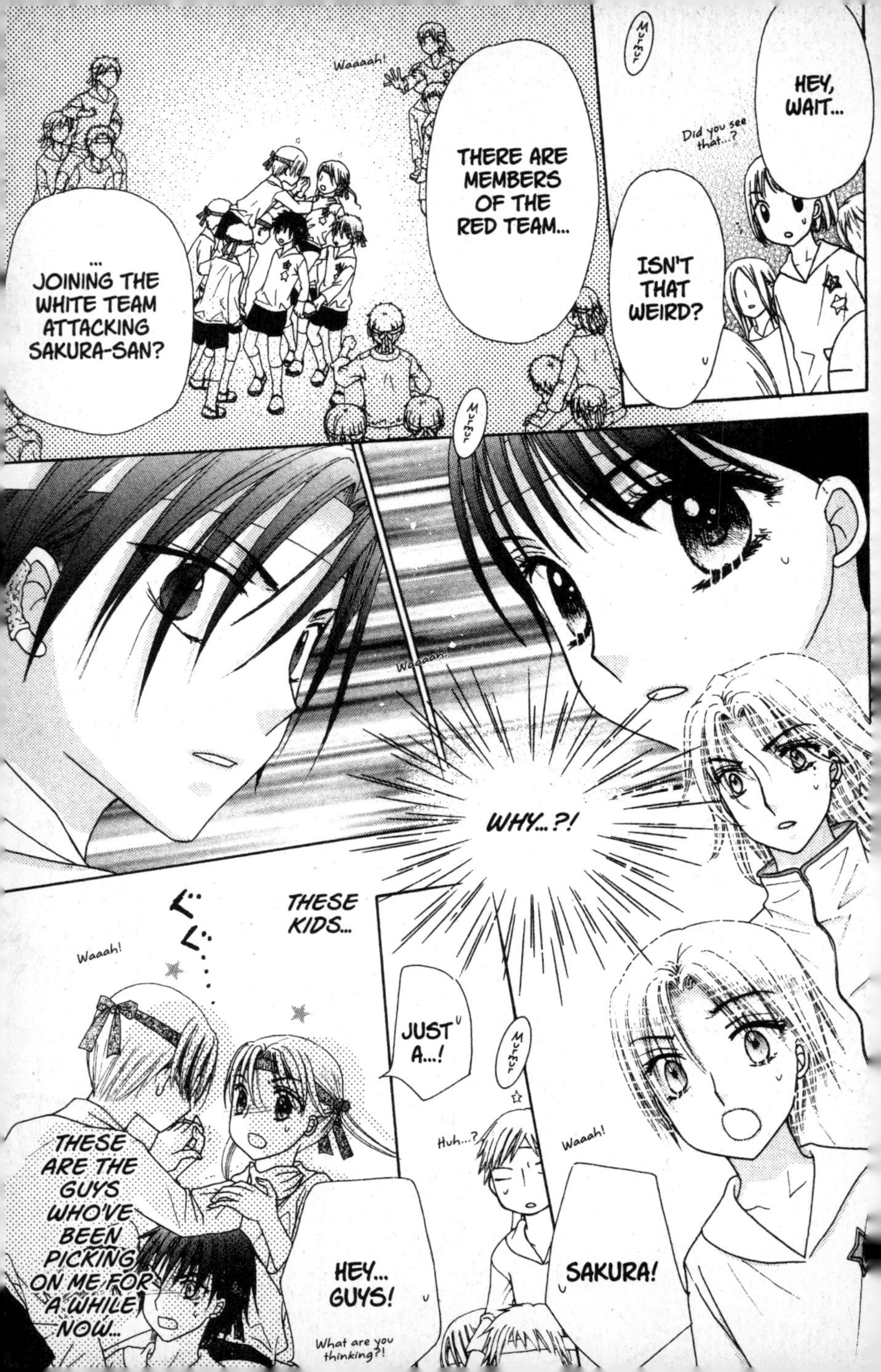
HEY, WAIT...
Did you see that...?
ISN'T THAT WEIRD?
Murmur
THERE ARE MEMBERS OF THE RED TEAM...
Waaaah!
...JOINING THE WHITE TEAM ATTACKING SAKURA-SAN?
Murmur
Waaaah
WHY...?!
SAKURA!
Waaah!
Huh...?
Murmur
JUST A...!
HEY... GUYS!
What are you thinking?!
THESE KIDS...
Waaah!
THESE ARE THE GUYS WHO'VE BEEN PICKING ON ME FOR A WHILE NOW...

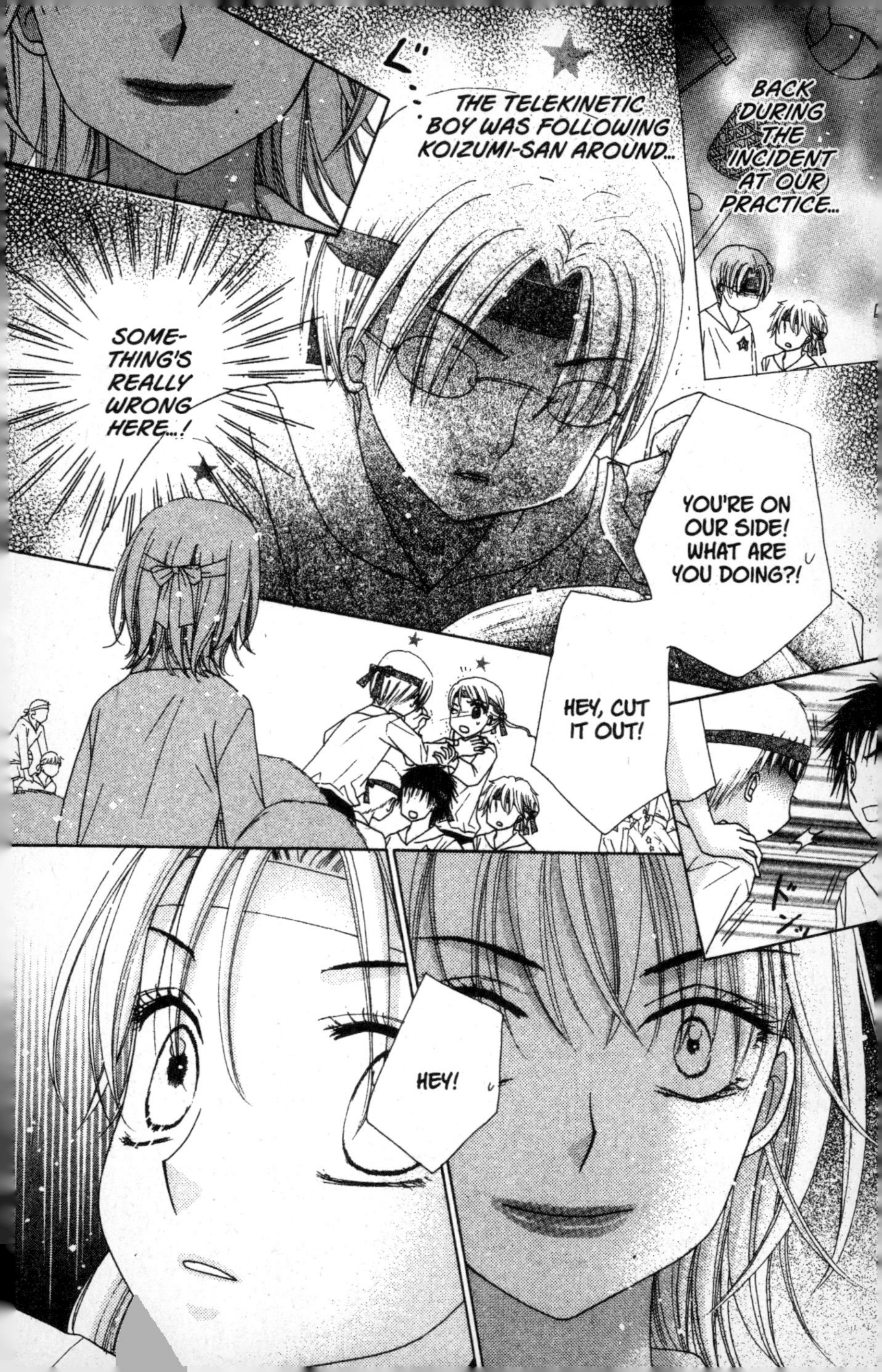
BACK DURING THE INCIDENT AT OUR PRACTICE...
THE TELEKINETIC BOY WAS FOLLOWING KOIZUMI-SAN AROUND...
SOME-THING'S REALLY WRONG HERE...!
YOU'RE ON OUR SIDE! WHAT ARE YOU DOING?!
HEY, CUT IT OUT!
HEY!

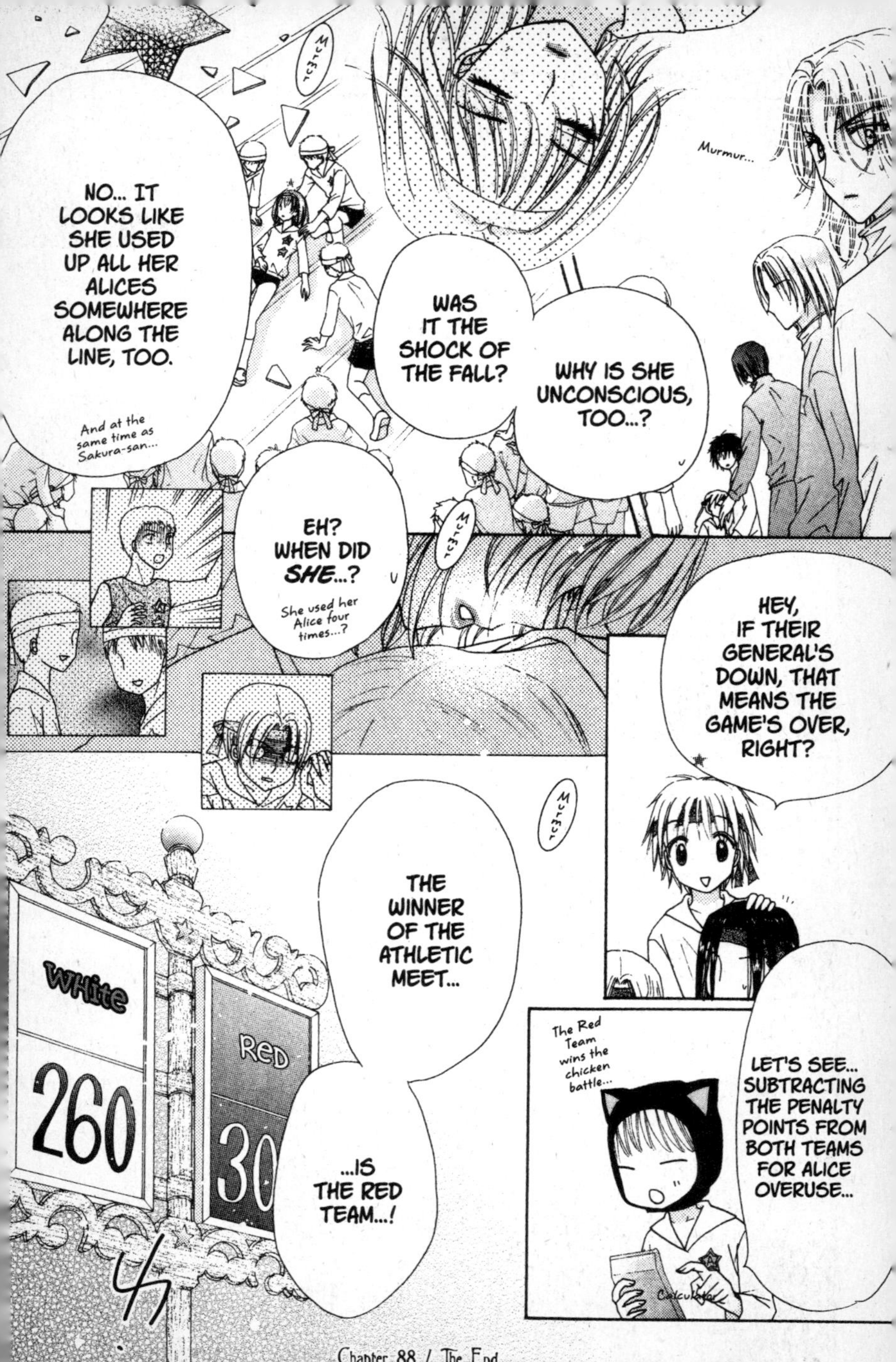
Murmur...
WHY IS SHE UNCONSCIOUS, TOO...?
WAS IT THE SHOCK OF THE FALL?
Murmur
NO... IT LOOKS LIKE SHE USED UP ALL HER ALICES SOMEWHERE ALONG THE LINE, TOO.
And at the same time as Sakura-san...
HEY, IF THEIR GENERAL'S DOWN, THAT MEANS THE GAME'S OVER, RIGHT?
Murmur
EH? WHEN DID *SHE*...?
She used her Alice four times...?
The Red Team wins the chicken battle...
LET'S SEE... SUBTRACTING THE PENALTY POINTS FROM BOTH TEAMS FOR ALICE OVERUSE...
Calculator
Murmur
THE WINNER OF THE ATHLETIC MEET...
...IS THE RED TEAM...!
White
260
Red
30

Chapter 88 / The End

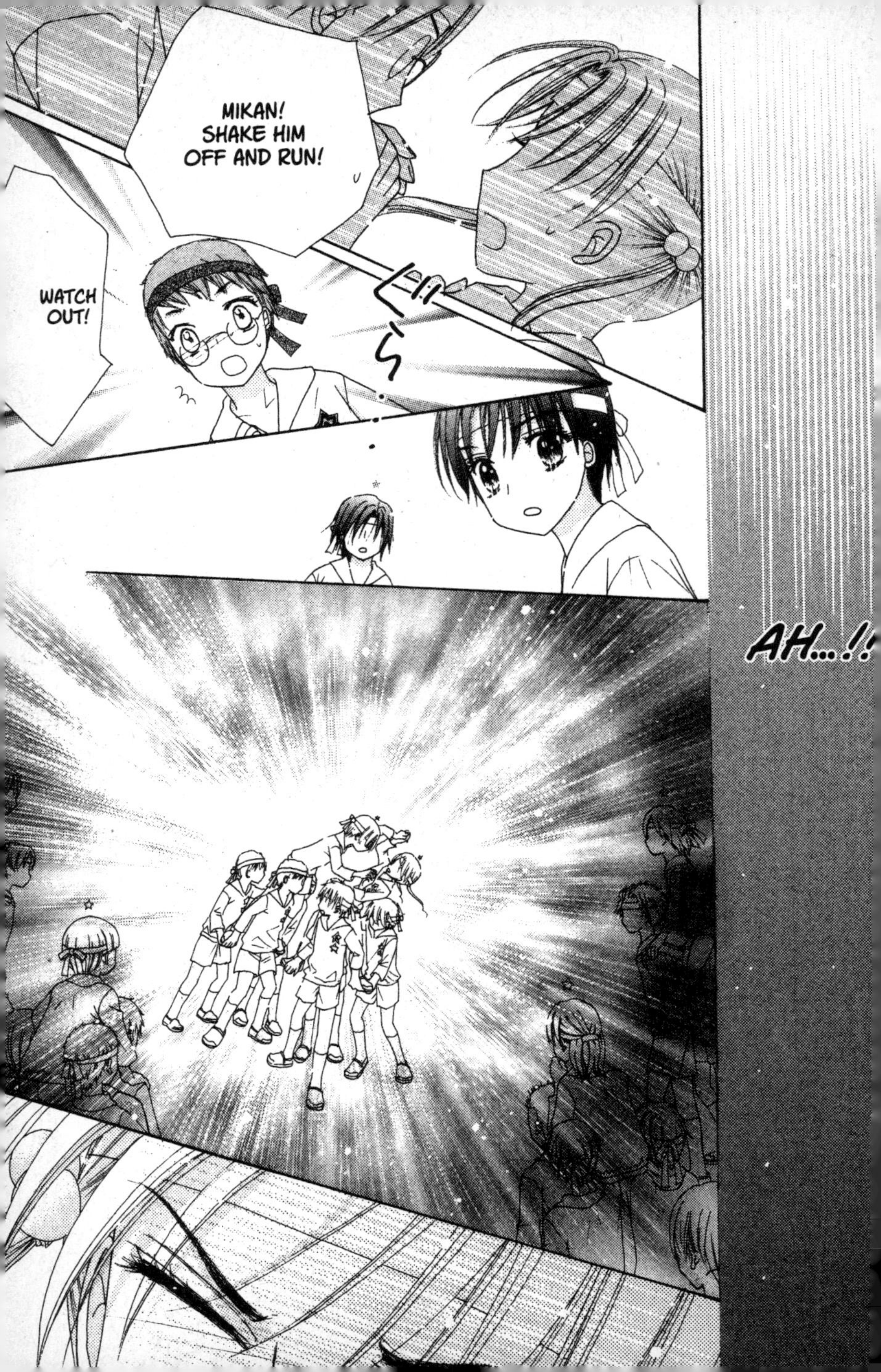
MIKAN! SHAKE HIM OFF AND RUN!
WATCH OUT!
ぐら
AH...!!

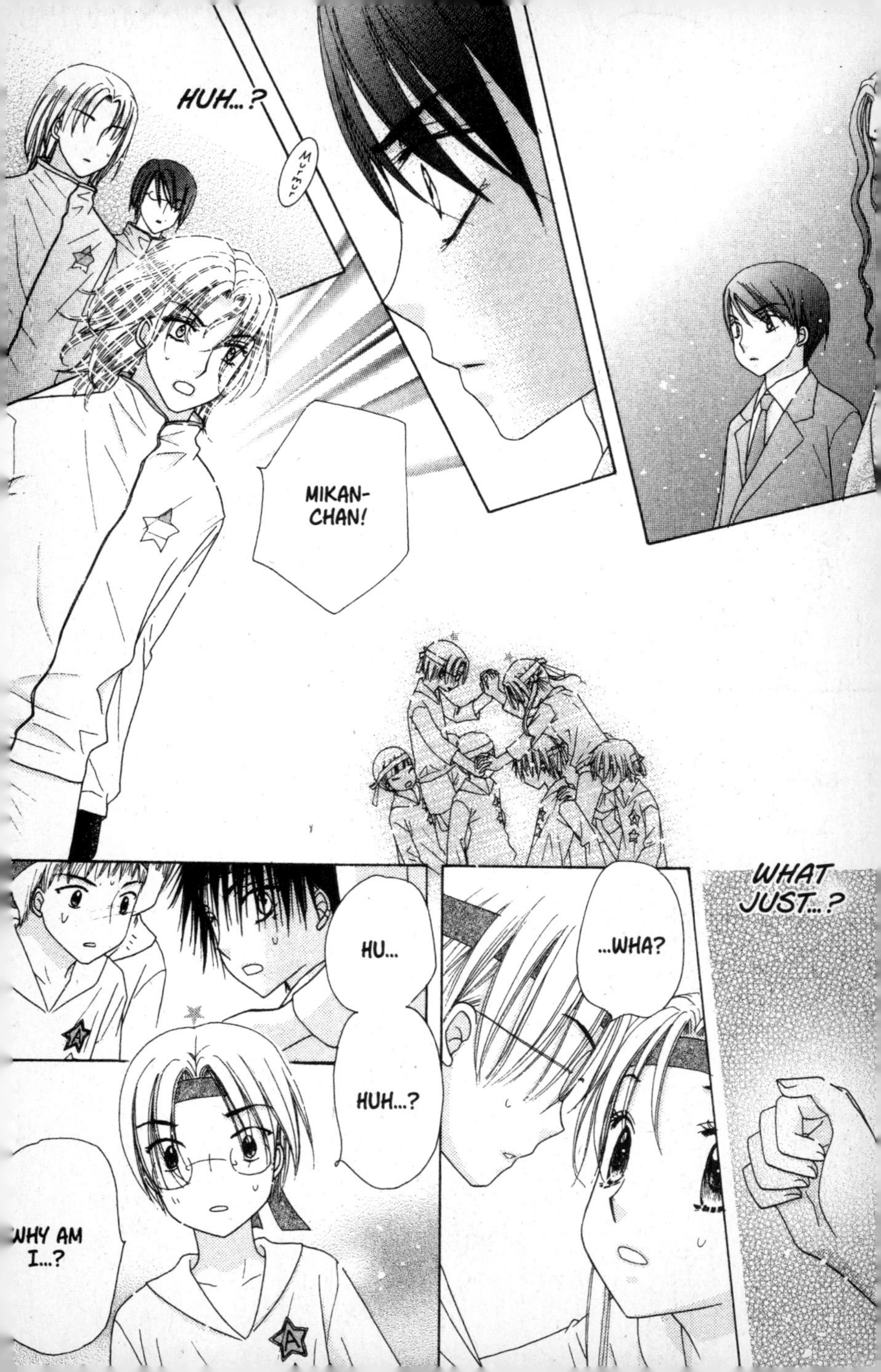
HUH...?
MIKAN-CHAN!
WHAT JUST...?
...WHA?
HU...
HUH...?
WHY AM I...?

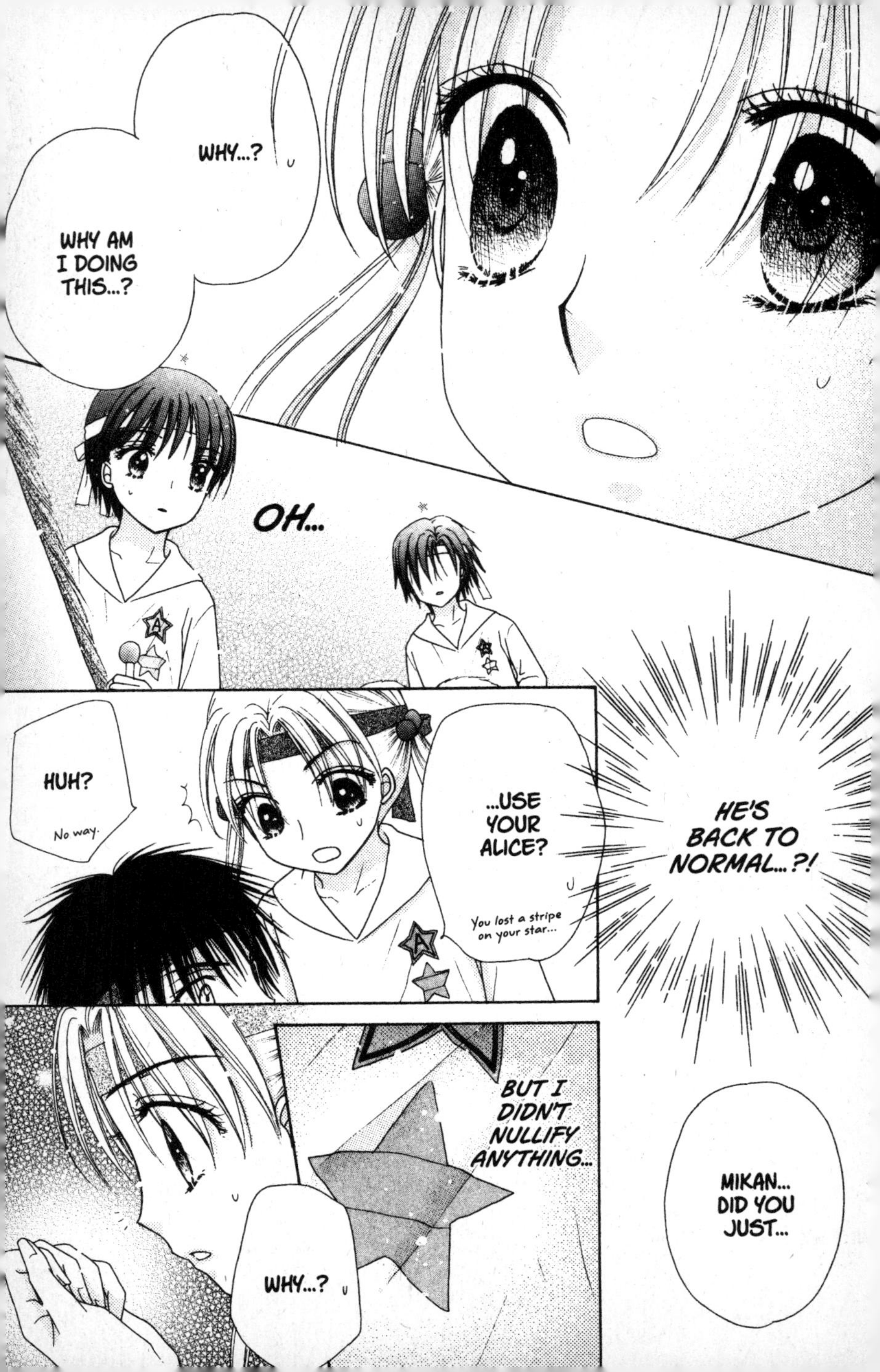
WHY...?
WHY AM I DOING THIS...?
OH...
HE'S BACK TO NORMAL...?!
MIKAN... DID YOU JUST...
...USE YOUR ALICE?
You lost a stripe on your star...
HUH?
No way.
BUT I DIDN'T NULLIFY ANYTHING...
WHY...?

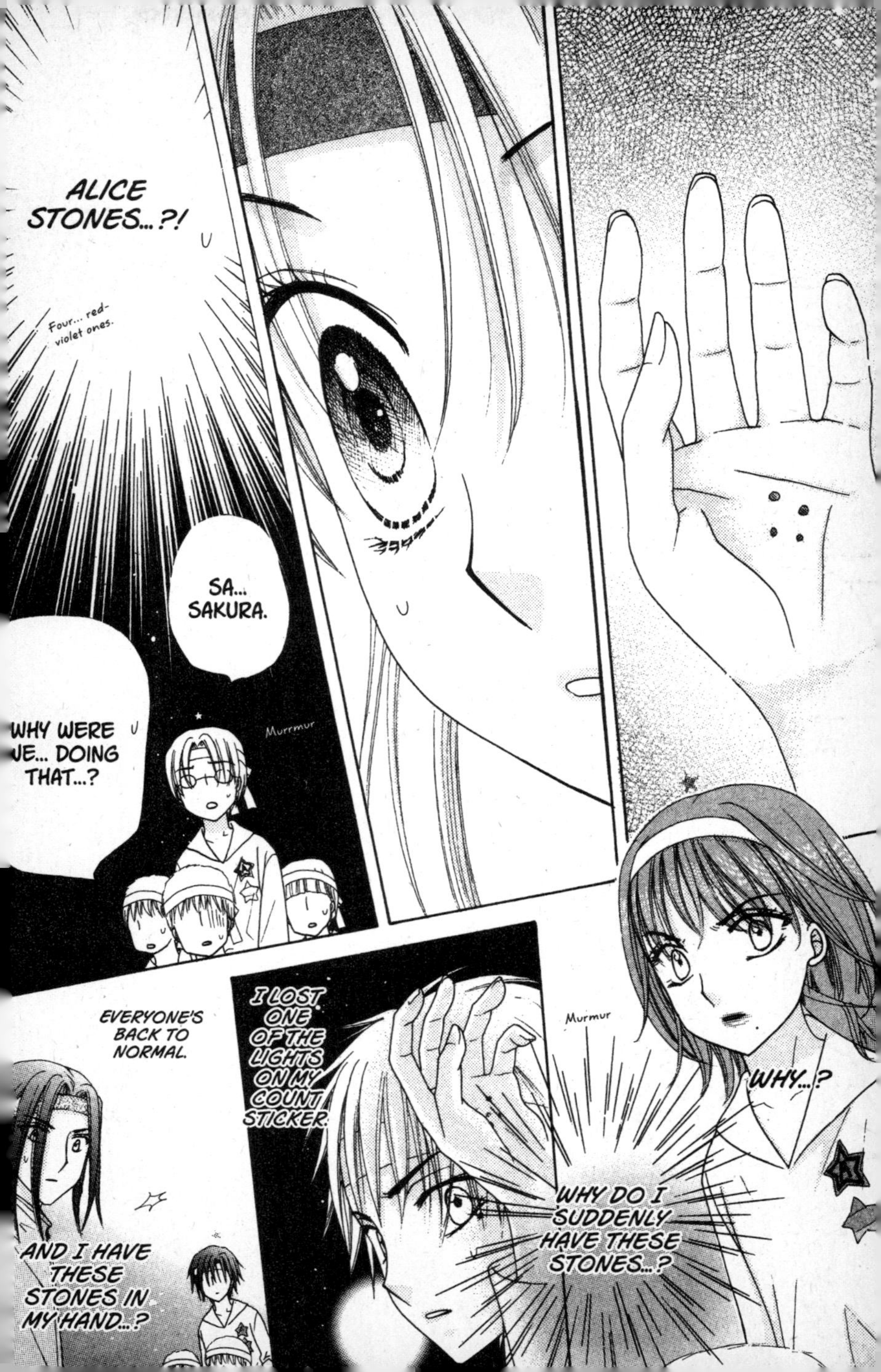
ALICE STONES...?!
Four... red-violet ones.
SA... SAKURA.
Murrmur
WHY WERE E... DOING THAT...?
Murmur
WHY...?
WHY DO I SUDDENLY HAVE THESE STONES...?
I LOST ONE OF THE LIGHTS ON MY COUNT STICKER.
EVERYONE'S BACK TO NORMAL.
AND I HAVE THESE STONES IN MY HAND...?

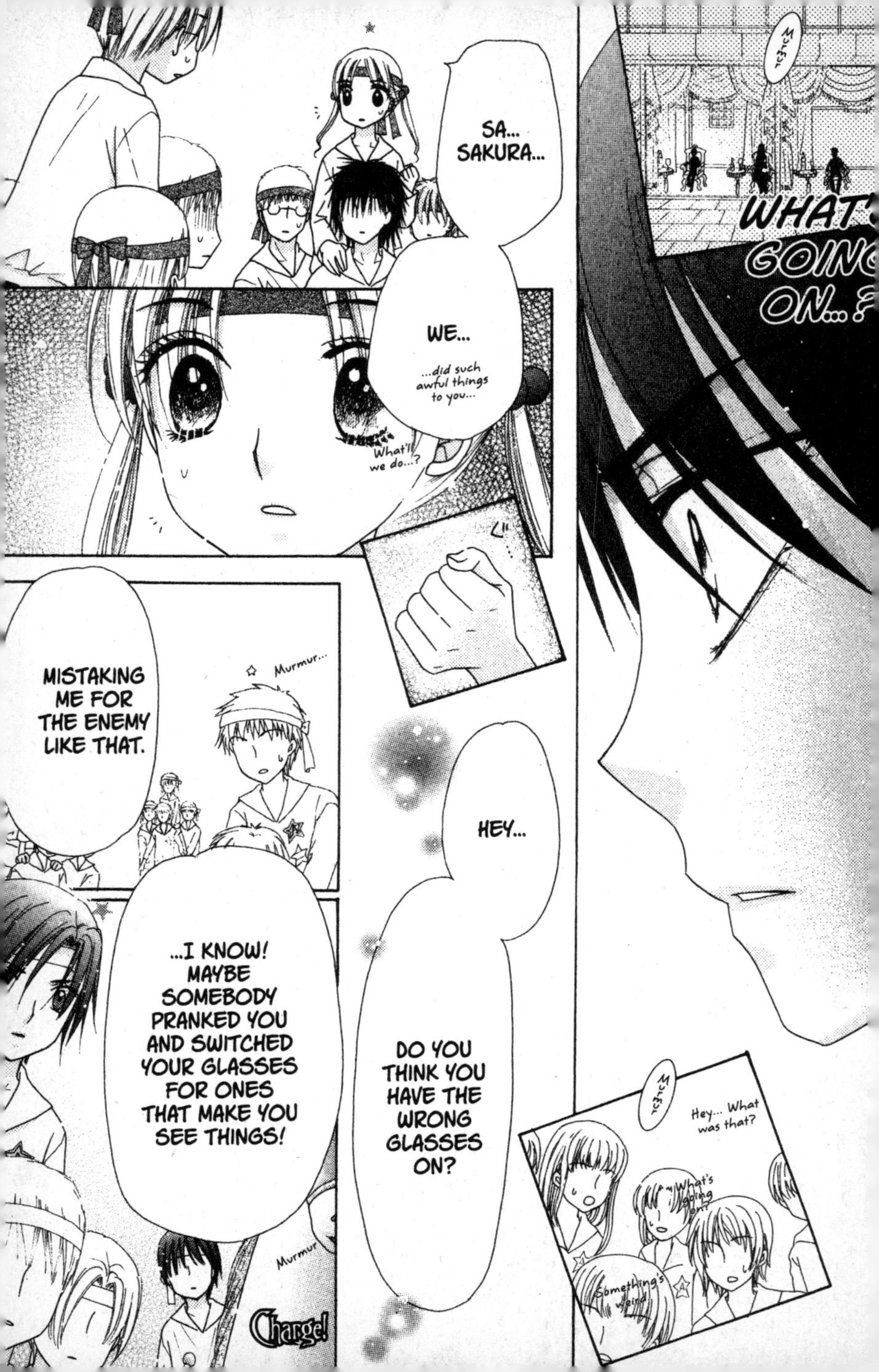
Murmur
WHAT'S GOING ON...?
Murmur
Hey... What was that?
What's going on?
Something's weird
SA... SAKURA...
WE...
...did such awful things to you...
What'll we do...?
HEY...
DO YOU THINK YOU HAVE THE WRONG GLASSES ON?
MISTAKING ME FOR THE ENEMY LIKE THAT.
Murmur...
...I KNOW! MAYBE SOMEBODY PRANKED YOU AND SWITCHED YOUR GLASSES FOR ONES THAT MAKE YOU SEE THINGS!
Murmur

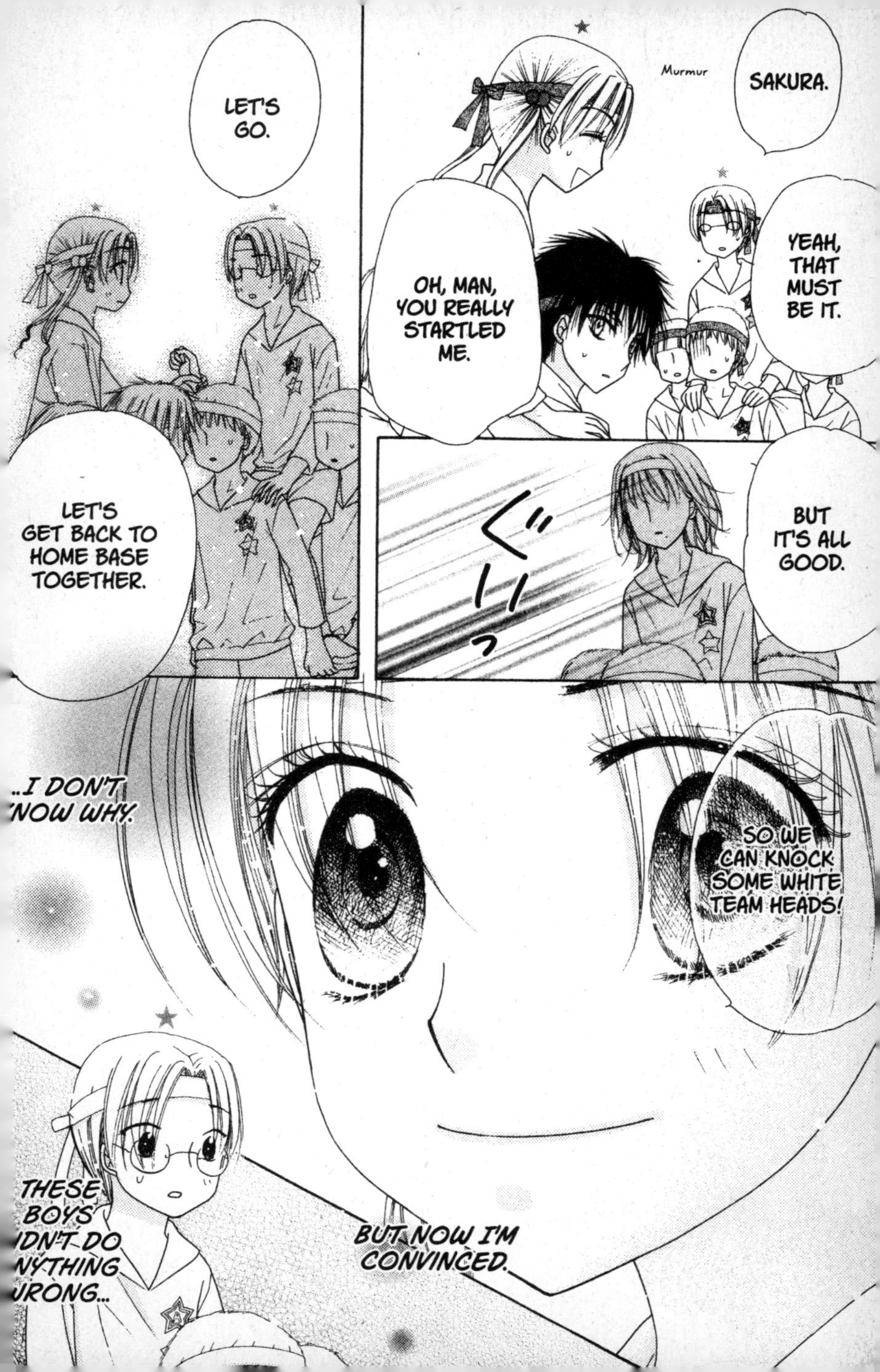
SAKURA.
Murmur
YEAH, THAT MUST BE IT.
OH, MAN, YOU REALLY STARTLED ME.
BUT IT'S ALL GOOD.
ぐいっ
LET'S GO.
LET'S GET BACK TO HOME BASE TOGETHER.
SO WE CAN KNOCK SOME WHITE TEAM HEADS!
..I DON'T NOW WHY.
BUT NOW I'M CONVINCED.
THESE BOYS IDN'T DO NYTHING URONG...

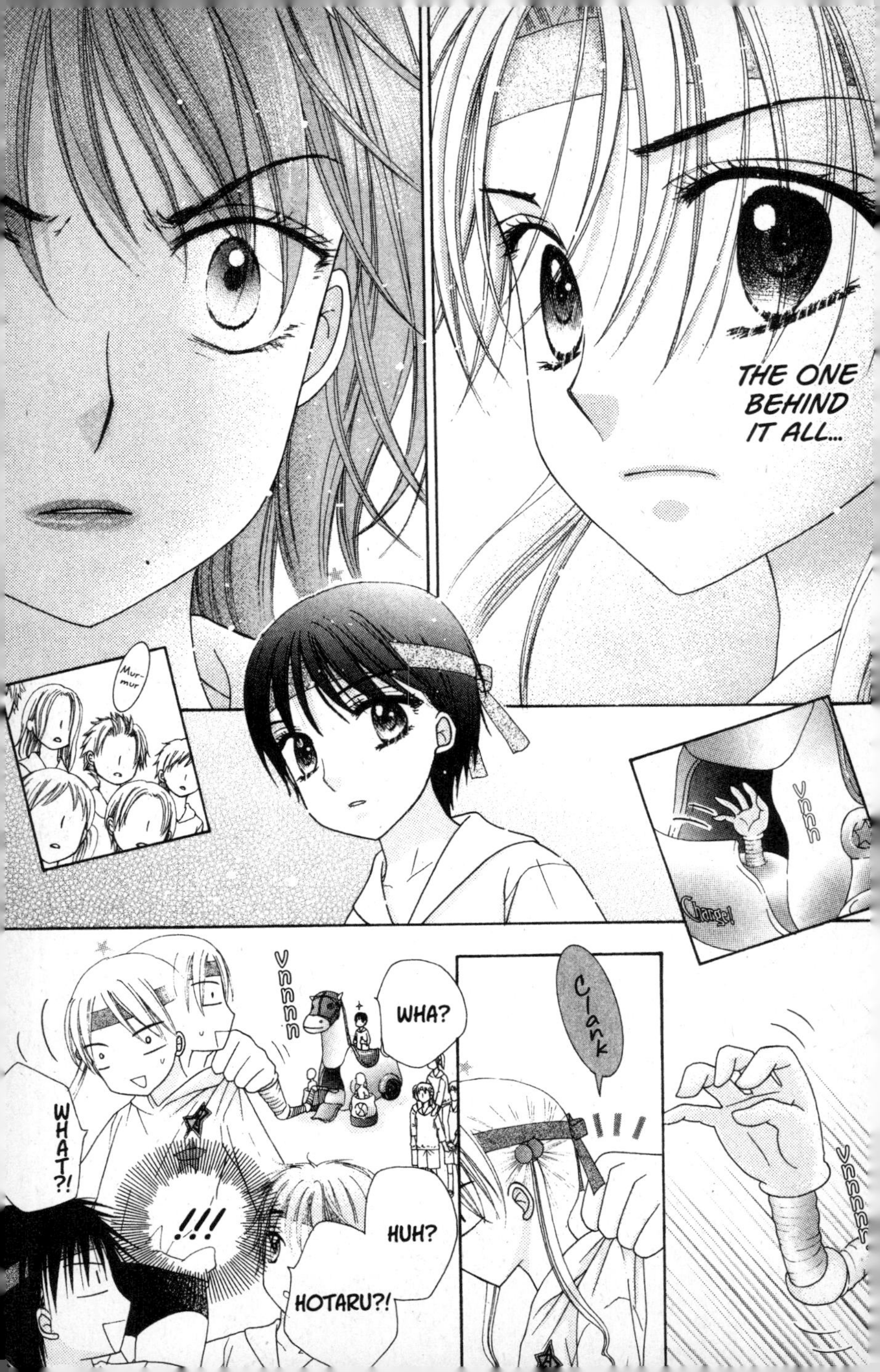
THE ONE BEHIND IT ALL...
Vnnn
Change!
Mur-mur
Vnnnn
Clank
WHA?
Vnnnn
WHAT?!
!!!
HUH?
HOTARU?!

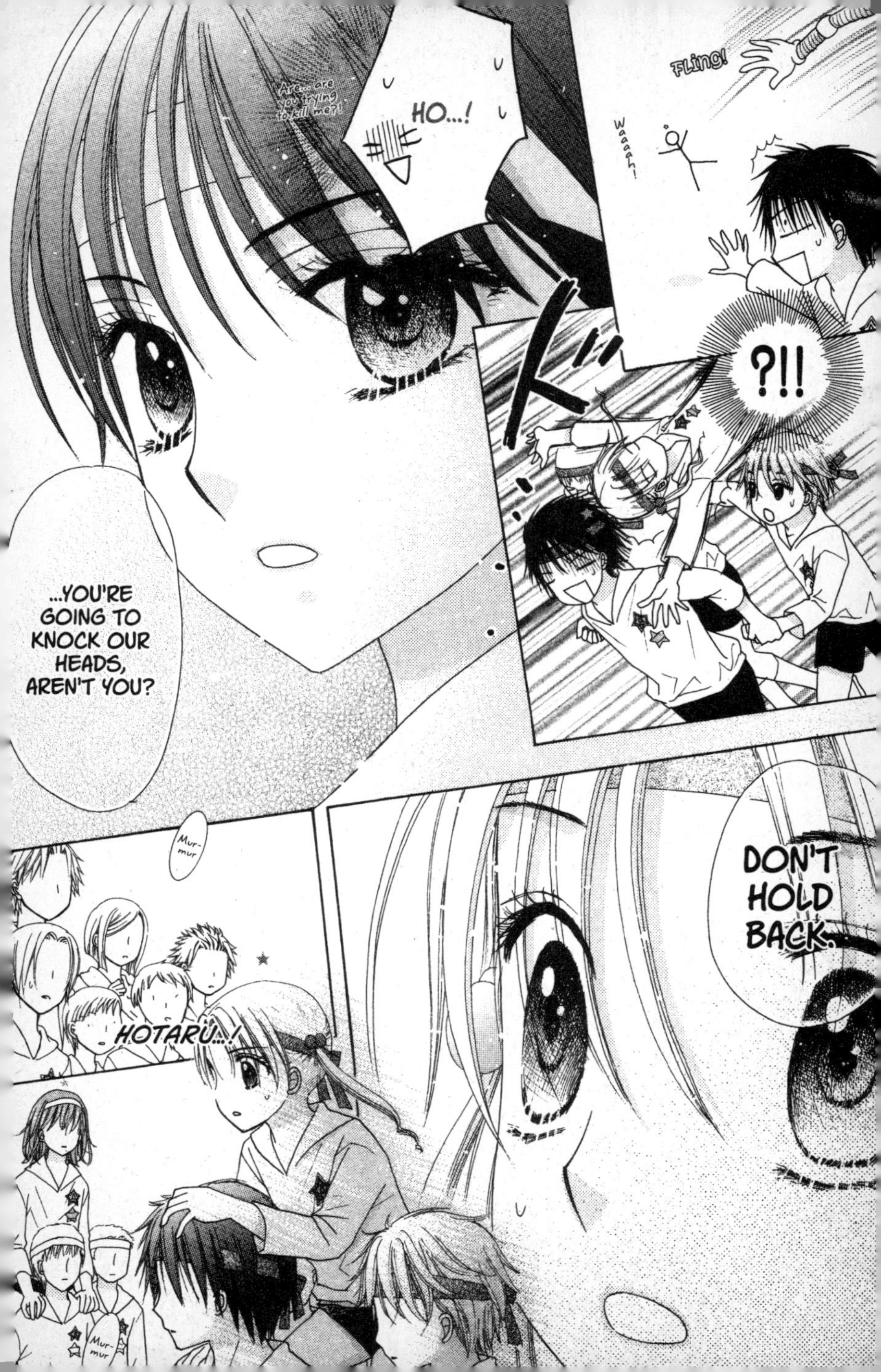

FLING!
Waaaah!
HO...!
Are... are you trying to kill me?!
?!!
...YOU'RE GOING TO KNOCK OUR HEADS, AREN'T YOU?
DON'T HOLD BACK.
Mur-mur
HOTARU...!
Mur-mur

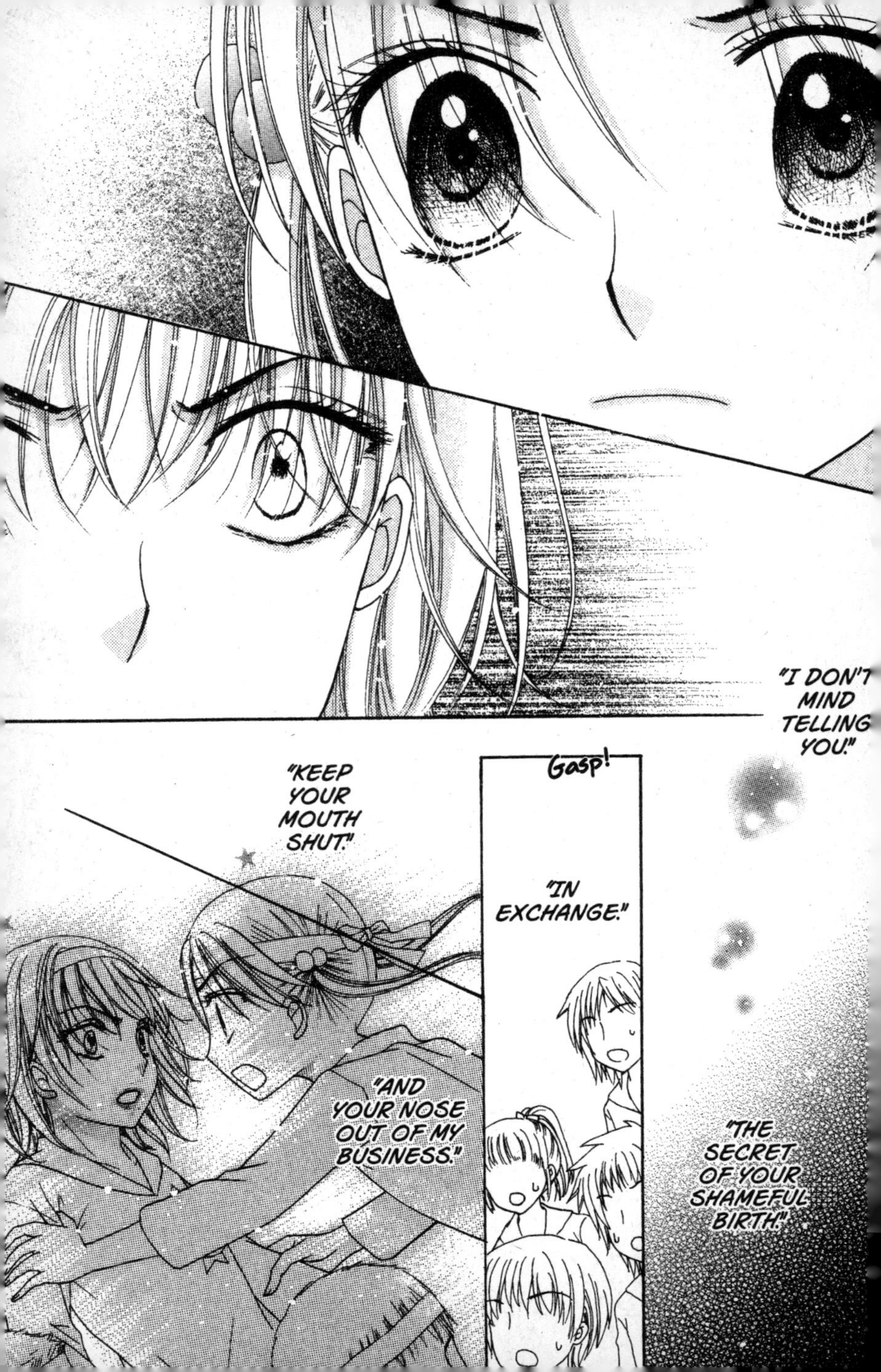
"I DON'T MIND TELLING YOU."
"THE SECRET OF YOUR SHAMEFUL BIRTH."
Gasp!
"IN EXCHANGE."
"KEEP YOUR MOUTH SHUT."
"AND YOUR NOSE OUT OF MY BUSINESS."

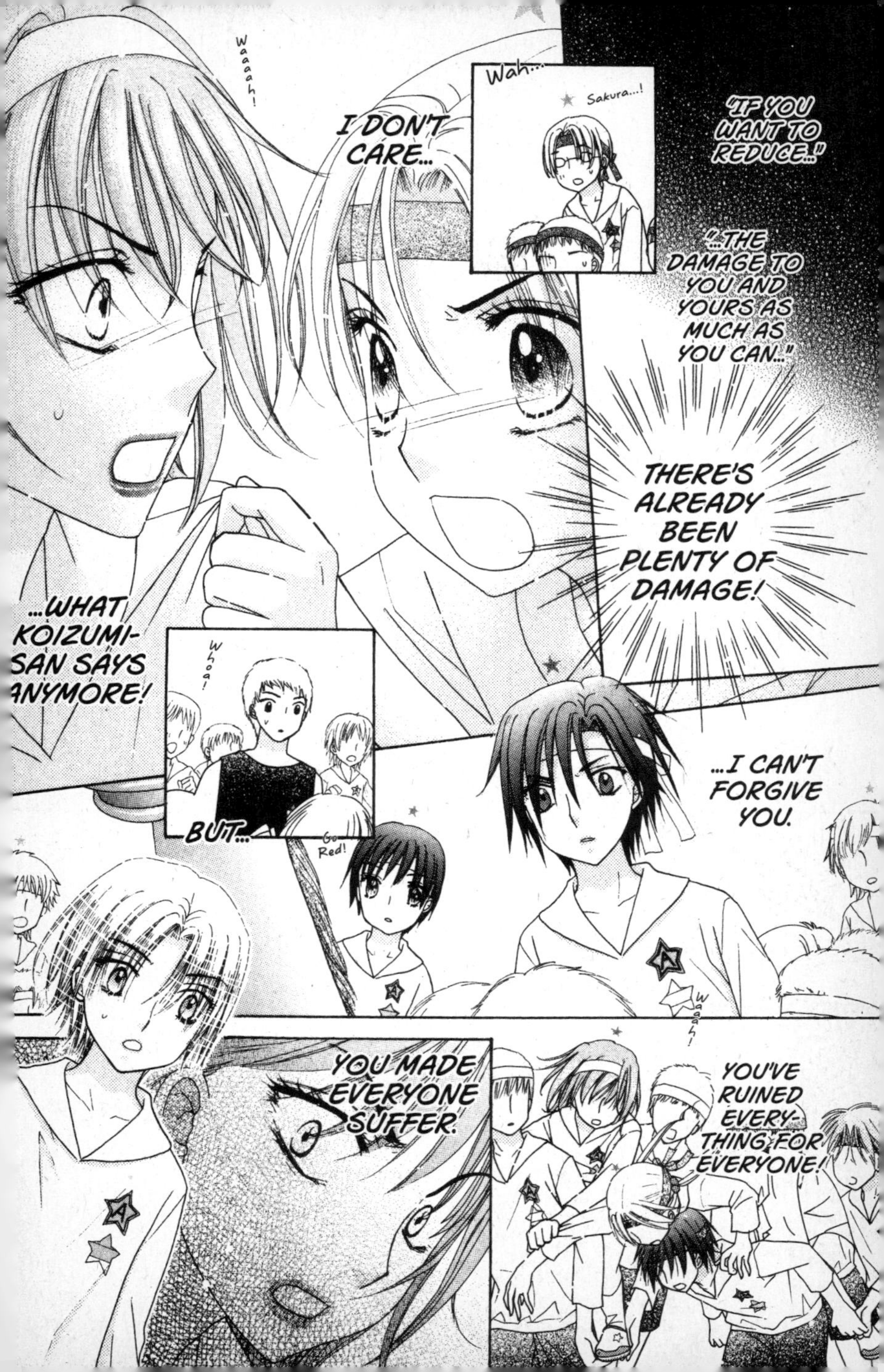

"IF YOU WANT TO REDUCE..."
"...THE DAMAGE TO YOU AND YOURS AS MUCH AS YOU CAN..."
Wah...
Sakura...!
I DON'T CARE...
Waaaah!
THERE'S ALREADY BEEN PLENTY OF DAMAGE!
...WHAT KOIZUMI-SAN SAYS ANYMORE!
...I CAN'T FORGIVE YOU.
Go Red!
Whoa!
BUT...
Waaah!
YOU'VE RUINED EVERY-THING FOR EVERYONE!
YOU MADE EVERYONE SUFFER.

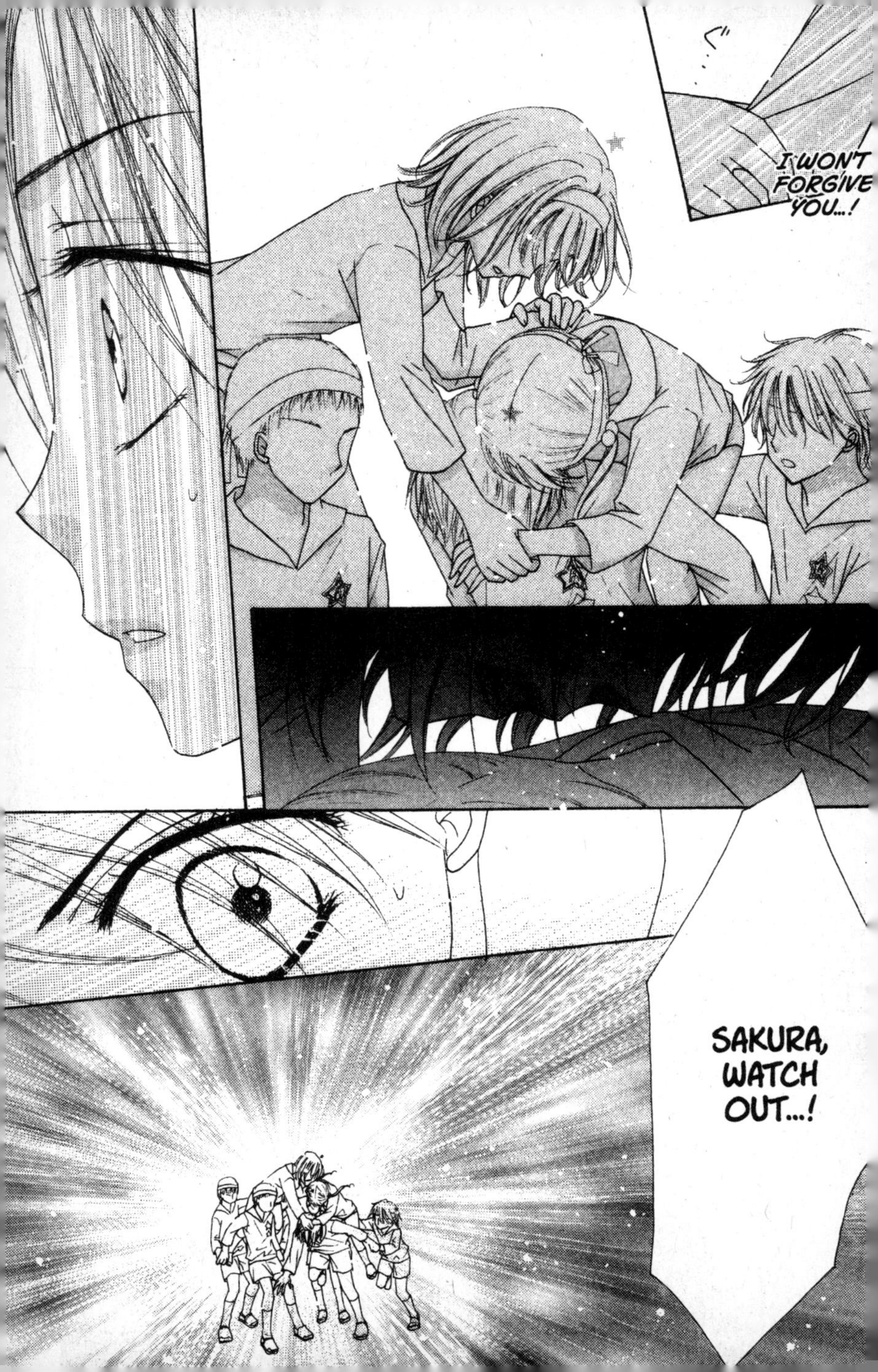
I WON'T FORGIVE YOU...!
SAKURA, WATCH OUT...!

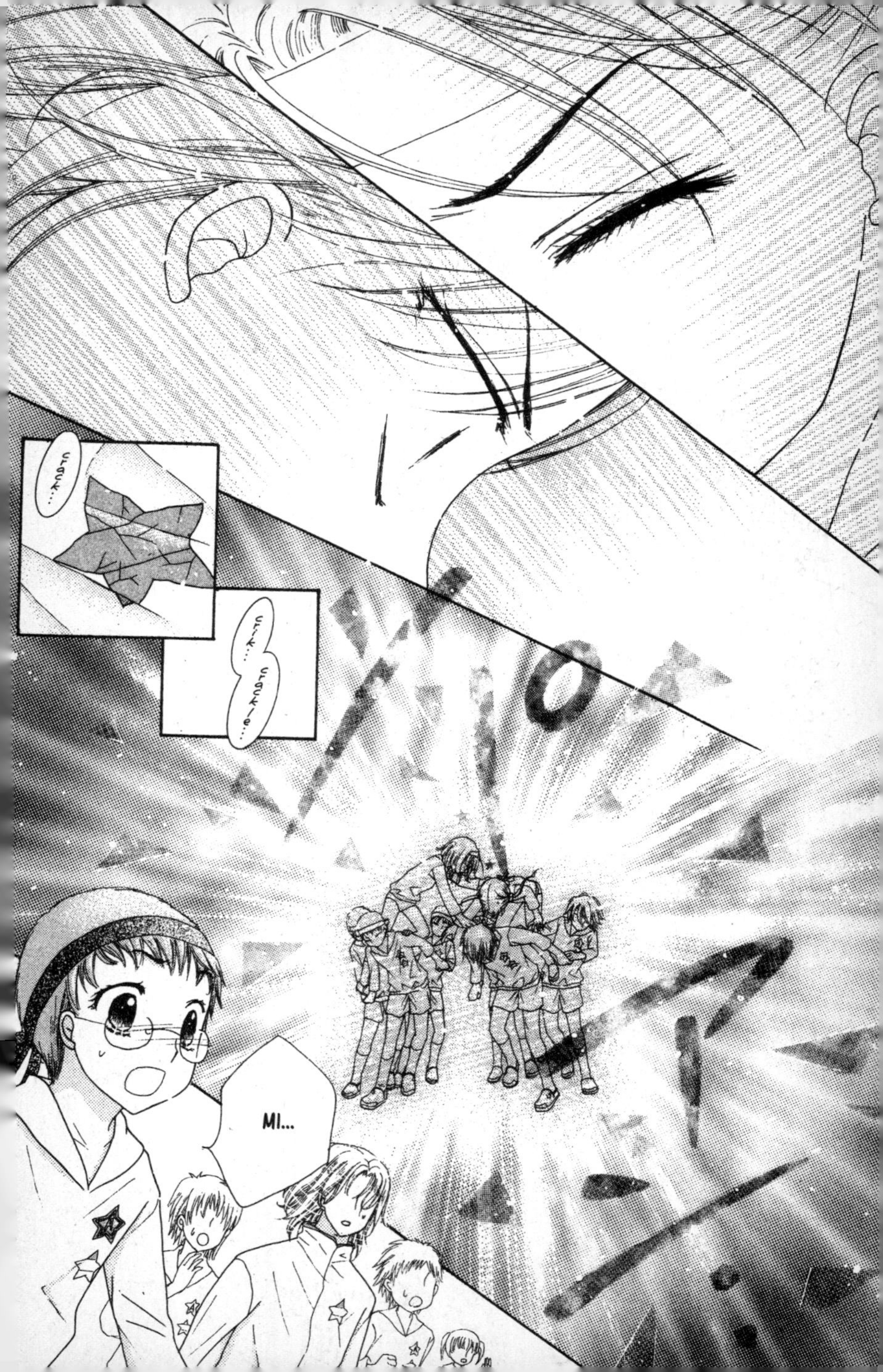
crack...
crik... crackle...
MI...

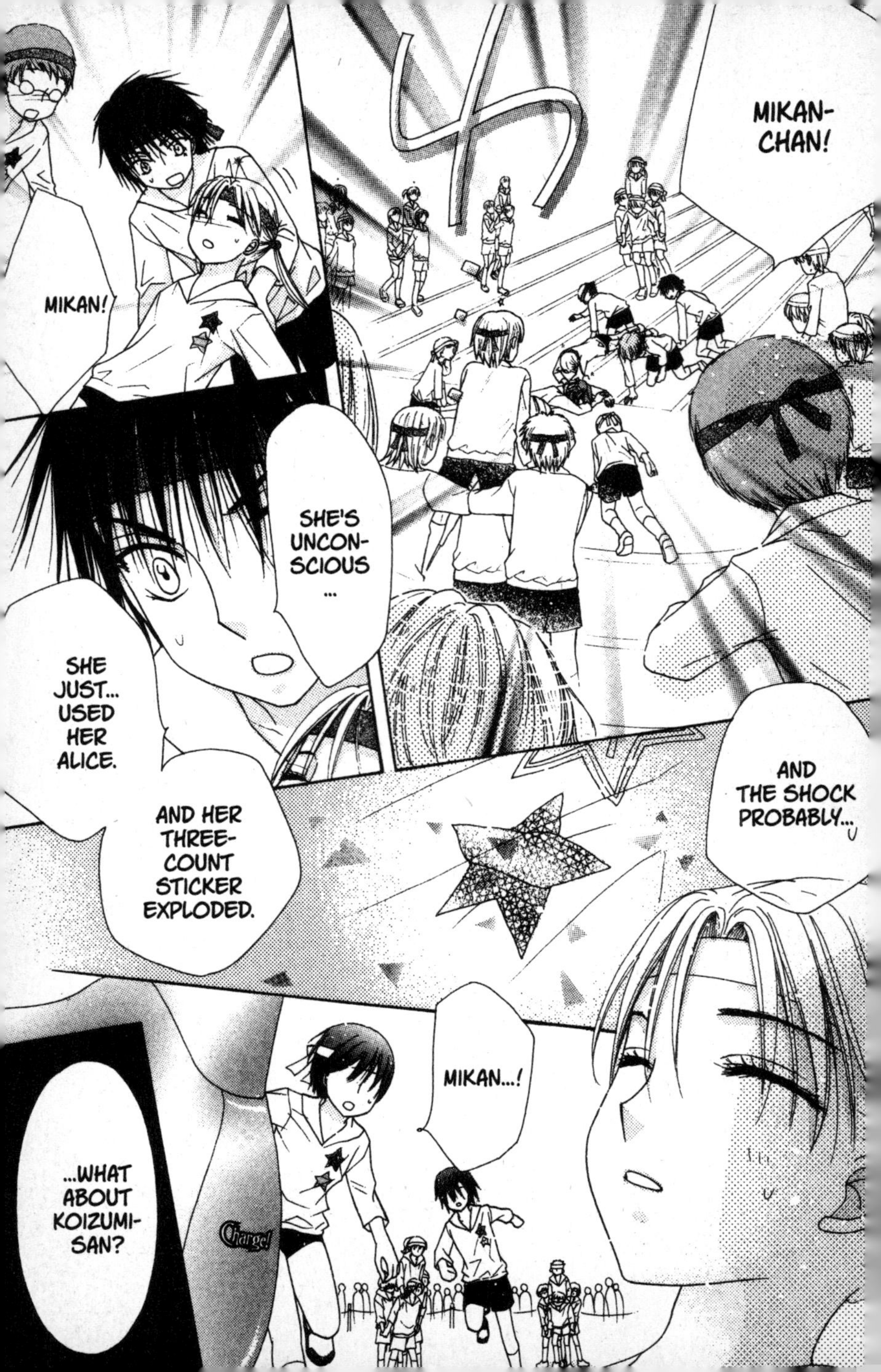
MIKAN-CHAN!
MIKAN!
SHE'S UNCONSCIOUS...
SHE JUST... USED HER ALICE.
AND THE SHOCK PROBABLY...
AND HER THREE-COUNT STICKER EXPLODED.
MIKAN...!
Charge!
...WHAT ABOUT KOIZUMI-SAN?

Time for a Character Psychology Test (15)

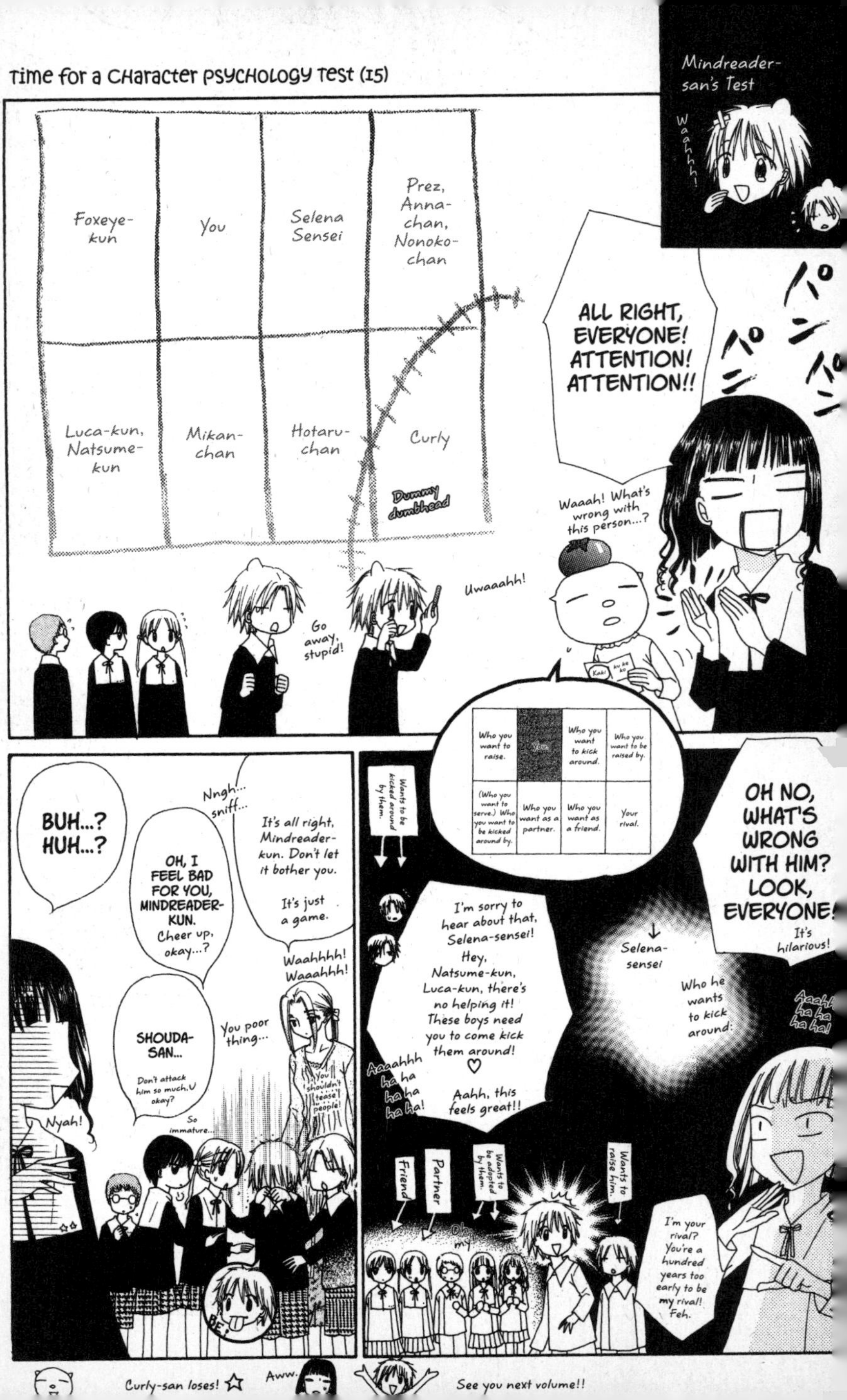
Mindreader-san's Test
Waahhh!
ALL RIGHT, EVERYONE! ATTENTION! ATTENTION!!
Waaah! What's wrong with this person...?
Uwaaahh!
Foxeye-kun
You
Selena Sensei
Prez, Anna-chan, Nonoko-chan
Luca-kun, Natsume-kun
Mikan-chan
Hotaru-chan
Curly
Dummy dumbhead
Go away, stupid!
OH NO, WHAT'S WRONG WITH HIM? LOOK, EVERYONE!
It's hilarious!
Who you want to raise.
You
Who you want to kick around.
Who you want to be raised by.
(Who you want to serve.) Who you want to be kicked around by.
Who you want as a partner.
Who you want as a friend.
Your rival.
Selena-sensei
Who he wants to kick around.
Aaahh ha ha ha ha!
Wants to be kicked around by them.
I'm sorry to hear about that, Selena-sensei! Hey, Natsume-kun, Luca-kun, there's no helping it! These boys need you to come kick them around! ♡
Aahh, this feels great!!
Aaaahhh ha ha ha ha ha!
I'm your rival? You're a hundred years too early to be my rival! Feh.
Wants to raise him.
Wants to be adopted by them.
Partner
Friend
Oh my
BUH...? HUH...?
Nngh... sniff...
It's all right, Mindreader-kun. Don't let it bother you.
It's just a game.
OH, I FEEL BAD FOR YOU, MINDREADER-KUN. Cheer up, okay...?
Waahhhh! Waaahhh!
SHOUDA-SAN...
Don't attack him so much, okay?
You poor thing...
You shouldn't tease people!
Nyah!
So immature...
BE
Curly-san loses! ☆
Aww.
See you next volume!!

THANKS

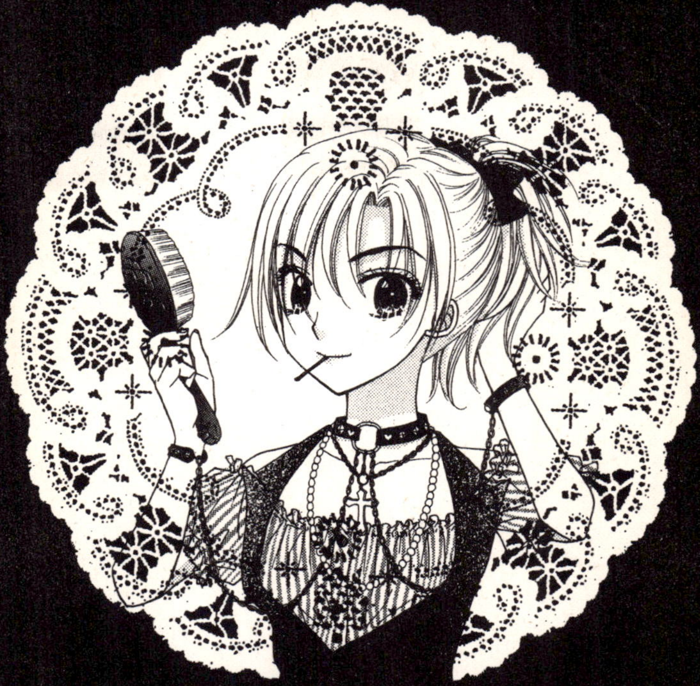

Thank you very much for reading this far.

SPECIAL THANKS

Nakamura-san, Ida-san, Morita-san, Miyoshi-san, Suu-san, Family-san, Friends-san, Editor-san, and my readers.

SEE YOU AGAIN

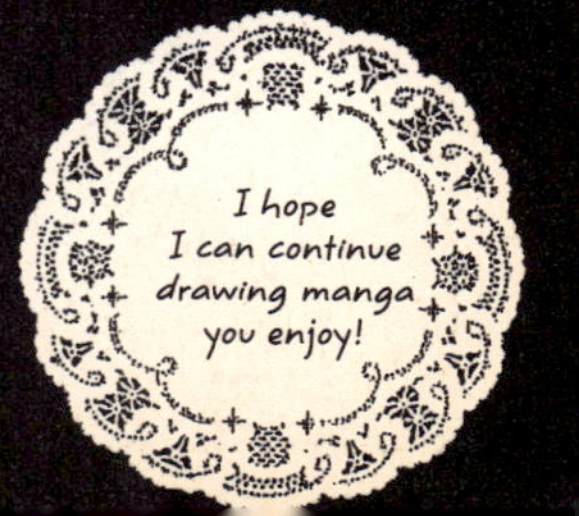
I hope
I can continue
drawing manga
you enjoy!

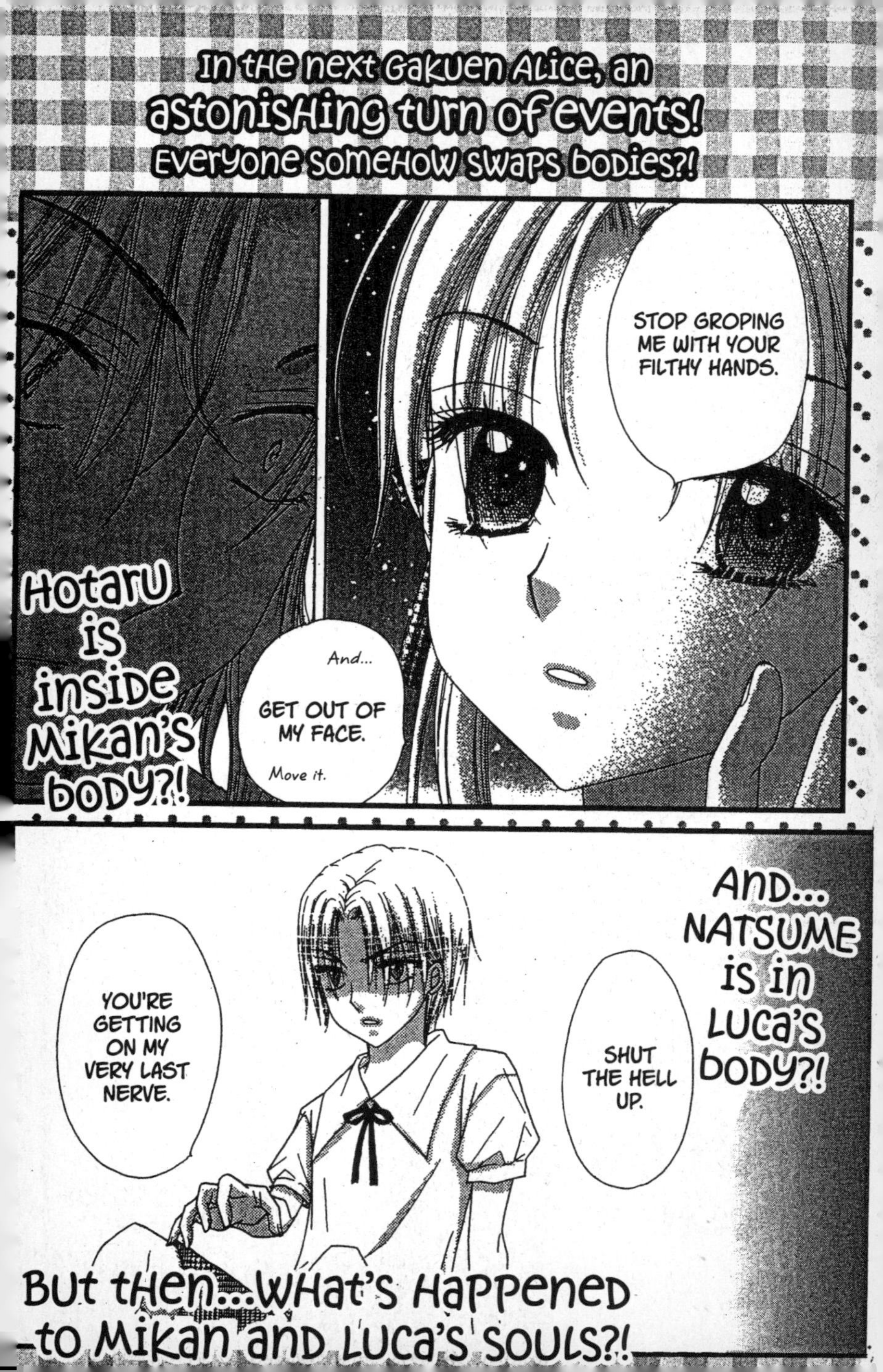
In the next Gakuen Alice, an astonishing turn of events! Everyone somehow swaps bodies?!
STOP GROPING ME WITH YOUR FILTHY HANDS.
And...
GET OUT OF MY FACE.
Move it.
Hotaru is inside Mikan's body?!
AND... NATSUME IS in LUCA'S BODY?!
SHUT THE HELL UP.
YOU'RE GETTING ON MY VERY LAST NERVE.
BUT THEN...WHAT'S HAPPENED TO MIKAN AND LUCA'S SOULS?!

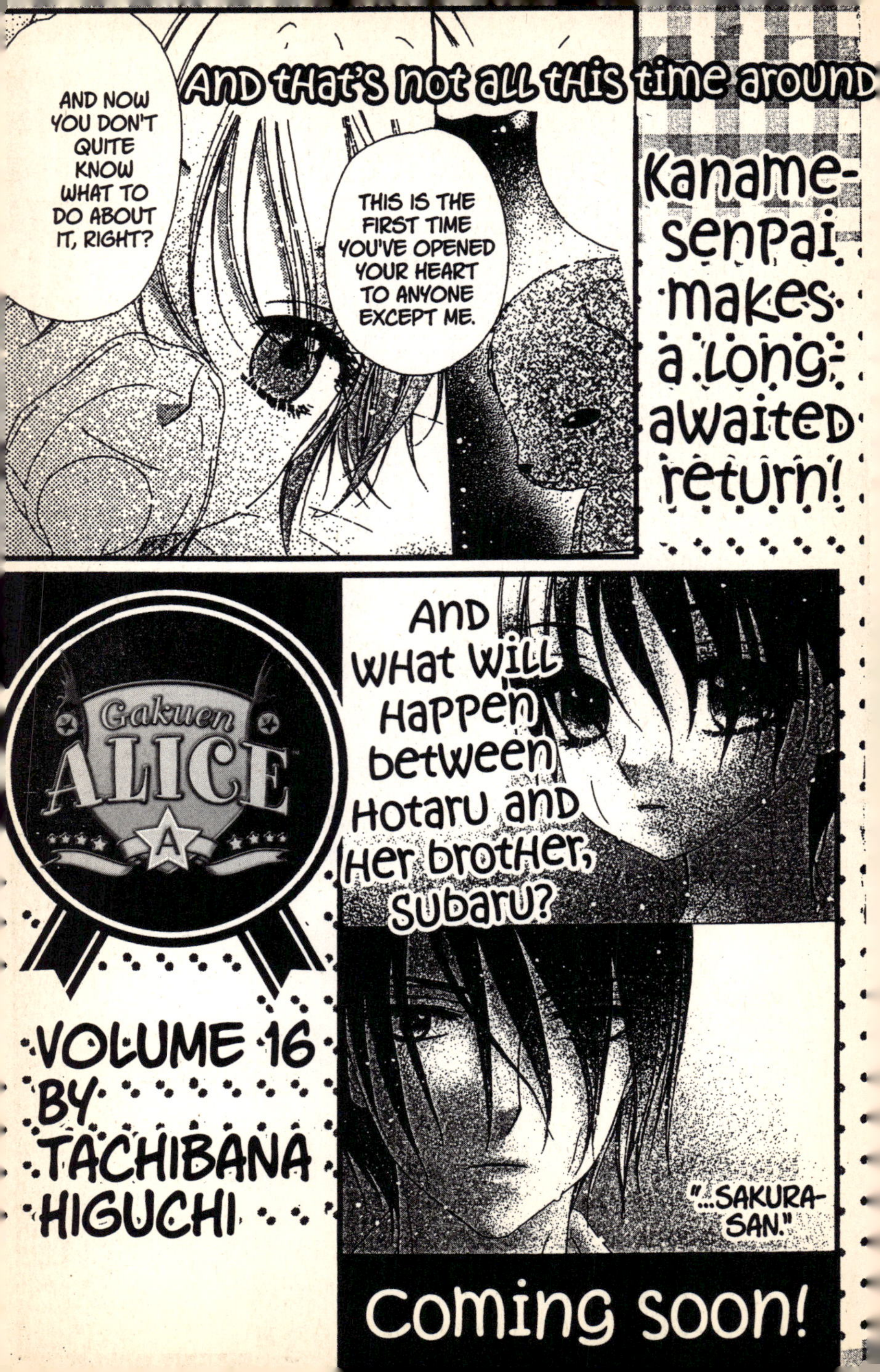
And that's not all this time around
Kaname-senpai makes a long-awaited return!
THIS IS THE FIRST TIME YOU'VE OPENED YOUR HEART TO ANYONE EXCEPT ME.
AND NOW YOU DON'T QUITE KNOW WHAT TO DO ABOUT IT, RIGHT?
And what will happen between Hotaru and her brother, Subaru?
"...SAKURA-SAN."
Coming soon!
Gakuen ALICE
VOLUME 16 BY TACHIBANA HIGUCHI

DOWNLOAD THE REVOLUTION.

Get the free TOKYOPOP app for manga, anytime, anywhere!

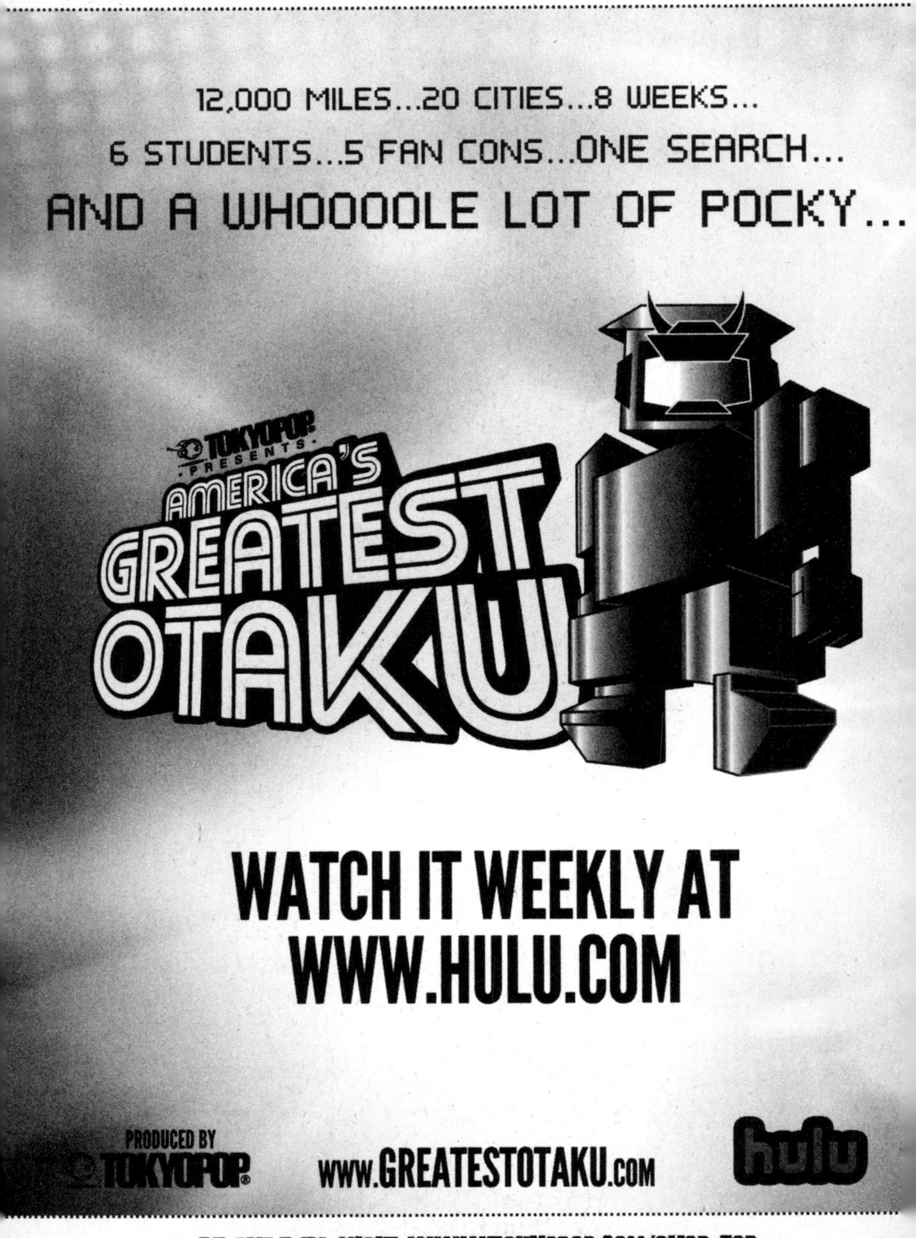
12,000 MILES...20 CITIES...8 WEEKS...
6 STUDENTS...5 FAN CONS...ONE SEARCH...
AND A WHOOOOLE LOT OF POCKY...
TOKYOPOP PRESENTS
AMERICA'S GREATEST OTAKU
WATCH IT WEEKLY AT
WWW.HULU.COM
PRODUCED BY TOKYOPOP
WWW.GREATESTOTAKU.COM
hulu

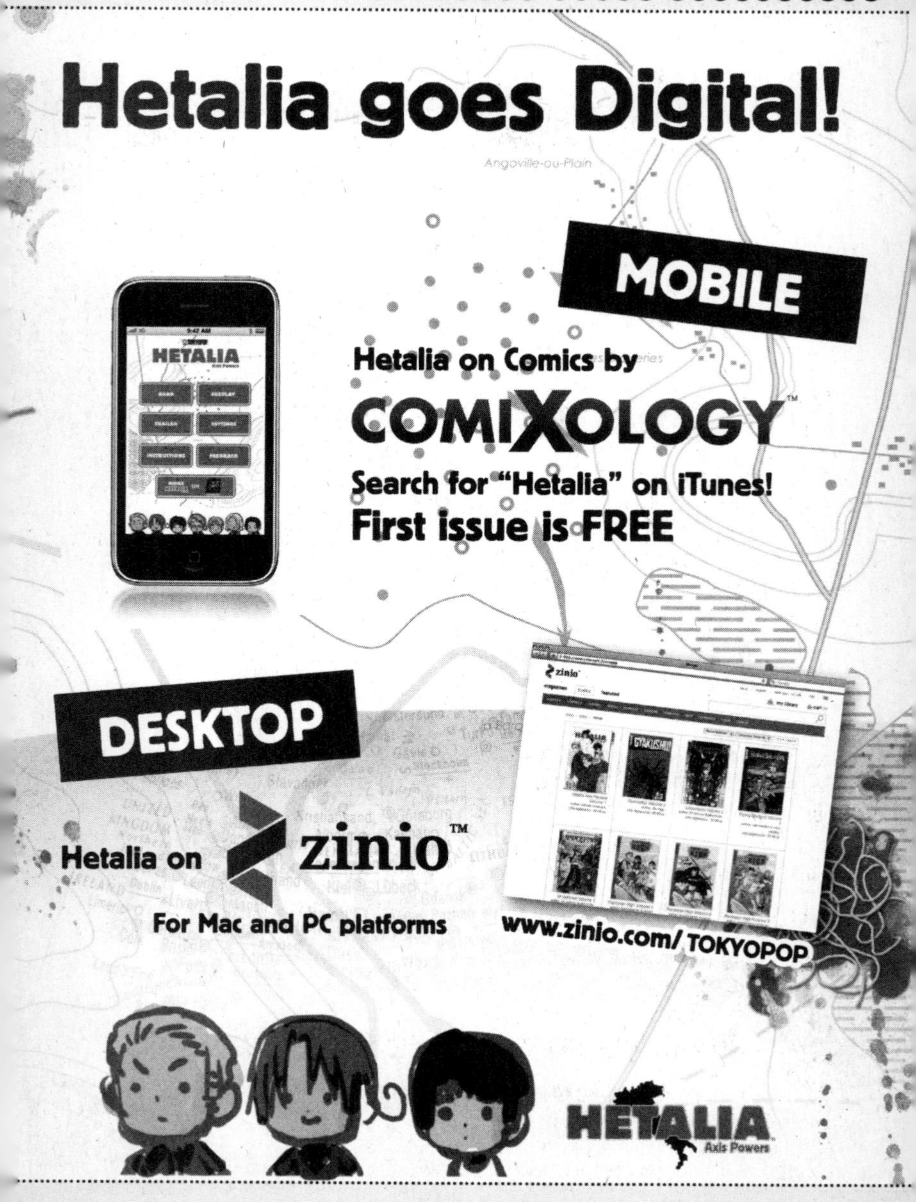
Hetalia goes Digital!
MOBILE
Hetalia on Comics by
COMIXOLOGY™
Search for "Hetalia" on iTunes!
First issue is FREE
DESKTOP
Hetalia on zinio™
For Mac and PC platforms
www.zinio.com/ TOKYOPOP
HETALIA
Axis Powers

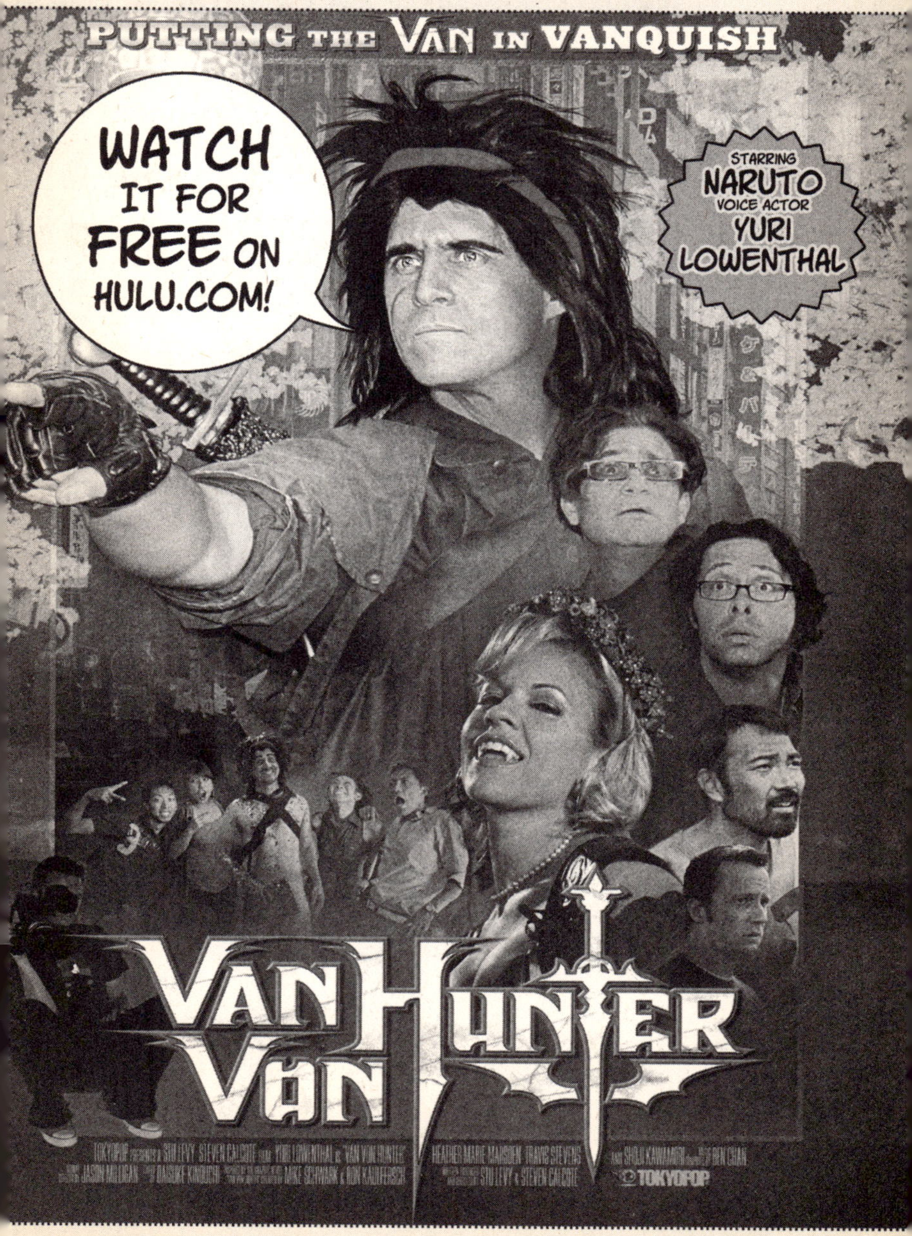
PUTTING THE VAN IN VANQUISH
WATCH IT FOR FREE ON HULU.COM!
STARRING NARUTO VOICE ACTOR YURI LOWENTHAL
VAN VON HUNTER
TOKYOPOP
STU LEVY STEVEN CALCOTE
YURI LOWENTHAL
HEATHER MARIE MARSDEN TRAVIS STEVENS
SHOJI KAWAMORI
BEN CHAN
JASON MILLIGAN
DAISUKE KINOUCHI
MIKE SCHWARK
STU LEVY STEVEN CALCOTE
TOKYOPOP

TOKYOPOP MANGA SUPPLEMENT

WARNING: Nosebleeds Ahead!!!

Karin is back!

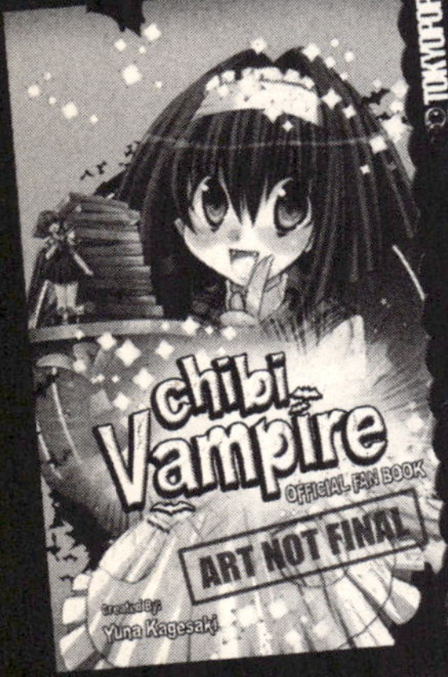
TOKYOPOP
chibi Vampire
OFFICIAL FAN BOOK
ART NOT FINAL
Created By:
Yuna Kagesaki

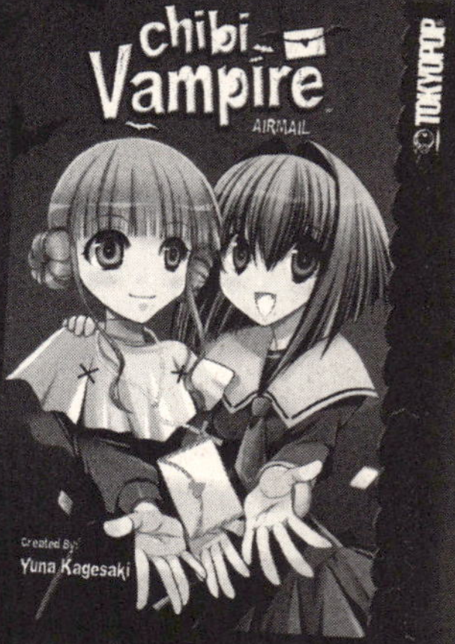
chibi Vampire
AIRMAIL
TOKYOPOP
Created By:
Yuna Kagesaki

Relive the laughter, romance and bittersweet moments in this must have book for Chibi Vampire fans. Loads of never before seen character sketches, maps and story highlights on the manga, anime and novels.

CHIBI VAMPIRE
Official Fanbook available January 2011!

A collection of manga stories that follows the continuing adventures of our favorite vampire. Finally find out what happened to Karin and her friends in these sweet tales and scary legends!

CHIBI VAMPIRE: AIRMAIL
available NOW in bookstores everywhere!

COMEDY
OT OLDER TEEN AGE 16+

BE SURE TO VISIT WWW.TOKYOPOP.COM/SHOP FOR EVERYTHING YOU COULD EVER WANT!

Learn From the Best!

Featuring the artists behind ***Fruits Basket***, ***Vampire Knight***, ***Maid Sama*** and **many more!**

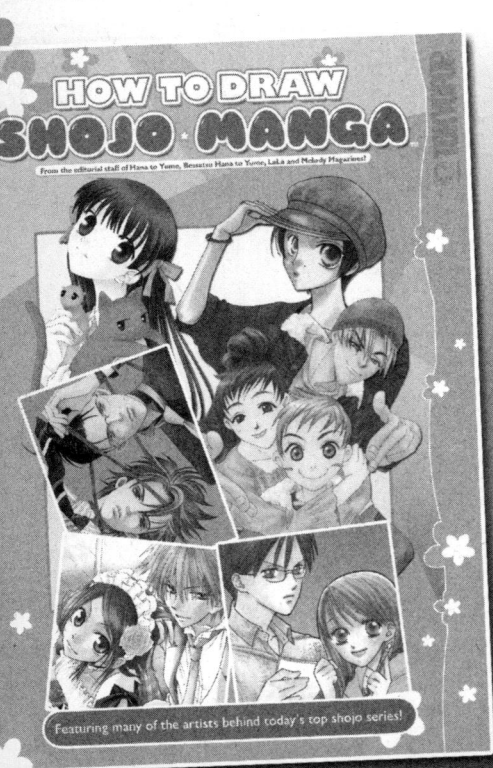

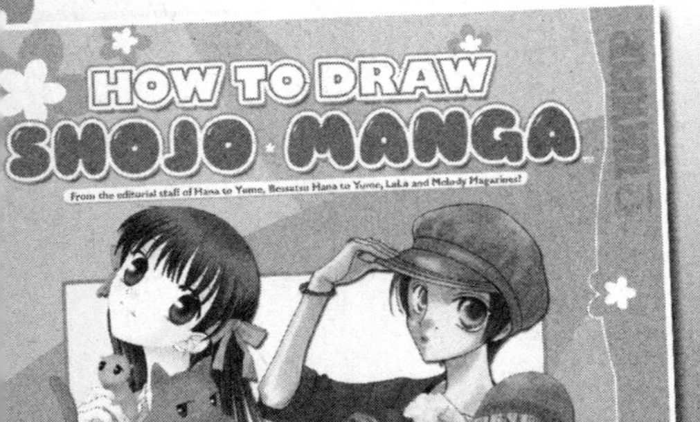
HOW TO DRAW
SHOJO MANGA
From the editorial staff of Hana to Yume, Bessatsu Hana to Yume, LaLa and Melody Magazines!
Featuring many of the artists behind today's top shojo series!

Wanna draw your own shojo manga but not quite sure where to start? The editors at Hakusensha Publishing, home of such beloved shojo series as *Fruits Basket*, *Vampire Knight*, *Maid Sama* and *Ouran High School Host Club*, have assembled a book jam-packed with useful tips and practical advice to help you develop your skills and go from beginner to ready for the manga big leagues!

Join aspiring artist Ena as she strives to make her big break drawing manga. Aided by her editor, Sasaki, and some of the best shojo artists in Japan, follow along as Ena creates a short story from start to finish, and gets professional feedback along the way. From page layout and pacing to pencils and perspective, this guide covers the basics, and then challenges you to go to the next level! Does Ena (and you!) have what it takes to go pro? Pick up this book and learn from the best!

ROMANCE

T
TEEN AGE 13+

FOR MORE INFORMATION VISIT: www.TOKYOPOP.com

Happy CAFE

Enjoy VOL 4

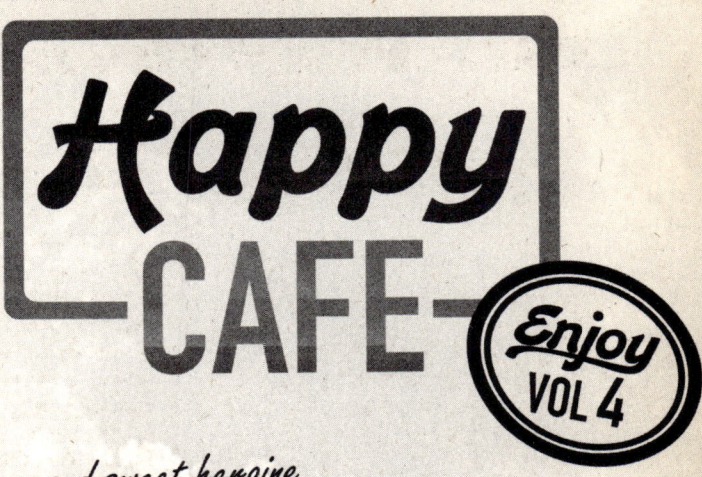

Our strong and sweet heroine continues to spread happiness at Café Bonheur . . .

Happy
CAFE
Enjoy
VOL 4
TOKYOPOP
Kou Matsuzuki

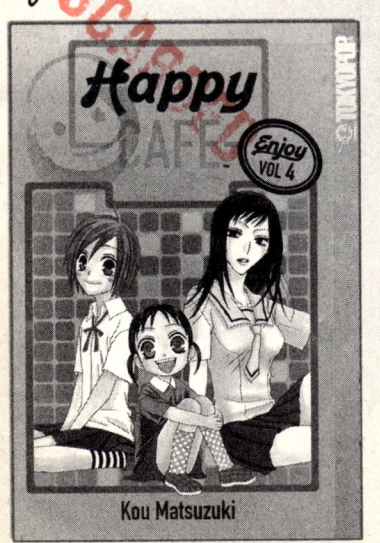

Uru finds herself stuck in Shindo's apartment during a blackout. As the evening wears on, she accidentally falls asleep on his shoulder, keeping him up all night and eventually getting him sick! Can Uru help cure his ills?

If you like Me and My Brothers, you'll definitely enjoy Happy Café!

BE SURE TO VISIT WWW.TOKYOPOP.COM/SHOP FOR EVERYTHING YOU COULD EVER WANT!

TOKYOPOP MANGA SUPPLEMENT

Let the Banquet Begin!

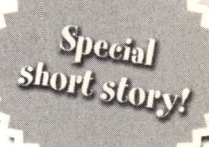

Never-before-seen creator interview!

Special short story!

Includes:
- *16 beautifully colored pages of the best Furuba artwork, including a gorgeous two-page spread of Kyo and Tohru!
- *Celebrated scenes from your favorite chapters
- *Furuba-themed zodiac games
- *Odd couple pairings
- *An impressive line-up of Fruits Basket books published all around the world!

© 1998 Natsuki Takaya / HAKUSENSHA, Inc.

FOR MORE INFORMATION VISIT: WWW.TOKYOPOP.COM

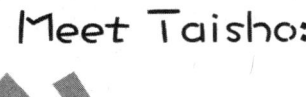

STOP!

This is the back of the book.
You wouldn't want to spoil a great ending!

This book is printed "manga-style," in the authentic Japanese right-to-left format. Since none of the artwork has been flipped or altered, readers get to experience the story just as the creator intended. You've been asking for it, so TOKYOPOP® delivered: authentic, hot-off-the-press, and far more fun!

1
2
3
4
5
6
7
8
9
10

DIRECTIONS

If this is your first time reading manga-style, here's a quick guide to help you understand how it works.

It's easy... just start in the top right panel and follow the numbers. Have fun, and look for more 100% authentic manga from TOKYOPOP®!

THE MANGA REVOLUTION • LEADING THE MANGA REVOLUTION • LEADING

漫画革命